HORNS

HORNS

JOE HILL

GOLLANCZ

LONDON

Copyright © Joe Hill 2010
All rights reserved

The right of Joe Hill to be identified as the author of
this work has been asserted by him in accordance with
the Copyright, Designs and Patents Act 1988.

First published in Great Britain in 2010
by Gollancz
An imprint of the Orion Publishing Group
Orion House, 5 Upper St Martin's Lane,
London WC2H 9EA

An Hachette UK Company

A CIP catalogue record for this book is available
from the British Library

ISBN 978 0 575 07916 8 (Cased)
ISBN 978 0 575 07917 5 (Export Trade Paperback)

3 5 7 9 10 8 6 4 2

Typeset by Input Data Services Ltd,
Bridgwater, Somerset

Printed and bound in the UK by
CPI Mackays, Chatham ME5 8TD

The Orion Publishing Group's policy is to use papers that
are natural, renewable and recyclable products and made
from wood grown in sustainable forests. The logging and
manufacturing processes are expected to conform to the
environmental regulations of the country of origin.

www.joehillfiction.com
www.orionbooks.co.uk

To Leanora – love, always

Satan is one of us; so much more so than Adam or Eve

MICHAEL CHABON, *On Daemons & Dust*

HELL

1

Ignatius Martin Perrish spent the night drunk and doing terrible things. He woke the next morning with a headache, put his hands to his temples, and felt something unfamiliar, a pair of knobby pointed protuberances. He was so ill – wet-eyed and weak – he didn't think anything of it at first, was too hungover for thinking or worry.

But when he was swaying above the toilet, he glanced at himself in the mirror over the sink and saw he had grown horns while he slept. He lurched in surprise, and for the second time in twelve hours he pissed on his feet.

2

~e~

He shoved himself back into his khaki shorts – he was still wearing yesterday's clothes – and leaned over the sink for a better look.

They weren't much as horns went, each of them about as long as his ring finger, thick at the base but soon narrowing to a point as they hooked upwards. The horns were covered in his own too-pale skin, except at the very tips, which were an ugly, inflamed red, as if the needle points at the ends of them were about to poke through the flesh. He touched one and found the point sensitive, a little sore. He ran his fingers along the sides of each and felt the density of bone beneath the stretched-tight smoothness of skin.

His first thought was that somehow he had brought this affliction upon himself. Late the night before, he had gone into the woods beyond the old foundry, to the place where Merrin Williams had been killed. People had left remembrances at a diseased black cherry tree, its bark peeling away to show the flesh beneath. Merrin had been found like that, clothes peeled away to show the flesh beneath. There were photographs of her placed delicately in the branches, a vase of pussy willows, Hallmark cards warped and stained from exposure to the elements. Someone – Merrin's mother, probably – had left a decorative cross with yellow nylon roses stapled to it and a plastic Virgin who smiled with the beatific idiocy of the functionally retarded.

He couldn't stand that simpering smile. He couldn't stand the cross either, planted in the place where Merrin had bled to death from her smashed-in head. A cross with yellow roses. What a fucking thing. It was like an electric chair with floral-print cushions, a bad joke. It bothered him that someone wanted to bring Christ out here. Christ was a year too late to do any good. He hadn't been anywhere around when Merrin needed Him.

Ig had ripped the decorative cross down and stamped it into the dirt. He'd had to take a leak, and he did it on the Virgin, drunkenly urinating on his own feet in the process. Perhaps that was blasphemy enough to bring on this transformation. But no – he sensed that there had been more. What else, he couldn't recall. He'd had a lot to drink.

He turned his head this way and that, studying himself in the mirror, lifting his fingers to touch the horns, once and again. How deep did the bone go? Did the horns have roots, pushing back into his brain? At this thought the bathroom darkened, as if the lightbulb overhead had briefly gone dim. The welling darkness, though, was behind his eyes, in his head, not in the light fixtures. He held the sink and waited for the feeling of weakness to pass.

He saw it then. He was going to die. Of course he was going to die. Something was pushing into his brain, all right: a tumour. The horns weren't really there. They were meta-phorical, imaginary. He had a tumour eating his brain, and it was causing him to see things. And if he was at the point of seeing things, then it was probably too late to save him.

The idea that he might be going to die brought with it a surge of relief, a physical sensation, like coming up for air after being underwater too long. Ig had come close to drowning once and had suffered from asthma as a child, and, to him, contentment was as simple as being able to breathe.

'I'm sick,' he whispered. 'I'm dying.'

It improved his mood to say it aloud.

He studied himself in the mirror, expecting the horns to vanish now that he knew they were hallucinatory, but it didn't work that way. The horns remained. He fretfully tugged at his hair, trying to see if he could hide them, at least until he got to the doctor's, then quit when he realised how silly it was to try to conceal something no one would be able to see but him.

He wandered into the bedroom on shaky legs. The bed-clothes were shoved back on either side and the bottom sheet still bore the rumpled impression of Glenna Nicholson's curves. He had no memory of falling into bed beside her, didn't even remember getting home – another missing part of the evening. It had been in his head until this very moment that he'd slept alone and that Glenna had spent the night somewhere else. *With* someone else.

They had gone out together, the night before, but after he'd been drinking awhile, Ig had just naturally started to think about Merrin, the anniversary of her death coming up in a few days. The more he drank, the more he missed her – and the more conscious he was of how little like her Glenna was. With her tattoos and her paste-on nails, her bookshelf full of Dean Koontz novels, her cigarettes and her rap sheet, Glenna was the un-Merrin. It irritated Ig to see her sitting there on the other side of the table, seemed a kind of betrayal to be with her, although whether he was betraying Merrin or himself, he didn't know. Finally he had to get away – Glenna kept reaching over to stroke his knuckles with one finger, a gesture she meant to be tender but for some reason pissed him off. He went to the men's room and hid there for twenty minutes. When he returned, he found the booth empty. He sat drinking for an hour before he understood that she was not coming back and that he was not sorry. But at some point in the evening, they had both wound up here in the same bed, the bed they'd shared for the last three months.

He heard the distant babble of the TV in the next room. Glenna was still in the apartment then, hadn't left for the salon yet. He would ask her to drive him to the doctor. The brief feeling of relief at the thought of dying had passed and he was already dreading the days and weeks to come: his father struggling not to cry, his mother putting on false cheer, IV drips, treatments, radiation, helpless vomiting, hospital food.

Ig crept into the next room, where Glenna sat on the living-room couch, in a Guns N' Roses tank-top and faded pyjama bottoms. She was hunched forward, elbows on the coffee table, tucking the last of a doughnut into her mouth with her fingers. In front of her was the box, containing three-day-old super-market doughnuts, and a two-litre bottle of Diet Coke. She was watching daytime talk TV.

She heard him and glanced his way, eyelids low, gaze disapproving, then returned her stare to the tube. 'My Best Friend Is a Sociopath!' was the subject of today's programme. Flabby rednecks were getting ready to throw chairs at one another.

She hadn't noticed the horns.

'I think I'm sick,' he said.

'Don't bitch at me,' she said. 'I'm hungover too.'

'No. I mean … look at me. Do I look all right?' Asking because he had to be sure.

She slowly turned her head towards him again and peered at him from under her eyelashes. She had on last night's mascara, a little smudged. Glenna had a smooth, pleasantly round face and a smooth, pleasantly curvy body. She could've almost been a model, if the job were modelling plus sizes. She outweighed Ig by fifty pounds. It wasn't that she was grotesquely fat, but that he was absurdly skinny. She liked to fuck him from on top, and when she put her elbows on his chest, she could push all the air out of him, a thoughtless act of erotic asphyxiation. Ig, who so often struggled for breath, knew every famous person who had ever died of erotic asphyxiation. It was a surprisingly common end for musicians. Kevin Gilbert. Hideto Matsumoto, probably. Michael Hutchence, of course, not someone he wanted to be thinking about at this particular moment. The devil inside.

'Are you still drunk?' she asked.

When he didn't reply, she shook her head and looked back at the television.

That was it, then. If she had seen them, she would've come screaming to her feet. But she couldn't see them because they weren't there. They existed only in Ig's mind. Probably if he looked at himself now in a mirror, he wouldn't see them either. But then Ig spotted a reflection of himself in the window, and the horns were still there. In the window he was a glassy, transparent figure, a demonic ghost.

'I think I need to go to the doctor,' he said.

'You know what I need?' she asked.

'What?'

'Another doughnut,' she said, leaning forward to look into the open box. 'You think another doughnut would be okay?'

He replied in a flat voice he hardly recognised, 'What's stopping you?'

'I already had one, and I'm not even hungry anymore. I just want to eat it.' She turned her head and peered up at him, her eyes glittering in a way that suddenly seemed both scared and pleading. 'I'd like to eat the whole box.'

'The whole box,' he repeated.

'I don't even want to use my hands. I just want to stick my face in and start eating. I know that's gross.' She moved her finger from doughnut to doughnut, counting. 'Six. Do you think it would be okay if I ate six more doughnuts?'

It was hard to think past his alarm and the feeling of pressure and weight at his temples. What she had just said made no sense, was another part of the whole unnatural bad-dream morning.

'If you're screwing with me, I wish you wouldn't. I told you, I don't feel good.'

'I want another doughnut,' she said.

'Go ahead. I don't care.'

'Well. Okay. If you think it's all right,' she said, and she took a doughnut, pulled it into three pieces, and began to eat, shoving in one chunk after another without swallowing.

Soon the whole doughnut was in her mouth, filling her cheeks. She gagged, softly, then inhaled deeply through her nostrils and began to swallow.

Iggy watched, repelled. He had never seen her do anything like it, hadn't seen anything like it since junior high, kids grossing out other kids in the cafeteria. When she was done, she took a few panting, uneven breaths, then looked over her shoulder, eyeing him anxiously.

'I didn't even like it. My stomach hurts,' she said. 'Do you think I should have another one?'

'Why would you eat another one if your stomach hurts?'

''Cause I want to get really fat. Not fat like I am now. Fat enough so you won't want to have anything to do with me.' Her tongue came out, and the tip touched her upper lip, a thoughtful, considering gesture. 'I did something disgusting last night. I want to tell you about it.'

The thought occurred again that none of it was really happening. If he was having some sort of fever dream, though, it was a persistent one, convincing in its fine details. A fly crawled across the TV screen. A car shushed past out on the road. One moment naturally followed the last, in a way that seemed to add up to reality. Ig was a natural at addition. Maths had been his best subject in school, after ethics, which he didn't count as a real subject.

'I don't think I want to know what you did last night,' he said.

'That's why I want to tell you. To make you sick. To give you a reason to go away. I feel so bad about what you've been through and what people say about you, but I can't stand waking up next to you anymore. I just want you to go, and if I told you what I did, this disgusting thing, then you'd leave and I'd be free again.'

'What do people say about me?' he asked. It was a silly question. He already knew.

She shrugged. 'Things about what you did to Merrin. How you're like a sick sex pervert and stuff.'

Ig stared at her, transfixed. It fascinated him, the way each thing she said was worse than the one before and how at ease she seemed to be with saying them. Without shame or awkwardness.

'So what did you want to tell me?'

'I ran into Lee Tourneau last night after you disappeared on me. You remember Lee and I used to have a thing going, back in high school?'

'I remember,' Ig said. Lee and Ig had been friends in another life, but all that was behind Ig now, had died with Merrin. It was difficult to maintain close friendships when you were under suspicion of being a sex murderer.

'Last night at the Station House, he was sitting in a booth in back, and after you disappeared, he bought me a drink. I haven't talked to Lee in forever. I forgot how easy he is to talk to. You know Lee, he doesn't look down on anyone. He was real nice to me. When you didn't come back after a while, he said we ought to look for you in the parking lot, and if you were gone, he'd drive me home. But then when we were outside, we got kissing kind of hot, like old times, like when we were together – and I got carried away and went down on him, right there with a couple of guys watching and everything. I haven't done anything that crazy since I was nineteen and on speed.'

Ig needed help. He needed to get out of the apartment. The air was too close, and his lungs felt tight and pinched.

She was leaning over the box of doughnuts again, her expression placid, as if she had just told him a fact of no particular consequence: that they were out of milk or had lost the hot water again.

'You think it would be all right to eat one more?' she asked. 'My stomach feels better.'

'Do what you want.'

She turned her head and stared at him, her pale eyes glittering with an unnatural excitement. 'You mean it?'

'I don't give a fuck,' he said. 'Pig out.'

She smiled, cheeks dimpling, then bent over the table, taking the box in one hand. She held it in place, shoved her face into it and began to eat. She made noises while she chewed, smacking her lips and breathing strangely. She gagged again, her shoulders hitching, but kept eating, using her free hand to push more doughnut into her mouth, even though her cheeks were already swollen and full. A fly buzzed around her head, agitated.

Ig edged past the couch, heading for the door. She sat up a little, gasping for breath, and rolled her eyes towards him. Her gaze was panicky, and her cheeks and wet mouth were gritted with sugar.

'*Mm*,' she moaned. '*Mmm.*' Whether she moaned in pleasure or misery, he didn't know.

The fly landed at the corner of her mouth. He saw it there for a moment – then Glenna's tongue darted out, and she trapped it with her hand at the same time. When she lowered her hand, the fly was gone. Her jaw worked up and down, grinding everything in her mouth into paste.

Ig opened the door and slid himself out. As he closed the door behind him, she was lowering her face to the box again ... a diver who had filled her lungs with air and was plunging once more into the depths.

3

He drove to the Modern Medical Practice Clinic, where they had a walk-in service. The small waiting room was almost full, and it was too warm, and there was a child screaming. A little girl lay on her back in the centre of the room, producing great howling sobs in between gasps for air. Her mother sat in a chair against the wall and was bent over her, whispering furiously, frantically, a steady stream of threats, imprecations and act-now-before-it's-too-late offers. Once she tried to grip her daughter's ankle and the little girl kicked her hand away with a black buckled shoe.

The other people in the waiting room were determinedly ignoring the scene, looking blankly at magazines or at the muted TV in the corner. It was 'My Best Friend Is a Sociopath!' here, too. Several of them glanced at Ig as he entered, a few in a hopeful sort of way, fantasising, perhaps, that the little girl's father had arrived to take her outside and deliver a brutal spanking. But as soon as they saw him, they looked away, knowing in a glance that he wasn't there to help.

Ig wished he'd brought a hat. He cupped a hand to his forehead, as if to shade his eyes from a bright light, hoping to conceal his horns. If anyone noticed them, however, they gave no sign of it.

At the far end of the room was a window in the wall and a woman sitting at a computer on the other side. The receptionist had been staring at the mother of the crying child, but when Ig appeared before her, she looked up and her lips twitched, formed a smile.

'What can I do you for?' she asked. She was already reaching towards a clipboard with some forms on it.

'I want a doctor to look at something,' Ig said, and lifted his hand slightly to reveal the horns.

She narrowed her eyes at them and pursed her lips in a sympathetic moue. 'Well, that doesn't look right,' she said, and swivelled to her computer.

Whatever reaction Ig expected – and he hardly knew what he expected – it wasn't this. She had reacted to the horns as if he'd shown her a broken finger or a rash – but she had *reacted* to them, had seemed to see them ... only if she'd *really* seen them, he could not imagine her simply puckering her lips and looking away.

'I just have to ask you a few questions. Name?'

'Ignatius Perrish.'

'Age?'

'Twenty-six.'

'Do you see a doctor locally?'

'I haven't seen a doctor in years.'

She lifted her head and peered at him thoughtfully, frowning again, and he thought he was about to be scolded for not having regular check-ups. The little girl shrieked even more loudly than before and Ig looked back in time to see her bash her mother in the knee with a red plastic fire truck, one of the toys stacked in the corner for kids to play with while waiting. Her mother yanked it out of her hands. The girl dropped onto her back again and began to kick at the air like an overturned cockroach, wailing with renewed fury.

'I want to tell her to shut that miserable brat up,' the receptionist remarked, in a sunny, passing-the-time tone of voice. 'What do you think?'

'Do you have a pen?' Ig asked, mouth dry. He held up the clipboard. 'I'll go fill these out.'

The receptionist's shoulders slumped and her smile went out.

'Sure,' she said to Ig, and shoved a pen at him.

He turned his back to her and looked down at the forms clipped to the board, but his eyes wouldn't focus.

She had seen the horns but hadn't thought them unusual. And then she'd said that thing about the girl who was crying and her helpless mother: *I want to tell her to shut that miserable brat up.* She had wanted to know if he thought it would be okay. So had Glenna, wondering if it would be all right to stick her face in the box of doughnuts and feed like a pig at the trough.

He looked for a place to sit. There were two empty chairs, one on either side of the mother. As Ig approached, the girl reached deep into her lungs and dredged up a shrill scream that shook the windows and caused some in the waiting area to flinch. Advancing forward into that sound was like moving into a knee-buckling gale.

As Ig sat, the girl's mother slumped in her chair, swatting herself on the leg with a rolled-up magazine – which was not, Ig felt, what she really wanted to hit with it. The little girl seemed to have exhausted herself with this final cry and now lay on her back with tears running down her red, ugly face. Her mother was red in the face, too. She cast a miserable, eye-rolling glance at Ig. Her gaze seemed to briefly catch on his horns, and then shifted away.

'Sorry about the ridiculous noise,' she said, and touched Ig's hand in a gesture of apology.

And when she did, when her skin brushed his, Ig knew that her name was Allie Letterworth and that for the last four months she'd been sleeping with her golf instructor, meeting him at a motel down the road from the links. Last week they had fallen asleep after an episode of strenuous fucking and Allie's cell phone had been off, and so she had missed the increasingly frantic calls from her daughter's summer day camp, wondering where she was and when she would be by to pick up her little girl. When she finally arrived, two hours late, her daughter was in hysterics, snot boiling from her nose, her bloodshot eyes wild, and Allie had to get her a sixty-dollar Webkinz and a banana split to calm her down and buy her silence; it was the only way to keep Allie's husband from finding out. If she had known what a drag a kid was going to be, she never would've had one.

Ig pulled his hand away from her.

The girl began to grunt and stamp her feet on the floor. Allie Letterworth sighed and leaned towards Ig and said, 'For what it's worth, I'd love to kick her right in her spoiled ass, but I'm worried about what all these people would say if I hit her. Do you think—?'

'No,' Ig said.

He couldn't know the things he knew about her but he knew them anyway, the way he knew his cell-phone number or his address. He knew, too, with utter certainty, that Allie Letterworth would not talk about kicking her daughter's spoiled ass with a total stranger. She had said it like someone talking to herself.

'No,' repeated Allie Letterworth, opening her magazine and then letting it fall shut. 'I guess I can't do that. I wonder if I ought to get up and go. Just leave her here and drive away. I could stay with Michael, hide from the world, drink gin and fuck all the time. My husband would get me on abandonment, but, like, who cares? Would you want partial custody of *that*?'

'Is Michael your golf instructor?' Ig asked.

She nodded dreamily and smiled at him and said, 'The funny thing is, I never would've signed up for lessons with him if I knew Michael was a nigger. Before Tiger Woods there weren't any jigaboos in golf except if they were carrying your clubs – it was one place you could go to get away from them. You know the way most blacks are, always on their cell phones with f-word this and f-word that, and the way they look at white women. But Michael is educated. He talks just like a white person. And it's true what they say about black dicks. I've screwed tons of white guys, and there wasn't one of 'em who was hung like Michael.' She wrinkled her nose and said, 'We call it the five-iron.'

Ig jumped to his feet and walked quickly to the receptionist's window. He hastily scribbled answers to a few questions and then offered her the clipboard.

Behind him the little girl screamed, '*No!* No, I *won't* sit up!'

'I feel like I *have* to say something to that girl's mother,' said the receptionist, looking past Ig at the woman and her daughter, paying no attention to the clipboard. 'I know it's not her fault her daughter is a screechy puke, but I really want to say just one thing.'

Ig looked at the little girl and at Allie Letterworth. Allie was bent over her again, poking her with the rolled-up magazine, hissing at her. Ig returned his gaze to the receptionist.

'Sure,' he said, experimentally.

She opened her mouth, then hesitated, gazing anxiously into Ig's face. 'Only thing is, I wouldn't want to start an ugly scene.'

The tips of his horns pulsed with a sudden unpleasant heat. Some part of him was surprised – already, and he hadn't even had the horns for an hour – that she hadn't immediately given in when he offered his permission.

'What do you mean, *start* one?' he asked, tugging restlessly at the little goatee he was cultivating, curious now to see if he could make her do it. 'It's amazing how people let their kids act these days, isn't it? When you think about it, you can hardly blame the child if the parent can't teach them how to act.'

The receptionist smiled: a tough, grateful smile. At the sight of it, he felt another sensation shoot through the horns, an icy thrill.

She stood and glanced past him, to the woman and the little girl. 'Ma'am?' she called. 'Excuse me, ma'am?'

'Yes?' said Allie Letterworth, looking up hopefully, probably expecting that her daughter was about to be called to her appointment.

'I know your daughter is very upset, but if you can't quiet her down, do you think you could show some fucking consideration to the rest of us and get off your wide ass and take her outside where we won't all have to listen to her squall?' asked the receptionist, smiling her plastic, stapled-on smile.

The colour drained out of Allie Letterworth's face, leaving furious spots glowing on her waxy cheeks. She held her daughter by the wrist. The little girl was pulling to get free, digging her fingernails at Allie's hand.

'What?' Allie asked. 'What did you say?'

'My head!' the receptionist shouted, dropping the smile and tapping furiously at her right temple. 'Your kid won't shut up, and my head is going to explode, and—'

'Fuck you!' shouted Allie Letterworth, coming to her feet, swaying.

'—if you had any consideration for anyone else—'

'Shove it up your ass!'

'—you'd take that shrieking pig of yours by the hair and drag her the fuck out—'

'You dried-up twat!'

'—but *oh no*, you just sit there *diddling* yourself—'

'Come on, Marcy,' said Allie, yanking at her daughter's wrist.

'No!' said the little girl.

'I said come on!' said her mother, dragging her towards the exit.

At the threshold to the street, Allie Letterworth's daughter wrenched her wrist free from her mother's grip. She bolted across the room but caught her feet on the fire truck and crashed onto her hands and knees. The girl began to scream once again, her most piercing screams yet, and rolled onto her side, holding a bloody knee. Her mother paid no mind. She threw down her purse and began to yell at the receptionist, and the receptionist hollered shrilly back. Ig's horns throbbed with a curiously pleasurable feeling of fullness and weight.

Ig was closer to the girl than anyone, and her mother wasn't coming over. He took her wrist to help her to her feet. When he touched her, he knew that her name was Marcia Letterworth and that she had dumped her breakfast into her mother's lap on purpose that morning, because her mother was making her go to the doctor to have her warts burned off and she didn't want to go and it was going to hurt and her mother was mean and stupid. Marcia turned her face up towards his. Her eyes, full of tears, were the clear, intense blue of a blowtorch.

'I hate Mommy,' she told Ig. 'I want to burn her in her bed with matches. I want to burn her all up gone.'

4

~♥

The nurse who took Ig's weight and blood pressure told him her ex-husband was dating a girl who drove a sporty yellow Saab. The nurse knew where she parked and wanted to go over on her lunch break and put a big long scratch in the side with her car keys. She wanted to leave dog shit in the driver's seat. Ig sat perfectly still on the exam table, his hands balled into fists, and offered no opinion.

When the nurse removed the blood-pressure cuff, her fingers brushed his bare arm and Ig knew that she had vandalised other people's cars, many times before: a teacher who'd flunked her for cheating on a test, a friend who had blabbed a secret, her ex-husband's lawyer, for being her ex-husband's lawyer. Ig could see her in his head, at the age of twelve, dragging a nail along the side of her father's black Oldsmobile, gouging an ugly white line that ran the length of his car.

The exam room was too cold, air-conditioner blasting, and Ig was trembling from the chill and his nervousness by the time Dr Renald entered the room. Ig lowered his head to show him the horns. He told the doctor he couldn't tell what was real and what wasn't. He said he thought he was having delusions.

'People keep telling me things,' Ig said. 'Awful things. Telling me things they want to do, things no one would *ever* admit to wanting to do. A little girl just told me she wanted to burn her mother up in her bed. Your nurse told me she wants to ruin some poor girl's car. I'm scared. I don't know what's happening to me.'

The doctor studied the horns, worry lines furrowed across his brow. 'Those are horns,' he said.

'I know they're horns.'

Dr Renald shook his head. 'They look inflamed at the points. Do they hurt?'

'Like hell.'

'Ha,' said the doctor. He rubbed a hand across his mouth. 'Let me measure them.' He ran the tape around the circumference, at the base, then measured from temple to point and from tip to tip. He scratched some numbers on his prescription pad. He ran his callused fingertips over them, feeling them, his face attentive, considering, and Ig knew something he didn't want to know. He knew that Dr Renald had, a few days before, stood in the dark of his bedroom, peering around a curtain and out of his bedroom window, masturbating while he watched his seventeen-year-old daughter's friends cavorting in the swimming pool.

The doctor stepped back again, his old grey eyes worried. He seemed to be coming to a decision. 'You know what I want to do?'

'What?' Ig asked.

'I want to grind up some OxyContin and have a little snort. I promised myself I'd never snort any at work, because I think it makes me stupid, but I don't know if I can wait six more hours.'

It took Ig a moment before he realised that the doctor was waiting for his thoughts on the matter.

'Can we just talk about these things on my head?' Ig said.

The doctor's shoulders sank. He turned his face away and let out a slow, seething breath.

'Listen,' Ig said. 'Please. I need help. Someone has to help me.'

Dr Renald reluctantly looked up at him.

Ig said, 'I don't know if this is happening or not. I think I'm going crazy. How come people don't react more when they see the horns? If I saw someone with horns, I'd piss down my own leg.' Which, in fact, was exactly what he *had* done when he first saw himself in the mirror.

'They're hard to remember,' the doctor said. 'As soon as I look away from you, I forget you have them. I don't know why.'

'But you see them now.'

Renald nodded.

'And you've never seen anything like them?'

'Are you sure I can't have a little sniff of Oxy?' the doctor asked. He brightened. 'I'd share. We could get fucked up together.'

Ig shook his head. 'Listen, please.'

The doctor made an ugly face but nodded.

'How come you aren't calling other doctors in here? How come you aren't taking this more seriously?'

'To be honest,' Renald said, 'it's a little hard to concentrate on your problem. I keep thinking about the pills in my briefcase and this girl my daughter hangs out with. Nancy Hughes. God I want her ass. I feel sort of sick when I think about it, though. She's still in braces.'

'Please,' Ig said. 'I'm asking for your medical opinion – your help. What do I do?'

'Fucking patients,' the doctor said. 'All any of you care about is yourselves.'

5

He drove. He didn't think where, and for a while it didn't matter. It was enough to be moving.

If there was a place left to Ig that he could call his own, it was this car, his 1972 AMC Gremlin. The apartment belonged to Glenna. She had lived there before him and would continue to live there after they were through with each other, which was apparently now. He had moved back in with his parents for a time, immediately after Merrin was killed, but he'd never felt at home, no longer belonged there. What was left to Ig now was the car, which was a vehicle but also a place of habitation, a space in which much of his life had been lived, good and bad.

The good: making love to Merrin Williams in it, banging his head on the roof and his knee on the gearshift. The rear shocks were stiff and screeched when the car jolted up and down, a sound that would cause Merrin to bite her lip to keep from laughing, even as Ig moved between her legs. The bad: the night Merrin was raped and killed, out by the old foundry, while he'd been sleeping drunk in this car, hating her in his dreams.

The AMC had been a place to hang out when there was nowhere else to go, when there was nothing to do except drive around Gideon, wishing something would happen. Nights when Merrin worked or had to study, Ig would cruise around with his best friend, tall, lean, half-blind Lee Tourneau. They'd drive down to the sandbar, where sometimes there would be a campfire and people they knew, a couple of trucks parked on the embankment, a cooler full of Coronas. They would sit on the hood of the car and watch the flames reflected in the black, swiftly moving water while sparks from the fire sailed up to vanish into the night. They would talk about bad ways to die – a natural subject for them, parked so close to the Knowles River. Ig said drowning would be worst, and he had personal experience to back it up. The river had swallowed him once, held him under, forced itself down his throat, and it had been Lee Tourneau who swam in to pull him out. Lee said there was lots worse than drowning and that Ig had no imagination. Lee said burning had drowning beat any day of the week, but then he *would* say that, having had an unfortunate run-in with a burning car. Both of them knew what they knew.

Best of all were nights in the Gremlin with Lee and Merrin both. Lee would accordion himself in the rear – he was courtly by nature and always let Merrin sit with Ig up front – and then lie stretched out, with the back of his hand draped over his brow, Oscar Wilde lounging in despair on his davenport. They'd go to the Paradise Drive-In, drink beer while madmen in hockey masks chased half-naked teenagers, who would fall under the chainsaw to cheers and honking horns. Merrin called these 'double dates' – Ig was there with her, and Lee was there with his right hand. For Merrin, half the fun of going out with Ig and Lee was ragging Lee's ass, but the morning Lee's mother died, Merrin was the first to his house, to hold him while he wept.

For half an instant, Ig thought of paying a visit to Lee now; he had pulled Ig out of the deep water once, maybe he could again. But then he remembered what Glenna had told him an hour ago, the terrible bad-dream thing she had confessed over doughnuts: *I got carried away and went down on him, right there with a couple of guys watching and everything.* Ig tried to feel the things he was supposed to feel, tried to hate them both, but couldn't even manage low-grade loathing. He had other concerns at the moment. They were growing out of his fucking head.

And anyway: it wasn't as if Lee were stabbing him in the back, swiping his beloved out from under him. Ig wasn't in love with Glenna and he didn't think she was or ever had been in love with him – whereas Lee and Glenna had history, had been sweethearts once upon a very long time ago.

It was still maybe not the sort of thing one friend would do to another, but then Lee and Ig weren't friends anymore. After Merrin had been killed, Lee Tourneau had casually, without overt cruelty, cut Ig out of his life. There had been some expressions of quiet, sincere sympathy in the days right after Merrin's body was found, but no promises that Lee would be there for him, no offers to meet. Then, in the weeks and months that followed, Ig noticed he only ever called Lee, not the other way around, and that Lee did not work too hard to hold up his end of a conversation. Lee had always affected a certain emotional disengagement, and so it was possible Ig did not immediately register how fully and completely he'd been dropped. After a while, though, Lee's routine excuses for not coming over, for not meeting, added up. Ig was maybe not smart about other people, but he'd always been good at maths. Lee was the aide to a New Hampshire congressman and couldn't have a relationship with the lead suspect in a sex-murder case. There were no fights, no ugly moments between them. Ig understood, let it be over without begrudging him. Lee – poor, wounded, studious, lonely Lee – had a future. Ig didn't.

Maybe because he'd been thinking of the sandbar, he wound up parked off Knowles Road, at the base of the Old Fair Road Bridge. If he were looking for a place to drown himself, he couldn't have hunted down a better spot. The sandbar reached a hundred feet into the current before dropping off into deep, fast, blue water. He could fill his pockets with stones and wade right in. He could also climb onto the bridge and jump; it was high enough. Aim for the rocks instead of the river if he wanted to do the job right. Just the thought of the impact made him wince. He got out and sat against the hood and listened to the hum of trucks high above him, rushing south.

He had been here lots of times. Like the old foundry on Route 17, the sandbar was a destination for people too young to have a destination. He remembered another time down here, with Merrin, and how they had got caught out in the rain and sheltered under the bridge. They were in high school then. Neither of them could drive, and they had no car to run to. They shared a soggy basket of fried clams, sitting up on the weedy cobblestone incline under the bridge. It was so cold they could see their breath, and he held her wet, frozen hands in his.

Ig found a stained, two-day-old newspaper, and when they got bored of not really reading it, Merrin said they should do something inspiring with it. Something that would lift the spirits of everyone everywhere who looked out on the river in the rain. They sprinted up the hill, through the drizzle, to buy birthday candles at the 7-Eleven, and then they ran back. Merrin showed him how to make boats out of the pages of the newspaper, and they lit the candles and put them in and set them off, one by one, into the rain and gathering twilight – a long chain of little flames, gliding serenely through the water-logged darkness.

'Together we are inspiring,' she said to him, her cold lips so close to his earlobe that it made him shiver, her breath all clams. She trembled continuously, struggling with a laughing fit. 'Merrin Williams and Iggy Perrish, making the world a better, more wonderful place, one paper ship at a time.'

She either didn't notice or pretended not to see the boats filling with rain and sinking less than a hundred yards offshore, the candles in them winking out.

Remembering how it had been, and who he had been when they were together, stopped the frantic, out-of-control whirl of thoughts in his head. Perhaps for the first time all day, Ig found he could take stock, to consider without panic what was happening to him.

He considered again the possibility that he had suffered a break with what was real, that everything he'd experienced over the course of the day had only been imagined. It wouldn't be the first time he'd confused fantasy with reality, and he knew from experience that he was especially prone to unlikely religious delusions. He had not forgotten the afternoon he spent in the Tree House of the Mind. Hardly a day had passed in eight years that he hadn't thought about it. Of course, if the tree house had been a fantasy – and that was the only explanation that ever made sense – it had been a shared one. He and Merrin had discovered the place together, and what had happened there was one of the secret silken knots that bound them to each other, a thing to puzzle over when a drive got dull, or in the middle of the night after being woken by a thunderstorm, when neither of them could get back to sleep. 'I know it's *possible* for people to have the same hallucination,' Merrin said once. 'I just never saw myself as the type.'

The problem with thinking that his horns were nothing but an especially persistent and frightening delusion, a leap into madness that had been a long time coming, was that he could only deal with the reality in front of him. It did no good to tell himself that it was all in his head if it went on happening anyway. His belief was not required; his disbelief was of no consequence. The horns were always there when he reached up to touch them. Even when he didn't touch them, he was aware of the sore, sensitive tips sticking out into the cool riverside breeze. They had the convincing and literal solidity of bone.

Lost in his thoughts, Ig didn't hear the car rolling down the hill until it crunched to a stop behind the Gremlin and the cop behind the wheel gave the siren a brief whoop. Ig's heart lunged painfully and he quickly turned. One of the policemen was leaning out of the passenger window of his cruiser.

'What's the story, Ig?' said the cop, who was not just any cop but the one named Sturtz.

Sturtz wore short sleeves that showed off his toned forearms, toasted a golden brown from routine exposure to the sun. It was a tight shirt, and he was a good-looking man. With his windblown blond hair and his eyes hidden behind his mirrored sunglasses he could've been on a billboard advertising cigarettes.

His partner, Posada, behind the steering wheel, was trying for the same look but couldn't carry it off. His build was too slight, his Adam's apple too prominent. They both had moustaches, but on Posada it was dainty and vaguely comical, the sort of thing that belonged on the face of a French maître d' in a Cary Grant comedy.

Sturtz grinned. Sturtz was always glad to see him. Ig was never glad to see any cop, but in particular he preferred to avoid Sturtz and Posada, who had, ever since Merrin's death, made a hobby out of hassling Ig, pulling him over for going five miles above the limit and searching his car, ticketing him for littering, loitering, living.

'No story. Just standing here,' Ig said.

'You been standing there for half an hour,' Posada called to him as the partners got out of their cruiser. 'Talking to yourself. The woman lives back that way brought her kids in because you were freaking her out.'

'Think how freaked out she'd be if she knew who he is,' Sturtz said. 'Your friendly neighbourhood sex deviant and murder suspect.'

'On the bright side, he's never killed any kids.'

'Not yet,' Sturtz said.

'I'll go,' Ig said.

Sturtz said, 'You'll stay.'

'What do you want to do?' Posada asked Sturtz.

'I want to run him in for something.'

'Run him in for what?'

'I don't know. Anything. I'd like to plant something on him. Bag of coke. Unregistered gun. Whatever. Too bad we don't have anything. I really want to fuck with him.'

'I want to kiss you on the mouth when you talk dirty,' Posada said.

Sturtz nodded, unperturbed by this admission. That was when Ig remembered the horns. It was starting again, like the doctor and the nurse, like Glenna and Allie Letterworth.

'What I really want,' Sturtz said, 'is to bust him for something and have him put up a struggle. Have an excuse to knock his fucking teeth out of his sorry mouth.'

'Oh, yeah. I'd like to watch that scene,' Posada said.

'Do you guys even know what you're saying?' Ig asked.

'No,' Posada said.

'Kind of,' Sturtz said. He squinted, as if trying to read something printed on a distant sign. 'We're talking about whether we ought to bust you just for the fun of it, but I don't know why.'

'You don't know why you want to bust me?'

'Oh I know why I want to bust you. I mean I don't know why we're talking about it. It's not the kind of thing I usually discuss.'

'Why do you want to bust me?'

'Because of that faggot look you've always got on your face. That faggot look pisses me off. I'm not a big fan of homos,' Sturtz told him.

'And I want to bust you because maybe you'll struggle and then Sturtz will bend you over the hood of the car to put the cuffs on,' Posada said. 'That'll give me something to beat off over tonight, only I'll be picturing both of you naked.'

'So you don't want to bust me because you think I got away with killing Merrin?' Ig asked.

29

Sturtz said, 'No. I don't even think you did it. You're too much of a pussy. You would've confessed.'

Posada laughed.

Sturtz said, 'Put your hands on the roof of the car. I want to poke around. Have a look in the back.'

Ig was glad to turn away from them and stretch his arms out over the roof of the car. He pressed his forehead to the driver's-side window. The cool of the glass was soothing.

Sturtz made his way around to the hatchback. Posada stood behind Ig.

'I need his keys,' Sturtz said.

Ig took his right hand off the roof and went to dig them out of his pocket.

'Keep your hands on the roof,' Posada said. 'I'll get them. Which pocket?'

'Right,' Ig said.

Posada eased his hand into Ig's front pocket and curled a finger through his keyring. He jangled them out, tossed them to Sturtz. Sturtz clapped his hands around them and popped the hatchback.

'I'd like to put my hand in your pocket again,' Posada said. 'And leave it there. You don't know how hard it is not to use my position of power to cop a feel. No pun intended. Cop. Ha. I never imagined how much of my job would involve handcuffing fit, half-naked men. I have to admit, I haven't always been good.'

'Posada,' Ig said, 'you should really let Sturtz know how you feel about him sometime.' As he said it, the horns throbbed.

'You think?' Posada asked. He sounded surprised but curious. 'Sometimes I've thought— but then I think, you know, he'd probably pound the snot out of me.'

'No way. I bet he's been waiting for you to do it. Why do you think he leaves the top button of his shirt open like that?'

'I've noticed he never gets that button.'

'You should just unzip his fly and go down on him. Surprise him. Give him a thrill. He's probably only waiting on you to make the first move. But don't do anything until I'm gone, okay? Something like that, you're going to want your privacy.'

Posada cupped his hands around his mouth and exhaled, sampling the odour of his breath.

'Hot damn,' he said. 'I didn't brush this morning.' Then he snapped his fingers. 'But there's some Big Red in the glove compartment.' He turned and hurried over to the cruiser, muttering to himself.

The hatchback slammed. Sturtz made his way to Ig's side.

'I wish I had a reason to arrest you. I wish you'd put a hand on me. I could lie and say you touched me. Propositioned me. I've always thought you looked more'n half queer, with your swishy walk and those eyes that always look like you're going to start crying. I can't believe Merrin Williams ever let you in her jeans. Whoever raped her probably gave her the first good fuck of her life.'

Ig felt as if he had swallowed a coal and it was stuck halfway down, behind his chest.

'What would you do,' Ig asked, 'if a guy touched you?'

'I'd shove my nightstick up his asshole. Ask Mr Homo how he likes that.' Sturtz considered a moment, then said, 'Unless I was drunk. Then I'd probably let him blow me.' He paused another second before asking, in a hopeful sort of voice, 'Are you going to touch me so I can shove my—?'

'No,' Ig said. 'But I think you're right about the gays, Sturtz. You've got to draw the line. You let Mr Homo get away with touching you, they'll think you're a homo, too.'

'I know I'm right. I don't need you to tell me. We're done here. Go on. I don't want to find you hanging around under the bridge anymore. Got me?'

'Yes.'

'Actually, I *do* want to find you hanging around here. With drugs in your glove compartment. Do you understand?'

'Yes.'

'Okay. Long as we got that straight. Now beat it.' Sturtz dropped Ig's car keys in the gravel.

Ig waited for him to walk away before he bent and collected them and climbed behind the wheel of the Gremlin. He took a last glance at the cruiser in the rearview mirror. By then Sturtz was sitting in the passenger seat holding a clipboard in both hands and frowning down at it, trying to decide what to write. Posada was turned sideways in the seat so he was facing his partner and was looking at the other man with a mix of yearning and greed. As Ig pulled away, Posada licked his lips, then lowered his head, ducking under the dash and out of sight.

6

He had gone down to the river to work out a plan, but for all the thinking he had done, Ig was as mixed up now as he'd been an hour ago. He thought of his parents and even got as far as driving a couple of blocks in the direction of their house. But then he nervously jerked the wheel, turning the car off course and down a side road. He needed help but didn't think they'd be able to give him any. It unnerved him to think about what they might offer him instead . . . what secret desires they might share. What if his mother harboured an urge to fuck little boys? What if his father did!

And anyway, it had been different between them in the time since Merrin died. It hurt them to see what had happened to him in the aftermath of her murder. They didn't want to know about how he was living, had never once been inside Glenna's place. Glenna asked why they never had a meal together, and insinuated that Ig was ashamed to be with her, which he was. It hurt them, too, the shadow he had cast over them, because it was a well-known fact in town that Ig had raped and murdered Merrin Williams and got away with it because his rich and connected parents had pulled strings, called in favours and twisted arms to interfere with the investigation.

His father had been a small-time celebrity for a while. He had played with Sinatra and Dean Martin, was on their records. He had cut records of his own, for Blue Tone, in the late sixties and early seventies, four of them, and had scored a Top 100 hit with a dreamy, cool-cat instrumental called 'Fishin' with Pogo'. He married a Vegas showgirl, played himself on TV variety shows and in a handful of movies, and finally resettled in New Hampshire so Ig's mom could be close to her family. Later he became a celebrity professor at Berklee College of Music who sat in on occasion with the Boston Pops.

Ig had always liked to listen to his father, to watch him while he played. It was almost wrong to say his father played. It often seemed the other way around: that the horn was playing him. The way his cheeks swelled out, then caved in as if he were being inhaled into it, the way the golden keys seemed to grab his fingers like little magnets snatching at iron filings, causing them to leap and dance in unexpected, startling fits. The way he shut his eyes and bent his head and twisted back and forth at the hips, as if his torso were an auger, screwing its way deeper and deeper into the centre of his being, pulling the music up from somewhere in the pit of his belly.

Ig's older brother had gone into the family line of work with a vengeance. Terence was on TV every night, star of his own music-and-comedy late-night show, *Hothouse*, which had come out of nowhere to mop the floor with the other late, late guys. Terry played horn in apparently death-defying situations, had done 'Ring of Fire' in a ring of fire with Alan Jackson, had played 'High & Dry' with Norah Jones, the two of them in a tank filling with water. It hadn't sounded good, but it was great TV. Terry was making it hand over fist these days.

He had his own way of playing, too, different from their father. His chest strained so hard his shirt looked as if at any moment it would pop a button. His eyes bulged from his sockets so he looked perpetually surprised. He jerked back and forth at the waist like a metronome. His face glistened with happiness, and sometimes it sounded as if his horn were screaming with laughter. He had inherited their father's most precious gift: the more he practised at a thing, the less practised it sounded and the more natural and unexpected and lively it became.

Ig had hated to listen to his brother play when they were teenagers and would make up any excuse to avoid going with his parents to Terry's performances. He got indigestion from jealousy, couldn't sleep the night before Terry put on a big show at the school or, later, at local clubs. He had hated especially to be with Merrin watching Terry perform, could hardly stand to see the delight in her face, to see her in thrall to his music. When she swayed to Terry's swing music, Ig imagined his brother reaching for her hips with invisible hands. He was over that now, though. He had been over it for a long time; in fact the only part of his day he enjoyed now was watching *Hothouse* when Terry played.

Ig would've played, too, but for his asthma. He could never capture enough air in his chest to make the horn wail that way. He knew that his father wanted him to play, but when Ig pushed himself, he ran out of oxygen and his chest grew sickeningly tight and a darkness rose up at the edge of his vision. He had occasionally pushed himself until he fainted.

When it was clear he wasn't getting anywhere with the trumpet, Ig had tried piano, but it had gone badly. The teacher, a friend of his father's, was a drunk with bloodshot eyes who stank of pipe smoke and who would leave Ig to practise some hopelessly complex piece on his own while he went into the next room to nap. After that, Ig's mother had suggested bass, but by then Ig wasn't interested in mastering an instrument. He was interested in Merrin. Once he was in love with her, he didn't need his family's horns anymore.

He was going to have to see them sometime: his father and his mother, and Terry, too. With *Hothouse* on summer hiatus, his brother had come in on the red-eye. He was in town for their grandmother's eightieth birthday tomorrow. It was Terry's first time back to Gideon since Merrin had died, and he wasn't staying long, was going back the day after tomorrow. Ig didn't blame him for wanting a quick getaway. The scandal had come just as the show was taking off and it could've cost him everything; it said something about Terry that he would return to Gideon at all, a place where he would be at risk of being photographed with his sex-murderer brother, a picture that would be worth a grand at least to the *Enquirer*. But then, Terry had never believed that Ig was guilty of anything. Terry had been Ig's loudest and angriest defender, at a time when the network would've preferred him to issue a terse 'No comment' and move on.

Ig could avoid them for now, but sooner or later he would have to risk facing them. Maybe, he thought, it would be different with his family. Maybe they would be immune to him, and their secrets would stay secrets. They loved him, and he loved them. Love had to count for something. Maybe he could learn to control it, to turn it off, whatever 'it' was. Maybe the horns would go away. They had come without warning, why shouldn't they go the same way?

He pushed a hand back through his limp, thinning hair – thinning at twenty-six! – then squeezed his head between his palms. He hated the frantic scurry of his thoughts, how desperately one idea chased after another. His fingertips brushed the horns and he cried out in fright. It was on his lips to say, *God, please God, make them go away* . . . but then he caught himself and said nothing.

A crawly sensation worked its way up his forearms. If he was a devil now, could he still speak of God? Would lightning strike him, shatter him in a white flash? Would he burn?

'God,' he whispered.

Nothing happened.

'God, God, God,' he said. He cocked his head, listening, waiting for some response.

'Please, God, make them go away. I'm sorry if I did

something to piss you off last night. I was drunk. I was angry,' Ig said.

He held a breath, lifted his eyes, looked at himself in the rearview mirror. There were the horns. He was getting used to the sight of them now. They were becoming a part of his face. This thought caused him to shiver with revulsion.

At the edge of his vision, slipping past on his right, he saw a blaze of white and yanked the wheel, pulling up to the kerb. Ig had been driving without thinking, paying no mind to where he was and with no idea where he was going. He had arrived, without meaning to, at the Sacred Heart of Mary, where he'd gone with his family to church for more than two-thirds of his life, and where he'd seen Merrin Williams for the first time.

He stared at the Sacred Heart with a dry mouth. He hadn't been in there, or in any other church, since Merrin was killed, had not wanted to be part of a crowd, to be stared at by other parishioners. Nor had he wanted to get right with God; he felt God needed to get right with him.

Maybe if he walked in there and prayed to God, the horns would go away. Or maybe – maybe Father Mould would know what to do. Ig had an idea then. Father Mould might be immune to the influence of the horns. If anyone could resist the power of them, Ig thought, wouldn't it be a man of the cloth? He had God on his side, and the protection of God's house. Maybe an exorcism could be arranged. Father Mould had to know people he could contact about something like that. A sprinkle of holy water and a few Our Fathers and Ig might be right back to normal.

He left the Gremlin at the kerb and walked up the concrete path to the Sacred Heart. He was reaching for the door when he caught himself, drew his hand back. What if, when he touched the latch, his hand began to burn? What if he couldn't go in? he wondered. What if when he tried to step through the door, some black force repelled him, threw him back on his ass?

He saw himself staggering through the nave, smoke boiling from under his shirt collar, his eyes bulging from their sockets like a character's in a cartoon, imagined suffocation and lacerating pain.

He forced himself to reach out and take the latch. One leaf of the door opened to his hand – a hand that did not burn, or sting, or feel any pain at all. He looked into the dimness of the nave, out over the rows of dark-varnished pews. The place smelled of seasoned wood and old hymnals with sun-worn leather covers and brittle pages. He had always liked the smell and was surprised to find he still liked it now, that the odour didn't cause him to choke.

Ig stepped through the door. He spread his arms and waited. He looked down the length of one arm, then the other, watching to see if any smoke would come trickling out of his shirt cuffs. None did. He lifted a hand to the horn at his right temple. It was still there. He expected them to tingle, to pulse, something – but there was nothing. The church was a cavern of silence and darkness, lit only by the pastel glow of the stained-glass windows. Mary at her son's feet as He died on the cross. John baptising Jesus in the river.

He thought he should approach the altar, kneel there, and plead with God for a break. He felt a prayer forming on his lips: *Please, God, if You make the horns go away, I'll always serve You, I'll come back to church, I'll be a priest, I'll spread the Word, I'll spread the Word in hot Third World countries where everyone has leprosy, if anyone has leprosy anymore, just please, make them go away, make me who I was again.* He didn't get around to saying it, though. Before he took a step, he heard a gentle clang of iron on iron and turned his head.

He was still in the entrance to the atrium, and there was a door to his left, slightly ajar, which looked into a staircase. There was a little gym down there, available to the parishioners for various functions. Iron banged softly again. Ig touched the door, and as it eased back, opening wider, a trickle of country music spilled out.

'Hello?' he called, standing in the doorway.

Another ding of iron, and a breathless gasp.

'Yes?' called Father Mould. 'Who is it?'

'Ig Perrish, sir.'

A moment of silence followed. It lasted a little too long.

Father Mould said, 'Come on down and see me.'

Ig went down the stairs.

At the far end of the basement, a bank of fluorescent lights shone down on a puffy floor mat, some giant inflatable balls, a balance beam – equipment for a kids' tumbling class. Here by the stairwell, though, some of the lights were out and it was darker. Arranged along the walls was a circuit of cardiovascular machines. Close to the foot of the stairs was a weight bench, Father Mould stretched out on his back upon it.

Forty years before, Mould had been a wingman for Syracuse and afterwards a marine, served a tour of duty in the Iron Triangle, and he still had the mass and overwhelming physical presence of a hockey player, the self-assured authority of a soldier. He was slow on his feet, hugged people when they amused him, and was lovable in the way of a gentle old St Bernard who likes to sleep on the furniture even though he knows he isn't supposed to. He was dressed in a grey warm-up suit and ancient beat-up Adidas. His cross hung from one end of the weight bar, swinging softly as he dropped the bar and then ponderously raised it again.

Sister Bennett stood behind the bench. She was built a little like a hockey player herself, with broad shoulders and a heavy, mannish face, her short, curly hair held back by a violet sweatband. She wore a purple tracksuit that matched. Sister Bennett had taught an ethics class at St Jude's and liked to draw flow charts on the chalkboard, showing how certain decisions led inexorably to salvation (a rectangle she filled with fat, puffy clouds) or inexorably to hell (a box filled with flames).

Ig's brother, Terry, had mocked her relentlessly, drawing flow charts of his own, for the amusement of his classmates, showing how, after a variety of grotesque lesbian encounters, Sister Bennett would wind up arriving in hell herself, where she would be only too glad to indulge in disturbing sexual practices with the devil. These had made Terry the hit of the St Jude's cafeteria – an early taste of celebrity. It had also been his first brush with notoriety, as he'd eventually been ratted out (by an anonymous tipster, whose identity was unknown to this day). Terry had been invited to Father Mould's office. Their meeting took place behind closed doors, but that was not enough to muffle the sound of his wooden paddle striking Terry's ass or, after the twentieth stroke, Terry's cries. Everyone in school heard. The sounds carried through the vents of the outdated heating system to every classroom. Ig had writhed in his chair, in agony for Terry. He had eventually stuck his fingers into his ears so he wouldn't have to hear. Terry was not allowed to perform at the year-end recital – for which he'd been practising for months – and was flunked in ethics.

Father Mould sat up, wiping his face with a towel. It was darkest there at the foot of the steps, and the thought crossed Ig's mind that Father Mould genuinely couldn't see the horns.

'Hello, Father,' Ig said.

'Ignatius. Seems like it's been forever. Where have you been keeping yourself?'

'I've got a place downtown,' Ig said, his voice hoarsening with emotion. He had been unprepared for Father Mould's solicitous tone, his easy, avuncular affection. 'It isn't far, really. I keep meaning to stop in, but—'

'Ig? Are you all right?'

'I don't know. I don't know what's happening to me. It's my head. Look at my head, Father.'

Ig stepped forward and bowed slightly, leaning into the

light. He could see the shadow of his head on the swept cement floor, the horns a pair of small pointed hooks sticking out from his temples. He was afraid almost to see Father Mould's reaction and glanced at him shyly. The ghost of a polite smile remained on Father Mould's face. His brow furrowed in thought as he studied the horns with a kind of glassy bewilderment.

'I was drunk last night, and I did terrible things,' Ig said. 'And when I woke up, I was like this, and I don't know what to do. I don't know what I'm becoming. I thought you could tell me what to do.'

Father Mould stared for another long moment, open-mouthed, baffled. 'Well, kiddo,' he said at last. 'You want me to tell you what to do? I think you ought to go home and hang yourself. That'd probably be the best thing for you, for your family – really, for everyone. There's rope in the storeroom behind the church. I'd go get it for you if I thought that would point you in the right direction.'

'Why—?' Ig started, and then had to clear his throat before he went on, 'Why do you want me to kill myself?'

'Because you killed Merrin Williams and your daddy's big-shot Jew lawyer got you off. Sweet little Merrin Williams. I had a lot of affection for her. Not much of a rack, but she did have one fine little ass. You should've gone to jail. I wanted you to go to jail. Sister, spot me.' He stretched out on his back for another set of reps.

'But, Father,' Ig said, 'I didn't do it. I didn't kill her.'

'Oh, you big kidder,' said Father Mould as he put his hands on the bar above him. Sister Bennett settled into position at the head of the bench press. 'Everyone knows you did it. You might as well kill yourself. You're going to hell anyway.'

'I'm there already.'

Father Mould grunted as he lowered the bar to his chest and heaved it up again. Ig noticed Sister Bennett staring at him.

'I wouldn't blame you for killing yourself,' she said without preamble. 'Most days I'm ready to commit suicide by lunchtime. I hate how people look at me. The lesbian jokes they make about me behind my back. I could use that rope in the shed if you don't want it.'

Father Mould shoved the bar up with a gasp. 'I think about Merrin Williams all the time. Usually when I'm balling her mother. Her ma does a lot of work for me here in the church these days, you know. Most of it on her hands and knees.' He grinned at the thought. 'Poor woman. We pray together most every day. Usually for you to die.'

'You . . . you took a vow of chastity,' Ig said.

'Chastity shmastity. I figure God is just glad I keep it in my pants around the altar boys. Way I see it, the lady needs comfort from someone, and she sure isn't going to get any from that four-eyed sad sack she's married to. Not the right kind of comfort anyway.'

Sister Bennett said, 'I want to be someone different. I want to run away. I want someone to like me. Did you ever like me, Iggy?'

Ig swallowed. 'Well . . . I guess. Somewhat.'

'I want to sleep with someone,' Sister Bennett continued, as if he hadn't said anything. 'I want someone to hold me in bed at night. I don't care whether it's a man or a woman. I don't care. I don't want to be alone anymore. I can write cheques for the church. Sometimes I want to empty the account and run away with the money. Sometimes I want to do that so bad.'

'I'm surprised,' Father Mould said, 'that no one in this town has stepped up to make an example out of you for what you did to Merrin Williams. Give you a taste of what you gave her. You'd think some concerned citizens would pay you a visit some night, take you for a relaxing tour of the countryside. Right back to that tree where you killed Merrin and string you up

42

from it. If you won't do the decent thing and hang yourself, then that'd be the next-best thing.'

Ig was surprised to find himself relaxing, unbunching his fists, breathing more steadily. Father Mould wobbled with the bench press. Sister Bennett caught the bar and settled it in its cradle with a clank.

Ig lifted his gaze to her and said, 'What's stopping you?'

'From what?' she asked.

'From taking the money and leaving.'

'God,' she said. 'I love God.'

'What's He ever done for you?' Ig asked her. 'Does He make it hurt less − when people laugh at you behind your back? Or more − because for His sake you're all alone in the world? How old are you?'

'Sixty-one.'

'Sixty-one is old. It's almost too late. *Almost*. Can you wait even one more day?'

She touched her throat, her eyes wide and alarmed. Then she said, 'I'd better go,' and turned and hurried past him to the stairs.

Father Mould hardly seemed aware she was going. He was sitting up now, wrists resting on his knees.

'Were you done lifting?' Ig asked him.

'One more rep to go.'

'Let me spot you,' Ig said, and came around behind the bench.

As he handed Father Mould the bar, Ig's fingers brushed his knuckles and he saw that when Mould was twenty, he and a few other guys on the hockey team had pulled ski masks over their faces and driven after a car full of Nation of Islam kids who had come up from New York City to speak at Syracuse about civil rights. Mould and his friends forced the kids off the road and chased them into the woods with baseball bats. They caught the slowest of them and shattered his legs in eight different places. It was two years before the kid walked again without the help of a walker.

'You and Merrin's mother – have you really been praying for me to die?'

'More or less,' Father Mould said. 'To be honest, most of the time when she's calling to God, she's riding my dick.'

'Do you know why He hasn't struck me down?' Ig asked. 'Do you know why God hasn't answered your prayers?'

'Why?'

'Because there is no God. Your prayers are whispers to an empty room.'

Father Mould lifted the bar again – with great effort – and lowered it and said, 'Bullshit.'

'It's all a lie. There's never been anyone there. You're the one who ought to use that rope in the shed.'

'No,' Father Mould said, 'you can't make me do that. I don't want to die. I love my life.'

So. He couldn't make people do anything they didn't already want to do. Ig had wondered if this might not be the case.

Father Mould made a face and grunted but couldn't lift the bar again. Ig turned from the weight bench and started towards the stairs.

'Hey,' Father Mould said, 'need some help here.'

Ig put his hands in his pockets and began to whistle 'When the Saints Go Marching In'. For the first time all morning he felt good. Father Mould gasped and struggled behind him, but Ig did not look back as he climbed the steps.

Sister Bennett passed Iggy as he stepped into the atrium. She was wearing red slacks and a sleeveless shirt with daisies on it and she had her hair up. She startled at the sight of him and almost dropped her purse.

'Are you off?' Ig asked her.

'I ... I don't have a car,' she said. 'I want to take the church car, but I'm scared of getting caught.'

'You're cleaning out the local account. What's a car matter?'

She stared at him for a moment, then leaned forward and kissed Ig at the corner of his mouth. At the touch of her lips, Ig knew about the awful lie she had told her mother when she was nine, and about the terrible day she had impulsively kissed one of her students, a pretty sixteen-year-old named Britt, and about the private, despairing surrender of her spiritual beliefs. He saw these things and understood and did not care.

'God bless you,' Sister Bennett said.

Ig had to laugh.

7

~e

There was nothing left for him but to go home and see his parents. He pointed the car towards their house and drove.

The silence of the car made him restless. He tried the radio, but it was worse than the quiet, jangled his nerves. His parents lived fifteen minutes outside of town, which gave him too much time to think. He had not been so unsure what to expect of them since the night he'd spent in jail, brought in for questioning about Merrin's rape and murder.

The detective, a man named Carter, had begun the interrogation by sliding a photo of her across the table between them. Later, when he was alone in his cell, that picture was waiting for Ig every time he closed his eyes. Merrin was white against the brown leaves, on her back, her feet together, her arms at her sides, her hair spread out. Her face was darker than the ground, and her mouth was full of leaves, and there was a dark dried trickle of blood that ran from under her hairline and down the side of her face to trace her cheekbone. She still wore his tie, the broad strip of it demurely covering her left breast. He couldn't drive the image from his mind. It worked on his nerves and on his cramping stomach, until sometime – who knew when, there was no clock in his cell – he fell to his knees in front of the stainless-steel toilet bowl and was sick.

He was afraid to see his mother the next day. It was the worst night of his life, and he thought it was likely also the worst night of hers. He had never been in trouble for anything. She wouldn't sleep, and he imagined her sitting up in the kitchen, in her nightdress, with a cup of cold herbal tea, red-eyed and waxy. His father, Derrick Perrish, wouldn't sleep either, would stay up to be with her. He wondered if his father would sit beside her quietly, the two of them scared and still, with nothing to do but wait, or if he would be agitated and bad-tempered, pacing the kitchen, telling her what they were going to do and how they were going to fix it, who he was going to come down on like a sack of motherfucking cinderblocks.

Ig had been determined not to cry when he saw his mother, and he didn't. Neither did she. His mother had made herself up as if for a luncheon with the board of trustees at the university, and her slim, narrow face was alert and calm. His father was the one who looked as if he'd been crying. Derrick had trouble focusing his stare. His breath was bad.

His mother said, 'Don't talk to anyone except the lawyer.' That was the first thing out of her mouth. She said, 'Don't admit to anything.'

His father repeated it – 'Don't admit to anything' – and hugged him and began to weep. Then, through his sobs, Derrick blurted, 'I don't care what happened,' and that was when Ig realised that they believed he had done it. It was the one notion that had never occurred to him. Even if he *had* done it – even if he'd been caught in the act – Ig had thought his parents would believe in his innocence.

Ig walked out of the Gideon police station later that afternoon, his eyes hurting in the strong, slanting October light. He hadn't been charged. He was never charged. He was never cleared. He was, to this day, considered a 'person of interest'.

Evidence had been collected on scene, DNA evidence, maybe – Ig wasn't sure, since the police kept the details to themselves – and he had believed with all his heart that once it was analysed, he would be publicly cleared of all wrong-doing. But there was a fire at the state lab in Concord, and the samples taken from around Merrin's corpse were ruined. This news poleaxed Ig. It was hard not to be superstitious, to feel that there were dark forces lined up against him. His luck was poison. The only surviving forensic evidence was a tyre imprint from someone's Goodyear. Ig's Gremlin had Michelins on it. But this was not decisive one way or another, and if there was no solid proof that Ig had committed the crime, there was nothing to take him off the hook either. His alibi – that he'd spent the night alone, passed out drunk in his car behind a derelict Dunkin' Donuts in the middle of nowhere – sounded like a desperate, threadbare lie, even to himself.

In those first months after he moved home, Ig was looked after and cared for, as if he were a child again, home with flu, and his parents intended to see him through his sickness by providing him with soup and books. They crept through their own house, as if afraid that the business and noise of their everyday lives might unnerve him. It was curious that they should feel so much concern for him, when they thought it possible he'd done such horrible things to a girl they too had loved.

But after the case against him fell apart and the immediate threat of prosecution had passed, his parents drifted away from him, retreating into themselves. They had loved him and been ready to go to the mattresses for him when it looked as if he was going to be tried for murder, but they seemed relieved to see the back of him as soon as they knew he wasn't going to jail.

He lived with them for nine months but did not have to

think long when Glenna asked if he wanted to split her rent. After he moved out, he saw his parents only when he came by the house to visit. They didn't meet in town for lunches, or go to the movies, or to shop, and they never came to the apartment. Sometimes, when Ig stopped by the house, he would discover that his father was away, in France for a jazz festival or in LA to work on a soundtrack. He never knew about his father's plans in advance, and his father didn't call to say he was going out of town.

Ig had harmless chats on the sun porch with his mother in which nothing of any importance was discussed. He had been about to begin a job in England when Merrin died, but that part of his life had been derailed by what happened. He told his mother he was going to go back to school, that he had applications for Brown and Columbia. And he really did; they were sitting on top of the microwave in Glenna's apartment. One of them had been used as a paper plate for a slice of pizza, and the other was stained with dried brown crescents from the bottom of a coffee cup. His mother was willing to play along, to encourage and approve, without asking uncomfortable follow-up questions, such as if he was ever going to visit these schools for an interview, if he had any notions of getting a job while he waited to hear from admissions. Neither of them wanted to rattle the fragile illusion that things were getting back to normal, that everything still might work out for Ig, that his life was going to resume.

On his occasional visits home, he was really only ever at ease when he was with Vera, his grandmother, who lived with his parents. He wasn't sure she even remembered that once he had been arrested for a sex murder. She was in a wheelchair most of the time, following a hip replacement that had inexplicably left her no better off, and Ig took her for walks on the gravel road through the woods north of his parents' house to a view of Queen's Face, a high shelf of rock that hang-gliders leaped from. On a warm, windy day in July, there might be five or six of them riding the updraughts, distant, tropically coloured kites weaving and bobbing in the sky. When Ig was with his grandmother and they watched the hang-gliders daring the winds off Queen's Face, he almost felt like the person he'd been when Merrin was alive, someone who was glad to do for others, who was glad for the smell of the outdoors.

As he rolled up the hill to the house, he saw Vera in the front yard, in the wheelchair, a pitcher of iced tea on an end-table set out next to her. Her head was bent at a crooked angle; she was asleep, had dozed off in the sun. Ig's mother had maybe been sitting outside with her – there was a rumpled plaid blanket spread on the grass. The sun struck the pitcher of iced tea and turned the rim into a hoop of brilliance, a silver halo. It was as peaceful a scene as could be, but no sooner had Ig stopped the car than his stomach started to churn. It was like the church. Now that he was here, he didn't want to get out. He dreaded seeing the people he'd come to see.

He got out. There was nothing else to do.

A black Mercedes he didn't recognise was parked to one side of the drive, Alamo plates on it. Terry's rent-a-car. Ig had offered to meet him at the airport, but Terry said it didn't make sense, he was getting in late and wanted to have a car of his own, and they could see each other the next day. So Ig had gone out with Glenna instead and wound up drunk and alone at the old foundry.

Of all the people in Ig's family, he was least afraid to see Terry. Whatever Terry might have to confess, whatever secret compulsions or shames, Ig was ready to forgive him. He owed him that. Maybe, on some level, Terence was who he had really come to see. When Ig was in the worst trouble of his life, Terry had been in the papers every day, saying that the case against him was a sham, utter nonsense, saying that his brother didn't have it in him to hurt someone he loved. Ig thought if anyone could find it in himself to help him now, it would have to be Terry.

Ig padded across the turf to Vera's side. His mother had left her turned to face the long grassy slope, slanting down and away to the old log fence at the bottom of the hill. Vera's ear rested against her shoulder and her eyes were closed and her breath whistled softly. He felt some of the tension drain out of him, seeing her at rest that way. He wouldn't have to talk to her, at least, wouldn't have to hear her babble her secret, most dreadful urges. That was something. He stared into her thin, worn, lined face, feeling almost sick with fondness for her, for the mornings they had spent together with tea and peanut-butter cookies and *The Price Is Right*. Her hair was bound behind her head but coming loose from its pins, so that long strands the colour of moonglow wandered across her cheeks. He put his hand gently over hers – forgetting for a moment what a touch could bring.

His grandmother, he learned then, had no hip pain at all but liked people pushing her here and there in the wheelchair and waiting on her hand and foot. She was eighty years old and entitled to some things. She especially liked to order around her daughter, who thought her shit didn't stink because she was rich enough to wipe with twenty-dollar bills, wife of the big has-been and mother of a showbiz phoney and a depraved sex killer. Although Vera supposed that was better than what Lydia had been, a cheap prostitute who'd been lucky to bag a small-time celebrity john with a sentimental streak. It was still a surprise to Vera that her daughter had come out of her Vegas years with a husband and a purse full of credit cards, not ten years in jail and an incurable venereal disease. It was Vera's privately held belief that Ig knew what his mother had been – a cheap whore – and that it had led to a pathological hatred of women and was the real reason he had raped and killed Merrin

Williams. These things were always so Freudian. And of course the Williams girl, she had been a frisky little gold digger, had been waving her little tail in the boy's face from day one, looking for a ring and Ig's family money. In her short skirts and tight tops, Merrin Williams had been hardly more than a whore herself, in Vera's opinion.

Ig let go of her wrist as if it were a bare wire that had given him an unexpected jolt, cried out, and took a stumbling step backwards. His grandmother stirred in her chair and opened one eye.

'Oh,' she said. 'You.'

'I'm sorry. I didn't mean to wake you.'

'I wish you hadn't. I wanted to sleep. I was happier asleep. Do you think I wanted to see *you*?'

Ig felt cold seeping behind his breastbone. His grandmother turned her head away from him.

'When I look at you, I want to be dead.'

'Do you?' he asked.

'I can't see any of my friends. I can't go to church. Everyone stares at me. They all know what you did. It makes me want to die. And then you show up here to take me for walks. I hate when you take me for walks and people see us together. You don't know how hard it is to pretend I don't hate you. I always thought there was something wrong with you. The screamy way you'd be breathing after you ran anywhere. You were always breathing through your mouth, like a dog, especially around pretty girls. And you were slow. So much slower than your brother. I tried to tell Lydia. I said I don't know how many times that you weren't right. She didn't want to hear it, and now look what's happened. We all have to live with it.'

She put her hand over her eyes, her chin trembling. As Ig backed away across the yard, he could hear her beginning to cry.

He walked across the front porch and through the open door and into the cave darkness of the front hall. He had ideas about going up to his old bedroom and lying down. He felt like he could use some time to himself, in the shadowy cool, surrounded by his concert posters and childhood books. But then, on his way past his mother's office, he heard the sound of shuffling papers, and he swivelled towards it automatically to look in on her.

His mother was bent over her desk, finger-walking through a handful of pages, occasionally plucking one out and slipping it into her soft leather briefcase. Leaning over like that, she had her pinstripe skirt pulled tight across her rear. His father had met her when she danced in Vegas, and she still had a showgirl's can. Ig flashed again to what he'd glimpsed in Vera's head, his grandmother's private belief that Lydia had been a whore and worse, and then he just as quickly discounted it as senile fantasy. His mother served on the New Hampshire State Council for the Arts and read Russian novels and even when she was a showgirl at least had worn ostrich feathers.

When Lydia saw Ig staring at her from the doorway, her briefcase tilted off her knee. She caught it, but by then it was too late. Papers spilled out, cascading to the floor. A few drifted down, swishing from side to side, in the aimless, no-hurry way of snowflakes, and Ig thought of the hang-gliders again. People jumped off Queen's Face, too. It was beloved of suicides. Maybe he would drive there next.

'Iggy,' she said. 'I didn't know you were coming by.'

'I know. I've been driving around and around. I didn't know where else to go. I've been having a hell of a morning.'

'Oh, baby,' she said, her brow furrowing with sympathy. It had been so long since he'd seen a sympathetic look, and he wanted sympathy so badly that he felt shaky, almost weak to be looked at that way.

'Something terrible is happening to me, Mom,' he said, his voice cracking. For the first time all morning, he felt close to tears.

'Oh, baby,' she said again. 'Why couldn't you have gone somewhere else?'

'Excuse me?'

'I don't want to hear about any more of your problems.'

The stinging sensation at the back of his eyeballs began to abate, the urge to cry draining away as quickly as it had come. The horns throbbed with a tender-sore feeling of ache, not entirely unpleasant.

'I'm in trouble, though.'

'I don't want to listen to this. I don't want to know.' She squatted on the floor and began picking up her papers and stuffing them into her briefcase.

'Mother,' he said.

'When you talk, I want to sing!' she shouted, and let go of her briefcase and clapped her hands over her ears. '*Lalala-la-la-la!* When you talk, I don't want to hear it. I want to hold my breath until you go away.'

She took a great swallow of air and held her breath, her cheeks popping out.

He crossed the room to her and sank down before her, where she would have to look at him. She crouched with her hands over her ears and her mouth squeezed tight. He took her briefcase and began to put her papers into it.

'Is this how you always feel when you see me?'

She nodded furiously, her eyes bright and staring.

'Don't suffocate yourself, Mom.'

His mother stared at him for a moment longer, then opened her mouth and drew a deep, whistling breath. She watched him put her papers into her bag.

When she spoke, her voice was small and shrill and rapid, words running together. 'I want to write you a letter a very nice letter with very nice handwriting on my special stationery to tell you how much Dad and I love you and how sorry we are you aren't happy and how much better it would be for everyone if you'd just go.'

He put the last of her papers into her briefcase and then squatted there, holding it across his knees. 'Go where?'

'Didn't you want to hike in Alaska?'

'With Merrin.'

'Or see Vienna?'

'With Merrin.'

'Or learn Chinese? In Beijing?'

'Merrin and I talked about going to Vietnam to teach English. But I don't think we were ever really going to do it.'

'I don't care *where* you go. As long as I don't have to see you once a week. As long as I don't have to hear you talk about yourself like everything's okay, because it's not okay, it's never going to be okay again. It makes me too unhappy to see you. I just want to be happy again, Ig.'

He gave her the briefcase.

'I don't want you to be my kid anymore,' she said. 'It's too hard. I wish I just had Terry.'

He leaned forward and kissed her cheek. And when he did, he saw how she had quietly resented him for years, for giving her stretch marks. He had single-handedly spoiled her *Playboy*-centrefold figure. Terry had been a small baby, considerate, and left her shape and skin intact, but Ig had fucked it all up. She had been offered five grand for a single night by an oil sheik in Vegas once, back before she had children. Those were the days. Easiest and best money she ever made.

'I don't know why I told you all that,' Lydia said. 'I hate myself. I was never a good mother.' Then she seemed to realise she had been kissed, and she touched her cheek, smoothing one palm across it. She was blinking back tears, but when she felt the kiss on her skin, she smiled. 'You kissed me. Are you ... are you going to go away, then?' Her voice unsteady with hopefulness.

'I was never here,' he said.

8

When he was back in the front hallway, he looked at the
screen door to the porch and the sunlit world beyond
and thought he ought to go, go now, get out of here before he
ran into someone else, his father or his brother. He had changed
his mind about looking for Terry, had decided to avoid him
after all. Considering the things his mother had said to him, Ig
thought it was better not to test his love for anyone else.

Yet he did not walk back out through the front door but
instead turned and began to climb the stairs. He was here, he
thought he should look in his room and see if there was anything
he wanted to take with him when he left. Left for where? He
didn't know yet. He wasn't sure, though, that he would ever be
coming back.

The stairs were a century old and creaked and muttered as
Ig climbed. No sooner had he reached the top of them than a
door across the hall, to the right, popped open, and his father
stuck out his head. Ig had seen this a hundred times before.
His father was distractible by nature and couldn't stand for
anyone to go by on the stairs without looking out to see who it
was.

'Oh,' he said. 'Ig. I thought you might be . . .' but his voice
trailed off. His gaze drifted from Iggy's eyes and on to the horns.
He stood there in a white wifebeater and striped suspenders, his
feet bare.

'Just tell me,' Ig said. 'Here's the part where you tell me something awful you've been keeping to yourself. Probably something about me. Just say it, and we'll get it out of the way.'

'I want to pretend I was doing something important in my studio, so I don't have to talk to you.'

'Well. That's not so bad.'

'Seeing you is too hard.'

'Gotcha. Just covered all this with Mom.'

'I think about Merrin. About what a good girl she was. I loved her, you know, in a way. And envied you. I was never in love with anyone the way you two were in love with each other. Certainly not your mother – status-obsessed whore. Worst mistake I ever made. Every bad thing in my life has come out of my marriage. But Merrin. Merrin was the sweetest little thing. You couldn't hear her laugh without smiling. When I think about the way you fucked her and killed her, I want to throw up.'

'I didn't kill her,' Ig said, dry-mouthed.

'And the worst part,' Derrick Perrish said, 'she was my friend and looked up to me, and I helped you get away with it.'

Ig stared.

'It was the guy who runs the state forensics lab, Gene Lee. His son died of leukaemia a few years back, but before he croaked, I helped him get tickets to Paul McCartney and arranged for Gene and his kid to meet him backstage and everything. After you were arrested, Gene got in touch. He asked me if you did it, and I said – I told him – that I couldn't give him an honest answer. And two days later there was that fire in the state lab up in Concord. Gene wasn't in charge there – he works out of Manchester – but I've always assumed ...'

Ig felt his insides turn over. If the forensic evidence gathered from the scene had not been destroyed, it might've been possible to establish his innocence. But it had gone up in flames – like every other hope Ig had held in his heart, like every good thing in Ig's life. In paranoid moments he had imagined there was an elaborate and secret conspiracy to condemn and destroy him. Now he saw he was right, there *had* been a secret agency at work, only it had been a conspiracy of people who wanted to protect him.

'How could you have done that? How could you have been so stupid?' Ig asked, breathless with a shock that wavered on the edge of hate.

'That's what I ask myself. Every day. I mean, when the world comes for your children, with the knives out, it's your job to stand in the way. Everyone understands that. But this. *This.* Merrin was like one of my kids, too. She was in our house every day for ten years. She *trusted* me. I bought her popcorn at movies and went to her lacrosse games and played cribbage with her, and she was beautiful and loved you, and you bashed her fuckin' brains in. It wasn't right to cover for you, not for that. You should've gone to jail. When I see you in the house, I want to slap that morose look right off your stupid face. Like you have anything to be sad about. You got away with murder. Literally. And dragged me into it. You make me feel unclean. You make me want to wash, scrub myself with steel wool. My skin crawls when you talk to me. How could you do that to her? She was one of the best people I ever knew. She was sure as shit my favourite thing about you.'

'Me, too,' Ig said.

'I want to go back into my office,' his father said, his mouth open, breathing heavily. 'I see you and I just want to go away. Into my office. Off to Vegas. Or Paris. *Anywhere.* I'd like to go and never come back.'

'And you really think I killed her. You don't sometimes wonder if maybe the evidence you had Gene burn up could've saved me? All the times I told you I didn't do it, you didn't sometimes think maybe – just maybe – I was innocent?'

59

His father stared, for a moment couldn't reply. Then he said, 'No. Not really. Tell the truth, I was surprised you didn't do something to her sooner. I always thought you were a weird little shit.'

9

⌒℮

He stood in the doorway of his bedroom for a full minute but did not enter the room, didn't lie down, as he had imagined doing. His head hurt again, in the temples, at the base of the horns. There was a feeling of pressure mounting behind them. Darkness twitched at the edges of his vision, in time to the beat of his pulse.

More than anything, he wanted rest, wanted no more madness. He wanted the touch of a cool hand on his brow. He wanted Merrin back – wanted to cry with his face buried in her lap and her fingers moving over the nape of his neck. All thoughts of peace were wrapped up in her. Every restful memory seemed to include her. A breezy July afternoon, lying in the grass above the river. A rainy October, drinking cider with her in her living room, huddled together under a knitted blanket, Merrin's cold nose against his ear.

He cast his gaze around the room, considering the detritus of the life he'd lived here. He spied his old trumpet case, sticking out a little from under the bed, and picked it up, set it on the mattress. Within was his silver horn. It was tarnished, the keys worn smooth, as if it had seen hard use.

It had. Even after he knew that his weak lungs would not allow him to play the trumpet – ever – Ig had, for reasons he no longer understood, continued to practise. After his parents sent him to bed, he would play in the dark, lying on his back under the sheets, his fingers flying over the keys. He played Miles Davis and Wynton Marsalis and Louis Armstrong. But the music was only in his head. For while he placed the mouthpiece to his lips, he did not dare blow, for fear of bringing on a wave of light-headedness and a storm of black snow. It seemed now an absurd waste of time, all that practise to no useful end.

He emptied the case onto the floor in a sudden convulsion of fury, cast out the trumpet and the rest of his horn paraphernalia – lead pipes and valve oil, spare mouthpiece – chucking it all. The last thing he grabbed was a mute, a Tom Crown, a thing that looked like a great Christmas ornament made out of brushed copper. He meant to launch it across the room, and he even made the throwing motion, but his fingers wouldn't open, wouldn't allow it to be flung. It was a beautiful piece of metalwork, but that wasn't why he held on to it. He didn't know why he held on to it.

What you did with a Tom Crown, you shoved it down into the bell of the horn to choke off the sound; if used properly, it produced a lascivious, hand-up-the-skirt squall. Ig stared down at it now, frowning, an imperceptible *something* tugging at his consciousness. It wasn't an idea, not yet. It wasn't even half an idea. It was a drifting, confused notion. Something about horns. Something about the way they were played.

Finally Ig set the mute aside, turned again to the trumpet case. He pulled out the foam padding, packed in a change of clothes, then went looking for his passport. Not because he thought he was leaving the country but because he wanted to take everything that was important with him, so he wouldn't have to come back later.

His passport was tucked in the fancy-pants Bible, a King James with a white leather cover and the words of Jesus printed in gold, kept in the top drawer of his dresser. Terry called it his Neil Diamond Bible. He had won it as a child, playing Scriptural Jeopardy in his Sunday school class. When faced with answers from the Bible, Ig had all the right questions.

Ig picked his passport out of the Good Book, then paused, looking at a column of dots and lines in blurred pencil, scrawled on the endpapers. It was a key to Morse Code. Ig had copied it into the back of the Neil Diamond Bible himself, more than ten years before. He once believed that Merrin Williams had sent him a message in Morse Code, and he spent two weeks working out a reply to be sent the same way. The response he had come up with was still scribbled there in a string of circles and dashes: his favourite prayer in the book.

He threw the Bible into the trumpet case as well. There had to be something in there, some useful tips for his situation, a homeopathic remedy you could apply when you came down with a bad case of the devil.

It was time to go, to get out before he saw anyone else, but at the bottom of the stairs he noticed how dry and tacky his mouth felt, and that it was painful to swallow. Ig detoured into the kitchen and drank from the sink. He cupped his hands together and splashed water into his face and then held the sides of the sink with his face dripping and shook himself like a dog. He rubbed his face dry with a dish towel, enjoying the rough feel of it against his raw, cold-shocked skin. At last Ig tossed down the towel and turned, to find his brother standing behind him.

10

~e

Terry leaned against the wall, just inside the swinging door. He didn't look so well – the jet lag, maybe. He needed a shave, and his eyelids had a puffy, swollen look, as if he were suffering from allergies. Terry was allergic to everything – pollen, peanut butter; he had once nearly died of a bee sting. His black silk shirt and tweed slacks hung loose on his frame, as if he had lost weight.

They regarded each other. Ig and Terry had not been in the same room together since the weekend Merrin had been killed, and Terry hadn't looked much better then, had been inarticulate with grief for her, and for Ig. Terence had left for the West Coast shortly after – supposedly for rehearsals, although Ig suspected he'd been summoned for a damage-control meeting with the execs at Fox – and had not been back since, and no surprise. Terry had not much cared for Gideon even before the murder.

Terry said, 'I didn't know you were here. I didn't hear you come in. Did you grow horns? While I was gone?'

'I thought it was time for a new look. Do you like them?'

His brother shook his head. 'I want to tell you something,' Terry said, and his Adam's apple jugged up and down in his throat.

'Join the club.'

'I want to tell you something, but I *don't* want to tell you. I'm afraid.'

'Go ahead. Spill it. It probably isn't so bad. I don't think anything you could have to say would bother me much. Mom just told me she never wants to see me again. Dad told me he wishes I had gone to jail forever.'

'No.'

'Yes.'

'Oh, Ig,' Terry said. His eyes were watering. 'I feel so bad. About everything. About how things turned out for you. I know how much you loved her. I loved her, too, you know. Merrin. She was a hell of a kid.'

Ig nodded.

'I want you to know—' Terry said in a choked voice.

'Go ahead,' Ig said gently.

'I didn't kill her.'

Ig stared, a pins-and-needles sensation beginning to spread across his chest. The thought that Terry might have raped and killed her had never crossed his mind, was impossible.

Ig said, 'Of course you didn't.'

'I loved you two guys and wanted you to be happy. I never would've done anything to hurt her.'

'I know that,' Ig said.

'And if I had any idea Lee Tourneau was going to kill her, I would've tried to stop it,' Terry said. 'I thought Lee was her friend. I've wanted to tell you so bad, but Lee made me keep quiet. He made me.'

'*EEEEEEEEEE,*' Ig screamed.

'He's awful, Ig,' Terry said. 'You don't know him. You think you do, but you don't have any idea.'

'*EEEEEEEEEEEE,*' Ig went on.

'Lee fixed you and me both, and I've been in hell ever since,' Terry said.

Ig fled into the hallway, ran through the dark for the front door, slammed through the screen, stumbled out into the sudden blinding glare of day, eyes blurring with tears, missed the steps, fell into the yard. He picked himself up, gasping. He had dropped his trumpet case – had hardly even been aware he was still carrying it – and he snatched it back up out of the grass.

He lurched across the lawn, barely looking where he was going. The corners of his eyes were damp, and he thought he might be crying, but when he touched his fingers to his face, they came away bloody. He lifted his hands to his horns. The points had ruptured through the skin and blood was trickling down his face. He was aware of a steady throbbing in the horns, and although there was a feeling of soreness in them, there was also a kind of nervous thrill shooting through his temples, a sensation of release not unlike orgasm. He staggered along, and from his mouth poured a stream of curses, choked obscenities. He hated how hard it was to breathe, hated the sticky blood on his cheeks and hands, the too-bright blue sky, the smell of himself, hated, hated, *hated*.

Lost in his own head, he didn't see his grandmother's wheelchair until he had almost crashed into it. He pulled up short, staring down at her. She had dozed off again, a soft snore burring in her nostrils. She was smiling faintly, as at some pleasant, dreamy thought, and the look of peace and happiness on her face made Ig's stomach roil with fury. He stomped on the brake on the back of her wheelchair and gave it a shove.

'Bitch,' he said as it began to roll forward, down the hill.

She lifted her head from her shoulder, put it back, then lifted it again, stirring weakly. The wheelchair thudded through the green, groomed grass, one wheel hitting a rock, juddering over it, going on, and Ig thought of being fifteen, the day he'd ridden the shopping cart down the Evel Knievel trail: the essential turning point of his life, really. Had he been going this fast then? It was something, the way the wheelchair picked up speed, the way a person's life picked up speed, the way a life was like a bullet aimed at one final target, impossible to slow or turn aside, and, like the bullet, you were ignorant of what you were going to hit, would never know anything except the rush and the impact. Vera was probably doing forty when she hit the fence at the bottom.

Ig walked on towards his car, breathing easily again, the tight, pinched feeling behind his breastbone gone as quickly as it had come. The air smelled of fresh grass, warmed in the late-August sun, and green leaves. Ig didn't know where he was going next, only that he was going. A garter snake slithered across the lawn behind him, black and green and wet-looking. It was joined by a second, and then a third. He didn't notice.

As Ig climbed in behind the wheel of the Gremlin, he began to whistle. It really *was* a fine day. He turned the Gremlin around in the drive and started down the hill. The highway was waiting where he'd left it

CHERRY

11

She was sending him a message.

At first he didn't know it was her, didn't know who was doing it. He didn't even know it was a message. *It* began about ten minutes after the start of services: a flash of golden light at the periphery of his vision, so bright it caused him to flinch. He rubbed at his eye, trying to massage away the glowing blot that now floated before him. When his sight had cleared somewhat, he glanced around, looking for the source of the light but unable to find it.

The girl sat across the aisle, one pew up from him, and she wore a white summer dress, and he had never seen her before. His gaze kept shifting to her, not because he thought she had anything to do with the light but because she was the best thing to look at on that side of the aisle. He wasn't the only one who thought so either. A lanky boy with cornsilk hair so pale it was almost white sat directly behind her and sometimes seemed to be leaning forward to look over her shoulder and down the front of her dress. Iggy had never seen the girl before but vaguely recognised the boy from school, thought he might be a year older.

Ignatius Martin Perrish searched furtively for a wristwatch or a bracelet that might be catching the light and reflecting it into his eyeball. He examined people in metal-framed eye-glasses, women with hoops dangling from their earlobes, but could not pinpoint what was causing that bothersome flash. Mostly, though, he looked at the girl, with her red hair and bare white arms. There was something about the whiteness of those arms that made them seem more naked than the bare arms of other women in church. A lot of redheads had freckles, but she looked as if she had been carved from a block of soap.

Whenever he gave up searching for the source of the light and turned his face forward, the gold flash returned, a blinding flare. It was maddening, this *flash-flash* in his left eye, like a moth of light circling him, fluttering in his face. Once he even batted at it, trying to swat it aside.

That was when she gave herself away, snorting helplessly, quivering with the effort it took to contain laughter. Then she gave him the look – a slow, sidelong gaze, self-satisfied and amused. She knew she had been caught and that there was no point in keeping up a pretence. Ig knew, too, that she had *planned* to get caught, to continue until she was found out, a thought that gave his blood a little rush. She was very pretty, about his age, her hair braided into a silky rope the colour of cherries. She was fingering a delicate gold cross around her throat and she turned it just so, into the sunlight, and it shone, became a cruciform flame. She lingered on the gesture, making it a kind of confession, then turned the cross away.

After that Ig was no longer able to pay the slightest attention to what Father Mould was saying behind the altar. He wanted more than anything for her to glance his way again, and for a long time she didn't do it, a kind of sweet denial. But then she took another sly, slow, sidelong peek at him. Staring straight at him, she flashed the cross in his eyes, two short and one long. A moment passed, and she flashed a different sequence, three short this time. She held her gaze on his while she winked the cross at him, smiling, but in a dreamy sort of way, as if she'd forgotten what she was smiling about. The intentness of her stare suggested she was *willing* him to understand something, that what she was doing with the cross was important.

'I think it's Morse Code,' said Ig's father out of the side of his mouth, in a low voice: one convict talking to another in the jail yard.

Ig twitched, a nervous reflex reaction. In the last few minutes, the Sacred Heart of Mary had become a TV show playing in the background, with the volume turned down to an inaudible murmur. But when his father spoke, Ig was jolted out of the moment and back into an awareness of where he was. He also discovered, to his alarm, that his penis had stiffened slightly in his pants and was lying hot against his leg. It was important that it go back down. Any moment they would stand for the final hymn, and it would be tenting out the front of his pants.

'What?' he asked.

'She's telling you, "Stop looking at my legs",' Derrick Perrish said, side of the mouth again, movie wiseguy. '"Or I'll give you a black eye".'

Ig made a funny sound trying to clear his throat.

By now Terry was trying to see. Ig sat on the inside of the aisle, with his father on his right and then his mother and then Terry, so his older brother had to crane his neck to see the girl. He considered her merits – she had turned to face forward again – then whispered loudly, 'Sorry, Ig. No chance.'

Lydia thumped him in the back of his head with her hymnal.

Terry said, 'Damn, Mom,' and she thumped him in the head with the book again.

'You won't use that word here,' she whispered.

'Why don't you hit Ig?' Terry whispered. 'He's the one checking out little redheads. Thinking lustful thoughts. He's coveting. Look at him. You can see it on his face. Look at that coveting expression.'

'Covetous,' Derrick said.

Ig's mother looked at him, and Ig's cheeks burned. She

73

shifted her gaze from him to the girl, who minded them not at all, pretending to be interested in Father Mould. After a moment Lydia sniffed and looked towards the front of the church.

'That's all right,' she said. 'I was starting to wonder if Ig was gay.'

And then it was time to sing, and they all stood, and Ig looked at the girl again, and as she came to her feet, she rose into a shaft of sunshine and a crown of fire settled on her brushed and shining red hair. She turned and looked at him again, opening her mouth to sing, only she gave a little cry instead, soft yet carrying. She had been about to flash him with the cross when the delicate gold chain came loose and spilled into her hand.

Ig watched her while she bowed her head and tried to fix it. Then something happened to give him an unhappy turn. The good-looking blond kid standing behind her leaned in and made a hesitant, fumbling gesture at the back of her neck. He was trying to fasten the necklace for her. She flinched and stepped away from him, gave him a startled, not particularly welcome look.

The blond did not flush or seem embarrassed. He looked less like a boy, more like classical statuary, with the delicate, stern, preternaturally calm, just slightly dour features of a young Caesar, someone who could, with a simple thumbs-down, turn a gang of bloodied Christians into lion food. Years later his hairstyle, that close-cropped cap of pale white, would be popularised by Marshall Mathers, but in that year it looked sporty and unremarkable. He also had on a tie, which was class. He said something to the girl, but she shook her head. Her father leaned in and smiled at the boy and began to work on the necklace himself.

Ig relaxed. Caesar had made a tactical error, touching her when she wasn't expecting it, had annoyed instead of charmed her. The girl's father worked at the necklace for a while but then laughed and shook his head because it couldn't be fixed, and she laughed, too, and took it from him. Her mother glared sharply at both of them, and the girl and her father began to sing again.

The service ended, and conversation rose like water filling a tub, the church a container with a particular volume, its natural quiet quickly displaced by noise. Ig's best subject had always been maths, and he reflexively thought in terms of capacity, volume, invariants and, above all, absolute values. Later he turned out to be good at logical ethics, but that was perhaps only an extension of the part of him that was good at keeping equations straight and making numbers play nice.

He wanted to talk to her but didn't know what to say, and in a moment he had lost his chance. As she stepped out from between the pews and into the aisle, she gave him a look, suddenly shy but smiling, and then the young Caesar was at her side, towering over her and telling her something. Her father intervened again, nudging her forward and somehow inserting himself between her and the junior emperor. Her dad grinned at the kid, pleasant, welcoming – but as he spoke, he was pushing his daughter ahead of him, marching her along, increasing the distance between her and the boy with the calm, reasonable, noble face. The Caesar did not seem troubled and did not try to reach her again but nodded patiently, even stepped aside, to allow the girl's mother and some older ladies – aunts? – to slip past him.

With her father nudging her along, there was no chance to talk to her. Ig watched her go, wishing she would look back and wave to him, but she didn't, of course she didn't. By then the aisle was choked with people departing. Ig's father put a hand on his shoulder to let him know they were going to wait for things to clear out. Ig watched young Caesar go by. He was there with his own father, a man with a thick blond moustache that grew right into his sideburns, giving him the look of the bad guy in a Clint Eastwood Western, someone to stand to the left of Lee Van Cleef and get shot in the opening salvo of the final battle.

Finally traffic in the aisle shrank to a trickle, and Ig's father took his hand off Ig's shoulder to let him know they could proceed. Ig stepped out from the pew and allowed his parents past him, as was his habit, so he could walk out with Terry. He looked, longingly, at the girl's pew, as if somehow she might've reappeared there – and when he did, his right eyeball filled with a flash of golden light, like it was starting up all over again. He flinched, shut his eye, then walked towards her pew.

She had left her little gold cross, lying atop the puddled gold chain, in a square of light. Maybe she had put it down and then forgotten about it, with her father rushing her away from the blond boy. Ig collected it, expecting it to be cold. But it was hot, delightfully hot, a penny left all day in the sun.

'Iggy?' called his mother. 'Are you coming?'

Ig closed his fist around the necklace, turned, and began quickly down the aisle. It was important to catch up to her. She had left him a chance to impress her, to be the finder of lost things, to be both observant and considerate. But when he reached the door, she was gone. He had a glimpse of her in the back of a wood-panelled station wagon, sitting with one of her aunts, her parents in the front, pulling away from the kerb.

Well. That was all right. There was always next Sunday, and when Ig gave it back to her it wouldn't be broken anymore and he would know just what to say when he introduced himself.

12

Three days before Ig and Merrin met for the first time, Sean Phillips, a retired serviceman who lived on the north side of Pool Pond, woke at one in the morning to a steely, eardrum-stunning detonation. For a moment, muddled up with sleep, he thought he was on the USS *Eisenhower* again and that someone had just launched a RAM. Then he heard squealing tyres and laughter. He got off the floor – he had fallen out of bed and bruised his hip – and pushed aside the blind in time to see someone's shitty Road Runner peeling away. His mailbox had been blown off its post and lay deformed and smoking in the gravel. It was so full of holes it looked as if it had caught a blast from a shotgun.

Late the following afternoon, there was another explosion, this time in the dumpster behind Woolworth's. The bomb went off with a ringing boom and spewed gouts of burning garbage thirty feet into the air. Flaming newspaper and packing material came down in a fiery hail, and several parked cars were damaged.

On the Sunday that Ig fell in love – or at least in lust – with the strange girl sitting across the aisle from him in the Sacred Heart, there was yet another explosion in Gideon. A cherry bomb with an explosive force roughly equal to a quarter stick of trinitrotoluene erupted in a toilet at the McDonald's on Harper Street. It blew the seat off, cracked the bowl, shattered the tank, flooded the floor, and filled the men's room with greasy black smoke. The building was evacuated until the fire marshal had determined it was safe to re-enter. The incident was reported on the front page of Monday's *Gideon Ledger*, in an article that closed with a plea from the marshal for those responsible to quit before someone lost some fingers or an eye.

Things had been blowing up all around town for weeks. It had started a couple of days before the Fourth of July and continued well after the holiday, with increasing frequency. Terence Perrish and his friend Eric Hannity *weren't* the primary culprits. They had never destroyed any property except their own, and they were both too young to be out joyriding at one in the morning, blowing up mailboxes.

But.

But Eric and Terry *had* been at the beach in Seabrook when Eric's cousin Jeremy Rigg walked into the fireworks warehouse there and came out with a case of forty-eight vintage cherry bombs, which he claimed had been manufactured in the good old days before the power of such explosives was limited by child-safety laws. Jeremy had passed six of them on to Eric, as a late birthday present, he said, although his real motive might've been pity. Eric's father had been out of work for more than a year and was an unwell man.

It is possible that Jeremy Rigg was patient zero at the centre of a plague of explosions and that all of the many bombs that went off that summer could in some way be traced back to him. Or maybe Rigg only bought them because other boys were buying them, because it was the thing to do. Maybe there were multiple points of infection. Ig never learned, and in the end it didn't matter. It was like wondering how evil had come into the world or what happens to a person after he dies: an interesting philosophical exercise, but also curiously pointless, since evil and death happened, regardless of the why and the how and the what-it-meant. All that mattered was that by early August both Eric and Terry had the fever to blow things up, like every other teenage male in Gideon.

The bombs themselves were called Eve's Cherries, red balls the size of crabapples with the fine-grained texture of a brick and the silhouette of an almost-naked woman stamped on the side. She was a pert-breasted honey with the unlikely proportions of a girl on a mudflap: tits like beach balls and a wasp waist thinner than her thighs. As a gesture towards modesty, she wore what looked like a maple leaf over her crotch, leading Eric Hannity to conclude she was a fan of the Toronto Maple Leafs and therefore a fuckin' Canuck slut who was just asking to get her tits lit up.

The first time Eric and Terry used one was in Eric's garage. They chucked a cherry into a trash can and beat feet. The explosion that followed knocked the can over, spun it across the concrete, and fired the lid up into the rafters. The lid was smoking when it came back down, bent in the middle as if someone had tried to fold it in two. Ig wasn't there but heard all about it from Terry, who said that afterwards their ears were ringing so badly neither of them could hear the other one whooping. Other items followed in a chain of demolitions: a life-size Barbie, an old tyre that they sent rolling down a hill with a bomb taped inside it, and a watermelon. Ig was present for exactly none of the detonations in question, but his brother was always sure to fill him in, at great length, on what he'd missed. Ig knew, for example, that there had been nothing left of the Barbie except for one blackened foot, which fell from the sky to rattle about on the blacktop of Eric's driveway, doing a mad disembodied tap dance, and that the stink of the burning tyre had made everyone who smelled it dizzy and ill, and that Eric Hannity was standing too close to the watermelon when it exploded and needed a shower as a result. The details thrilled and tormented Ig, and by mid-August he was half desperate to see something vapourised himself.

So on the morning Ig walked into the pantry and found Terry trying to zip a twenty-eight-pound frozen Butterball turkey into his school backpack, he knew right away what it was for. Ig didn't ask to come along, and he didn't bargain with threats: *Let me go with you or I'll tell Mom.* Instead he watched while Terry struggled with his backpack and then, when it was clear it wasn't going to fit, said they should make a sling. He got his windbreaker from the mudroom, and they rolled the bird up in it, and then each of them took a sleeve. Hauling it between them that way, it was no trouble to carry, and just like that, Ig was going with him.

The sling got them as far as the edge of the town woods, and then, not long after they started along the trail that led to the old foundry, Ig spotted a shopping cart, half sunk in a bog to the side of the path. The front right wheel shimmied furiously, and rust flaked off the thing in a continuous flurry, but it beat lugging all that turkey a mile and a half. Terry made Ig push.

The old foundry was a sprawling medieval keep of dark brick with a great twisting chimney stack rising from one end and the walls Swiss-cheesed with holes that had once held windows. It was surrounded by a few acres of ancient parking lot, the macadam fissured almost to the point of disintegration and tummocky bunches of grass growing up through it. The place was busy that afternoon, kids skateboarding in the ruins, a fire burning in a trash can out back. A group of teenage derelicts – two boys and a skaggy girl – stood around the flames. One of them had what looked like a misshapen wiener on a stick. It was blackened and crooked, and sweet blue smoke poured off it.

'Lookit,' said the girl, a pudgy blonde with acne and low-riding jeans. Ig knew her. She was in his grade. Glenna someone. 'Here comes dinner.'

'Looks like fuckin' Thanksgiving,' said one of the boys, a

kid in a HIGHWAY TO HELL T-shirt. He gestured expansively towards the fire in the trash can. 'Throw that scrumptious bitch on.'

Ig, just fifteen and uncertain around strange older kids, could not speak, his windpipe shrivelling as if he were already suffering an asthma attack. But Terry was smooth. Two years older and possessed of a driver's permit, Terry already had a certain sly grace about him and the eagerness of a showman to amuse an audience. He spoke for the both of them. He always spoke for the both of them: that was his role.

'Looks like dinner's done,' Terry said, nodding at the thing on the stick. 'Your hot dog is turning black.'

'It's not a hot dog!' shrieked the girl, doubling over and screaming with laughter. 'It's a turd! Gary's cookin' a dog turd!' Her jeans were old and worn, and her too-small halter looked like a half-price item from K-mart, but over it she wore a handsome black leather jacket with a European cut. It didn't go with the rest of her outfit, or with the weather, and Ig's first thought was that it was stolen.

'You want a bite?' asked the kid in the HIGHWAY TO HELL shirt. He swung the stick away from the fire and offered it in Terry's direction. 'Cooked to perfection.'

'C'mon, man,' Terry said. 'I'm a high-school virgin, I play trumpet in the marching band, and I got a teeny weenie. I eat enough shit as it is.'

The derelicts erupted into laughter, maybe less because of what had been said than because of who was saying it – a slender, good-looking kid with a faded American-flag bandanna tied around his head to hold back his shaggy black hair – and the way it was said, in a tone of exuberance, as if he were joyfully putting down someone else and not himself. Terry used jokes like judo throws, as a way to deflect the energy of others from himself, and if he couldn't find any other target for his humour, he was glad to pull the trigger on himself – an inclination that would serve him well years later, when he was doing interviews on *Hothouse*, begging Clint Eastwood to punch him in the face and then autograph his broken nose.

Highway to Hell looked past Terry, across the broken asphalt, to a boy standing at the top of the Evel Knievel trail. 'Hey, Tourneau. Your lunch is done.'

More laughter – although the girl, Glenna, looked suddenly uneasy. The boy at the top of the trail didn't even glance their way but stood looking down the hill, clutching a big mountain board under one arm.

'Are you going?' Highway to Hell shouted when there was no response. 'Or do I need to cook you up a pair of nuts?'

'Go, Lee!' shouted the girl, and she held an encouraging fist in the air. 'Let 'er rip!'

The boy at the top of the trail cast a brief, disdainful look at her, and in that moment Ig recognised him, knew him from church. It was young Caesar. He had been dressed in a tie then, and he wore one now, along with a button-up short-sleeved shirt, khaki shorts and Converse high-tops with no socks. Just by virtue of holding a mountain board he managed to make the costume look vaguely alternative, the act of wearing a tie an ironic affectation, the kind of thing the lead singer in a punk band might do.

'He ain't going,' said the other boy who stood at the trash can, a long-haired kid. 'Jesus, Glenna, he's got a bigger pussy'n you.'

'Fuck you,' she said. To the bunch around the trash can, the look of hurt on her face was the funniest thing yet. Highway to Hell laughed so hard the stick shook, and his cooked turd fell into the flames.

Terry lightly slapped Ig's arm and they moved on. Ig wasn't sorry to be going, found something almost unbearably sad about the crew of them. They had nothing to do. It was terrible that this was the sum total of their summer afternoon, a burned shit and hurt feelings.

They approached the willowy blond boy – Lee Tourneau, apparently – slowing again as they reached the top of the Evel Knievel trail. The hill fell steeply away here, towards the river, a dark blue gleam visible through the black trunks of the pines. It had been a dirt road once, although it was difficult to imagine anyone driving a car down it, it was so steep and eroded, a vertiginous drop ideal for producing a rollover. Two half-buried and rusting pipes showed through the ground, and between them was a worn-smooth groove of packed earth, a kind of depression that had been polished to a hard gloss by the passage of a thousand mountain bikes and ten thousand bare feet. Ig's grandmother Vera had told him that in the thirties and forties, when people didn't care what they put into the river, the foundry had used those pipes to wash the dross into the water. They looked almost like rails, like tracks, lacking only a coal car or a roller-coaster kart to ride them. On either side of the pipes, the trail was all crumbling sun-baked dirt and protruding stones and trash. The hard-packed path between the pipes offered the easiest way down, and Ig and Terry slowed, waiting for Lee Tourneau to go.

Only he didn't go. He was never going to go. He put the board on the ground – it had a cobra painted on it, and big, thick, knobby tyres – and pushed it back and forth with one foot, as if to see how it rolled. He squatted and picked up the board and pretended to check the spin on one wheel.

The derelicts weren't the only ones giving him a hard time. Eric Hannity and a loose collection of other boys stood at the bottom of the hill squinting up at him and occasionally hollering taunts. Someone yelled at him to stick a manpon in his mangina and go, already. From over by the trash can, Glenna screamed again: 'Ride 'er, cowboy!' Beneath her rowdy cheer, though, she sounded desperate.

'Well,' Terry said to Lee Tourneau, 'it's like this. You can live life as a cripple or as a lame-ass.'

'What's that mean?' Lee asked.

Terry sighed. 'It means are you going to go?'

Ig, who had been down the trail many times on his mountain bike, said, 'It's okay. Don't be scared. The trail between the pipes is really smooth, and—'

'I'm not scared,' said Lee, as if Ig had made an accusation.

'So go,' Terry said.

'One of the wheels is sticking,' the kid said.

Terry laughed. He laughed mean, too. 'Come on, Ig.'

Ig pushed the cart past Lee Tourneau and into the trench between the pipes. Lee looked at the turkey, and his brow furrowed with a question that he didn't speak aloud.

'We're going to blow it up,' Ig said. 'Come see.'

'There's a baby seat in the shopping cart,' Terry said, 'in case you want a ride down.'

It was a shitty thing to say, and Ig grimaced sympathetically at Lee, but Lee's face was a Spock-on-the-bridge-of-the-*Enterprise* blank. He stood aside, holding his board to his chest, watching them go.

The boys at the bottom were waiting for them. There were a couple of girls, too, older girls, maybe old enough to be in college. They weren't on the riverbank with the boys, but sunning themselves out on Coffin Rock, in bikini tops and cutoffs.

Coffin Rock was forty feet offshore, a wide white stone that blazed in the sun. Their kayaks rested on a small sandbar that tailed upriver away from it. The sight of those girls, stretched upon the rock, made Ig love the world. Two brunettes – they might've been sisters – with tanned, toned bodies and a lot of leg, sitting up and talking to each other in low voices and staring at the boys. Even with his back turned to Coffin Rock Ig was aware of them, as if the girls, and not the sun, were the primary source of light cast upon the bank.

A dozen or so boys had collected for the show. They sat indifferently in tree branches hanging out over the water, or astraddle mountain bikes, or perched on boulders, all of them trying to look coolly unhappy. That was another side effect of those girls on the rock. Every boy there wanted to look older than every other boy, too old to really be there at all. If they could, with a dour look and a standoffish pose, somehow suggest they were only in the vicinity because they had to baby-sit a younger brother, all the better.

Possibly because he really *was* baby-sitting his younger brother, Terry was allowed to be happy. He hauled the frozen turkey out of the shopping cart and walked it towards Eric Hannity, who rose from a nearby rock, dusting off the back of his pants.

'Let's bake that bitch,' Hannity said.

'I call a drumstick,' Terry said, and some boys laughed in spite of themselves.

Eric Hannity was Terry's age, a rude, blunt savage with a harsh mouth and hands that knew how to catch a football, cast a rod, repair a small motor and smack an ass. Eric Hannity was a superhero. As a bonus, his father was an ex-state trooper who had actually been shot, albeit not in a gunfight, but in an accident at the barracks; another officer, on his third day, had dropped a loaded .30-06, and the slug had caught Bret Hannity in the abdomen. Eric's father had a business dealing baseball cards now, although Ig had hung around long enough to get a sense that his real business involved fighting his insurance company over a hundred-thousand-dollar settlement that was supposedly coming any day but that had yet to materialise.

Eric and Terry lugged the frozen turkey over to an old tree stump, rotted at the centre into a kind of a damp hole. Eric put a foot on the bird and pushed it down. It was a tight fit, and fat and skin bunched up around the edges of the hole. The two legs, pink bones wrapped in uncooked flesh, were squeezed together, pursing the turkey's stuffing cavity to a white pucker.

From his pocket Eric took his last two cherry bombs and set one aside. He ignored the boy who picked up the spare and the other boys who gathered around, staring at it and making appreciative noises. Ig had an idea Eric had set down his extra cherry just to get this precise reaction. Terry took the other bomb and jammed it into the Butterball. The fuse, almost six inches long, stuck obscenely out of that puckered hole in the turkey's rear end.

'You all'll want to find cover,' Eric said, 'or you're going to be wearing turkey dinner. And give me back that other one. If someone tries to walk off with my last cherry, this bird won't be the only one getting a piece of ordnance stuck up the ass.'

The boys scattered, crouching at the bottom of the embankment, sheltering behind tree trunks. Despite their best efforts to look disinterested, there was a helium-touched air of nervous anticipation hanging over them now. The girls on the rock were interested, too, could see something was about to happen. One of them rose to her knees and shaded her eyes with a hand, looking over at Terry and Eric. Ig wished, with a wistful pang, there was some reason for her to look at him instead.

Eric put a foot on the edge of the stump and produced a lighter, which ignited with a snap. The fuse began to spit white sparks. Eric and Terry remained for a moment, peering thoughtfully down, as if there were some doubt about whether it was going to catch. Then they began to back away, neither in any hurry. It was nicely done, a carefully managed bit of stagey cool. Eric had told the others to take cover, and they had all obliged by running for it. Which made Eric and Terry look steely and unflappable, the way they stayed behind to light the bomb and then made a slow, unhurried retreat from the blast area. They walked twenty paces but did not duck or hide behind anything, and they kept steady watch on the carcase. The fuse made a continuous sizzling sound for about three seconds, then stopped. And nothing happened.

'Shit,' Terry said. 'Maybe it got wet.'

He took a step back towards the stump.

Eric grabbed his arm. 'Hang on. Sometimes it—'

But Ig didn't hear the rest of the sentence. No one did. Lydia Perrish's twenty-eight-pound Butterball turkey exploded with a shattering crack, a sound so loud, so sudden and hard, that the girls out on the rock screamed. So did many of the boys. Ig would've screamed himself, but the blast seemed to force all the air out of his weak lungs and he could only wheeze.

The turkey was torn apart in a rising gout of flame. The stump half exploded as well. Smoking chunks of wood whirled through the air. The skies opened and rained meat. Bones, still garnished with quivering lumps of raw pink flesh, drizzled down, rattling through the leaves and bouncing off the ground. Turkey parts fell *pitter-plitter-plop* into the river. In stories told later, many boys would claim that the girls on Coffin Rock were decorated with chunks of raw turkey, soaked in poultry blood like the chick in fuckin' *Carrie*, but this was embellishment. The furthest-flung fragments of bird fell a good twenty feet short of the rock.

Ig's ears felt as if they were stuffed with cotton wool. Someone shrieked in excitement, a long distance off from him – or at least he thought it was a long distance off. But when he looked back over his shoulder, he found the shrieking girl standing almost directly behind him. It was Glenna in her awesomely awesome leather jacket and boob-clinging tank-top. She stood next to Lee Tourneau, clasping a couple of his fingers with one hand. Her other hand was raised high into the air and closed into a white-knuckled fist, a hillbilly gesture of triumph. When Lee noticed what she was doing, he wordlessly slipped his fingers out of her grip.

Other sounds rushed into the silence: yells, hoots, laughter. No sooner had the last of the turkey remains dropped from above than the boys were out of their hiding places and leaping around. Some grabbed splintered bones and threw them in the air and then pretended to duck, re-enacting the moment of detonation. Other boys leaped into low tree branches, pretending they had just stepped on land mines and were being blown into the sky. They swung back and forth from the boughs, howling. One kid was dancing around, playing air guitar for some reason, apparently unaware he had a flap of raw turkey skin in his hair. It looked like footage from a nature documentary. Impressing the girls out on the rock was, for the moment, inconsequential – for most anyway. No sooner had the turkey erupted than Ig had looked out at the river to see if they were all right. He regarded them still, watching them rise to their feet, laughing and chattering brightly to one another. One of them nodded downriver and then walked out on the sandbar to the kayaks. They would go soon.

Ig tried to think of some contrivance that would make them stay. He had the shopping cart, and he walked it up the trail a few feet and then rode it back down the hill, standing on the rear end, just something to do because he thought better when he was moving. He did this once, then again, so deep in his own head he was hardly aware he was doing it.

Eric, Terry, and other boys had loosely collected around the smouldering remains of the stump to inspect the damage. Eric rolled the last remaining cherry in one hand.

'Whatchu going to blow up now?' someone asked.

Eric frowned thoughtfully and did not reply. The boys around him began to offer suggestions, and soon they were shouting to be heard over one another. Someone said he could get a ham to explode, but Eric shook his head. 'We already done meat,' he said. Someone else said they ought to put the cherry in one of his little sister's dirty diapers. A third person said only if she was wearing it, to general laughter.

Then the question was repeated – *Whatchu going to blow up now?* – and this time there was a pause, while Eric made up his mind.

'Nothing,' he said, and put the cherry in his pocket.

The gathered boys made despairing sounds, but Terry, who knew his part in this scene, nodded his approval.

Then came offers and bargaining. One boy said he would trade his father's dirty movies for it. Another kid said he would trade his father's dirty *home* movies. 'Seriously, my mom is a fuckin' crazy bitch in the sack,' he said, and boys fell into one another, laughing helplessly.

'There's about as much chance of me giving up my last cherry,' Eric said, 'as there is of one of you homos climbing in that shopping cart and riding it naked down from the top of the hill.' Jerking his thumb over his shoulder at Ig and the shopping cart.

'I'll ride it down from the top of the hill,' Ig said. 'Naked.'

Heads turned. Ig stood several feet away from the knot of boys around Eric, and at first no one seemed to know who had spoken. Then there was laughter and some dis-believing hoots. Someone threw a turkey leg at Ig. He ducked and it sailed overhead. When Ig straightened up, he saw Eric Hannity staring intently at him while passing his last cherry bomb from hand to hand. Terry stood directly behind Eric, his face stony now, and he shook his head, almost imperceptibly: *No you don't.*

'Are you for real?' Eric asked.

'Will you let me have it if I ride this cart down the hill with no clothes on?'

Eric Hannity considered him through slitted eyes. 'All the way down. Naked. If the cart doesn't reach bottom, you get nothing. Doesn't matter if you break your fucking back.'

'Dude,' Terry said, 'I'm not letting you. What the fuck do

you think I'm going to tell Mom when you flay all the skin off your scrawny white ass?'

Ig waited for the howls of hilarity to subside before replying, simply, 'I'm not going to get hurt on the hill.'

Eric Hannity said, 'You got yourself a deal. I want to see this shit.'

'Wait, wait, wait,' Terry said, laughing, waving a hand in the air. He hustled across the dry ground to Ig, came around the cart and took his arm. He was grinning when he leaned in close to speak into Ig's ear, but his voice was low and harsh. 'Will you fuck off? You are *not* going to ride down this hill with your cock flapping around, making the both of us look like retarded assholes.'

'Why? We've been skinny-dipping down here. Half these guys have already seen me with my clothes off. The other half,' Ig said, glancing towards the rest of the gathering, 'don't know what they been missing.'

'You don't have a prayer of making it down the hill in this thing. It's a fucking shopping cart, Ig. It has wheels like *this*.' Holding up his thumb and index finger in the OK sign.

Ig said, 'I'm going to make it.'

Terry's lips parted to show his teeth in an angry, frustrated sneer. His eyes, though – his eyes were scared. In Terry's mind Ig had already left most of his face on the side of the hill and was lying in a tangled, squalling mess halfway down it. Ig felt a kind of affectionate pity for Terry. Terry was cool, cooler than Ig would ever be, but he was afraid. His fear narrowed his vision, so that he couldn't see anything except what he stood to lose. Ig wasn't built that way.

Now Eric Hannity was starting forward himself. 'Let him go if he wants to. It's no skin off your back. Off his, probably, but not yours.'

Terry went on arguing with Ig for another moment, not with words but with his stare. What finally caused Terry to look away was a sound, a soft, dismissive snort. Lee Tourneau was turning to whisper to Glenna, raising his hand to cover his mouth. But for some reason the hillside was, in that moment, unaccountably silent, and Lee's voice carried, so everyone within ten feet of him could hear him saying, '—we don't want to be around when the ambulance turns up to scrape dipshit off the hill—'

Terry spun on him, his face shrivelling in a look of rage. 'Oh, don't go anywhere. You stand right there with that mountain board of yours you're too chickenshit to ride and check out the show. You might want to see what a pair of balls look like. Take notes.'

The gathered boys burst into laughter. Lee Tourneau's cheeks became inflamed, darkened to the deepest red Ig had ever seen in a human face, the colour of a devil in a Disney cartoon. Glenna gave her date a look that was both pained and a little disgusted, then took a step away from him, as if his case of uncool might be catching.

In the tumult of amusement that followed, Ig slipped his arm from Terry's grip and turned the cart up the hill. He pushed it through the weeds at the side of the trail, because he didn't want the boys coming up the slope behind him to know what he knew, to see what he had seen. He didn't want Eric Hannity to have a chance to back out. His audience hurried after him, shoving and shouting.

Ig had not gone far before the little wheels of the cart snagged in some brush and it started to veer violently to one side. He struggled to right it. Behind him there was a fresh outburst of hilarity. Terry was walking briskly at Ig's side and he grabbed the front end of the cart and pointed it straight, shaking his head. He whispered *Jesus* under his breath. Ig walked on, shoving the cart before him.

A few more steps brought him to the crest of the hill. He had settled himself to doing it, so there was no reason to hesitate or be embarrassed. He let go of the cart, grabbed the waistband of his shorts and jerked them down, along with his underwear, showing the boys down the hill below his scrawny white ass. There were cries of shock and exaggerated disgust. When Ig straightened, he was grinning. His heartbeat had quickened, but only a little, like that of a man moving from a swift walk to a light jog – hurrying to catch his cab before someone else could get it. He kicked off his shorts without removing his sneakers and stripped off his shirt.

'Well,' Eric Hannity said, 'don't be shy now.'

Terry laughed – a little shrilly – and looked away. Ig turned to face the crowd: fifteen and naked, balls and cock, shoulders hot in the afternoon sunshine. The air carried on it a whiff of smoke from the trash-can fire, where Highway to Hell still stood with his long-haired pal.

Highway to Hell threw up one hand, his pinkie and his index finger extended in the universal symbol of the devil's horns, and shouted, 'Fuckin' yeah, baby! Lap dance!'

For some reason this affected the boys more than anything that had been said so far, so that several clutched at themselves and doubled over, gasping for breath, as if in reaction to some airborne toxin. For himself, however, Ig was surprised at how relaxed he felt, naked except for his loose tennis sneakers. He did not care if he was unclothed in front of other boys, and the girls on Coffin Rock would catch only the briefest glimpse of him before he flew into the river – which did not worry him either. The thought, in fact, gave him a gleeful tickle of excitement, low down, in the pit of the stomach. Of course, there was *one* girl looking at him already: Glenna. She stood on tiptoes at the back of the crowd, her jaw hanging open in an expression that mingled surprise with bemusement. Her boyfriend, Lee, wasn't with her. He had not followed them up the hill, had apparently *not* wanted to see what balls looked like.

Ig rolled the cart forward and manoeuvred it into place, using the moment of chaos to prepare for the ride. No one paid any notice to the careful way he lined up the shopping cart with the half-buried pipes.

What Ig had discovered, riding the cart for short distances at the bottom of the hill, was that the two old and rusted pipes sticking out of the dirt were roughly a foot and a half apart and that the little back wheels of the shopping cart fit precisely between them. There was about a quarter inch of room on either side, and when one of the front wheels shimmied and tried to turn the cart off-course, Ig had noticed it would strike a pipe and be turned back. It was very possible, on the steep pitch of the path, that the cart would hit a stone and flip over. It would not swerve off course and roll, however. *Could* not swerve off course. It would ride the inside of those pipes like a train on its rails.

He still had his clothes under one arm, and he turned and tossed them to Terry. 'Don't go anywhere with them. This'll be over soon.'

'You said it,' Eric told him, which set off a fresh ripple of laughter – but which didn't elicit quite the roar of amusement it maybe deserved.

Now that the moment had come and Ig was holding the handle of the cart, preparing to push off into space, he saw a few alarmed faces among the watching boys. Some of the older, more thoughtful-looking kids were half smiling in a quizzical way, and there was worried knowledge in their eyes, the first uneasy awareness that perhaps someone ought to put a stop to this thing before it went any further and Ig got himself seriously hurt. The thought came to Ig that if he didn't go – *now* – someone might raise a sensible objection.

'See you,' Ig said before anyone could try to stop him, and he nudged the cart forward, stepping lightly onto the back.

It was a study in perspective, the two pipes leading away

downhill, narrowing steadily to a final point, the bullet and the barrel. Almost from the moment he stepped onto the cart, he found himself plunging forward into a euphoric near-silence, the only sounds the shrieking wheels and the rattle and bang of the steel frame. Rushing at him from below, he saw the Knowles River, its black surface diamonded with sunlight. The wheels clattered right, then left, struck the pipes, and were turned back on course, just as Ig had known they would be.

In a moment the shopping cart was going too fast for him to do anything but hold on. There was no possibility of stopping, dismounting. He had not anticipated how quickly he would accelerate. The wind sliced at his bare skin so keenly it burned, he burned as he fell, Icarus ignited. The cart struck something, a squarish rock, and the left side vaulted off the ground, and this was it, it was going to overturn at whatever magnificent, fatal speed he was doing, and his naked body would be flung over the bars, and the earth would sand the skin off him and shatter his bones as the turkey bones had shattered, in a sudden, explosive slam. Only the front left wheel scraped the upper curve of the pipe and rode it back down onto the track. The sound of those wheels, spinning faster and faster, had risen to a mad, tuneless whistle, a lunatic piping.

When he glanced up, he saw the end of the trail, the pipes narrowing to their final point just before the dirt ramp that would launch him out over the water. The girls stood on the sandbar, by their kayaks. One of them was pointing at him. He imagined himself sailing overhead, hey diddle diddle, the cat and the fiddle, Ig jumped over the moon.

The cart came screaming from between the pipes and shot at the ramp like a rocket leaving its gantry. It hit the dirt incline, and he was flung into the air, and the sky opened to him. The sunlit day caught Ig as if he were a ball lightly tossed into a glove, held him in its gentle clasp for one moment – and then the shopping cart snapped up and back and the steel frame struck him in the face and the sky let him go, dumped him into blackness.

13

Ig had a fragmentary memory of the time he was underwater that he later assumed was false, because how could he remember anything about it if he'd been unconscious?

What he remembered was everything dark and roaring noise and a whirling sense of motion. He was poured forth into a thunderous torrent of souls, ejected from the earth and any sense of order and into this other, older chaos. He was in horror of it, appalled by the thought that this might be what waited after death. He felt he was being swept away, not just from his life but from God, the idea of God, or hope, or reason, the idea that things made sense, that cause followed effect, and it ought not to be like this, Ig felt, death ought not to be like this, even for sinners.

He struggled in that furious current of noise and nothing. The blackness seemed to shatter and peel away to show a muddy glimpse of sky but then closed back over him. When he felt himself weakening and sinking away, he had the sense of being grabbed and tugged along from beneath. Then, abruptly, there was something more solid under him. It felt like mud. A moment later he heard a far-off cry and was struck in the back.

The force of the impact shocked him, knocked the darkness out of him. His eyes sprang open, and he stared into a painful brightness. He retched. The river came out of his mouth, his nostrils. He was turned on his side on the mud, ear against the ground, so he could hear what was either the pounding of approaching feet or the slam of his own heart. He was downstream from the Evel Knievel trail, although in that first blurred moment of consciousness he wasn't sure how far. A length of black rotted fire hose slithered across the liquid earth, three inches from his nose. Only after it was gone did he know that it had been a snake, sliding past him down the bank.

The leaves above began to come into focus, flitting gently against a background of bright sky. Someone was kneeling beside him, a hand on his shoulder. Boys began to crash into sight, tumbling through the brush and then hitching up when they saw him.

Ig couldn't see who was kneeling beside him but felt sure it was Terry. Terry had pulled him out of the water and got him breathing again. He rolled onto his back to look into his brother's face. A skinny, sallow boy with a cap of icy blond hair stared expressionlessly back at him. Lee Tourneau was absentmindedly smoothing his tie against his chest. His khaki shorts were soaking wet. Ig didn't need to ask why. In that moment, staring into Lee's face, Ig decided he was going to begin wearing ties himself.

Terry came through the bushes, saw Iggy, and put on the brakes. Eric Hannity was right behind him and ran into him so hard he almost knocked him down. By now almost twenty boys were gathered around.

Ig sat up, drawing his knees close to his chest. He looked at Lee again and opened his mouth to speak, but when he tried, there was a bitter snap of pain in his nose, as if it were being broken all over again. He hunched and snorted a red splash of blood onto the dirt.

'Excuse me,' he said. 'Sorry about the blood.'

'I thought you were dead. You looked a little dead. You weren't breathing.' Lee was shivering.

'Well,' Ig said, 'I'm breathing now. Thank you.'

'What'd he do?' Terry asked.

'He pulled me out,' Ig said, gesturing at Lee's soaked shorts. 'He got me breathing again.'

'You swam in for him?' Terry said.

'No,' Lee said. He blinked, seemed utterly baffled, as if Terry had asked him a much more difficult question: the capital of Iceland, the state flower. 'He was already in the shallows by the time I saw him. I didn't swim out for him or ... or anything really. He was already—'

'He pulled me out,' Ig said over him, would have none of Lee's stammering humility. He remembered quite clearly the feeling of someone in the water with him, moving close beside him. 'I wasn't breathing.'

'And you did mouth-to-mouth?' Eric Hannity asked, with unmistakable incredulity.

Lee shook his head, still confused. 'No. No, it wasn't like that. All I did was smack his back when he, you know ... when he was ...' He floundered there, didn't seem to know how to go on.

Ig continued, 'That's what made me cough it up. I swallowed most of the river. My whole chest was full of it, and he pounded it out of me.' He spoke through gritted teeth. The pain in his nose was a series of sharp, bitter shocks, little electrical jolts. They even seemed to have colour; when he closed his eyes, he saw neon-yellow flashes.

The gathered boys looked upon Ig and Lee Tourneau with a quiet, dumbstruck wonder. What had just transpired was a thing that happened only in daydreams and TV shows. Someone had been about to die, and someone else had rescued him, and now the saved and the saviour were marked as special, stars in their own movie, which made the rest of them extras, or supporting cast at best. To have actually saved a life was to have *become* someone. You were no longer Joe Schmo, you were Joe Schmo who pulled Ig Perrish naked out of the Knowles

River the day he almost drowned. You would be that person for the rest of your life.

For himself, looking up into Lee's face, Ig felt the first bud of obsession beginning to open in him. He had been saved. He had been about to die, and this pale-haired boy with questioning blue eyes had brought him back. In evangelical churches you went to the river and were submerged and then lifted up into your new life, and it seemed to Ig now that Lee had saved him in this sense as well. Ig wanted to buy him something, to give him something, to find out his favourite rock band so it could be Ig's favourite rock band, too. He wanted to do Lee's homework for him.

There was noisy crashing in the brush, as if someone were driving a golf cart towards them. Then the girl, Glenna, appeared among them, out of breath, her face blotchy. She bent at the waist, put one hand on her round thigh, and gasped, 'Jesus. Look at his face.' Her gaze shifted to Lee, and her brow furrowed. 'Lee? What are you doing?'

'He pulled Ig out of the water,' Terry said.

'He got me breathing,' Ig said.

'*Lee?*' she asked, screwing up her face in an expression that suggested utter disbelief.

'I didn't do anything,' Lee said, shaking his head, and Ig could not help but love him.

The pain that had been beating in the bridge of Ig's nose had flowered, opening behind his forehead, between his eyes, penetrating deeper into the brain. He was beginning to see those neon-yellow flashes even with his eyes open. Terry sank down on one knee at his side, put a hand on his arm.

'We better get you dressed and back home,' Terry said. He sounded chastened in some way, as if he, and not Ig, were guilty of idiot recklessness. 'I think your nose is broken.' He looked up then at Lee Tourneau and gave him a brief nod of acknowledgment. 'Hey. Looks like maybe I was full of shit back

99

on the hill. Sorry about what I said a couple minutes ago. Thanks for helping my brother out.'

Lee said, 'Skip it. It's not worth making a big deal.'

Ig almost shivered at the calm cool of it, his unwillingness to bask in the appreciation of others.

'Will you come with us?' Ig asked Lee, gritting his teeth against the pain. He looked at Glenna. 'Both of you? I want to tell my parents what Lee did.'

Terry said, 'Hey, Ig. Let's not, and say we did. We don't want Mom and Dad to know this happened. You fell out of a tree, okay? There was a slippery branch, and you face-planted. That's just . . . just easier.'

'Terry – we *have* to tell them. I'd be drowned if he didn't pull me out.'

Ig's brother opened his mouth to argue, but Lee Tourneau beat him to the punch.

'No,' he said, almost sharply, and looked up at Glenna with wide eyes. She stared back at him with much the same look and grabbed strangely at her black leather jacket. Then he was on his feet. 'I'm not supposed to be here. I didn't do anything anyway.' Hurrying across the little clearing to grab Glenna's chubby hand and tug her towards the trees. With his other hand, he carried his brand-new mountain board.

'Wait,' Ig said, getting to his feet. When he stood, a bright neon flash burst behind his eyes, carrying with it a feeling like he had a nose full of packed broken glass.

'I got to go. We both got to go.'

'Well. Will you come over to the house sometime?'

'Sometime.'

'Do you know where it is? It's on the highway, just about—'

'Everyone knows where it is,' Lee said, and then he was gone, billygoating away through the trees, pulling Glenna after him. She cast a final, distressed look back at the boys before allowing herself to be led off.

The pain in Ig's nose was more intense now and coming in steady, rolling waves. He cupped his hands to his face for a moment, and when he took them away, his palms were painted in crimson.

'Come on, Ig,' Terry said. 'We better go. You need to see a doctor about your face.'

'You and me both,' Ig said.

Terry smiled and tugged Ig's shirt loose from the ball of laundry he was holding. Ig was startled to see it, had forgotten, until that moment, that he was standing there naked. Terry pulled it on over Ig's head, dressing him as if he were five and not fifteen.

'Probably need a surgeon to remove Mom's foot from my ass, too. She'll be ready to kill me after she gets a look at you,' Terry said. As Ig's head came through the shirt hole, he found his brother peering into his face with unmistakable anxiety. 'You aren't going to tell, are you? For real, Ig. She'd murder me for letting you ride that fucking cart down the hill. Sometimes it's just better not to tell.'

'Oh, man, I'm no good at lying. Mom always knows. She knows the second I open my mouth.'

Terence looked relieved. 'So who said open your mouth? You're in pain. Just stand there and cry. Leave the bullshit to me. It's what I'm good at.'

14

~e~

Lee Tourneau was shivering and soaking wet the next time Ig saw him as well, two days later. He wore the same tie, the same shorts, had his mountain board under one arm. It was as if he'd never dried off, as if he'd only just waded out of the Knowles.

It had started to rain, and Lee had been caught out in it. His almost-white hair was soaked flat, and he had the sniffles. He carried a wet canvas satchel over his shoulder; it gave him the look of a newsboy out to hawk some papers in an old *Dick Tracy* strip.

Ig was alone in the house, an uncommon occurrence. His parents were in Boston to attend a cocktail party at John Williams' town house. Williams was in his last year as the conductor of the Boston Pops, and Derrick Perrish was going to perform with the orchestra in the farewell concert. They had left Terry in charge. Terry had spent most of the morning in his pyjamas in front of MTV, on the phone, carrying on a series of conversations with equally bored friends. His tone at first was cheerfully lazy, then alert and curious, then, finally, clipped and flat, the toneless tone he used to express his highest levels of disdain. Ig had gone by the living room to see him pacing, an unmistakable sign of agitation. Finally Terry had banged down the phone and launched himself up the stairs. When he came back down, he was dressed and tossing the keys to their father's Jag in one hand. He said he was going to Eric's. He said it with his upper lip curled, the look of someone with a dirty job to do, someone who has come home to find the trash cans knocked over and garbage spread all over the yard.

'Don't you need someone with a licence to go with you?' Ig asked. Terry had his permit.

'Only if I get pulled over,' Terry said.

Terry walked out the door, and Ig closed it behind him. Five minutes later Ig was opening it again, someone thumping on the other side. Ig assumed it was Terry, that he had forgotten something and come back to get it, but it was Lee Tourneau instead.

'How's your nose?' Lee asked.

Ig touched the tape across the bridge of his nose, then dropped his hand. 'I wasn't that pretty to begin with. You want to come in?'

Lee took a step in through the door and stood there, a pool forming under his feet.

'Looks like *you're* the one who drowned,' Ig said.

Lee didn't smile. It was as if he didn't know how. It was as if he'd put his face on for the first time that morning and didn't know how to use it.

'Nice tie,' Lee said.

Ig looked down at himself, had forgotten he was wearing it. Terry had rolled his eyes at Ig when Ig came downstairs Tuesday morning with his blue tie knotted around his throat. 'What's that?' Terry had asked derisively.

Their father had been wandering through the kitchen at that exact moment and looked over at Ig, then said, 'Class. You ought to put some on sometime, Terry.' Ig had worn a tie every day since, but there'd been no more discussion of the matter.

'What are you selling?' Ig asked, nodding at the canvas bag.

'They're six bucks,' Lee said. He folded back the flap and withdrew three different magazines. 'Take your pick.'

The first was called, simply, *The Truth!* The cover showed a groom and his bride kneeling before the altar in a vast church. Their hands were clasped in prayer, their faces raised into the light slanting through stained-glass windows. Their expressions suggested that the both of them had been sucking laughing gas; they wore identical looks of maniacal joy. A grey-skinned alien stood behind them, tall and naked. He had placed a three-fingered hand on each of their heads – it looked as if he might be about to smash their skulls together and kill them both, much to their joy. The cover line read 'Married by Aliens!'. The other magazines were *Tax Reform Now* and *Modern American Militia.*

'All three for fifteen,' Lee said. 'They're to raise money for the Christian Patriots' Food Bank. *The Truth!* is really good. It's all great celebrity sci-fi stuff. There's a story about how Steven Spielberg got to tour the real Area 51. And there's another one about the guys from Kiss, when they were on an airplane that got hit by lightning and the engines conked out. They were all praying to Christ to save them, and then Paul Stanley saw Jesus on the wing, and a minute later the engines started up again and the pilot was able to pull out of the dive.'

'The guys in Kiss are Jewish,' Ig said.

Lee didn't seem troubled by this news. 'Yeah. I think most of what they publish is bullshit. It was still a good story.'

This struck Ig as a remarkably sophisticated observation.

'Did you say it's fifteen for all three?' he said.

Lee nodded. 'If you sell enough, you're eligible for prizes. That's how I wound up with the mountain board I was too chickenshit to use.'

'*Hey,*' Ig said, surprised at the calm, flat way Lee copped to being a coward. It was worse hearing him say it about himself than it was hearing Terry say it on the hill.

'No,' Lee said, unperturbed. 'Your brother had me right. I thought I'd impress Glenna and her pals, showing the thing off, but when I was on the hill, I couldn't make myself risk it. I just hope if I run into your brother again, he won't hold it against me.'

Ig felt a brief but intense flash of hate for his older brother. 'Like he's got room to talk. He almost pissed himself when he thought I was going to go home and tell Mom what really happened to me. One thing about my brother: in any given situation you can always count on him to cover his ass first and worry about other people second. Come on in. I got money upstairs.'

'You want to buy one?'

'I want to buy all three.'

Lee narrowed one eye to a squint. 'I can see *Modern American Militia*, because it's all stuff about guns and how to tell a spy satellite from a normal satellite. But are you sure you want *Tax Reform Now?*'

'Why not? I'll have to pay taxes someday.'

'Most of the people who read this magazine try not to.'

Lee followed Ig to his room but then stopped in the hall, peering cautiously within. Ig had never thought of the room as particularly impressive – it was the smallest on the second floor – but wondered now if it looked like the bedroom of a rich kid to Lee and if this would count against him. Ig had a glance around the place himself, trying to imagine how Lee saw it. The first thing he noticed was the view of the swimming pool out the window, the rain dimpling its vivid blue surface. Then there was the autographed poster of Mark Knopfler over the bed; Ig's father had played horns on the last Dire Straits album.

Ig's own horn was on the bed, resting in an open case. The trumpet case contained an assortment of other treasures: a wad of money, tickets to a George Harrison show, a photo of his mother in Capri, and the redheaded girl's cross on its broken chain. Ig had made an effort to fix it with a Swiss Army knife, which got him exactly nowhere. Finally he had put it aside and turned to a different but related task. Ig had borrowed the M volume of Terry's *Encyclopaedia Britannica* and looked up the key to Morse Code. He still remembered the exact sequence of short and long flashes the redheaded girl had aimed at him, but when he translated them, his first thought was that he had to be wrong. It was a simple enough message, a single short word, but so shocking it caused a cool, sensuous prickle to race up his back and over his scalp. Ig had begun to try to work out an adequate response, lightly pencilling strings of dots and dashes into the endpapers of his Neil Diamond Bible, trying different replies. Because, of course, it wouldn't do to just talk to her. She had spoken to him in flashes of daylight, and he felt he ought to reply in kind.

Lee took it all in, his gaze darting here and there, finally settling on four chrome towers filled with CDs that stood against the wall. 'That's a lot of music.'

'Come in.'

Lee shuffled in, bowed by the weight of the dripping canvas bag.

'Sit down,' Ig said.

Lee sat on the edge of Ig's bed, soaking the duvet. He twisted his head to look over his shoulder at the towers of CDs.

'I've never seen so much music. Except maybe in a record store.'

'Who do you like to listen to?' Ig asked.

Lee shrugged.

This was an inexplicable reply. Everyone listened to something.

'What albums do you have?' Ig asked.

'I don't.'

'Nothing?'

'Just never been that interested, I guess,' Lee said calmly. 'CDs are expensive, aren't they?'

It bewildered Ig, the idea that a person could not be interested in music. It was like not being interested in happiness; like being colour-blind. Then he registered Lee's follow-up – *CDs are expensive, aren't they?* – and for the first time it came to him that Lee didn't have money to spend on music, or anything else. Ig thought of Lee's brand-new mountain board – but that had been a prize for his charity work, he'd just said. There were his ties and his button-up short-sleeved shirts – but probably his mother made him wear them when he went out peddling his magazines, expected him to look clean-cut and responsible. Poor kids often dressed up. It was rich kids who dressed down, carefully assembling a blue-collar costume: eighty-dollar designer jeans that had been professionally faded and tattered and worn-out T-shirts straight off the rack from Abercrombie & Fitch. Then there was Lee's association with Glenna and Glenna's friends, a crowd that gave off a trailer-park vibe; country-club kids just didn't hang out at the foundry, burning shit on a summer afternoon.

Lee raised one eyebrow – he definitely gave off a bit of a Spock vibe – seeming to pick up on Ig's surprise. He said, 'What do you listen to?'

'I don't know. Lots of stuff. I've been on a big Beatles kick lately.' By 'lately' Ig meant the last seven years. 'You like them?'

'Don't really know them. What are they like?'

The notion that anyone in the world might not know the Beatles staggered Ig. He said, 'You know ... like, *the Beatles.* John Lennon and Paul McCartney.'

'Oh, them,' Lee said, but the way he said it, Ig knew he was embarrassed and only *pretending* to know. Not pretending too hard either.

Ig didn't speak but went to the rack of CDs and studied his Beatles collection, trying to decide where Lee ought to start. First he thought *Sgt Pepper* and pulled it out. But then he wondered if Lee would really enjoy it or if he'd find all the horns and accordions and sitars disorienting, if he'd be turned off by the lunatic mix of styles, rock jams turning into English pub sing-alongs turning into mellow jazz. He'd probably want something easier to digest, a collection of clear, catchy melodies, something recognisable as rock 'n' roll. *The White Album*, then. Except coming in at *The White Album* was like walking into a movie in the last twenty minutes. You'd get action, but you wouldn't know who the characters were or why you were supposed to care. Really, the Beatles were a story. Listening to them was like reading a book. You had to start with *Please Please Me*. Ig pulled down the whole stack and put them on the bed.

'That's a lot of stuff to listen to. When do you want them back?'

Ig didn't know he was giving them away until the moment Lee asked the question. Lee had pulled him out of the roaring darkness and pounded the breath back into his chest and for it had been given nothing. A hundred dollars of CDs was nothing. Nothing.

'You can have them,' Ig said.

Lee gave him a confused look. 'For the magazines? You have to pay for those in cash.'

'No. Not for the magazines.'

'What then?'

'Not letting me drown.'

Lee looked at the tower of CDs, put a tentative hand on top of them.

'Thank you,' he said. 'I don't know what to say. Except maybe you're crazy. And you don't need to.'

Ig opened his mouth, then closed it, briefly stricken with emotion, with liking Lee Tourneau too much to manage a simple reply. Lee gave him another puzzled, curious stare, then quickly looked away.

'Do you play same as your dad?' Lee asked, pulling Ig's trumpet out of his case.

'My brother plays. I know how, but I don't really myself.'

'Why not?'

'I can't breathe.'

Lee frowned.

'I mean, I have asthma. I run out of air when I try to play.'

'I guess you'll never be famous.' He didn't say it unkindly. It was just an observation.

'My dad isn't famous. My dad plays jazz. You can't get famous playing jazz.' *Anymore*, Ig silently added.

'I've never heard one of your dad's records. I don't know much about jazz. It's like the stuff that's always playing in the background in movies about old-time gangsters, right?'

'Usually.'

'I bet I'd like that. Music for a scene with gangsters and those girls in the short straight skirts. Flappers.'

'Right.'

'And then the killers walk in with machine guns,' Lee said, looking excited for the first time since Ig had met him. 'Killers in fedoras. And they hose the place down. Blow away a bunch of champagne glasses and rich people and old mobsters.' Miming a tommy gun as he said it. 'I think I like that kind of music. Music to kill people to.'

'I've got some stuff like that. Hang on.' Ig pulled out a disc by Glenn Miller and another by Louis Armstrong. He put them with the Beatles. Then, because Armstrong was filed below AC/DC. Ig asked, 'Did you like *Back in Black*?'

'Is that an album?'

Ig grabbed *Back in Black* and put it on Lee's growing pile. 'Got a song on it called "Shoot to Thrill". Perfect for gunfights and breaking stuff.'

But Lee was bent over the open trumpet case, looking at Ig's other treasures – picking at the redhead's crucifix on the slender golden chain. It bothered Ig to see him touching it, and he was gripped by an urge to slam the trumpet case shut . . . on Lee's fingers if he pulled his hand away too slowly. Ig brushed the impulse aside, as briskly as if it were a spider on the back of his hand. He was disappointed in himself for feeling such a thing, even for a moment. Lee looked like a child displaced by a flood – cold water still dripping off the tip of his nose – and Ig wished he had stopped in the kitchen to make cocoa. He wanted to give Lee a cup of hot soup and some buttered toast. There were any number of things he wanted Lee to have. Just not the cross.

He moved patiently around to the side of the bed and reached into the case to collect his stack of bills, turning his shoulder so Lee had to straighten up and take his hand away from the cross. Ig counted off a five and ten ones. He had about six dollars left.

'For the magazines,' Ig said.

Lee folded the money and tucked it into his pocket. 'You like pictures of snatch?'

'Snatch?'

'Pussy.' He said it without awkwardness – they might've still been talking music.

Ig had missed a transition somewhere. 'Sure. Who doesn't?'

'My distributor has all kinds of magazines. I've seen some strange stuff in his storeroom. Stuff that'll turn your head around. There's a whole magazine of pregnant women.'

'*Ugh!*' Ig cried, joyously disgusted.

'We live in troubled times,' Lee said, without any notable disapproval. 'There's one of old women, too. *Still Horny* is a big one. That's chicks over sixty fingering themselves. You got any porn?'

Ig's answer was in his face.

'Let's see,' Lee said.

Ig got Candy Land out of his closet, one of a dozen games stuffed in the back.

'Candy Land,' Lee said. 'Nice.'

Ig didn't understand at first, then he did. He'd never thought about it, had only stuck his jack-off literature there because no one played Candy Land anymore, not because it had any symbolic meaning.

He set it on the bed and removed the lid and the board, took out the plastic tray that held the pieces. Beneath was a Victoria's Secret catalogue, and the *Rolling Stone* with Demi Moore naked on the cover.

'This is pretty tame material,' Lee said, not unkindly. 'I'm not sure you even need to hide this stuff, Ig.'

Lee shifted aside the *Rolling Stone* and discovered an issue of *Uncanny X-Men* beneath it, the one with Jean Grey dressed in a black corset. He smiled placidly.

'This is a good one. Because Phoenix is so sweet and good and caring, and then *bam!* Out comes the black leather. That your thing? Cute girls with the devil inside?'

Ig said, 'I don't have a thing. I don't know how that got in there.'

'Everyone has a thing,' Lee said, and of course he was right. Ig had been thinking almost exactly this when Lee said he didn't know what music he liked. 'Still, whacking off over comics ... that's unwell.' He said it calmly, with a certain appreciation. 'You ever had anyone do it for you? Jerk you off?'

For a moment the room seemed to expand around Ig, as if it were the inside of a balloon filling with air. The thought crossed his mind that Lee might be about to offer a hand job, and if that were to happen – a terrible, diseased thing to contemplate – then Ig would tell him he had nothing against gay people, he just wasn't one himself.

But Lee went on, 'Remember the girl I was with, Monday? She's done it to me. She gave a little scream when I finished. Funniest thing I ever heard. I wish I had it on tape.'

'Seriously?' Ig asked, both relieved and shaken. 'Has she been your girlfriend for a long time?'

'We don't have a relationship like that. Not a boyfriend-girlfriend thing. She just comes over now and then to talk about boys and the people who are mean to her at school and stuff. She knows my door is open.' Ig almost laughed at this last statement, which he assumed was ironic, but then held back. Lee seemed to mean it genuinely. He went on, 'The times she's whacked me off were kind of a favour she did. It's a good thing, too. If not for that, I'd probably club her to death, the way she gabs on all the time.'

Lee gently put the *Uncanny X-Men* back into the box, and Ig reassembled Candy Land and replaced it in his closet. When he came back to the bed, Lee was holding the cross in one hand, had picked it out of the trumpet case. At the sight, Ig's heart took the elevator to the basement.

'This is pretty,' Lee said. 'Belong to you?'

'No,' Ig said.

'No. I didn't think. Looks like something a girl would wear. Where'd you get it?'

The easiest thing to do would've been to lie, to say it belonged to his mother. But lies turned Ig's tongue to clay, and anyway, Lee had saved his life.

'In church,' Ig said, knowing that Lee would figure out the rest. He did not know why it felt so catastrophically wrong to simply tell the truth about such a little thing. It was never wrong to tell the truth.

Lee had looped both ends of the golden chain around his index finger so the cross dangled across his palm. 'It's broken,' he said.

'That's how I found it.'

'Was a redhead wearing it? Girl about our age?'

'She left it. I was going to fix it for her.'

'With this?' Lee asked, knuckling the Swiss Army knife that

Ig had been using to bend and twist at the chain's gold rings. 'You can't fix it with this. For something like this, you probably need a pair of needle-nose pliers. You know, my dad has some precision tools. I bet I could fix it up in five minutes. I'm good at that: fixing things.'

Lee turned his gaze to Ig at last. He didn't need to ask outright for Ig to know what he wanted. Ig felt ill at the thought of giving it to him, and his throat was unaccountably tight, the way it sometimes got at the onset of an asthma attack. But there was really only one possible reply that would allow him to keep his own sense of himself as a decent and selfless person.

'Sure,' Ig said. 'Why don't you take it home and see if you can do something with it?'

Lee said, 'Okay. I'll fix it up, and give it back to her on Sunday.'

'Would you?' Ig asked. It felt as if there were a smooth wooden shaft going through the pit of his stomach, with a crank on one end, and someone was beginning to turn it, methodically twisting his insides around it.

Lee nodded and returned his gaze to the cross. 'Thanks. I'd like that. I was asking you what your thing is. You know, what kind of girl you like. She's *my* kind of thing. There's something about her, you can just tell she's never been naked in front of any guy except her father. You know I saw it break? The necklace. I was standing in the pew right behind her. I tried to help her with it. She's cute, but a little snotty. I think it's fair to say most pretty girls are snotty until they get their cherry popped. Because, you know, it's the most valuable thing they're ever going to have. It's the thing that keeps boys sniffing around them and thinking about them – the idea of getting to be the one. But after someone does it, they can relax and act like a normal girl. Anyway. I appreciate you letting me have this. It'll give me a nice in with her.'

'No prob,' Ig said, feeling as if he'd given away something much more special than a cross on a gold necklace. It was fair – Lee deserved something good after saving Ig's life and not getting any credit. But Ig wondered why it didn't *feel* fair.

He said Lee should come over when it wasn't raining and swim sometime, and Lee said all right. Ig felt a certain disconnect from his own voice, as if it were coming from some other source in the room – the radio, perhaps.

Lee was partway to the door with his satchel over his shoulder when Ig saw he had left his CDs. 'Take your music,' he said. He was glad Lee was going. He wanted to lie on his bed for a while and rest. His stomach hurt.

Lee glanced at them and then said, 'I don't have anything to listen to them on.'

Ig wondered again how poor Lee was – if he had an apartment or a trailer, if he woke at night to screams and banging doors, the cops arresting the drunk next door for beating his girlfriend again. Another reason not to resent him for taking the cross. Ig hated that he could not be happy for Lee, that he could not take pleasure in what he was giving away, but he wasn't happy, he was jealous.

Shame turned him around and got him rummaging in his desk. He stood up with the portable Walkman disc player he'd gotten for Christmas, and a pair of headphones.

'Thanks,' Lee said when Ig handed the disc player to him. 'You don't have to give me all this stuff. I didn't do anything. I was just standing there and . . . you know.'

Ig was surprised at the intensity of his own reaction, a lightening of the heart, a rush of affection for the skinny, pale kid with the unpractised smile. Ig remembered that moment that he'd been saved. That every minute of his life from here on out was a gift, one Lee had offered to him. The tension uncoiled from his stomach and he was able to breathe easy once again.

Lee stuffed the CD player and headphones and discs into his satchel before hoisting his bag. Ig watched from an upstairs window as Lee rode down the hill on his mountain board, through the drizzle, the fat wheels throwing up rooster tails of water from the gleaming asphalt.

Twenty minutes later Ig heard the Jag pull in with that sound he liked, a smooth revving noise right out of an action movie. He returned to the upstairs window again and looked down at the black car, expecting the doors to open and spill out Terry, Eric Hannity and some girls, in a gush of laughter and cigarette smoke. But Terry got out alone and stood by the Jaguar awhile, then walked to the door slowly, as if he had a stiff back, as if he were a much older man who'd been driving for hours instead of just across town.

Ig was halfway down the stairs when Terry let himself in, water glittering in his messy thatch of black hair. He saw Ig staring down at him and gave him a tired smile.

'Hey, bro,' Terry said. 'Got something for you.' And lobbed it, a dark roundness, the size of a crabapple.

Ig clapped his hands around it, then looked at the white silhouette of the naked girl wearing the maple leaf over her crotch. The bomb was heavier than he imagined it would be, the grain rough, the surface cold.

'Your winnings,' Terry said.

'Oh,' Ig said. 'Thanks. With what happened, I guess Eric forgot to pay up.' In fact, Ig had, days ago, casually come to accept that Eric Hannity was never going to pay, that he had got his nose broke for nothing.

'Yeah. Well. I reminded him.'

'Everything okay?'

'Now that he paid up it is.' Terry paused, one hand on the newel post, then said, 'He didn't want to fork over because you wore sneakers when you went down the hill or some such shit.'

'Well. That's weak. That's the weakest thing I've ever heard,' Ig said. Terry did not reply, just stood there rubbing his thumb against the edge of the newel post. 'Still. Did you guys really get into it? It's just a firecracker.'

'No, it isn't. You see what it did to the turkey?'

This struck Ig as a funny thing to say, missing the point. Terry gave Ig a guilty-sorry sort of smile and said, 'You don't know what he was going to do with that. There's a kid from school Eric doesn't like. A kid I know from band. Good kid. Ben Townsend. But, see, Ben's mother is in the insurance business. Like, answers phones or something. So Eric has a hate on for him.'

'Just because his mom works in insurance?'

'You know Eric's father isn't doing too well, right? Like, he can't lift things and he can't work and he has trouble . . . he has trouble taking a dump. It's just really sad. They were supposed to get all this insurance money, but they haven't yet. I guess they're never going to. And so Eric wants to get even with someone, and he sort of fixed on Ben.'

'Just because his mother works for the insurance company that's screwing Eric's dad?'

'No!' Terry cried. 'That's the part of this that is most fucked. She works for a *completely different* insurance company.'

'That doesn't make any sense.'

'*No*. It *doesn't*. And don't spend too much time trying to work it out, because it never will. Eric was gonna use this thing to blow something up that belonged to Ben Townsend, and he called me to see if I wanted in.'

'What was he going to blow up?'

'His cat.'

Ig felt a little exploded himself, blown up with a kind of horror that bordered on wonder. 'No. Maybe that's what Eric *said*, but he was screwing with you. I mean, c'mon . . . a cat?'

'He tried to *pretend* he was screwing with me when he saw how pissed I was. And he only gave me that cherry bomb when I threatened to tell his father about the shit we've been doing. Then he threw it at my head and told me to get the fuck out. I know for a fact Eric's daddy has perpetrated several acts of police brutality on Eric's ass.'

'Even though he can't take a shit?'

'He can't take a shit, but he can swing a belt. I hope to God that Eric is never a cop. Him and his dad are just alike. You'd have the right to remain silent with his boot on your throat.'

'Would you really have told his dad about—?'

'What? No. No way. How could I tattle about all the stuff Eric's blown up when I was in on it myself? That's, like, the first rule of blackmail.' Terry was silent a moment, then said, 'You think you know someone. But mostly you just know what you want to know.' He looked up at Ig with clear eyes and said, 'He *is* a badass. Eric. And I always felt kind of like a badass when I was with him. You're not in band, so you don't know, Ig. It's hard to be desired by women and feared by men when your primary skill is playing "America the Beautiful" on the trumpet. I liked the way people looked at us. That's what was in it for me. I couldn't tell you what was in it for him. Except he liked that I'd pay for things and that we know some famous people.'

Ig rolled the bomb around and around in his hand, feeling that there was something he ought to say but not knowing how to say it. What came to him at last was hopelessly inadequate. 'What do you think I should blow up with this?'

'I don't know what. Just don't leave me out, okay? Sit on it a few weeks. After I have my licence, I'll drive us down to Cape Cod with a bunch of the guys. We can have a bonfire on the beach and find something there.'

'Last big explosion of the summer,' Ig said.

'Yeah. Ideally I'd like to see us leave a swathe of destruction that can be seen from orbit. Barring that, let's at least try to destroy something precious and beautiful that can never be replaced,' Terry said.

15

The whole way to church, Ig's palms were sweating, felt tacky and strange. His stomach was upset, too. He knew why, and it was ridiculous – he didn't even know her name and had never spoken a word to her.

Except that she had signalled him. A church full of people, many her own age, and she had looked right at him and had sent him a message with her cross of burning gold. Even now he wasn't sure why he'd let her go, how he could've given her away like a baseball card or a CD. He told himself Lee was a lonely trailer-park kid who needed someone, that things had a way of working out how they were supposed to. He tried to feel good about what he had done, but there was instead, rising within him, a black wall of horror. He could not imagine what had compelled him to allow Lee to take her cross away from him. Lee would have it with him today. He would give it to her, and she would say thank you, and they would talk after church. In his mind they were already walking out together; as she went by, the redhead glanced Ig's way, but her gaze slid over him without any recognition at all as the repaired cross glittered in the hollow of her throat.

Lee was there, in the same pew, and he was wearing her cross around his *own* throat. It was the first thing Ig noticed, and his reaction was simple and biochemical. It was as if he had downed a painfully hot cup of coffee, all at once. His stomach knotted and burned. His blood surged furiously, as if hopping with caffeine.

The pew in front of Lee remained empty until the last moments just before the service began, and then three stout old ladies with big hair slid in where the girl had sat the week before. Lee and Ig spent much of the first twenty minutes craning their heads, searching for her, but she wasn't there. That hair of hers, a rope of braided copper wire, would have been impossible to miss. Finally Lee looked across the aisle at Ig and lifted his shoulders in a comical shrug, and Ig gave an exaggerated shrug back, as if he were Lee's co-conspirator in his attempt to connect with Morse Code Girl.

Ig wasn't, though. He bowed his head when it was time to say the Lord's Prayer, but what Ig was praying for wasn't a part of the standard text. He wanted the cross back. It didn't have to be right. He wanted it more than he'd ever wanted anything, more than he'd wanted to breathe when he was lost in that fatal rush of black water and roaring souls. He didn't know her name, but he knew they were good at having fun together, at being together; the ten minutes when she'd been flashing that light into his face were the best ten minutes he'd ever spent in church. Some things you didn't give away, no matter how much you owed.

When the services were over, Ig stood with his father's hand on his shoulder, watching people file past. His family was always among the last to leave any crowded place: church, a movie theatre, a baseball stadium. Lee Tourneau went by and dipped his head to Ig in a dismissive sort of nod that seemed to say, *Somes you win and somes you lose.*

As soon as the aisle was clear, Ig crossed to the pew where the girl had sat the week before and then sank to one knee there and began to tie his shoe. His father looked back at him, but Ig nodded that they should go on and he would catch up. He watched until his family had moved out of the nave before quitting with the shoe.

The three stout old ladies who had settled in Morse Code Girl's former pew were still there, collecting purses and arranging summer shawls over their shoulders. As he glanced up at them now, it came to Ig that he had seen them before. They had walked out with the girl's mother last Sunday, in a chattering, social pack, and at the time Ig had wondered if they were aunts. Had one of them even been in the car with the girl after the services? Ig wasn't sure. He wanted to think so, but suspected he was letting wishful thinking colour memory.

'Excuse me,' Ig said.

'Yes?' asked the lady closest to him, a big woman, hair dyed a metallic shade of brown.

Ig wagged a finger at the pew and shook his head. 'There was a girl here. Last Sunday. She left something by accident, and I was going to give it back. Red hair?'

The woman didn't reply but remained where she was, even though the aisle was clear enough to allow her to exit. Finally Ig realised she was waiting for him to make eye contact. When he did, and saw the knowing, narrow-eyed way she was looking at him, he felt his pulse flutter.

'Merrin Williams,' said the woman, 'and her parents were only in town last weekend to take possession of their new house. I know because I sold it to them and showed them this church as well. They're back in Rhode Island now, packing their things. She'll be here next Sunday. I'm sure I'll be seeing them again, soon enough. If you want, I could pass along whatever it is Merrin left here.'

'No,' Ig said. 'That's okay.'

'Mm,' said the woman. 'I thought you'd rather give it to her yourself. You have that look about you.'

'What . . . what look?' Ig asked.

'I'd say it,' said the woman, 'but we're in church.'

16

~ℰ~

The next time Lee came over, they went into the pool and played basketball in the shallow end until Ig's mother came out with grilled ham-and-Brie sandwiches on a plate. Lydia couldn't just make a grilled ham-and-cheese with yellow American like other moms – it had to have a pedigree, express in some way her own more sophisticated and worldly palate. Ig and Lee sat eating them on reclining patio chairs, with water puddling under their seats. For some reason one or the other of them was always dripping wet when they were together.

Lee was polite to Ig's mother, but after she walked away, he peeled back the toast and looked at the milky melted cheese on the ham.

'Someone came all over my sandwich,' he said.

Ig choke-laughed on a bite, which turned into a coughing fit, harsh, painful in his chest. Lee automatically thumped him on the back, rescuing Ig from himself. It was getting to be a habit, an integral part of their relationship.

'For most people it's just lunch. For you it's another chance to get yourself killed.' Lee squinted at him in the sunlight and said, 'You're probably the most death-prone person I know.'

'I'm harder to finish off than I look,' Ig said. 'Like a cockroach.'

'I liked AC/DC,' Lee said. 'If you were going to shoot

someone, you'd really want to do it while you were listening to them.'

'What about the Beatles? Did you feel like shooting anyone listening to them?'

Lee considered seriously for a moment, then said, 'Myself.'

Ig laughed again. Lee's secret was that he never strained for the laugh, didn't even always seem to know that the things he said were amusing. He had a restraint, an aura of glassy and unflappable cool, that made Ig think of a secret agent in a movie, defusing a warhead – or programming one. At other times he was such a blank – he never laughed, not at his own jokes, not at Ig's – it was as if Lee were an alien scientist, come to earth to learn about human emotions. Kind of like Mork.

At the same time he was laughing, Ig was distressed. Not liking the Beatles was almost as bad as not knowing about them at all.

Lee saw the chagrin on his face and said, 'I'll give them back. You should have them back.'

'No,' Ig said. 'Keep 'em and listen to them some more. Maybe you'll hear something you like.'

'I did like some of it,' Lee said, but Ig knew he was lying. 'There was that one ...' and his voice trailed off, leaving Ig to guess at which of maybe sixty songs he might be referring to.

And Ig guessed it. '"Happiness Is a Warm Gun"?'

Lee pointed a finger at him, cocked his thumb and blew him away.

'What about the jazz? Did you like any of that?'

'Kind of. I don't know. I couldn't really hear the jazz stuff.'

'What do you mean?'

'I kept forgetting it was on. It's like the music in the supermarket.'

Ig shivered. 'So are you going to be a hit man when you grow up?' he asked.

'Why?'

'Cause you only like music you can murder people to.'

'No. Just it ought to set the scene. Isn't that the whole point of music? It's like the background to what you're doing.'

He wasn't going to argue with Lee, but ignorance like that pained him. Hopefully, over the years of being best friends, Lee would learn the truth about music: that it was the third rail of life. You grabbed it to shock yourself out of the dull drag of hours, to feel something, to burn with all the emotions you didn't get to experience in the ordinary run of school and TV and loading the dishwasher after dinner. Ig supposed that growing up in a trailer park, Lee had missed out on a lot of the good things. It was going to take him a few years to catch up.

'So what *are* you going to do when you grow up?' Ig asked.

Lee tucked away the rest of his sandwich and, with his mouth stuffed full, said, 'I'd like to be in Congress.'

'For real? To do what?'

'I'd like to write a law that says irresponsible bitches who do drugs have to get sterilised so they can't have kids they aren't going to take care of,' Lee said, without heat.

Ig had wondered why he didn't talk about his mother.

Lee's hand drifted to the cross around his neck, nestled just above his clavicles. After a moment he said, 'I've been thinking about her. Our girl from church.'

'I bet,' Ig said, trying to make it sound funny, but it came off a little harsh and irritated, even to his own ears.

Lee appeared not to notice. His eyes were distant, unfocused. 'I bet she isn't from around here. I've never seen her in church before. She was probably visiting family or something. Bet we never see her again.' He paused, then added, 'The one that got away.' Not melodramatically, but with a knowing sense of humour about it.

The truth caught in Ig's throat, like that lump of sandwich that wouldn't go down. It was there, waiting to be told – *she'll be back next Sunday* – but he couldn't say it. He couldn't lie either, didn't have the nerve. He was the worst liar he knew.

What he said instead was, 'You fixed the cross.'

Lee didn't look down at it but idly picked at it with one hand while staring out at the light dancing across the surface of the pool. 'Yeah. I've been keeping it on, just in case I run into her while I'm out selling my magazines.' He paused, then continued, 'You know the dirty magazines I told you about? The ones my distributor has in his storeroom? There's one called *Cherries*, all these girls who are supposed to be eighteen-year-old virgins. That's my favourite, girl-next-door types. You want a girl where you can imagine what it would be like to be the first. Of course the girls in *Cherries* aren't *really* virgins. You can tell just by looking at them. They'll have a tattoo on their hip or wear too much eyeshadow, and they'll have stripper names. They're just dressing up all innocent for the photo shoot. The next photo shoot they'll dress up as sexy cops or cheerleaders, and it'll be just as fake. The girl in church, now, she's the real deal.' He lifted the cross from his chest and rubbed it between his thumb and forefinger. 'The thing I'm hung up on is the idea of seeing something real. I don't think most people feel half the things they pretend to feel. I think especially girls in a relationship tend to put on attitudes like clothes, just to keep a guy interested. Like Glenna keeping me interested with the occasional hand job. It isn't because she loves hand jobs. It's because she *doesn't* love being lonely. When a girl loses her virginity, though, it may hurt, but it's real. It might be the realest, most private thing you could ever see in another person. You wonder who she'll be in that moment, when you finally get past all the pretend. That's what I think about when I think about the girl in church.'

Ig was sorry about the half a sandwich he had eaten. The cross around Lee's neck was flashing in the sunlight, and when Ig closed his eyes, he could still see it, a series of glowing after-images, signalling a dreadful warning. He felt a headache coming on.

When he opened his eyes, he said, 'So politics doesn't work out, you going to kill people for a living?'

'I guess.'

'How would you do it? What's your MO?' Wondering how he would kill Lee himself, to get back the cross.

'Who are we talking about? Some skag who owes her dealer money? Or the president?'

Ig let out a long, slow breath. 'Someone who knows the truth about you. A star witness. If he lives, you're going to jail.'

Lee said, 'I'd burn him to death in his car. Do it with a bomb. I'm on the kerb across the street from him, watching as he climbs behind the wheel. The moment he pulls out, I press the button on my remote control, so after the explosion the car keeps rolling, this big burning wreck.'

Ig said, 'Hey. Wait a minute. I got to show you something.'

He ignored the puzzled look Lee gave him, rose, and trotted inside. He returned three minutes later, right hand closed into a fist. Lee looked up, brow furrowed, as Ig settled back into his deckchair.

'Check it out,' Ig said, and opened his right hand to show the cherry bomb.

Lee looked at it, his face blank as a plastic mask, but his indifference didn't fool Ig, who was learning to read him. When Ig had opened his hand and Lee saw what he was holding, he sat up in spite of himself.

'Eric Hannity paid up,' Ig said. 'This is what I got for riding the cart down the hill. You saw the turkey, didn't you?'

'It rained Thanksgiving for an hour.'

'Wouldn't it be cool to stick it in a car? Say you found a wreck somewhere. I bet you could blow the hood off with this thing. Terry told me these are pre-CPL.'

'Pre-what?'

'Child-protection laws. The fireworks they make nowadays are like farts in a bathtub. Not these.'

'How could they sell 'em if they're against the law?'

'It's only against the law to manufacture new ones. These are from a box of old ones.'

'Is that what you're going to do? Find a wreck and blow it up?'

'No. My brother's making me wait until we go to Cape Cod, Labor Day weekend. He's taking me after he gets his licence.'

'It's not my business, I guess,' Lee said, 'but I don't see how he has any say.'

'No. I have to wait. Eric Hannity wasn't even going to give it to me, because I was wearing sneakers when I went down the hill. He said I wasn't really naked. But Terry said that was bullshit and got Eric to cough up. So I owe him. And Terry wants to wait for Cape Cod.'

For the first time in their brief friendship, Lee seemed irritated by something. He grimaced, wiggled around on his deckchair, as if he had suddenly noticed something digging into his back. He said, 'Kind of stupid they're called Eve's Cherries. Shoulda called 'em Eve's Apples.'

'Why?'

''Cause of the Bible.'

'The Bible only says they ate fruit from the Tree of Knowledge. It never says it's an apple. Could've been a cherry.'

'I don't believe that story.'

'No,' Ig admitted. 'Neither do I. Dinosaurs.'

'You believe in Jesus?'

'Why not? As many people wrote about him as wrote about Caesar.' He looked sidelong at Lee, who himself so resembled Caesar that his profile might've been stamped on a coin, was only missing the crown of laurel leaves.

'Do you believe he could do miracles?' Lee asked.

'Maybe. I don't know. If the rest is true, does that part even matter?'

'I did a miracle once.'

Ig found this a not terribly remarkable thing to admit. Ig's father said he had seen a UFO once in the Nevada desert, when he was out there drinking with the drummer from Cheap Trick. Instead of asking what miracle Lee had performed, Ig said, 'Was it cool?'

Lee nodded, his very blue eyes distant, a little unfocused. 'I fixed the moon. When I was a little kid. And ever since, I've been good at fixing other things. It's what I'm best at.'

'How'd you fix the moon?'

Lee narrowed one eye to a squint, lifted one hand towards the sky, pinched an imaginary moon between thumb and fore-finger, and gave it a half turn. He made a soft click. 'All better.'

Ig didn't want to talk religion; he wanted to talk demolition. 'It's going to be pretty miraculous when I light the fuse on this thing,' he said, and Lee's gaze swivelled back to the cherry bomb in Ig's hand. 'I'm going to send something home to God. Any suggestions what?'

The way Lee looked at the cherry bomb, Ig thought of a man sitting at a bar drinking something boozy and watching the girl onstage tug down her panties. They had not been buddies for long, but a pattern had been established – this was the moment Ig was supposed to offer it to him, the way he had given Lee his money, his CDs and Merrin Williams' cross. But he didn't offer it, and Lee couldn't ask for it. Ig told himself he didn't give it to Lee because he had embarrassed him last time, with his gift of CDs. The truth was something different: Ig felt a mean urge to hold something over him, to have a cross of his own to wear. Later, after Lee left, Ig would be ashamed of this impulse – a rich kid with a swimming pool, lording his treasures over a kid from a single-parent home in a trailer park.

'You could stick it in a pumpkin,' Lee said, and Ig replied,

'Too much like the turkey,' and they were off and running, Lee suggesting things, Ig considering them in turn.

They discussed the merits of throwing the bomb into the river to see if they could kill fish with it, dropping it into an outhouse to see if it would make a shit geyser, using a slingshot to shoot it into the bell tower of the church to see what kind of gong it made when it went off. There was the big billboard outside of town that read WILD BASS WAREHOUSE – FISHING AND BOATING SUPPLIES; Lee said it would be hilarious to tape the bomb to the *B* and see if they could make it the WILD ASS WAREHOUSE. Lee had lots of ideas.

'You keep trying to figure out what kind of music I like,' Lee said. 'I'll tell you what I like. The sound of things blowing up and tinkling glass. Music to my ears.'

17

Ig was waiting for his turn in the barber's chair when he heard a tapping from behind him and looked over his shoulder and saw Glenna standing on the sidewalk, staring in at him from an inch away, her nose smooshed to the window. She was so close she would've been breathing on his neck if there weren't a plate of glass between them. Instead she breathed on the glass, turning it white with condensation. She wrote in it with one finger: I SEEN YOUR PP. Beneath this she drew a cartoonish dangling cock.

Ig's heart lurched, and he quickly glanced around to see if his mother was close by, if she had noticed. But Lydia stood across the room from him, behind the barber's chair, giving instructions to the hairdresser. Terry was up in the seat, wearing the apron, waiting patiently to be made even more beautiful. Cutting Ig's own rat's snarl was like clipping a deformed hedge. It couldn't be made pretty, only manageable.

Ig looked back at Glenna, shaking his head furiously: *Go away.* She wiped the message off the glass with the sleeve of her awesomely awesome leather jacket.

She wasn't alone. Highway to Hell was there, too, along with the other derelict who'd been a part of their group at the foundry, a long-haired kid in his late teens. The two boys were on the other side of the parking lot, rooting in a garbage can. What was it with the two of them and garbage cans?

Glenna rattled her fingernails against the window. They were painted the colour of ice, long and pointed, witch fingernails. He looked again at his mother but could see at a glance he wouldn't be missed. Lydia was wrapped up in what she was saying, shaping something in the air, the perfect head of hair or maybe an imaginary sphere, a crystal ball, and in the ball was a future in which the nineteen-year-old hairdresser received a big tip if she could just stand there and nod her head and chew her gum and let Lydia tell her how to do her job.

When Ig came outside, Glenna had turned her back to the window and planted her firm, round bottom against the glass. She was staring at Highway to Hell and his long-haired buddy. They stood with the trash can between them and a garbage bag pulled open. The long-haired kid kept reaching up to touch Highway to Hell's face, tenderly almost. He laughed, a big, goofy guffaw, every time the kid caressed him.

'Why did you give Lee that cross?' Glenna said.

It jolted Ig – of all the things she could've said. He had been asking himself the same question for over a week.

'He said he was going to fix it,' Ig said.

'It's fixed. So why doesn't he give it back?'

'It isn't mine. It's— This girl dropped it in church. I was going to fix it and give it back, but I couldn't, and Lee said he could with his dad's tools, and now he's wearing it in case he runs into her when he's going door-to-door for his charity.'

'His charity,' she said, and snorted. 'You ought to ask for it back. You should ask for your CDs back, too.'

'He doesn't have any music.'

'He doesn't *want* any music,' Glenna said. 'If he wanted some, he'd get himself some.'

'I don't know. CDs are pretty expensive and—'

'So? He's not *poor*, you know,' Glenna said. 'He lives in Harmon Gates. My dad does their yard work. That's how I know him. My dad sent me over there to plant peonies one day by myself. Lee's parents have plenty of money. Did he tell you he can't afford CDs?'

It disoriented Ig, the idea that Lee lived in Harmon Gates, had a man to do his yard work, a mother. A mother especially. 'His parents live together?'

'It doesn't seem like it sometimes, because his mother works at Exeter Hospital and has a really long commute and isn't around so much. It's probably better that way. Lee and his mom don't get along.'

Ig shook his head. It was like Glenna was talking about a completely different person, someone Ig didn't know. He had formed a very clear picture of Lee Tourneau's life, the trailer he shared with his pickup-driving father, the mother who had disappeared when he was a child to smoke crack and sell herself in the Combat Zone down in Boston. Lee had never told Iggy that he lived in a trailer or that his mother was a drug-addicted hoor, but Ig felt that these things were implied by Lee's view of the world, by the subjects he never discussed.

'Did he tell you he doesn't have any money for things?' Glenna asked again.

Ig shook his head.

'I didn't think,' she said. She toed a stone on the ground for a moment, then looked up and said, 'Is she prettier than me?'

'Who?'

'The girl from church. The girl who used to wear that cross.'

Ig tried to think what to say, mentally flailing for some graceful and considerate lie – but he had never been any good at lying, and his silence was a kind of answer in and of itself.

'Yeah,' Glenna said, smiling ruefully. 'I thought so.'

Ig looked away from her, too distressed by that unhappy smile to maintain eye contact. Glenna seemed all right, direct and no bullshit.

Highway to Hell and the long-haired kid were laughing over the trash can – the loud, sharp cries of crows. Ig had no idea why.

'Do you know a car you could set fire to,' Ig said, 'and get away with it? Not like a car someone owns. Just a wreck?'

'Why?'

'Lee wants to set fire to a car.'

She frowned, trying to figure out why Ig had shifted the conversation to *this*. Then she looked at Highway to Hell. 'Gary's dad, my uncle, has a bunch of junkers in the woods, out behind his house in Derry. He's got a home auto-parts business. Or at least he *says* he has an auto-parts business. I don't know if he's ever had any customers.'

'You should mention them to Lee sometime,' Ig said.

A fist rapped on the glass behind him, and both of them turned to look up at Ig's mother. Lydia smiled down at Glenna and lifted one hand in a stiff little wave, then shifted her gaze to Ig and opened her eyes in a wide, strained look of impatience. He nodded, but when his mother turned her back to them, Ig did not immediately move to re-enter the salon.

Glenna cocked her head to an inquisitive angle. 'So if we get some arson going, you want in?'

'No. Not really. You kids have fun.'

'You kids,' she said, and her smile broadened. 'What are you going to do with your hair?'

'I don't know. Probably what I always do.'

'You ought to shave it off,' she said. 'Go bald. You'd look cool.'

'Huh? No. No, my mom—'

'Well, you ought to at least clip it short and punk it up. Bleach the tips or something. Your hair is part of who you are. Don't you want to be someone interesting?' She reached out and ruffed up his hair. 'You could be someone interesting with a little effort.'

'I don't think I get a say. My mom is going to want me to stick with what works.'

'Ah, that's too bad. I like me some crazy hair myself,' Glenna said.

'Yeah?' said Gary, a.k.a. Highway to Hell. 'You're going to fucking love my ass.'

They both swivelled their heads to look at Highway to Hell and the long-haired boy, who had just wandered over from the trash can. They had collected hair clippings from the garbage and glued them to Gary's face, making a tufty reddish brown beard, the sort van Gogh wore in his self-portraits. It didn't match the blue bristle of Gary's shaved head.

Glenna's face shrivelled in a look of pain. 'Oh, God. That ain't going to fool anyone, you asshole.'

'Give me your jacket,' Gary said. 'I put your jacket on, I bet I could pass for at least twenty.'

Glenna said, 'You could pass for retarded. And you aren't getting arrested in this jacket.'

Ig said, 'That really is a nice jacket.'

Glenna gave him a mysteriously miserable look. 'Lee gave it to me. He's a very generous person.'

18

Lee opened his mouth to say something, then changed his mind and closed it.

'What?' Ig asked.

Lee opened his mouth again and closed it and opened it and said, 'I like that rat-a-tat-tat Glenn Miller song. You could make a corpse dance to that song.'

Ig nodded and didn't reply.

They were in the pool, because August was back. No more rain, no more unseasonable cool. It was almost a hundred degrees, not a cloud in the sky, and Lee was wearing a strip of white zinc oxide down the bridge of his nose to keep it from burning. Ig was in a life ring, and Lee hung off an inflatable pool mattress, both of them floating in still, tepid water so heavily chlorinated that the fumes stung their eyes. It was too hot to horse around.

The cross still hung from Lee's neck. It was spread out on the mattress, stretching away from his throat and towards Ig – as if Ig's stare had the power of magnetism and was tugging it in his direction. The sun caught it and flashed gold in Ig's eyes, producing a steady staccato signal. Ig didn't need to know Morse Code to know what it was signalling him now. It was Saturday, and Merrin Williams would be in church tomorrow. *Last chance*, the cross flashed. *Last chance, last chance.*

Lee's lips parted slightly. He seemed to want to say more

but did not know how to proceed. Finally he said, 'Glenna's cousin Gary is having a bonfire in a couple of weeks. At his place. Sort of an end-of-the-summer party. He's got some bottle rockets and stuff. He says he might have beer, too. You think you'd want to come?'

'When?'

'It's the last Saturday this month.'

'I can't. My dad is playing a show with John Williams at the Boston Pops. It's opening night. We always go to his opening-night shows.'

'Yeah, I understand that,' Lee said.

Lee put the cross in his mouth and sucked on it, thinking. Then he dropped it and finally said the thing he wanted to say. 'Would you ever sell it?'

'Sell what?'

'Eve's Cherry. The bomb. There's a junker at Gary's. Gary says no one will care if we trash the thing. We might put lighter fluid on it and blow it up.' He caught himself, then added, 'That's not why I asked if you could come. I asked because it'll be more fun if you're there.'

'No. I know,' Ig said. 'Just, I wouldn't feel right selling it to you.'

'Well. You can't keep giving me things either. If you were going to sell it, how much would you want? I've got a little money saved up from tips on the magazine sales.'

Or you could borrow a twenty from your mama, Ig thought, in an almost-sly, silky voice that he hardly recognised as his own.

'I don't want your money,' Ig said. 'But I'll trade you.'

'For what?'

'For that,' Ig said, and nodded at the cross.

There. It was said. Ig's next breath held in his lungs, a hot, chlorine-flavoured capsule of oxygen, chemical and strange. Lee had saved his life, pulled him out of the river when he was unconscious and pounded the air back into him, and Ig was ready to give back, felt he owed Lee anything and everything – except for this. She had signalled *him*, not Lee. Ig understood there was no right in bargaining with Lee like this, no moral defence, no way to sell it as the act of a decent person. No sooner had he asked for the cross back than he felt a kind of shrivelling inside; he had always thought of himself as the good guy in his own story, the clear hero. But the good guy wouldn't do this. Maybe some things were more important than being the good guy, though.

Lee stared, a slight half smile pulling at the corners of his lips. Ig felt a blaze of heat in his face and was not entirely sorry, was glad to be embarrassed for her. He said, 'I know this is coming out of nowhere, but I think I have a crush on her. I would've said something earlier, but I didn't want to be in your way.'

Without hesitation Lee reached behind his neck and undid the clasp. 'All you ever had to do was ask. It's yours. It was always yours. You found it, not me. All I did was fix it. And if it gets you in with her, I'm glad to fix that, too.'

'I thought she was your sort of thing, though. You aren't—?'

Lee waved a hand through the air. 'Going to compete with a friend over some girl whose name I don't know. All the stuff you've given me, all the CDs? Even if they mostly sucked, I appreciate it. I'm not an ungrateful person, Ig. You ever see her again, you're all over it. I'm behind you all the way. I don't think she's coming back, though.'

'She is,' Ig said softly.

Lee looked at him.

The truth had come out before Ig could help himself. He had to know that Lee didn't care, because they were friends now. Were going to be friends for the rest of their lives.

When Lee didn't speak – just floated there with that half smile on his long, narrow face – Ig went on, 'I met someone who knows her. She wasn't there last Sunday because her family is moving up from Rhode Island and they had to go back and get the rest of their stuff.'

Lee finished removing the cross and tossed it lightly to Ig, who caught it when it hit the water.

'Go get her, tiger,' Lee said. 'You're the one who found that thing, and for whatever reason she didn't seem to take a shine to me. Besides. I have all I can handle in the lady department these days. Glenna came over to see me yesterday, to tell me about the car at Gary's, and while she was over, she took the whole thing in her mouth. Only for a minute. But she did it.' Lee beamed – the smile of a child with a new balloon. 'What a fucking slut, huh?'

'That's awesome,' Ig said, and smiled weakly.

19

Ig saw Merrin Williams and then pretended he hadn't: no
easy task, his heart leaping inside him, throwing itself into
his ribcage like an angry drunk assaulting the bars of his holding
cell. He had thought of this moment not just every day but
nearly every hour of every day, since he had last seen her, and
it was almost too much for his nervous system, was overloading
the grid. She wore cream-coloured linen slacks and a white
blouse with the sleeves folded back, and her hair was loose this
time, and she looked right at him as he came up the aisle with
his family, but he pretended not to see her.

Lee and his father came in a few minutes before the service
began and settled into a pew on Ig's side, close to the front. Lee
turned his head and gave her a long look, up and down. She
didn't seem to notice, was gazing intently at Ig. After Lee had
finished inspecting her, he peered back over his shoulder, to
look at Ig himself from under heavy-lidded eyes. He shook his
head in mock disapproval before pivoting away.

Merrin stared at Iggy for the entire first five minutes of the
service, and in all that time he did not once look at her directly.
He clenched his hands together, his palms slick with sweat,
and kept his eyes fixed on Father Mould.

She didn't give up staring at him until Father Mould said,
'Let us pray.' She slid off the pew to kneel and put her hands
together, and that was when Ig slipped the cross out of his

pocket. He held it in the cup of his hand, found some sunshine and pointed it at her. A spectral golden cross of light drifted over her cheekbone and struck the corner of her eye. She blinked the first time he flashed her with it, flinched the second time, and looked back at him the third time. He held the piece steady, so a golden cross of pure light burned in the centre of his hand and its reflection shone on her cheek. She regarded him with unexpected solemnity, the radio operator in a war movie, receiving a life-or-death signal from a comrade-in-arms.

Slowly and deliberately, he tilted it this way and that, flashing the Morse Code message he had memorised over the course of the last week. It felt important to get it exactly right, and he handled the cross as if it were a thimbleful of nitroglycerin. When the message was complete, he held her gaze for a moment longer and then closed his hand around the cross and looked away again, his heart slamming so loudly he felt sure his father must be able to hear it, kneeling next to him. But his father was praying over his hands, his eyes closed.

Ig Perrish and Merrin Williams took care not to look at each other again throughout the rest of the service. Or, to be more exact, they did not look into each other's face, although he was conscious of her watching him from the corner of her eye, as he watched her, enjoying the way she stood to sing, with her shoulders back. Her hair burned in the daylight.

Father Mould blessed them all and bade them to love one another, which was precisely Ig's goal. As people began to file out, Ig remained where he was, his father's hand on his shoulder, as always. Merrin Williams stepped into the aisle, her own father behind her, and Ig expected her to stop and thank him for rescuing her cross, but she did not even look at him. Instead she stared back and up at her father, chatting with him as they went out. Ig opened his mouth to speak to her – and then his gaze was drawn to her left hand, her index finger extended to point behind her, back towards her pew. It was such a casual gesture she could've just been swinging her arm, but Ig was sure she was telling him where to wait for her.

When the aisle was clear, Ig stepped out and aside, to let his father and mother and brother go on ahead. But instead of following them, he turned and walked towards the altar and the chancel. When his mother shot a look at him, he pointed in the direction of the back hall, where there was a restroom. You could only pretend you needed to tie your shoe so many times. She went on, her hand on Terry's arm. Terry was looking back at Ig with narrow-eyed suspicion but allowed himself to be marched away.

Ig hung out in the shadowy back hall that led to Father Mould's office, watching for her. She returned soon enough, and by then the church was practically empty. She looked around the nave but didn't see him, and he remained in the darkness, watching her. She walked to the altar of repose and lit a candle and crossed herself and knelt and prayed. Her hair fell to hide her face, and so Ig did not think she saw him as he started forward. He did not feel as if he was walking towards her at all. His legs were not his own. It was more like being carried, as if he were on the shopping cart again; there was that same giddy but nauseating feeling of plunge in his stomach, of dropping off the very edge of the world, of sweet risk.

He did not interrupt her until she lifted her head and looked up.

'Hey,' he said, as she rose. 'I found your cross. You left it. I was worried when I didn't see you last Sunday that I wouldn't have a chance to give it back.' He was already holding it out to her.

She tugged the cross and its slender chain of gold from his hand and held it in hers.

'You fixed it.'

'No,' Ig said. 'My friend Lee Tourneau fixed it. He's good at fixing things.'

'Oh,' she said. 'Tell him I said thanks.'

'You can tell him yourself if he's still around. He goes to this church, too.'

'Will you put it on?' she asked. She turned her back to him and lifted her hair and bent her head forward to show him the white nape of her neck.

Ig smoothed his palms across his chest to dry them and then opened the necklace and gently pulled it around her throat. He hoped she wouldn't see that his hands were shaking.

'You met Lee, you know,' Ig said, so he'd have something to say. 'He was sitting behind you the day it broke.'

'That kid? He tried to put it back on me after it snapped. I thought he was going to strangle me with it.'

'I'm not strangling you, am I?' Ig asked.

'No,' she said.

He was having trouble linking the clasp to the chain. It was his nervous hands. She waited patiently.

'Who were you lighting a candle for?' Ig asked.

'My sister.'

'You have a sister?' Ig asked.

'Not anymore,' she said in a clipped, emotionless sort of way, and Ig felt a sick twinge, knew he shouldn't have asked.

'Did you figure out the message?' he blurted, feeling an urgent need to move the conversation to something else.

'What message?'

'The message I was flashing you. In Morse Code. You know Morse Code, don't you?'

She laughed – an unexpectedly rowdy sound that almost caused Ig to drop the necklace. In the next moment, his fingers discovered what to do, and he fastened the chain around her throat. She turned. It was a shock how close she was standing.

'No. I went to Girl Scouts a couple of times, but I quit before we got to anything interesting. Besides, I already know everything I need to know about camping. My father was in the Forest Service. What were you signalling me?'

She flustered him. He had planned this whole conversation in advance, with great care, working out everything she'd ask and every smooth reply he'd give her, but it was all gone now.

'But weren't *you* flashing something to *me*?' he asked. 'The other day?'

She laughed again. 'I was just seeing how long I could flash you in the eyes before you figured out where it was coming from. What message did you *think* I was sending you?'

But Ig couldn't answer her. His windpipe was bunching up again, and there was a dreadful suffusion of heat in his face, and for the first time he realised how ridiculous it was to have imagined she had been signalling *anything*, let alone what he had talked himself into believing – that she was flashing the word 'us'. No girl in the world would've signalled such a thing to a boy she had never spoken to before. It was obvious, now that he looked at it straight on.

'I was saying, "This is yours",' Ig told her at last, deciding that the only safe thing to do was to ignore the question she had just asked him. Furthermore, this was a lie, although it sounded true. He had been signalling her a single short word as well. The word had been 'yes'.

'Thanks, Iggy,' she said.

'How do you know my name?' he asked, and was surprised at the way her face suddenly coloured.

'I asked someone,' she said. 'I forget why, I—'

'And you're Merrin.'

She stared, her eyes questioning, surprised.

'I asked someone,' he said.

She looked at the doors. 'My parents are probably waiting.'

'Okay,' he said.

By the time they reached the atrium, he had found out they were both in first-period English together, that her house was on Clapham Street, and that her mother had signed her up to be a volunteer at the blood drive the church was holding at the end of the month. Ig was working the blood drive, too.

'I didn't see you on the sign-up sheet,' she said. They walked three more steps before it occurred to Ig that this meant she had looked for his name on the sheet. He glanced over and saw her smiling enigmatically to herself.

When they came through the doors, the sunshine was so bright that for a moment Ig couldn't see anything through the harsh glare. He saw a dark blur rushing at him and lifted his hands and caught a football. As his vision cleared, he saw his brother and Lee Tourneau and some other boys – even Eric Hannity – and Father Mould fanning out across the grass, and Father Mould was shouting, 'Ig, right here!' His parents were standing with Merrin's parents, Derrick Perrish and Merrin's father talking cheerfully, as if their families had been friends for years. Merrin's mother, a thin woman with a pinched, colourless mouth, was shading her eyes with one hand and smiling at her daughter in a pained sort of way. The day smelled of hot tarmac, sun-baked cars, and fresh-cut lawn. Ig, who was not at all athletically inclined, cocked back his arm and threw the football with a perfect tight spin on it, and it cut through the air and dropped right into Father Mould's big, callused hands. Father Mould lifted it over his head, running across the green lawn in his black short-sleeved shirt and white collar.

Football lasted for most of half an hour, fathers and sons and Father chasing one another across the grass. Lee was drafted as a quarterback; he wasn't much of an athlete either, but he looked the part, falling back to go long with that look of perfect, almost icy calm on his face, his tie tossed over one shoulder. Merrin kicked off her shoes and played, the only girl among them. Her mother said, 'Merrin Williams, you'll get grass stains on your pants and we'll never get them out,' but her father waved his hand in the air and said, 'Let her have some fun.' It was supposed to be touch football, but Merrin threw Ig down on every play, diving at his feet, until it was a gag that cracked everyone up, Ig wiped out by this sixteen-year-old girl built like a blade of grass. No one thought it was funnier, or enjoyed it more, than Ig himself, who went out of his way to give her chances to cream him.

'You should drop your butt on the ground as soon as they snap the ball,' she said, the fifth or sixth time she wiped him out. "Cause I can do this all day. You know that? What's funny?' Because he was laughing.

She was kneeling over him, her red hair tickling his nose. She smelled of lemons and mint. The necklace hung from her throat, flashing at him again, transmitting a message of almost unbearable pleasure.

'Nothing,' he said. 'I think I'm reading you loud and clear.'

20

For all the rest of the summer, they had a habit of wandering into each other. When Ig went with his mother to the supermarket, Merrin was there with *her* mother, and they wound up walking together, drifting along a few feet behind their parents. Merrin got a bag of cherries, and they shared it while they walked.

'Isn't this shoplifting?' Ig asked.

'We can't get in trouble if we eat the evidence,' she said, and spat a pit into her hand and then handed it to him. She gave him all her pits, calmly expecting him to get rid of them, which he did by putting them in his pocket. When he got home, there was a sweet-smelling wet lump the size of a baby's fist in his jeans.

And when the Jag had to go into Masters Auto for an inspection, Ig tagged along with his father, because he knew by then that Merrin's dad worked there. Ig had no reason to believe that Merrin would be at the dealership as well, on a sunny Wednesday afternoon, but she was, sitting on her father's desk, swinging her feet back and forth, as if waiting for him, impatient for him to arrive. They got orange sodas from the vending machine and stood talking in a back hallway, under buzzing fluorescent lights. She told him she was hiking out to Queen's Face the next day, with her father. Ig said the path went right behind his house, and she asked if he would walk up with them.

Her lips were stained orange from the soda. It was no work to be together. It was the most natural thing in the world.

It was natural to include Lee also. He kept things from getting too serious. He invited himself along for the walk up Queen's Face, said he wanted to check it out for mountainboarding trails. He forgot to bring the board, though.

On the climb up, Merrin grabbed the collar of her T-shirt and pulled it away from her chest, twitching it back and forth to fan herself and mock-panting from the heat. 'You guys ever jump in the river?' Merrin asked, pointing at the Knowles through the trees. It wound through dense forest in the valley below, a black snake with a back of brilliantly glittering scales.

'Ig jumps in all the time,' Lee said, and Ig laughed. Merrin gave them both a puzzled, narrow-eyed look, but Ig only shook his head. Lee went on, 'Tell you what, though. Ig's pool is a lot nicer. When are you going to have her over swimming?'

Ig's face prickled with heat at the suggestion. He had fantasised just that thing, many times – Merrin in a bikini – but whenever he came close to asking her, his breath failed him.

They talked about her sister, Regan, just once in those first weeks. Ig asked why they had moved up from Rhode Island, and Merrin said with a shrug, 'My parents were really depressed after Regan died, and my mother grew up here, her whole family is here. And home didn't feel right anymore. Without Regan in it.'

Regan had died at twenty of a rare and particularly aggressive form of breast cancer. It took just four months to kill her.

'Must've been awful,' Ig murmured, a moronic generality but the only thing that felt safe. 'I can't imagine how I'd feel if Terry died. He's my best friend.'

'That's what I thought about Regan and me.' They were in Merrin's bedroom, and her back was to Ig, her head bent. She was brushing her hair. Without looking at him, she went on, 'But she said some things when she was sick – some really mean things. Things I never knew she thought about me. When she died, I felt like I hardly knew her. 'Course, I got off easy, compared to the things she said to my parents. I don't think I can ever forgive her for what she said to Dad.' She spoke this last bit lightly, as if they were discussing a matter of no real importance, and then was quiet.

It was years before they talked about Regan again. But when Merrin told him, a few days later, that she was going to be a doctor, Ig didn't need to ask what her speciality was going to be.

On the last day of August, Ig and Merrin were at the blood drive, across the street from the church, in the Sacred Heart Community Center, handing out paper cups of Tang and Lorna Doone sandwich cookies. A few ceiling fans pushed a sluggish current of hot air around the room, and Ig and Merrin were drinking as much juice as they were handing out. He was just working up his nerve to finally ask her over for a swim when Terry walked in.

He stood on the other side of the room, searching for Ig, and Ig lifted a hand to get his attention. Terry jerked his head: *Get over here.* There was something stiff and tense and worrisome in this gesture. In some ways it was worrisome enough just seeing Terry there. Terry wasn't the sort to come anywhere near a church function on a wide-open summer afternoon if he could avoid it. Ig was only half aware of Merrin following him across the room as he threaded his way between gurneys, donors stretched upon them, tubes in their arms. The room smelled of disinfectant and blood.

When Ig got to his brother, Terry gripped his arm, squeezing it painfully. He turned him through the door and out into the foyer, where they could be alone. The doors were open to the bright, hot, stillborn day.

'Did you give it to him?' Terry asked. 'Did you give him the cherry?'

Ig didn't have to ask who he was talking about. Terry's voice, thin and harsh, frightened him. Needles of panic prickled in Ig's chest.

'Is Lee okay?' Ig asked. It was Sunday afternoon. Lee had gone up to Gary's the day before. It came to Ig now that he had not seen Lee in church that morning.

'Him and some other jokers taped a cherry bomb to the windshield of a junked car and ran. But it didn't go off right away, and Lee thought the fuse went out. They do that. He was walking back to check on it when the windshield exploded and sprayed glass everywhere. *Ig*. They pulled a fucking sliver out of his left eye. They're saying he's lucky it didn't go into his brain.'

Ig wanted to scream, but something was happening in his chest. His lungs had gone numb, as if injected with a dose of Novocain. He couldn't speak, couldn't force any sound up through his throat at all.

'Ig,' said Merrin. 'Where's your inhaler?' Her voice was calm and steady. She already knew all about his asthma.

He struggled to pull it out of his pocket and dropped it. She got it for him, and he put it in his mouth and took a long, damp suck.

Terry said, 'Look, Ig. Ig, it's not just about his eye. He's in a lot of trouble. What I heard is some cops showed up with the ambulance. You know that mountain board of his? Turns out it's stolen. They pulled a two-hundred-dollar leather jacket off his girlfriend, too. The police asked his father for permission to search his room this morning, and it was *full* of stolen shit. Lee worked out at the mall for a couple weeks, at the pet store, and he had a key to an access hallway that runs behind the shops. He helped himself to piles of stuff. He had all these magazines he ripped off from Mr Paperback, and he was running a scam, selling them to people, pretending he was raising money for some made-up charity. Shit is messed up.

He'll be in juvie court if any of the stores press charges. In some ways, if he goes blind in one eye, it'll be the best thing for him. Might win him some sympathy, maybe he won't—'

'Oh, God,' Ig said, hearing *if he goes blind in one eye*, and *they pulled a fucking sliver out*; everything else was just noise, Terry playing an avant-garde riff on his trumpet. Ig was crying and squeezing Merrin's hand. When had she taken his hand? He didn't know.

'You're going to have to talk to him,' Terry said. 'You better have a word and make sure he's going to keep his mouth shut. We got to do some ass-covering here. If anyone finds out you gave him that cherry bomb – or that *I* gave it to *you* – oh, Jesus, Ig. They could throw me out of band.'

Ig couldn't speak, needed another long suck on his inhaler. He was shaking.

'Will you give him a second?' Merrin snapped. 'Let him get his breath back.'

Terry gave her a surprised, wondering look. For a moment his jaw hung slack. Then he closed his mouth and was silent.

'Come on, Ig,' she said. 'Let's go outside.'

Ig walked with her, down the steps, into the sunlight, his legs trembling. Terry hung back, let them go.

The air was still and weighted with moisture and a sense of building pressure. The skies had been clear earlier in the morning, but now there were heavy clouds in them, as dark and vast as a fleet of aircraft carriers. A hot gust of wind rose from nowhere and battered at them. That wind smelled like hot iron, like train tracks in the sun, like old pipes, and when Ig closed his eyes, he saw the Evel Knievel trail, the way the two half-buried pipes fell away down the slope like the rails of a roller coaster.

'It isn't your fault,' she said. 'He isn't going to blame you. C'mon. The blood drive is almost over. Let's get our stuff and go see him. Right now. You and me.'

Ig shrank at the thought of going with her. They had traded – the cherry bomb for her. It would be awful to bring her with him. It would be rubbing it in. Lee had only saved his life, and Ig had repaid him by taking Merrin away, and this was what happened, and Lee was blind in one eye, his eye was gone, and Ig had done that to him. Ig got the girl and his life, and Lee got a sliver of glass and ruin, and Ig took another deep suck off the inhaler, was having trouble breathing.

When he had enough air to speak, he said, 'You can't come with me.' A part of him was thinking already that the only way for him to atone was to be done with her, but another part of him, the same part that had traded for the cross in the first place, knew he wasn't going to do that. He had decided weeks ago, had made a deal, not just with Lee but with himself – that he would do what was necessary to be the boy walking next to Merrin Williams. Giving her up wouldn't make him the good guy in this story. It was too late to be the good guy.

'Why not? He's my friend, too,' she said, and Ig was at first surprised at her, then at himself, for not realising that this was true.

'I don't know what he'll say. He might be mad at me. He might say stuff about – about a trade.' As soon as he said it, he knew he shouldn't have said it.

'What trade?' He shook his head, but she asked again. 'What did you trade?'

'You won't be mad?'

'I don't know. Tell me, and then we'll see.'

'After I found your cross, I gave it to Lee so he could fix it. But then he was going to keep it, and I had to trade him to get it back. And the cherry bomb was what I traded.'

She furrowed her brow. 'So?'

He stared helplessly into her face, willing her to understand, but she didn't understand, so he said, 'He was going to keep it so he'd have a way to meet you.'

151

For one moment longer, her eyes were clouded, uncomprehending. Then they cleared. She did not smile.

'You think you traded—' she started, then stopped. A moment later she started again. She was staring at him with a cool, ball-shrivelling calm. 'You think you traded for *me*, Ig? Is that how you think all this worked? And do you think if he had returned the cross to me instead of you, then Lee and I would be—' But she didn't say that either, because to go any further would be to admit that she and Ig were together now, something they both understood but had not dared to say aloud. She started a third time. 'Ig. I left it on the pew for *you.*'

'You left it – what?'

'I was bored. I was so bored. And I was sitting there imagining a hundred more mornings, roasting in the sun in that church, dying inside one Sunday at a time while Father Mould blabbed away about my sins. I needed something to look forward to. Some reason to be there. I didn't just want listen to some guy talk about sin. I wanted to do some myself. And then I saw you sitting there like a little priss, hanging on every word like it was all so interesting, and I knew Ig, I just knew – that fucking with your head would present me with hours of entertainment.'

As it happened, in the end Ig did go and see Lee Tourneau alone. When Merrin and Ig started back to the Community Center, to clean up the pizza boxes and the empty juice bottles, there came a peal of thunder that lasted for at least ten seconds, a low, steady rumble that was not so much heard as felt. It caused the bones in Ig's body to shiver like tuning forks. Five minutes later the rain was clattering on the roof, so loudly he had to shout at Merrin to be heard over it, even when she was standing right next to him. It was so dark, the water coming down with such force, that it was difficult to see to the kerb from the open doors of the Community Center. They had thought they might be able to bike to Lee's, but Merrin's father turned up to bring her home in his station wagon, and there was no opportunity to go anywhere together.

Terry had got his licence two days before, passing the test on his first try, and the next day he drove Ig over to Lee Tourneau's. The storm had split trees and unscrewed telephone poles from the soil, and Terry had to steer the Jaguar around torn branches and overturned mailboxes. It was as if some great subterranean explosion, some final, powerful detonation, had rattled the whole town and left Gideon in a state of ruin.

Harmon Gates was a tangle of suburban streets, houses painted citrus colours, attached two-car garages, the occasional backyard swimming pool. Lee's mother, the nurse, a woman in her fifties, was outside the Tourneaus' Queen Anne, pulling branches off her parked Cadillac, her mouth puckered in a look of irritation. Terry let Ig out, said to call home when he wanted a ride back.

Lee had a large bedroom in their finished basement. Lee's mother walked Ig down and opened the door onto a cavernous gloom, in which the only light was the blue glow of a television. 'You've got a visitor,' she said, rather tonelessly.

She let Ig past her and closed the door behind him, so they could be alone.

Lee's shirt was off, and he sat on the edge of his bed, clutching the frame. A *Benson* rerun was on the tube, although Lee had the volume turned all the way down, so it was just a source of light and moving figures. A bandage covered his left eye and was wrapped around and around his skull, swaddling much of his head. The shades were pulled down. He did not look directly at Ig, or at the TV; his gaze pointed downwards.

'Dark in here,' Ig said.

'The sunlight hurts my head,' Lee said.

'How's your eye?'

'They don't know.'

'Is there any chance——?'

'They think I won't lose all the vision in it.'

'That's good.'

Lee sat there. Ig waited.

'You know everything?'

'I don't care,' Ig said. 'You pulled me out of the river. That's all I need to know.'

Ig was not aware that Lee was weeping until he made a snuffling sound of pain. He cried like someone enduring a small act of sadism – a cigarette ground out on the back of the hand. Ig took a step closer and kicked over a stack of CDs, discs he had given him.

'You want those back?' Lee asked.

'No.'

'What then? You want your money? I don't have it.'

'What money?'

'For the magazines I sold you. The ones I *stole*,' he said the last word with an almost-luxuriant bitterness.

'No.'

'Why are you here, then?'

'Because we're friends.' Ig took another step closer and then cried out softly. Lee was weeping blood. It stained the bandage and dribbled down the side of his left cheek. Lee touched two fingers absentmindedly to his face. They came away red.

'Are you all right?' Ig asked.

'It hurts when I cry. I'll have to learn how to stop feeling bad about things.' He breathed harshly, his shoulders rising and falling. 'I should've told you. About everything. It was shitty, selling you those magazines. Lying to you about what they were for. After I got to know you better, I wanted to take them back, but it was too late. That's not how friends treat friends.'

'We don't want to start with that. I wish like hell I never gave you the cherry bomb.'

'Forget it,' Lee said. 'I wanted it. I decided. You don't got to worry about that. Just don't decide you hate me. I really need someone to still like me.'

He didn't need to ask. The sight of the blood staining through the bandage made Ig's knees weak. It took a great effort of will not to think how he had teased Lee with the cherry, talking about all the things they could blow up together with it. How he had worked to take Merrin away from Lee, who had walked into the water and pulled him out when he was drowning, a betrayal for which there could be no expiation.

He sat down beside Lee.

'She'll tell you not to hang around me anymore,' Lee said.

'My mom? No. No, she's glad I came to see you.'

'Not your mom. *Merrin*.'

'What are you talking about? She wanted to come with me. She's worried about you.'

'Oh?' Lee quivered strangely, as if gripped by a chill. Then he said, 'I know why this happened.'

'It was a shitty accident. That's all.'

Lee shook his head. 'It was to remind me.'

Ig was quiet, waiting, but Lee didn't speak again.

'Remind you of what?' Ig asked.

Lee was struggling against tears. He wiped at the blood on his cheek with the back of one hand and left a long dark streak.

'Remind you what?' Ig asked again, but Lee was shivering with the effort it took to keep from sobbing and never got around to telling him.

THE FIRE SERMON

21

Ig drove away from his parents' house, from his grandmother's smashed body and smashed wheelchair, from Terry and Terry's awful confession, with no immediate notion of where he was going. He knew, rather, only where he *wasn't* going: to Glenna's apartment, to town. He could not bear to see another human face, hear another human voice.

He was holding a door shut in his mind, throwing all his mental weight against it, while two men pushed against the other side, trying to force their way into his thoughts: his brother and Lee Tourneau. It took all his will to keep the invaders from barging into his last refuge, to keep them out of his head. He didn't know what would happen when they pushed through that door at last, wasn't sure what he would do.

Ig followed the narrow state highway, across sunlit open pastures and under trees that overhung the road, into corridors of flickering darkness. He saw a shopping cart upended in a ditch at the side of the road and wondered how it was that shopping carts sometimes found their way out here, where there was nothing. It went to show that no one knew, when they abandoned a thing, what misuses it would be put to later by others. Ig had abandoned Merrin Williams one night – had walked away from his best friend in all the world, in a fit of immature, self-righteous anger – and look what had happened.

He thought about riding the Evel Knievel trail on the

shopping-cart express, ten years before, and his left hand rose unconsciously to touch his nose, still crooked where he'd broken it. His mind threw up an image, unbidden, of his grandmother riding her wheelchair down the long hill in front of the house, the rubber wheels banging over the rutted grassy slope. He wondered what she had broken when she finally slammed into the fence. He hoped her neck. Vera had told him that whenever she saw him, she wanted to be dead, and Ig lived to serve. He liked to think he had always been a conscientious grandson. If he had killed her, he would look at it as a good start. But there was still plenty of work ahead.

His stomach cramped, which he wrote off as a symptom of his unhappiness until it began to gurgle as well, and he had to admit to himself he was hungry. He tried to think where he could get food with a minimum of human interaction and at that moment saw The Pit gliding by on his left.

It was the place of their last supper, where he'd spent his final evening with Merrin. He had not been in there since. He doubted he was welcome. This thought alone was an invitation. Ig turned in to the parking lot.

It was early afternoon, the indolent, timeless period that followed lunch and came before people began to show up for their after-work drink. There were only a few parked cars, belonging, Ig guessed, to the more serious sort of alcoholic. The board out front read:

10¢ WINGS & 2$ BUD
LADYS NITE THURS COME AND SEE US GIRLS
RAH RAH GIDEON SAINTS

He stood from the car, the sun behind him, his shadow three yards long, pencilled on the dirt, a black-horned stick figure, the spurs of bone on his head pointing towards the red door of The Pit.

When he came through the door, Merrin was already there. Although it was crowded, the place full of college kids watching the game, he spotted her right away. She sat in their usual booth, turned to face him. The sight of her, as it always did – especially when they hadn't been together in a while – had the curious effect of reminding him of his own body, the bare skin under his clothes. He hadn't seen her in three weeks, and after tonight he wouldn't see her again until Christmas, but in between they would have shrimp cocktail and some beers and some fun in the cool, freshly laundered sheets of Merrin's bed. Merrin's father and mother were at their camp on Winnipesaukee, and they'd have her place all to themselves. Ig went dry in the mouth at the thought of what was waiting after dinner, and a part of him was sorry they were bothering with drinks and food at all. Another part of him, though, felt it was necessary to not be in a hurry, to take their time with the evening.

It wasn't as if they had nothing to talk about. She was worrying, and it didn't take a lot of insight to figure out why. He was leaving at eleven forty-five tomorrow morning on British Airways to take a job with Amnesty International and would be an ocean apart from her for half a year. They had never been without each other for so long.

He could always tell when she was worrying over something, knew all the signs. She withdrew. She smoothed things with her hands – napkins, her skirt, his ties – as if by ironing out such minute items she could smooth the path to some future safe harbour for both of them. She forgot how to laugh and became almost comically earnest and mature about things. The sight of her this way struck him as funny; it made him think of a little girl dressing up in her mother's clothes. He couldn't take her seriousness seriously.

It didn't make any logical sense for her to be worried,

although Ig knew that worry and logic rarely travelled together. But, really, he would not even have taken the job in London if she hadn't told him to take it, hadn't *pushed* him to take it. Merrin wouldn't let him pass on it, had relentlessly argued him out of every reservation. She told him there was no harm in trying it for six months. If he hated it, he could come home. But he wasn't going to hate it. It was exactly the sort of thing he'd always wanted to do, the dream job, and they both knew it. And if he liked the job – and he would – and wanted to remain in England, she would come to him. Harvard offered a transfer programme with the Imperial College London, and her mentor at Harvard, Shelby Clarke, selected the participants; there was no question she could get in. They could have a flat in London. She would serve him tea and crumpets in her knickers, and afterward they could have a shag. Ig was sold. He had always thought the word 'knickers' was a thousand times sexier than 'panties'. So he took the job and was sent off to New York City for a three-week summer training and orientation session. And now he was back, and she was smoothing things, and he was not surprised.

He made his way through the room to her, past the jostle and press of bodies. He bent across the table to kiss her before sliding into the booth opposite her. She didn't lift her mouth to him, and he had to settle for a peck on her temple.

There was an empty martini glass in front of her, and when the waitress came, she ordered another one, told her to bring a beer for Ig. He was enjoying the look of her, the smooth line of her throat, the dark shine of her hair in the low light, and at first just went along with the conversation, murmuring in the right places, only semi-listening. He didn't really start to focus in until Merrin told him he should look at his time in London as a vacation from their relationship, and even then he thought she was trying to be funny. He didn't know she was serious until she got to the part about how she felt it would be good for both of them to spend time with other people.

'With our clothes off,' Ig said.

'Couldn't hurt,' she said, and swallowed about half her martini.

It was the way she gulped at her drink, more than what she'd said, that gave him a cold shock of apprehension. That was a courage drink, and she'd already had at least one – maybe two – before he got here.

'You think I can't wait for a few months?' he asked. He was going to make a joke about masturbation, but a strange thing happened on the way to the punchline. His breath got caught in his throat, and he couldn't say any more.

'Well. I don't want to worry about what's going to happen a few months from now. We don't know how you're going to feel in a few months. Or how I'll feel. I don't want you thinking you have to come back home just so we can be together. Or assuming I'm going to transfer there. Let's just worry about what happens now. Look at it like this. How many girls have you been with? In your whole life?'

He stared. He had seen this look of frowning, pretty concentration on her face many times, but he had never been scared of it before.

'You know the answer to that,' he said.

'Just me. And no one does that. No one lives their entire life with the first person they slept with. Not these days. There isn't a man on the planet. There need to be other affairs. Two or three at least.'

'Is that your word for it? "Affairs"? That's tasteful.'

'Fine,' she said. 'You have to fuck a few other people.'

A cheer went up from the crowd, a roar of approval. Someone had slid home under the tag.

He was going to say something, but his mouth was too tacky, and he had to have a sip of beer. There was only one swallow left in the glass. He didn't remember the beer coming, and he didn't remember drinking it. It was lukewarm and salty, like a mouthful of the ocean. She had waited until today, twelve hours before he left to cross the ocean, to tell him this, to tell him—

'Are you breaking up with me? You want out – and you waited until *now* to tell me?'

The waitress stood at the side of their table with a basket of chips and a rigid smile.

'Would you like to order?' she asked. 'Something else to drink?'

'Another martini and another beer, please,' Merrin said.

'I don't want another beer,' Ig said, and didn't recognise his own thick, sullen, almost-childish voice.

'We'll both have Key lime martinis, then,' Merrin said.

The waitress retreated.

'What the hell is this? I have a plane ticket, a rented apartment, an office. They're expecting me to be there ready to work on Monday morning, and you lay this shit on me. What outcome are you hoping for here? Do you want me to call them up tomorrow and tell them, "Thanks for giving me a job that seven hundred other applicants wanted, but I have to pass"? Is this, like, a test to see what I value more, you or the job? Because if it is, you ought to know it's immature and insulting.'

'No, Ig. I want you to go, and I want you to—'

'Fuck someone else.'

Her shoulders jumped. He was a little surprised at himself, hadn't expected his own voice to sound so ugly.

But she nodded, and swallowed. 'Do it now or do it later, but you're going to do it anyway.'

Ig had a nonsensical thought, in his brother's voice: *Well, it's like this. You can live life as a cripple or a lame-ass.* Ig wasn't sure Terry had ever really said such a thing, thought the line might be completely imagined, and yet it came to him with the clarity of a line remembered from a favourite song.

The waitress gently set Ig's martini in front of him and he tipped it to his mouth, swallowing down a third of it in a gulp. He'd never had one before, and the sugary, harsh burn of it caught him by surprise. It sank slowly down his throat and expanded into his lungs. His chest was a furnace, and a sweat prickled on his face. His hand drifted up to his throat, found the knot of his tie. He struggled with it, pulling it loose. Why had he worn a button-up shirt? He was roasting in it. He was in hell.

'It'll always bother you, wondering what you missed out on,' Merrin said now. 'That's how men are. I'm just being practical. I'm not waiting to get married to you so I can fight through your midlife affair with our baby-sitter. I'm not going to be the reason for your regrets.'

He struggled for patience, to recover a tone of calm, of good humour. The calm he could manage. The good humour he could not.

'Don't tell me how other men think. I know what I want. I want the life we spent the last however many years day-dreaming about. How many times have we talked about what to name the kids? You think that was all bullshit?'

'I think it's part of the problem. You live like we already *have* kids, like we're *already* married. But we don't and we aren't. To you the kids already exist, because you live in your head, not in the world. I'm not sure I ever even wanted kids.'

Ig yanked off his tie, flung it on the table. He couldn't stand the feel of anything around his neck right now.

'You could've fooled me. It sounded like you were into the idea the last eight thousand times we talked about it.'

'I don't know *what* I'm into. I haven't had a chance to get clear of you and think about my own life since we met. I haven't had a single day—'

'So I'm suffocating you? Is that what you're telling me? That's horseshit.'

She turned her face away from him, stared blankly across the room, waiting for his anger to subside. He drew a long, whistling breath, told himself not to yell, and tried again.

'Remember the day in the tree house?' he asked. 'The tree house we could never find again, the place with the white curtains? You said this doesn't happen to ordinary couples. You said we were different. You said the love we had was marked out as special, that not two people out of a million were ever given anything like we were given. You said we were meant for each other. You said there was no ignoring the signs.'

'It wasn't a sign. It was just an afternoon lay in someone's tree house.'

Ig shook his head slowly from side to side. Talking to her now was like flailing his hands at a storm of hornets. It did nothing, and it stung, and yet he couldn't stop himself.

'Don't you remember we looked for it? We looked all summer, and we could never find it again? And you said it was a tree house of the mind?'

'That's what I said so we could *stop* looking for it. This is exactly what I'm talking about, Ig. You and your magical think-ing. A fuck can't just be a fuck. It always has to be a transcendent experience, life-changing. It's depressing and weird, and I'm tired of acting like it's normal. Will you listen to yourself? Why the fuck are we even *talking* about a tree house?'

'I'm getting sick of your mouth,' Ig said.

'You don't like it? You don't like to hear me talk about fucking? Why, Ig? Does it mess with your picture of me? You don't want a real person. You want a holy vision you can beat off to.'

The waitress said, 'I guess you still haven't made up your minds.' Standing beside their table again.

'Two more,' Ig said, and she went away.

They stared at each other. Ig was gripping the table and felt dangerously close to turning it over.

'We were kids when we met,' she said. 'We let it get a lot more serious than any high-school relationship should've been. If we spend some time with other people, it will put our relationship in perspective. Maybe we pick it up again later and see if we can love each other as adults the way we did as kids. I don't know. After some time has gone by, maybe we can take another look at what we have to offer each other.'

'"At what we have to offer each other"?' Ig said. 'You sound like a loan officer.'

She was rubbing her throat with one hand, her eyes miserable now, which was when Ig noticed she wasn't wearing her cross. He wondered if there was meaning in that. The cross had been like an engagement ring, long before either of them had ever discussed the idea of staying together their whole lives. He honestly could not remember ever seeing her without it – a thought that filled his chest with a sick, draughty sensation.

'So do you have someone picked out?' Ig asked. 'Someone you want to fuck in the name of putting our relationship in perspective?'

'I'm not thinking about it that way. I'm just—'

'Yes, you are. That's what this is all about, you said so yourself. We need to fuck other people.'

She opened her mouth, then closed it, then opened it again. 'Yes, I guess so, Ig. I guess that has to be part of it. I mean, I have to sleep with other people, too. Otherwise you'd probably go over there and live like a monk. It'll be easier for you to move on if you know I have.'

'So there is someone.'

'There's someone I've ... I've been out with. Once or twice.'

'While I was in New York.' Not asking it. Saying it. 'Who?'

'No one you've ever met. It doesn't matter.'

'I want to know anyway.'

'It isn't important. I'm not going to ask you any questions about what you're doing in London.'

'About *who* I'm doing,' he said.

'Right. Whatever. I don't want to know.'

'But I *do*. When did it happen?'

'When did what happen?'

'When did you start seeing this guy? Last week? What did you tell him? Did you say things would have to wait until I took off for London? Or *did* it wait?'

She parted her lips just slightly to reply, and he saw something in her eyes, something small and fearful, and in a rush of prickling heat he knew something he didn't want to know. He knew she'd been working towards this moment the whole summer, going all the way back to when she first started pushing him to take the job.

'How far has it gone? Have you already fucked him?'

She shook her head, but he couldn't tell if she was saying no or refusing to answer the question. She was blinking back tears. He didn't know when that had started. It was a surprise to feel no urge to comfort her. He was in the grip of something he didn't understand, a perverse mix of rage and excitement. Part of him was surprised to discover that it felt good to be wronged, to have a justification to hurt her. To see how much punishment he could inflict. He wanted to flay her with his questions. And at the same time, images had started to occur to him: Merrin on her knees in a tangle of sheets, lines of bright light from the half-shut Venetian blinds across her body, someone else reaching for her naked hips. The thought aroused and appalled in equal measure.

'Ig,' she said softly. 'Please.'

'Stop with your please. There are things you aren't telling me. Things I need to know. I need to know if you've fucked him already. Tell me if you've fucked him already.'

'No.'

'Good. Was he ever there? In your apartment, with you when I called from New York? Sitting there with his hand under your skirt?'

'No. We had lunch, Ig. That was all. We talk now and then. Mostly about school.'

'You ever think about him when I'm fucking you?'

'Jesus, no. Why would you even ask that?'

'Because I want to know *everything*. I want to know every shitty little thing you're not telling me, every dirty secret.'

'Why?'

'Because it'll make it easier for me to hate you,' Ig said.

The waitress stood rigidly at the side of their table, frozen in the act of setting down their fresh drinks.

'What the fuck are you looking at?' Ig asked her, and she took an unsteady step backwards.

The waitress wasn't the only one staring. At the other tables arranged around theirs, heads were turned. A few onlookers watched them seriously, while others, younger couples mostly, observed them with bright-eyed merriment, struggling not to laugh. Nothing was quite so entertaining as a noisy public break-up.

When Ig looked back at Merrin, she was up on her feet, standing behind her chair. She was holding his tie in her hands. She had picked it up when he threw it aside and had been restlessly folding and smoothing it ever since.

'Where are you going?' he asked, and caught her shoulder as she tried to slip by. She lurched into the table. She was drunk. They both were.

'Ig,' she said. 'My arm.'

Only then did he realise how hard he was squeezing her shoulder, digging in with his fingers with enough force to feel the bone. It took a conscious effort to open his hand.

'I'm not running away,' she said. 'I want a minute to clean up.' Gesturing at her face.

169

'We're not done talking about this. There's a lot you aren't telling me.'

'If there are things I don't want to tell you,' she said, 'it isn't out of meanness. I just don't want to see you hurt, Ig.'

'Too late.'

'Because I love you.'

'I don't believe you.'

He said it to hurt her – he didn't honestly know if he believed it or not – and felt a savage rush of excitement to see he had succeeded. Her eyes filled with bright tears and she swayed, put a hand on the table to steady herself once more.

'If I've been keeping things from you, it was to protect you. I know what a good person you are. You deserve better than what you got when you threw in with me.'

'Finally,' he said. 'Something we agree on. I deserve better.'

She waited for him to say more, but he couldn't, was short of breath again. She turned and navigated her way through the crowd, towards the ladies' room. He drank the rest of his martini, watching her go. She looked good, in her white blouse and pearl-grey skirt, and Ig saw a couple of college boys turn their heads to watch her, and then one of them said something, and the other laughed.

Ig's blood felt thick and slow and he was conscious of it pumping heavily in his temples. He wasn't aware of the man standing next to the table and didn't hear him saying 'sir', didn't see him until the guy bent over to look in Ig's face. He had a bodybuilder's physique, his sporty white tennis shirt pulled tight across his shoulders. Little blue eyes peeped out from under a bony crag of forehead.

'Sir,' he said again. 'We're going to have to ask you and your wife to leave. We can't have you abusing the staff.'

'She's not my wife. She's just someone I used to fuck.'

The big man – bartender? bouncer? – said, 'I don't need that language in my face. Take it someplace else.'

Ig got up and found his wallet and put two twenties on the table before setting out for the door. As he went, he felt a sensation of rightness settling over him. *Leave her*, was what he thought. Sitting across from her, he had wanted to force secrets out of her and to inflict as much unpleasantness as possible upon her in the process. But now that she was out of sight and he had breathing room, he felt it would be a mistake to give her any more time to justify what she'd decided to do to him. He didn't want to hang around and give her a chance to dilute his hate with tears, with more talk about how she loved him. He didn't want to understand, and he didn't want to sympathise.

She would come back and find the table empty. His absence would say more than he could ever hope to articulate if he remained. It did not matter that he was her ride. She was a grown-up, she could get a cab. Wasn't that her whole point in fucking someone else while he was away in England? To establish her bona fides as a grown-up?

He had never in all his life felt so sure that he was doing the proper thing, and as he got closer to the door, he heard a sound like applause rising to greet him, a low crashing of stomping feet and clapping hands that rose and rose until he opened the door at last and looked out into a thunderous downpour.

By the time he got to the car, his clothes were soaked through. He started backing up, even before he had the head-lights on. He flipped the wipers on, full speed, and they lashed at the rain, but still water ran down the windshield in a flood, distorting his view of things. He heard a crunch, glanced back and saw he had backed into a telephone pole.

He wasn't going to get out and look at the damage. That thought didn't even cross his mind. Before he spun onto the highway, though, he looked out the driver's-side window and through the water beaded on the glass he saw her standing ten feet away, hugging herself in the rain, her hair hanging in wet strings. She stared miserably across the lot at him but did not gesture for him to stop, to wait, to come back. Ig put his foot on the gas and drove away.

The world blurred past the window, an impressionistic muddle of greens and blacks. In the late afternoon, the temperature had climbed as high as ninety-eight degrees, falling just short of triple digits. The air-conditioner was set on high, where Ig had left it all day. He sat in its refrigerated blast, dimly aware that he was shivering in his wet clothes.

His emotions came in pulses, so on the exhale he hated her and wanted to tell her as much and see it sink into her face. On the inhale he felt a sick pang at the thought of driving away, leaving her in the rain, and he wanted to go back and tell her, in a quiet voice, to get into the car. In his mind she was still standing there in the rain, waiting for him. He lifted his gaze to the rearview mirror, as if he might see her back there, but of course The Pit was already half a mile away. Instead he saw a police car riding his bumper, a black cruiser with a bar across the roof.

He looked at the speedometer and discovered he was doing close to sixty in a forty. His thighs were by now trembling with an almost painful force. He eased off the gas, his pulse thudding, and when he saw the closed and boarded-up Dunkin' Donuts on the right of the road, he pulled off.

The Gremlin was still moving too quickly, and the tyres tore at dirt, slung rocks. In the side mirror, he saw the police cruiser go by. Only it wasn't a cruiser at all, just a black GTO with a roof rack.

He sat shuddering behind the wheel, waiting for his racing heart to slow down. After a bit he decided it might be a mistake to proceed in this weather, as drunk as he was. He would wait for the rain to stop; it was already slackening off. His next thought was that Merrin might try to call him at home, make sure he got in all right, and it would be satisfying for his mother to say, 'No, Merrin, he isn't here yet. Is everything okay?'

Then he remembered his cell phone. Merrin would probably try that first. He slipped it from his pocket and shut it off and threw it on the floor of the passenger seat. He didn't doubt she'd call, and the idea that she might imagine that something had happened to him – that he'd had an accident or, in his misery, put the car into a tree on purpose – was a good one.

The next thing to do was to stop shaking. He cranked his seat back and turned off the car, got a windbreaker from the back seat and spread it over his legs. He listened to the rain drumming slower and slower on the roof of the Gremlin, the energy of the storm already spent. He closed his eyes, relaxing to the deep, resonant beat of the downpour, and did not open them again until seven in the morning, sunlight showing through the trees.

He went home in a hurry, flung himself into the shower, dressed, collected his luggage. It was not the way he had meant to leave town. His mother and father and Vera were having breakfast together in the kitchen and his parents seemed amused to see him rushing around, flustered and disorganised. They didn't ask where he'd been all night. They thought they knew. Ig didn't have the heart or the time to tell them the truth of what had happened. His mother had a sly little smirk on her face, and he preferred to leave her smiling rather than looking sick for him.

Terry was home – *Hothouse* on summer hiatus – and he had promised he would drive Ig to Logan Airport, but he was still in bed. Vera said he'd been out with the old crowd all night and had not made it home until after sun-up. Vera had heard the car pull in and looked out in time to see Terry throwing up in the yard.

'Too bad he's home and not out there in LA,' his grandmother said. 'The paparazzi missed out on quite a photograph. Big TV star losing his dinner in the rosebushes. That would've been one for *People* magazine. He wasn't even dressed in the same clothes he went out in.'

Lydia Perrish looked a little less amused then and poked restlessly at her grapefruit.

Ig's father sat back in his chair, gazing into his son's face. 'You all right, Ig? You look like you have a touch of something.'

'I'd say Terence wasn't the only one who got his money's worth last night,' Vera said.

'You okay to drive? I could be dressed in ten minutes,' Derrick said. 'Take you myself.'

'Stay and eat your breakfast. I better get going now before it's too late. Tell Terry I hope no one died and I'll call him from England.'

Ig kissed them all and said he loved them and went out the door, into the cool of the morning, the dew bright in the grass. He drove the sixty miles to Logan Airport in forty-five minutes. He didn't see any traffic until the last few miles, when he was past the Suffolk Downs Racetrack and going by a high hill with a thirty-five-foot cross on the top of it. Ig got stuck behind a line of trucks for a while, in the shadow of that cross. It was summer everywhere else, but there in the deep gloom the giant cross cast across the road it was late fall, and he got briefly shivery. He had the curious, confused idea that it was called Don Orsillo's cross, only that couldn't be right. Don Orsillo was the announcer for the Red Sox.

The roads were clear, but the British Airways terminal was packed, and Ig's ticket was coach. He waited in line for a long time. The ticket area was full of echoing voices and the sharp clack of high heels ringing out across the marble floor and indecipherable announcements over the loudspeaker. He had checked his baggage and was waiting in yet another line, to clear security, when he felt rather than heard the disturbance behind him. He glanced around and saw people moving aside, making room for a contingent of policemen in flak vests and helmets, carrying M16s, walking in his direction. One of them was making hand gestures, pointing at the line.

When Ig turned away from them, he saw other policemen coming from the opposite direction. They were closing in from either side. Ig wondered if they were going to pull someone out of line. Someone waiting to clear security must've come up on Big Brother's threat list. Those guns were scary, but not as scary as the dead, dull look in their faces.

And there was one other thing he noticed, the funniest thing of all. The officer in charge, the one using hand gestures to tell his men to spread out, to cover the exits – sometimes Ig had the crazy impression the guy was pointing at him.

22

⁓ℰ

Ig stood just inside the door of The Pit, waiting for his eyes to adjust to the cavernous gloom, a shadowy space lit only by wide-screen TVs and digital poker machines. A couple sat at the bar, figures that seemed entirely formed from darkness. A bodybuilder moved behind the bar, hanging beer glasses upside down over the back counter. Ig recognised him as the bouncer who had chased him out on the night Merrin was murdered.

Other than that, the place was empty. Ig was glad. He didn't want to be seen. What he wanted was to get lunch without even placing an order, without speaking to anyone at all. He was trying to come up with a way to make that happen when his cell phone went off, burring softly.

It was his brother. The darkness flexed around Ig like a muscle. The thought of answering, of speaking to him, made Ig dizzy with hate and dread. He did not know what he would say, what he *could* say. He held the phone in his hand, watching it hum in his palm, until the ringing stopped.

No sooner had it gone silent than he began to wonder if Terry knew what he had confessed to a few minutes ago. And then there were the other things Ig could've found out by answering the phone, such as: if the horns needed to be *seen* to pervert people's minds. It might still be possible to have a normal conversation with someone over the phone. He wondered, too, if Vera was dead and Ig was, now, really the murderer everyone had always believed him to be.

No. He wasn't ready to find that one out, not yet. He needed some time to be alone in the dark, to dwell in isolation and ignorance.

Sure, came a voice in his mind, his own voice, but sly and mocking. *That's how you spent the last twelve months. What's one more afternoon?*

When his eyes were used to the yawning shadows of The Pit he spotted an empty corner booth where someone had eaten pizza, perhaps with kids; Ig noted plastic cups with bendy straws. A few wedges of the pizza remained. More importantly, the parent who had chaperoned this particular pizza party had left a half-full glass of pale beer. Ig slipped into the booth, the upholstery creaking, and helped himself. The beer was lukewarm. For all he knew, the last person to drink from the glass had had oozing cankers and a virulent case of hepatitis. After you'd grown horns from your temples, it seemed a little silly to be too fussy about possible exposure to germs.

A swinging door to the kitchen batted open and a waitress came through, emerging from a white-tiled space, brightly lit by fluorescents, into the darkness. She had a bottle of cleaning fluid in one hand and a rag in the other and came briskly across the room, headed straight for him.

Ig knew her, of course. It was the same woman who had served him and Merrin drinks on their last night together. Her face was framed by two wings of lank black hair that curled under her long, pointed chin, so she looked like the female version of the wizard who was always giving Harry Potter such a hard time in the movies. Professor Snail or something. Ig had been waiting to read the books with the children he and Merrin planned to have together.

She wasn't looking at the booth, and he shrank back into the red vinyl. It was already too late to slip out without being seen. He considered hiding under the table, then dismissed the idea as disturbing. In another moment she was bent over the table, collecting plates. A light hung directly above the booth, and even when he pressed himself all the way back into the seat, it still cast the shadow of his head, and the horns, upon the table. She saw the shadow first, then glanced up at him.

Her pupils shrank. Her face paled. She dropped the plates back on the table with a shocking crash, although it was perhaps more of a shock that none of them broke. She drew a sharp breath, preparing to cry out, and then her gaze found the horns. The shout seemed to die in her throat. She stood there.

'The sign said please seat yourself,' Ig told her.

'Yes. All right. Let me clean your table off and . . . and I'll bring you a menu.'

'Actually,' Ig said, 'I've already eaten.' Gesturing at the plates before him.

Her eyes shifted from his horns to his face, back and forth, several times. 'You're the guy,' she said. 'Ig Perrish.'

Ig nodded. 'You served my girlfriend and me a year ago, on our last evening together. I want to say I'm sorry for the things I said that night and the way I acted. I would tell you that you saw me at my worst, except who I was then is nothing compared to who I am now.'

'I don't feel even a little bad about it.'

'Oh. Good. I thought I made a terrible impression.'

'No,' she said. 'I mean I don't feel even a little bad about lying to the police. I'm just sorry they didn't believe me.'

Ig felt his insides clench. It was starting again. She was half talking to herself, or, maybe more accurately, talking with her own private devil, a demon that just also happened to have Ig Perrish's face. If he didn't find a way to control it – to mute the effect of the horns – he would go out of his mind soon, if he wasn't crazy already.

'What lies?'

'I told the police you threatened to strangle her. I said I watched you try to push her down.'

'Why would you tell them that?'

'So you wouldn't get away with it. So you wouldn't just walk away. And look at you. She's dead, and here you are. You got away with it anyhow, just like my father got away with what he did to my mother and me. I wanted you to go to jail.' She gave her head an unconscious toss, flipping her hair out of her face. 'Also, I wanted to be in the newspaper. I wanted to be a star witness. If they put you on trial, I would've been on TV.'

Ig stared.

'I tried my best,' she went on. 'When you left that night, your girlfriend went hurrying out after you, and she forgot her coat. I carried it outside to give it back to her, and I saw you drive away without her. But that's not what I told the police. I told them when I went outside I saw you pulling her into the car and then hauling ass out of here. That's what screwed me up. I guess you hit a telephone pole, backing up, and one of the customers heard the crunch and looked out a window to see what happened. They told the police they saw you leave her. The detective asked me to take a polygraph to confirm my story, and I had to take back that part. Then they didn't believe any of the other stuff I told them either. But I know what happened. I know you just turned around and came back to get her a couple minutes later.'

'You've got that wrong. Someone else picked her up.' When Ig thought who, he felt nauseated.

But the idea that she might've been wrong about him didn't seem to interest the waitress. When she spoke again, it was as if Ig had said nothing. 'I knew I'd see you again someday. Are you going to force me to go out in the parking lot with you? Are you going to take me somewhere to sodomise me?' Her tone was unmistakably hopeful.

'What? No. The fuck?'

Some of the excitement went out of her eyes. 'Are you at least going to threaten me?'

'No.'

'I could say you did. I could tell Reggie you warned me to watch my back. That'd be a good story.' Her smile faded a little more, and she shot a glum look at the bodybuilder behind the bar. 'He probably wouldn't believe me, though. Reggie thinks I'm a compulsive liar. I guess I am. I like to tell my little stories. Still. I never should've told Reggie that my boyfriend, Gordon, died in the World Trade Tower, after I told Sarah – she's another waitress here – that Gordy died in Iraq. I should've figured they'd swap notes. Still. Gordon *could* be dead somewhere. He's dead to me. He broke up with me by e-mail, so fuck him. Why am I telling you all this?'

'Because you can't help yourself.'

'That's right. I can't,' she said, and shivered, a response with unmistakably sexual connotations.

'What did your father do to your mother and you? Did he ... did he hurt you?' Ig asked, not sure he really wanted to know.

'He told us he loved us, but he lied. He ran away to Washington with my fifth-grade teacher. They started a family, and he had another daughter, one he likes better than he ever liked me. If he really loved me, he would've taken me with him instead of leaving me with my mother, who's a depressing, angry old bitch. He said he would always be a part of my life, but he isn't part of shit. I hate liars. Other liars, I mean. My own little stories don't hurt anyone. Do you want to know the little story I tell about you and your girlfriend?'

The pizza Ig had eaten sat in his stomach in a heavy, doughy lump. 'Probably not.'

Her face flushed with excitement and her smile returned. 'Sometimes people come in and ask about what you did to her. I can always tell in a glance how much they want to know, if

180

they just want the basics or some nasty details. The college kids usually want to know something nasty. I tell them after you beat her brains in, you turned her over and sodomised the corpse.'

Ig tried to stand up, clubbed his knees against the underside of the table, and at the same time clashed his horns against the stained-glass lampshade hanging over the tabletop. The lamp started to swing, and his horned shadow plunged towards the waitress and then shrank away from her, towards and away. Ig had to sit back down, pain throbbing behind his kneecaps.

'She wasn't—' Ig started. 'That didn't— You sick fucking bitch.'

'I am,' the waitress confessed, with a touch of pride. 'I am *so bad*. But you should see their faces when I tell them. The girls especially love that bit. It's always exciting to hear about someone being *defiled*. Everyone loves a good sex murder, and in my opinion there isn't a story yet that can't be improved by a little sodomy.'

'Do you understand you're talking about someone I loved?' Ig asked. His lungs felt scraped and raw, and it was hard to catch his breath.

'Sure,' she said. 'That's why you killed her. That's why people usually do it. It isn't hate. It's love. Sometimes I wish my father had loved my mother and me enough to kill *us*, and then himself. Then it would've been a big awful tragedy and not just another dull, depressing break-up. If he had the stomach for double homicide, we all could've been on TV.'

'I didn't kill my girlfriend,' Ig said.

At this the waitress finally showed a reaction, frowning, her lips pursing in a look of puzzled disappointment. 'Well. *That's* no fun. I just think you're a whole lot more interesting if you killed someone. Course, you've got horns growing out of your head. That's fun! Is it a mod?'

'Mod?'

'A body modification. Did you do it to yourself?'

Although he still could not remember the evening before – he could recall everything up until his drunken outburst in the woods by the foundry, but after that there was only a dreadful blank – he knew the answer to this one. It came to him instantly and without struggle.

'Yes,' he said. 'I did.'

23

The waitress said he'd be more interesting if he killed someone, so he decided, why not kill Lee Tourneau.

It was a joy to know where he was going, to climb back into the car with a certain destination. The tyres threw dirt as he peeled out. Lee worked in the congressman's office in Portsmouth, New Hampshire, forty minutes away, and Ig was in the mood for a drive. He could use the time on the road to figure out how he was going to do it.

First he thought he'd use his hands. Strangle him as he had strangled Merrin, Merrin who'd loved Lee, who'd been first to his house to console him the day his mother died, and Ig grabbed the steering wheel as if he were throttling Lee already and shook it back and forth hard enough to rattle the steering column. Hating Lee was the best feeling Ig had felt in years.

His second thought was that there had to be a tyre-iron in the trunk. He could put on his windbreaker – it was lying across the back seat – and stick the tyre-iron up his sleeve. When Lee was in front of him, he could let it slip down into his hand and give it to him across the head. Ig imagined the wet *thok!* of the tyre-iron connecting with Lee's skull and shivered with excitement.

His concern was that the tyre-iron might be too quick, that Lee might never know what hit him. In a perfect world, Ig would force Lee into the car and take him somewhere to drown him. Hold his head under the water and watch him struggle. Ig grinned at the thought, unaware that smoke was trickling from his nostrils. In the brightly lit cockpit of the car, it was just a pale summery haze.

After Lee had lost most of the sight in his left eye, he got quiet and kept his head down. He did twenty hours of unpaid volunteer work for every store he'd stolen from, regardless of how much he'd taken, a thirty-dollar pair of sneakers or a two-hundred-dollar leather jacket. He wrote a letter to the paper detailing each of his crimes and apologising to shopkeepers, his friends, his mother, his father and his church. He got religion – literally – and volunteered for every programme Sacred Heart offered. He worked every summer with Ig and Merrin at Camp Galilee.

And once every summer, Lee was a guest speaker at Camp Galilee's Sunday-morning services. He always began by telling the children that he was a sinner, that he had stolen and lied, used his friends and manipulated his parents. He told the children that once he was blind but now he saw. He said it while pointing into his half-ruined left eye. He delivered the same moral pep talk every summer. Ig and Merrin listened from the rear of the chapel, and when Lee pointed to his eye and quoted 'Amazing Grace', it inevitably caused Ig's back and arms to break out in goosebumps. Ig felt lucky knowing him, was proud to know him, to have a small piece of Lee's story.

It was a hell of a good story. Girls liked it especially. They liked both that Lee had been bad and that he had reformed; they liked that he could talk about his own soul and that children loved him. There was something unbearably noble about the way he could calmly admit to the things he had done, without showing any shame or self-consciousness. The girls he dated liked being the one temptation he still allowed himself.

Lee had been accepted to the seminary school in Bangor, Maine, but he gave up theology when his mother got sick and he came home to take care of her. By then his parents were divorced, his father off with his second wife in South Carolina. Lee brought his mother her meds, kept her sheets clean, changed her diapers and watched PBS with her. When he wasn't at his mother's bedside, he was at UNH, where he collected a major in media studies; on Saturdays he drove to Portsmouth to work in the office of New Hampshire's newest congressman.

He started as an unpaid volunteer, but by the time his mother died, he was a full-time employee, head of the congressman's religious-outreach programme. A lot of people thought that Lee was reason number one the congressman had been re-elected the last time out. His opponent, a former judge, had signed a waiver allowing a pregnant felon the right to receive a first-trimester abortion, which Lee dubbed capital punishment for the unborn. Lee went to half the churches in the state to speak about it. He looked good in the pulpit, in his tie and crisp white shirt, and he never missed a chance to call himself a sinner, and they all loved that.

Lee's work on the campaign had also resulted in the one and only fight he ever had with Merrin, although Ig wasn't sure it was a fight if one person wouldn't defend himself. Merrin ripped him up one side and down the other over the abortion thing, but Lee took it calmly and said, 'If you want me to quit my job, Merrin, I'll turn in my resignation tomorrow. Don't even need to think about it. But if I remain in the job, I have to do what I was hired to do, and I'm going to do it well.' She said Lee had no shame. Lee said sometimes he wasn't sure he had anything else, and she said, 'Oh, Christ, don't go earnest on me,' but after that she let him be.

Lee had liked to look at her, of course. Ig had seen him sometimes, checking Merrin out when she got up from a table, her skirt swishing at her legs. He had always liked looking at her. Ig had not minded that Lee looked. Merrin was his. And anyway, after what Ig had done to Lee's eye – over time he'd come to feel he was personally responsible for Lee's partial blindness – he could hardly begrudge him a glance at a pretty woman. Lee often said the accident could've blinded him completely and that he tried to enjoy each and every good thing he saw as if it were his last taste of ice cream. Lee had a knack for making statements like that, confessing plainly to his pleasures and mistakes, unafraid of being mocked. Not that anyone mocked him. Quite the opposite: everyone was rooting for Lee. His turnaround was in-fucking-spirational. Maybe someday soon he would run for political office himself. There had already been some talk along those lines, although Lee laughed off any suggestion that he might seek higher office, trotted out that Groucho Marx bit about how any group that would accept him as a member wasn't worth belonging to. Caesar had refused the throne three times as well, Ig remembered.

Something was beating in Ig's temples. It was like a hammer falling on hot metal, a steady ringing crash. He came off the interstate and followed the highway to the office park, where the congressman kept his offices in a building with a great wedge-shaped glass atrium thrusting outwards from the front of the building like the prow of some enormous glass tanker. Ig drove to the entrance around the back.

The blacktop lot behind the building, two-thirds empty, was baking in the afternoon heat. Ig parked and grabbed his blue nylon windbreaker from the back seat and climbed out. It was too warm for a coat, but he put it on anyway. He liked the feel of the sun on his face and head and the heat shimmering up off the asphalt beneath him. Gloried in it, really.

He opened the hatchback and raised the compartment in the floor. The tyre-iron was bolted to the underside of a metal panel, but the bolts were caked in rust and trying to twist them loose hurt his hands. He quit and looked in his roadside emergency kit. It held a magnesium flare, a tube wrapped in red paper, oily and smooth. He grinned. A flare beat the hell out of a tyre-iron. He could burn Lee's pretty face with it. Blind him in the other eye, maybe – that might be as good as killing him. Besides, Ig was more suited to a flare than a tyre-iron. Wasn't it well established that fire was the devil's only friend?

Ig crossed the blacktop through the shimmering heat. It was this summer that the seventeen-year locusts came out to mate, and the trees behind the parking lot were filled with their noise, a deep, resonating thrum, like the working of a great mechanical lung. The sound of them filled Ig's head, the sound of his headache, of madness, of his clarifying rage. A snippet of the Revelation to John came back to him: *Then from the smoke came locusts on the earth.* The locusts came every seventeen years to fuck and to die. Lee Tourneau was a bug, no better than the locusts – quite a bit worse, really. He had done the fucking part, and now he could die. Ig would help him. As he crossed the lot, he jammed the flare up into the sleeve of his coat and held it there with his right hand.

He approached a pair of Plexiglas doors imprinted with the Honorable Congressman of New Hampshire's name. They had a mirrored tint and he saw himself reflected there: a scrawny, sweating man in a windbreaker zipped to his throat, who looked as if he'd come to commit a crime. Not to mention he had horns. The points had split through the skin of his temples, and the bone beneath was stained pink with blood. Worse even than the horns, though, was the way he was grinning. If he had been standing on the other side of those doors and saw himself coming, he would've turned the lock and called 911.

He pushed into air-conditioned, carpeted quiet. A fat man with a flat-top haircut sat behind a desk, talking cheerfully into a headset. Just to the right of the desk was a security checkpoint where visitors were required to pass through a metal detector. A fifty-something state trooper sat behind the X-ray monitor, chewing gum. A sliding Plexiglas window behind the receptionist's desk looked into a small bare room with a map of New Hampshire tacked to the wall and a security monitor on a table. A second state trooper, an enormous, broad-shouldered man, sat in there at a folding table, bent over paperwork. Ig could not see his face, but he had a thick neck and a great white bald head that was somehow vaguely obscene.

Ig was unnerved by those state troopers and that metal detector. The sight of them brought back bad memories of Logan Airport, and his body tingled with an ill sweat. He had not been here to see Lee in well over a year, and didn't remember ever having to clear any kind of security before.

The receptionist said 'Good-bye, honey' into his headset, pressed a button on his desk, and looked at Ig. The receptionist had a big, round, moony face, and probably his name was Chet or Chip. Behind his square-framed glasses was a bright look of dismay or bafflement.

'Help you?' he asked Ig.

'Yes. Could you—?'

But then something else caught Ig's attention: the security monitor in that room on the other side of the Plexiglas window. It displayed a fish-eyed view of the reception area – the potted plants, the inoffensive plush couches, and Ig himself, his features clear and unmistakable. Only something was wrong with the monitor. Ig kept splitting into two overlapping figures and then jumping back together; that part of the image was flickering and unstable. The primary image of Ig showed him as he was, a pale, gaunt man with tragically receding hair, a goatee, and curving horns. But then there was that secondary shadow image, dark and featureless, which kept twitching in and out of existence. This second version of himself was *without* horns – an image not of who he was, but of who he had been. It was like watching his own soul trying to pry itself free from the demon to which it was anchored.

The state trooper who sat in that bare, brightly lit room with the monitor had noticed as well, had revolved in his office chair to study the screen. Ig still could not see the trooper's face; he had rotated far enough around so Ig could see only his ear and his polished white dome, a cannonball of bone and skin, resting on the thick, brutal plug of his neck. After a moment the state trooper reached out and banged his fist on the monitor, trying to correct the image, and hit it so hard that for a moment the whole picture blacked out.

'Sir?' said the receptionist.

Ig pulled his stare away from the monitor. 'Could ... could you page Lee Tourneau? Tell him Ig Perrish is here to see him.'

'I have to see your driver's licence and print you an ID tag before I can send you through,' he said in a flat, automatic sort of way, staring at the horns with blank-eyed fascination.

Ig glanced at the security checkpoint and knew he couldn't walk through it with a magnesium flare stuck up his sleeve.

'Tell him I'll wait out here. Tell him he's going to want to see me.'

'I don't think he will,' said the receptionist. 'I can't imagine anyone would want to. You're awful. You have horns, and you're awful. I wish I didn't even come into work today, just looking at you. I almost didn't come into work. Once a month I give myself a mental-health day and stay at home and put on my mother's underpants and get myself good and hot. For an old bird, she has some really dirty stuff. She's got a black satin corset with a whalebone back, lotta straps, real nice.' His eyes were glazed, and there was a little white spit at the corner of his mouth.

'I especially like that you think of it as a mental-health day,' Ig said. 'Get me Lee Tourneau, would you?'

The receptionist rotated ninety degrees to one side, turning his shoulder to Ig. He punched a button, then murmured into his headset. He listened for a moment, then said, 'Okay.'

He revolved back towards Ig. His round face gleamed with perspiration. 'He's in meetings all morning.'

'Tell him I know what he did. Use those exact words. Tell Lee if he wants to talk about it, I'll wait for five minutes in the parking lot.'

The receptionist gave him a blank stare, then nodded and turned slightly away again. Into his headset he said, 'Mr Tourneau? He says . . . he says he knows what you did?' Turning it into a question at the last moment.

Ig didn't hear what else the receptionist had to say, though, because in the next moment there was a voice in his ear, a voice he knew well but had not heard in several years.

'Iggy fucking Perrish,' said Eric Hannity.

Ig turned around and saw the bald state trooper who'd been sitting with the security monitor in the room on the other side of the Plexiglas window. At eighteen Eric had been a teenager straight out of an Abercrombie & Fitch catalogue, big and sinewy, with a head of close-cropped curly brown hair. He had liked to walk around with no shoes and his shirt off and his jeans slipping down around his hips. But at almost thirty, his face had lost its definition, becoming a fleshy block, and when his hair started to thin, he'd shaved it off rather than fight a battle he couldn't win. He was magnificent now in his baldness; if he'd had an earring in one ear, he could've played Mr Clean in a TV commercial. He had, perhaps inevitably, gone into his daddy's line of work, a trade that offered him both authority and legal cover to occasionally hurt people. Back when Ig and Lee were still friends (if they had ever really been friends), Lee had mentioned that Eric was in charge of the congressman's security. Lee said Eric had mellowed a lot. Lee had even been out fishing with him a time or two. ''Course, for chum he uses the livers of disembowelled protesters,' Lee had said. 'Make of that what you will.'

'Eric,' Ig said, stepping back from the desk. 'How are you?'

'Happy,' Eric Hannity said. 'Happy to see you. What about you, Ig? How you doing? Kill anyone this week?'

Ig said, 'I'm fine.'

'You don't look fine. You look like you forgot to take your pill.'

'What pill?'

'Well. You must be sick with *something*. It's ninety degrees out, but you're in a windbreaker and you're sweating like a hog. Plus, you've got horns growing out of your head, and I know *that's* not normal. 'Course, if you were a healthy person, you never would've beat your girlfriend's face in and left her in the woods. The little redheaded twat,' Hannity said. He regarded Ig with pleasure. 'I've been a fan of yours ever since, you know that, Ig? No shit. I've thought your rich-bitch family was due to come down a couple pegs for years. Your brother especially, all his fucking money, on TV with swimsuit models sitting in his lap every night, like he ever worked an honest day in his life. Then you go and do what you did. You shovelled shit all over your family name, and they aren't ever going to scrape it off. I love it. I don't know what you can do for an encore. What will you do for an encore, Ig?'

It was a struggle to keep his legs from shaking. Hannity loomed, outweighing him by a hundred pounds, towering over him by six inches. 'I'm just here to pass a word with Lee.'

'I know what you do for an encore,' Eric Hannity said, as if Ig had not replied. 'You show up at a congressman's office with a head full of crazy and a weapon hidden in your windbreaker. You've got a weapon, don't you? That's why you're wearing that jacket, to hide it. You've got a gun, and I'm going to shoot you and be on the front page of the *Boston Herald* for bagging Terry Perrish's mentally ill brother. Wouldn't that be something? Last time I saw your brother, he offered me free tickets to his show if I ever got out to LA. Rubbing it in my face about what a big shit he is. What I'd like is to be the guy who heroically shoots you in the fucking face before you can kill again. Then, at the funeral, I could ask Terry if he can still help me out with tickets. Just to see his expression. Come on, Ig. Step up to the metal detector so I can have an excuse to blow your mentally deficient ass away.'

'I'm not going in to see anyone. I'm going to wait outside,' Ig said, already backing for the door, conscious of a cool flop sweat under his arms. His palms were slippery. As he nudged the door open with one elbow, the flare slipped, and for one terrifying moment he thought it was going to slide out in front of Hannity and fall to the floor, but he was able to grab it with his thumb and hold it in place.

Eric Hannity watched with an almost animal look of hunger on his face as Ig backed out into the sunlight.

The transition from the chill of the office to the baking heat of the afternoon made Ig briefly dizzy. The sky brightened, then dimmed, then brightened again.

He had known just what he was doing when he drove to the congressman's office. It had seemed simple, had seemed right. He saw now, though, that it had been a mistake. He was not going to kill Lee Tourneau with a highway flare (itself a comically absurd idea). Lee wasn't even going to come out to talk to him.

As he crossed the lot, Ig's stride quickened, along with the beat of his heart. The thing to do was leave, take the back roads to Gideon. Find a place to be alone, to be quiet and do some thinking. Get his head right. After the day he'd been through, he desperately needed to get his head right. Coming here was an act so thoroughly reckless and impulsive that it frightened him to think he'd allowed himself to do it. There was a part of him that thought there was a good chance Eric Hannity was already rallying back-up and that if Ig didn't go soon, he wouldn't be able to go at all. (Another part, though, cooed softly, *In ten minutes Eric won't remember you were here. He was never even talking to* you. *He was talking with his own devil.*)

Ig tossed the flare into the back of the Gremlin, slammed the hatchback. He had made it around to the driver's side door before he heard Lee call to him.

'Iggy?'

Ig's internal temperature changed at the sound of Lee's voice, fell by several degrees, as if he had too quickly swallowed a very cold drink. Ig turned and stared. He saw Lee through the wavering heat rising off the blacktop, a rippled, distorted figure, flickering in and out of existence, a soul and not a man. His short hair burned hot and white, as if he were aflame. Eric Hannity stood next to him, his bald pate throwing glare, his arms crossed over his barrel chest, hands hidden beneath his armpits.

Hannity remained by the entrance to the congressman's offices, but Lee started towards Ig, seeming to walk not on the ground but on air, to be flowing like liquid through the smothering heat of day. As he got closer, however, his form became more solid, so that he was no longer a streaming, insubstantial spirit, a thing shaped out of heat and distorted sunlight, but finally only a man, with his feet on the ground. He wore jeans and a white shirt, a blue-collar costume that had the effect of making him look more like a carpenter than a political shill. He removed a pair of mirrored sunglasses as he came close. A thin gold chain glittered at his throat.

The blue of Lee's right eye was the exact shade of the burnt August sky above. The damage to the left eye had not resulted in the usual sort of cataract, which appeared as a creamy white film across the retina. Lee had developed a cortical cataract, which manifested itself as a sunburst of palest blue – a terrible white star opening in the black ink of his pupil. The right eye was clear and watchful, fixed upon Ig, but the other was turned slightly inwards and seemed to gaze off into the distance. Lee said he could see through it, if unclearly. He said it was like looking through a soap-covered window. Lee seemed to take Ig in with his right eye. Who knew what the left eye was looking at?

'I got your message,' Lee said. 'So. You know.'

Ig was taken aback, hadn't imagined that even under the influence of the horns Lee would admit to it so bluntly. It disarmed him, too, the shy, half-smiling look of apology on Lee's face, an expression that seemed almost embarrassed, as if raping and murdering Ig's girlfriend had been a graceless social faux pas, like tracking mud onto a new carpet.

'I know *every*thing, you fuck,' Ig said, his voice shaking.

Lee paled; spots of colour bloomed in his cheeks. He held up his left hand, palm out, in a wait-a-minute gesture. 'Ig. I'm not going to make excuses. I knew it was the wrong thing to do. I had a little too much to drink, and she looked like she needed a friend, and things got out of hand.'

'That's all you have to say for yourself? Things got out of fucking hand? You know I'm here to kill you.'

Lee stared for a moment, then glanced over his shoulder at Eric Hannity and back to Ig. 'Given your history, Ig, you shouldn't joke. After what you've been through over Merrin, you want to be careful what you say in the presence of a lawman. Especially a lawman like Eric. He really doesn't get irony.'

'I'm not being ironic.'

Lee picked at the golden chain around his throat and said, 'For what it's worth, I feel lousy about it. At the same time, a small part of me is glad you found out. You don't need her in your life, Ig. You're better off without her.'

Ig couldn't help himself, made a low, agonised sound of rage in his throat and started towards Lee. He expected Lee to back away, but Lee held his ground, just pointed another glance back at Eric, who nodded in return. Ig shot a look at Eric himself – and went still. For the first time, he saw that Eric Hannity's holster was empty. The reason it was empty was that he had the revolver in one hand and he was hiding it in his armpit. Ig couldn't actually see the gun but he sensed it there, could feel the weight of it, as if he held it himself. Eric would use it, too, Ig had no doubt. He wanted to shoot Terry Perrish's brother, get in the paper – HERO COP SLAYS ALLEGED SEX KILLER – and if Ig put his hands on Lee, it would be all the excuse he needed. The horns would do the rest, compelling Hannity to fulfil his ugliest impulses. That's how they worked.

'I didn't know you cared so much,' Lee said finally, taking slow, steady breaths. 'Jesus, Ig, she's trash. I mean, she has a good heart, but Glenna's always been trash. I thought the only reason you were living with her was to get out of your parents' house.'

Ig had no idea what he was talking about. For a moment the day seemed to catch in place; even the dreadful sawing of the locusts seemed to pause. Then Ig understood, remembered what Glenna had admitted to that morning, the first confession the horns had compelled. It seemed impossible it had been only that morning.

'I'm not talking about *her*,' Ig said. 'How could you think I'm talking about *her*?'

'Who are you talking about, then?'

Ig didn't understand. They all told. As soon as they saw Ig, saw his horns, the secrets tumbled forth. They couldn't help themselves. The receptionist wanted to wear his mother's underwear, and Eric Hannity wanted an excuse to shoot Ig and get in the paper, and now it was Lee's turn, and the only thing Lee had to confess to was being on the receiving end of a drunken blow job.

'Merrin,' Ig said hoarsely. 'I'm talking about what you did to Merrin.'

Lee tilted his head, just a little, so his right ear was pointed towards the sky – like a dog listening for a faraway sound. He let out a soft, sighing breath. Then he gave his head the tiniest shake.

'Lost me, Ig. What am I supposed to have done to—?'

'Fucking killed her. I *know* it was you. You killed her and made Terry keep quiet about it.'

Lee gave Ig a long, measured look. He glanced again towards Eric Hannity – checking, Ig thought, to see if Eric was close enough to hear their conversation. He was not. Then Lee looked back, and when he did, his face was dead and blank. The change was so jarring that Ig almost shouted in fear – a comical reaction, a devil afraid of a man, when it was supposed to be the other way around.

'Terry told you this?' Lee said. 'If he did, he's a goddamn liar.'

Lee was closed off from the horns in some way Ig didn't understand. There was a wall up, and the horns couldn't poke through. Ig tried to *will* the horns to work, and for a moment they filled with a dense swell of heat and blood and pressure, but it didn't last. It was like trying to play a trumpet with a mass of rags stuffed into it. Force as much air into it as you liked, it wasn't going to blow.

Lee went on, 'I hope he hasn't been telling anyone else that. And I hope you haven't either.'

'Not yet. But soon everyone will know what you did.' Could Lee even *see* the horns? He hadn't mentioned them. Hadn't even seemed to look at them.

'They'd better not,' Lee said. Then the muscles flexed at the corners of his jaw as an idea occurred to him, and he said, 'Are you recording this?'

'Yes,' Ig said, but he was too slow, and anyway, that was the wrong answer; no one who was attempting entrapment would admit to recording a conversation.

'No, you aren't. You never did learn to lie, Ig,' Lee said, and smiled. His left hand was fingering the gold chain around his throat. The other was in his pocket. 'Too bad for you, though. If you *were* recording this conversation, you might get somewhere. As it is, I don't think you can prove anything. Maybe your brother said something to you while he was drunk, I don't know, but whatever he told you, I'd just put it out of your mind. I definitely wouldn't go around repeating it. Tales out of school never do anyone any good. Think about it. Can you imagine Terry going to the police with some crazy story about me killing Merrin, with nothing but his word against mine, and him silent a whole year? No evidence to back him up? 'Cause there isn't any, Ig, it's all gone. If he goes out with that story, best-case scenario: it's the end of his career. Worst-case scenario: maybe we both wind up in jail. I promise there's no way I'd be going without him.'

Lee slipped a hand out of his pocket long enough to rub a knuckle in his good eye, as if to clear some dust from it. For a moment the right eye was shut and he was staring at Ig through the damaged eye, the eye shot through with those spokes of white. And for the first time, Ig understood what was so terrible about that eye, what had always been so terrible about it. It wasn't that it was *dead*. It was just ... occupied with other matters. As if there were two Lee Tourneaus. The first was the man who'd been Ig's friend for more than a decade, a man who could admit to children he was a sinner and who donated blood to the Red Cross three times a year. The second Lee was a person who gazed at the world around him with all the empathy of a trout.

Lee cleared whatever was in his right eye and let the hand fall to his side. He casually replaced it in his pocket. He was coming forward again. Ig retreated, staying out of arm's reach. He wasn't sure why he was backing off, didn't know why it suddenly seemed a matter of life and death to keep at least a few feet of blacktop between himself and Lee Tourneau. The locusts droned in the trees, a terrible, maddening buzz that filled Ig's head.

'She was your friend, Lee,' Ig said as he retreated around the front end of the car. 'She trusted you, and you raped her and killed her and left her in the woods. How could you do that?'

'You've got one thing wrong, Ig,' Lee said in a calm, steady, low voice. 'It wasn't rape. I'm sure you'd like to believe that, but honestly, she *wanted* me to fuck her. She was coming on to me for months. Sending me messages. Playing little word games. She had this whole cocktease business going on behind your back. She was just waiting for you to go to London so we could have our thing.'

'No,' Ig said, a sick heat rising to his face, rising behind the horns. 'She might've slept with someone else, but she wouldn't have slept with you, Lee.'

'She told you that she wanted to sleep with other people. Who do you think she was talking about? I mean, honestly, this seems to be a running theme with your girls, Ig. Merrin, Glenna – sooner or later they all wind up on the end of my dick.' Opening his mouth in a toothy, aggressive grin that had no humour in it.

'She fought you.'

'I know you probably won't believe this, Ig, but she wanted that too, wanted me to take the lead, push past her objections. Maybe she *needed* that. It was the only way she could get over her inhibitions. Everybody has a dark side. That was hers. You know she came when we fucked, don't you? Out there in the woods with me? She came hard. I think it was a fantasy of hers. Being taken in the gloomy ol' forest. A little bit of scratch and wrestle.'

'And then a rock in the head?' Ig asked. He had by now backed all the way around the front end of the Gremlin to the passenger side, and Lee had followed him step by step. 'That part of the fantasy?'

Lee stopped walking and stood there. 'You'll have to ask Terry. He was the one who did that part.'

'That's a lie,' Ig whispered.

'But there really is no truth. None that matters,' Lee said. His left hand came out of his shirt. He wore a delicate gold cross, which flashed in the sunlight. He put it in his mouth and sucked on it for a moment, then let it fall and said, 'No one knows what went down that evening. If I smashed her with the rock, or if Terry did it, or if *you* did it ... no one is ever going to know what *really* happened. You don't have a case to make, and I'm not going to cut some deal with either of you, so what do you want?'

'I want to see you die hopeless and scared in the dirt,' Ig said. 'Just like she did.'

Lee smiled, as if he had been offered a compliment.

'Do it, then,' he said. 'Come on and do it.' He took a quick step forward, lunging at Ig, and Ig opened the passenger door between them, flinging it into Lee.

It crashed into Lee's legs with a bang and something hit the asphalt – *rattle-clatter-tchok!* Ig had a glimpse of a red Swiss Army knife with a three-inch blade, spinning away across the ground. Lee staggered and made a harsh whuffing sound, exhaling sharply, and Ig used the chance to scramble into the car, across the passenger seat and behind the wheel. He didn't even bother to close the passenger door.

'Eric!' Lee shouted. 'Eric, he's got a knife!'

But the Gremlin came to life in a rasping, grinding burst and Ig's foot found the gas before he was even settled in the seat. The Gremlin lurched forward and the passenger door thudded shut. Ig's gaze darted to the rearview mirror and he saw Eric Hannity trotting across the lot, pistol in his hand, barrel pointed at the ground.

Chunks of asphalt flew from the back tyres and glittered in the sunlight, skeins of gold. As Ig pulled out, he shot another glance at the rearview mirror and saw Lee and Eric standing in the dust cloud. Lee's good right eye was closed again and he was waving a hand at the billowing grit. The half-blind left eye, though, was open and staring after Ig with an alien sort of fascination.

24

Ig stayed off the interstate on the way back – back where? He didn't know. He drove automatically, with no conscious thought to direction. He wasn't sure what had just happened to him. Or, rather, he knew what had happened but not what it meant. It wasn't anything Lee had said or done; it was what he hadn't said, hadn't done. The horns hadn't touched him. Lee alone, of all the people Ig had dealt with today, had told Ig only what he wanted to tell; his confession had been a considered decision, not a helpless impulse.

Ig wanted off the road, as soon as possible. Would Lee call the police and tell them Ig had shown up in a deranged state and come at him with a knife? No, actually, Ig didn't think he would. Lee wouldn't bring the law into this if he could avoid it. Still, Ig kept to the speed limit and watched his rearview mirror for police cruisers.

He wished he could be coolly in control, could handle his getaway like Dr Dre – be a stone-cold badass – but his nerves were jangled and his breath was short. He had finally come up against the edge of emotional exhaustion. Crucial systems were shutting down. He couldn't keep going like this. He needed to get a handle on what was happening to him. He needed a fucking *saw*, a sharp-toothed saw, needed to cut the miserable things off his head.

The sun beat at the window in flashes, a soothing, hypnotic

repetition. Images beat the same way in Ig's mind. The open Swiss Army knife on the ground, Vera riding her wheelchair down the hill, Merrin flashing her cross at him that day ten years ago in church, the horned image of himself in the security monitor at the congressman's office, the golden cross shining in the summer light at Lee's throat – and Ig twitched in surprise, knees knocking the steering wheel. A peculiar and unpleasant idea came to him, an impossible idea, that Lee was wearing *her* cross, had taken it off her dead body, a trophy. Only no, she hadn't been wearing it their last night together. Still: it was hers. It had been just a gold cross like any other, not a mark on it to show who it had belonged to, and yet he felt sure it was the same cross she'd been wearing the first day he saw her.

Ig restlessly twisted at his goatee, wondering if it might be as simple as that, if Merrin's cross had turned off the horns (muted them) in some way. Crosses held back vampires, didn't they? No, that was worse than garbage, that was nonsense. He had walked into the house of the Lord earlier that morning, and Father Mould and Sister Bennett had fallen all over themselves to tell him their secrets and ask his permission to sin.

But Father Mould and Sister Bennett hadn't been in the church. They had been *beneath* it. That wasn't a holy place. It was a gym. Had they worn crosses, had they dressed themselves in any sign of their faith? Ig remembered Father Mould's cross, hanging from one end of the twenty-pound bar set across the bench press, and Sister Bennett's scrawny bare throat. What do you say to *that*, Ig Perrish? Ig Perrish didn't say anything; he drove.

A boarded-up Dunkin' Donuts flashed by on his left, and he realised he was near the town woods, not far from the road running up to the old foundry. He was less than half a mile from where Merrin had been murdered, the very same place he'd gone last night to curse and rave and piss and pass out. It was as if the day's whole motion had merely described a great circle that was always, inevitably, going to lead him back to where he had started.

He slowed and turned. The Gremlin thudded down the single-lane gravel road with trees growing close on either side. Fifty feet from the highway, the lane was blocked by a chain, a BB-dented No Trespassing sign hanging from it. He drove off the road and around it and back up into the ruts.

Soon the foundry came into sight through the trees. It stood in an open field at the top of a hill and should've been in sunlight, but instead was dark, seemed to be in shadow. Maybe a cloud was across the sun; but no, when Ig squinted up through the windshield, he saw an impossibly clear late-afternoon sky.

He drove until he was at the edge of the meadow around the remains of the foundry, then stopped the car. He left the engine running and got out.

When Ig was a child, the foundry was the ruins of a castle, straight out of the Brothers Grimm, a place in the deep, dark forest where a wicked prince might lure an innocent to the slaughter – exactly what had happened here, it turned out. It was a surprise to discover as an adult that it wasn't so very far off in the woods after all, just maybe a hundred feet from the road. Ig started towards the place where her body had been found and where the memorial for her was kept by her friends and family. He knew the way, had been there often since her death. Snakes followed, but he pretended not to notice.

The black cherry tree was as he had left it the night before. He had yanked her pictures down out of the branches. They lay scattered among weeds and bushes. The bark, a pale, scaly crust, was peeling away to show the rotten reddish wood beneath. Ig had pulled his pecker out and pissed into the weeds, on his own feet, and into the face of the plastic Virgin Mary figurine that had been left in a natural hollow between two of the thickest roots. He had despised that Mary with her idiot smile, symbol of a story that meant nothing, servant of a God who was no good to anyone. He had no doubt that Merrin had called out to God here in this place while she was being raped and killed, in her heart if not with her voice. God's reply had been that due to the high volume of calls she could expect to be on hold until she was dead.

Ig glanced casually at the statue of Mary now, started to look away and then did a double take. The Holy Mother looked as if she had been held in flames. The right half of her smiling, beatific face was scabbed black, like a marshmallow left too long over a campfire. The other half of her face had run like wax. That side was frowning and deformed. The sight of her gave Ig a brief moment of light-headedness, and he swayed and put his foot on something round and smooth that rolled under his heel and—

—for a moment it was night and the stars were wheeling overhead and he was peering up into the branches and gently drifting leaves, and he said, 'I see you up there.' Talking to whom – God? Rocking on his heels in the warm night before he went—

—straight back on his ass, slamming butt-first into the dirt. He looked past his feet and saw he had stepped on a bottle of wine, the same bottle he'd brought out the night before. He bent and picked it up and shook it, and wine sloshed inside.

He got up and tipped his head back for an uneasy look into the branches of the black cherry tree. Leaves fluttered gently above. He moved his tongue around the tacky, bad-tasting cavity of his mouth, then turned and started back to the car.

Ig stepped over a snake or two on the way, still ignoring them. He uncorked the wine and had a swallow. It was hot from a day spent in the sun, but he didn't mind. It tasted like Merrin when he went down on her: a taste of oils and copper. It tasted like weeds, too, as if it had in some way absorbed the fragrance of the summer itself after an evening spent beneath the tree.

Ig drove on to the old foundry, bumping gently across the

overgrown meadow. As he rolled towards the building, he scanned it for signs of life. On a hot August evening in his own childhood, half the kids in Gideon would've been out here, looking to score something: a smoke, a beer, a kiss, a grope, or a sweet taste of their own mortality on the Evel Knievel trail. But the place was empty and isolated in the last of the day's light. Maybe since Merrin had been killed out here, kids didn't like to come around so much anymore. Maybe they thought the place was haunted. Maybe it was.

He rolled around to the rear of the building and put his car into park on one side of the Evel Knievel trail, positioning the Gremlin in the shade of an oak. A frilly blue skirt, a long black sock and someone's overcoat hung from the branches, as if the tree were fruiting mildewed laundry. Beyond the front bumper were the old and rusting pipes leading down to the water. He shut off the car and got out to look around.

Ig had not been inside for years, but it was much as he remembered it. The foundry lay open to the sky, brick arches and pillars rising away into the slanting reddish light. Thirty years of overlapping graffiti covered the walls. The individual messages were mostly incoherent, but then perhaps the individual messages were of no importance. It seemed to Ig that all such messages were the same at heart: *I Am; I Was; I Want to Be.*

Part of one wall had fallen in and Ig navigated his way around a mound of bricks, past a wheelbarrow piled with rusting tools. At the far side of the largest room was the chimney. The iron hatch to the blast furnace hung ajar, an opening just large enough to crawl into.

Ig approached it and peered in at a mattress and a collection of red candles, melted to fat stubs. A filthy and stained blanket that had once been blue was pushed to the side of the mattress. Further back were the charred remnants of a campfire in a circle of coppery light, centred directly beneath the chimney.

Ig picked up the blanket and sniffed it. It reeked of stale urine and smoke. He let it flop from his hands.

On his walk back to the car, to get his bottle and his cell phone, he finally had to admit that snakes were following him. He could *hear* them, the hiss their bodies made moving in the dry grass: almost a dozen of them in all. He grabbed a chunk of old concrete from amid the weeds and turned and threw it at them. One snake effortlessly weaved aside. None of them were struck. They went still, watching him in the last of the day's light.

He tried not to look at them but at the car, a two-foot rat snake dropped from the oak tree above and hit the hood of the Gremlin with a tinny bang. He recoiled with a scream, then lunged at it, grabbing at it to throw it off the car.

Ig thought he had it by the head, but he'd gripped it too low, mid-trunk, and it twisted on itself and fastened its teeth into his hand. It was like catching an industrial staple in the meat of his thumb. He grunted and flung it into the brush. He stuck his thumb into his mouth and tasted blood. He wasn't worried about poison. There were no poisonous snakes in New Hampshire. Or no, that wasn't quite right. Dale Williams had liked to take Ig and Merrin hiking in the White Mountains and had warned them to be on the lookout for timber rattlers. But he had always done so gleefully, his chubby cheeks bright red, and Ig had never heard of rattlers in New Hampshire from anyone else.

He spun on his entourage of reptiles. There were almost twenty of them now.

'Get the fuck away from me!' he roared at them.

They froze, watching him from the high grass with avid, slitted, gold-foil eyes – then began to scatter, veering aside and slipping into the weeds. Ig thought some cast disappointed looks back at him as they departed.

He stalked towards the foundry and pulled himself up

through a doorway several feet off the ground. He turned there for a last look into the deepening twilight. A single snake had not done as she was told and had trailed him all the way back to the ruin. She swished restlessly about directly below, a small, delicately marked garter, staring up with the excited, eager look of a groupie under a rock star's balcony, desperate to be seen and acknowledged.

'Go brumate somewhere!' he shouted.

Maybe he was imagining it, but she seemed to squiggle about even faster, almost ecstatically. It reminded him of sperm swimming up the birth canal, of loosened erotic energy – a disconcerting line of thought. He whirled around and got away from there as fast as he could without running.

He sat in the furnace with the bottle, and with each swallow of wine the darkness surrounding him opened and expanded, becoming lusher. When the last inch of merlot was gone and there was no point sucking on the bottle anymore, he sucked on his sore, snakebit thumb instead.

He didn't consider bedding down in the Gremlin – he had bad memories of the last time he'd dozed off there, and anyway, he did not want to wake up with a blanket of snakes covering the windshield.

Ig wished for a way to light the candles but wasn't sure it was worth going to the car to get the cigarette lighter. He didn't want to walk through a mess of snakes in the dark. He was sure they were still out there.

He thought there might be a lighter or a matchbook somewhere in the furnace with him, and he reached into his pocket for his cell phone, thinking he could use the light from the screen to look around. But when he put his hand in his pocket, he found something in there with his phone, a slim cardboard box that felt like, but couldn't be . . .

A box of matches. He slipped them out of his pocket and

stared at them, a prickle of gooseflesh spilling down his back, and not just because he didn't smoke and didn't know how he had come by this particular matchbox.

LUCIFER MATCHES it said on the cover in ornate black script, and showed the silhouette of a leaping black devil, his head tossed back, goatee curling from his chin, horns thrusting at the sky.

And for a moment it was there again, tantalisingly close, what had happened the night before, what he had done, but when he grasped at it, it slipped away. It was as slippery, and as hard to get a hand on, as a snake in the weeds.

He pushed open the little drawer in the box of Lucifer Matches. A few dozen matches, with evil-looking purply-black heads. Big, thick, kitchen-style matches. They had a smell on them, the odour of eggs beginning to go bad, and he thought they were old, so old it would be a miracle if he could get one to light. He dragged one across the strike strip, and it hissed to life on the first try.

Ig began lighting candles. There were six in all, arranged in a loose semicircle. In a moment they were throwing their reddish light upon the bricks and he saw his own shadow surging and falling against the curved roof above. His horns were unmistakable, his shadow's most striking feature. When he looked down, he saw that the match had burned itself out against his fingers. He hadn't noticed, hadn't felt any pain as it sizzled down to his skin. He rubbed thumb and index finger together and watched the blackened remains of the matchstick crumble away. His thumb didn't hurt anymore where the rat snake had bitten him. In the poor light, he couldn't even find the wound.

He wondered what time it was. He didn't own a watch, but he had the cell phone, and he turned it back on to see that it was almost nine. He had a low battery warning and five messages. He put the phone to his ear and played them.

The first: 'Ig, it's Terry. Vera's in the hospital. The brake on her wheelchair let go and she rolled down the hill and right into the fence. She's lucky to be alive. She broke her fuckin' face and cracked a couple of ribs. They got her in intensive care, and it's too early to get drunk. Call me.' A click and he was gone. No mention of their encounter in the kitchen that morning, but that didn't surprise Ig. For Terry it hadn't happened.

The second: 'Ig. It's your mother. I know that Terry told you about Vera. They're keeping her unconscious and on a morphine drip, but at least she's stable. I talked to Glenna. She wasn't sure where you are. Give me a call. I know we talked earlier today, but my head is a mess, and I can't remember when or about what. I love you.'

Ig laughed at that. The things people said. The effortless way they lied, to others, to themselves.

The third: 'Hey, kid. Dad. I guess you heard your Grandma Vera went through the fence like a runaway truck. I stretched out for an afternoon nap, and when I woke up, there was an ambulance in the front yard. You ought to talk to your mom. She's pretty upset.' After a pause his father said, 'I had the funniest dream about you.'

The next was Glenna. 'Your grandmother is in Emergency. Her wheelchair went out of control, and she rolled into the fence at your house. I don't know where you are or what you're doing. Your brother came by looking for you. If you get this message, your family needs you. You should go to the hospital.' Glenna burped softly. '*Unh.* Excuse me. I had one of those supermarket doughnuts this morning, and I think they were going bad. If a supermarket doughnut *can* go bad. My stomach has hurt all day.' She paused again and then said, 'I'd go to the hospital with you, but I've never met your grandma, and I barely know your parents. I was thinking today how strange that is, that I don't know them. Or not strange. Maybe it's not strange.

You're the nicest guy in the world, Ig. I've always thought that. But I think deep down you've always been sort of ashamed to be with me after all those years with *her*. Because she was so clean and good and never made any mistakes, and I'm all mistakes and bad habits. I don't blame you, you know. For being ashamed. For what it's worth, I don't think too much of me either. I'm worrying about you, bud. Take care of your grandma. And yourself.'

This message caught him off guard, or maybe it was his own reaction to it that caught him off guard. He had been prepared to hold her in contempt, to hate her, but not to remember why he'd liked her. Glenna had been casually free with her apartment and her body, had not held his self-pity and his wretched obsession with a dead girlfriend against him. And it was true: Ig had been with her because, on some level, it was a help to be around someone as fucked up as he was, someone he could look down his nose at just a little. Glenna was a sweet, shabby mess. She had a Playboy Bunny tattoo she didn't remember getting and stories about being pepper-sprayed by cops, fighting at concerts. She'd been in half a dozen relationships, all of them bad: a married man, an abusive pot dealer, a guy who'd taken pictures of her and shown them to friends. And of course there had been Lee.

He thought over the thing she'd confessed about Lee Tourneau that morning, Lee who had been her first crush, who stole for her. Ig had not imagined he could be sexually possessive about Glenna – he'd never believed that their relationship was going anywhere or was exclusive in some way. They were roommates who fucked, not a couple with a future – but the thought of Glenna falling to her knees in front of Lee Tourneau and Lee pushing himself into her mouth made Ig feel weak with a disgust that bordered on moral horror. The idea of Lee Tourneau anywhere near Glenna made him ill and afraid for her, but there was no time to dwell on it. The phone was cycling on to the last message, and an instant later Terry was speaking in Ig's ear again.

'Still at the hospital,' he said. 'Honestly, I'm more worried about you than I am about Vera. No one knows where you are, and you won't answer this fucking phone. I went by the apartment looking for you. Glenna said she hasn't seen you since last night. Did you two fight? She didn't look too good.' Terry paused, and when he spoke again, his words had a quality of being weighed and measured before they were spoken, selected with unnatural care. 'I know I talked to you, sometime since I got in, but I can't remember if we made plans. I don't know. My head isn't right. You get this message, call me. Let me know where you are.' Ig thought that was all. Ig thought now Terry would hang up. Instead there was an unsteady, indrawn breath, and then, in a rough, scared voice, his brother said, 'Why can't I remember what we talked about the last time we talked?'

Each candle cast its own shadow against the curved brick ceiling, so that six featureless devils crowded together above Ig, mourners in black, gathered over the casket. They swayed from side to side to a dirge only they could hear.

Ig chewed his beard, worrying about Glenna, wondering if Lee Tourneau would visit her tonight, looking for him. But when he called her, it switched over to voicemail without ringing. He didn't leave a message. He didn't know what to say. *Hey, babe, I won't be coming home tonight . . . I want to stay away until I figure out what to do about the horns growing out of my head. Oh, and by the way, don't suck Lee Tourneau's cock tonight. He's not a good guy.* If she wasn't answering the phone, she was already asleep. She had said she wasn't feeling well. Enough, then. Leave it. Lee wasn't going to batter in her door at midnight with an axe. Lee would want to remove Ig as a threat in some way that would expose himself to the bare minimum of risk.

Ig lifted the bottle to his lips, but nothing came out. He had drained it a good while ago, and it was still empty now. It pissed him off. Bad enough to be exiled from humanity, but he had to be sober, too. He turned to heave the bottle, then caught himself staring through the open furnace door.

The snakes had found their way into the foundry, so many it caused the breath to shoot out of him. Were there a hundred? He thought there might be, a shifting tangle that faced the door to the furnace, their black eyes glittering and avid in the candlelight. After a moment of hesitation, he completed the throw, and the bottle hit the floor before them, spraying glass. Most of the serpents went gliding away, vanishing into piles of brick or out of sight through one of the many doorways. Some, however, only retreated a short distance and then stopped, eyeing him in an almost accusatory way.

Ig slammed the door on them and flung himself down on the filthy bed, dragging the blanket over him. His thoughts were a riot of angry noise, people shouting at him, confessing their sins, and asking for permission to commit more, and he did not imagine he would ever find his way to sleep, but sleep found him, pulled a black bag over his head and choked the consciousness out of him. For six hours he could've been dead.

25

Iggy woke in the furnace, wrapped in the old piss-stained blanket. It was refreshingly cool at the bottom of the chimney, and he felt strong and well. As his head cleared, he had a thought, the happiest thought of his life. He had dreamt it – all of it. Everything that had come to pass the day before.

He had been drunk and wretched, had pissed on the cross and the Virgin Mary, had cursed God and his own life, had been consumed by an annihilating rage, yes; that had happened. But then, in the blank time afterwards, he had staggered here to the foundry and passed out. The rest had been a particularly vivid nightmare: discovering he'd grown horns; hearing one awful confession after another, leading up to the worst of all, Terry's terrible, impossible secret; loosening the wheelchair brake and shoving Vera down the hill; his visit to the congressman's office and his disorientating confrontation with Lee Tourneau and Eric Hannity; and then settling here at the foundry, hiding in the moribund blast furnace from a mob of lovestruck serpents.

Sighing with relief, Ig lifted his hands to his temples. His horns were hard as bone and filled with an unpleasant, fevery heat. He opened his mouth to scream, but someone else beat him to it.

The iron hatch and the curved brick walls muffled sound, but as from a great distance he heard a sharp, anguished cry, followed by laughter. It was a girl. She screamed, *'Please!'* She screamed, *'Don't, stop!'* Ig pushed open the iron door of the furnace, his pulse banging hard inside him.

He scrambled out through the hatch into the clear, clean light of the August morning. Another wavering cry of fear – or pain – came from his left, through a doorless opening that led outside. On some half-conscious level, Ig registered for the first time a throaty, hoarse quality to the shouting voice and understood that he wasn't hearing a girl at all, but a boy, one whose voice was shrill with panic. Ig did not slow, but flew barefoot across the concrete, past the wheelbarrow full of old and rusting tools. He grabbed the first instrument that came to hand without stopping or looking at it, just wanting something to swing.

They were outside, on the asphalt: three wearing clothes and one wearing only streaks of mud and a pair of too-small white jockey shorts. The boy in his underwear, scrawny and long in the torso, was perhaps as young as thirteen. The others were older boys, juniors or seniors in high school.

One of them, a kid with a shaved head shaped like a light-bulb, sat on top of the nearly naked boy, smoking a cigarette. A few paces behind him was a fat kid in a wifebeater. His face was sweaty and gleeful and he hopped from foot to foot, his fat-boy tits jiggling. The oldest of the boys stood to the left, holding a small, writhing garter snake by the tail. Ig recognised this snake – impossible but true – as the one that had given him the longing looks the day before. She twisted, trying to lift herself high enough to bite the boy who held her, but was unable. This third boy held a pair of garden shears in his other hand. Ig stood behind them all, in the doorway, looking down at them from six feet above the ground.

'No more!' screamed the boy in his underwear. His face was grimy, but clear lines of pink skin stood out where tears had cut tracks in the dirt. *'Stop, Jesse! It's enough!'*

The smoker, Jesse, sitting on top of him, flicked hot ash in the boy's face. 'Shut the fuck up, cumstain. It's enough when I say.'

Cumstain had already been burned with the cigarette several times. Ig could see three bright, shiny, red spots of inflamed tissue on his chest. Jesse moved the tip of the cigarette from burn mark to burn mark, holding it only an inch from Cumstain's skin. The glowing coal traced a rough triangle.

'You know why I burned a triangle?' Jesse asked. 'That's how the Nazis marked a fag. That's *your* mark. I woulda given you something not so bad, but you hadda squeal like you're taking it up the ass. Plus, your breath smells like fresh dick.'

'Ha!' shouted the fat boy. 'That's funny, Jesse!'

'I got just the thing to get rid of that dick smell,' said the boy with the snake. 'Something to wash his mouth out.'

As he spoke, he lifted the open blades of the shears and put them behind the head of the garter snake and, operating the handles with one hand, snapped her head off with a wet crunch. The diamond-shaped head bounced across the blacktop. It sounded hard, like a rubber ball. The trunk of the snake jerked and writhed, curling up on itself and then uncoiling in a series of mighty spasms.

'*Geeeee!*' screamed Fatboy, leaping up and down. 'You decapernated that fucker, Rory!'

Rory crouched beside Cumstain. Blood came from the snake's neck in quick arterial spurts.

'Suck it,' Rory said, shoving the snake in Cumstain's face. 'All you got to do is suck it and Jesse is done.'

Jesse laughed and inhaled deeply from his cigarette, so the coal at the tip brightened to an intense, poisonous red.

'*Enough*,' said Ig, his own voice unrecognisable to himself – a deep, resonant voice that seemed to come from the bottom of a chimney – and as he spoke, the cigarette in Jesse's mouth erupted like a firecracker, going up in a white flash.

215

Jesse screamed and flipped back off Cumstain, falling into the high grass. Ig jumped from the cement, landing into the weeds, and stabbed the handle of the tool he was holding into the fat boy's stomach. It was like poking a tyre, a feeling of springy, hard resistance shivering up the shaft. The fat kid coughed and went back on his heels.

Ig wheeled around and pointed the business end of the tool at the boy named Rory. Rory let go of the snake. She hit the blacktop and twisted desperately about, as if still alive and trying to squirm away.

Rory rose slowly to his feet and took a step back onto a low heap of wooden planks and old cans and rusting wire. The junk shifted underfoot, and he wobbled and sat down again. He stared at what Ig was pointing at him: an ancient pitchfork with three curved and rusting tines.

There was a stitch in Ig's lungs, a seared feeling, such as he often felt when one of his asthma attacks was coming on, and he exhaled, trying to breathe out the tightness in his chest. Smoke gushed from his nostrils. At the periphery of his vision, he saw the boy in jockey shorts rising to one knee and wiping at his face with both hands, trembling in his tightie-whities.

'I want to run,' said Jesse.

'Me, too,' the fat kid said.

'Just leave Rory here to die alone,' Jesse said. 'What'd he ever do for us?'

'He got me two weeks' detention for flooding the bathroom at school, and I didn't even plug the toilets up,' said the fat kid. 'I was just standing there. So fuck him. I want to live!'

'Then you better run,' Ig told them, and Jesse and Fatboy turned and sprinted for the woods.

Ig lowered the pitchfork and sank the points into the ground, leaned on the handle, looking over it at the teenage boy sitting on the trash heap. Rory did not attempt to rise but stared back with large, fascinated eyes.

'Tell me the worst thing you've ever done, Rory,' Ig asked him. 'I want to know if this is a new low for you, or if you've done worse.'

Speaking automatically, Rory said, 'I stole forty bucks from my mother to buy beer, and my older brother, John, beat her up when she said she didn't know what happened to the money. Johnnie thought she blew it on scratch tickets and was lyin', and I didn't say anything because I was afraid he'd beat me up, too. The way he hit her was like hearing someone kick a watermelon. Her face still isn't right, and I feel sick whenever I kiss her good night.' As he spoke, a dark stain began to spread across the crotch of Rory's denim shorts. 'Are you going to kill me?'

'Not today,' Ig said. 'Go. I release you.' The smell of Rory's urine appalled him, but he kept it from showing in his face.

Rory pushed himself back to his feet. His legs were shaking visibly. He slid sideways and began to retreat towards the tree-line, walking backwards, keeping his gaze on Ig and Ig's pitchfork. He wasn't watching where he was going and almost stumbled over Cumstain, who still sat on the ground in his underwear and a pair of unlaced tennis sneakers. Cumstain held an armful of laundry to his chest and was staring at Ig with the same look he might've given some dead and diseased thing, a carcase withered by infection.

'Do you want a hand up?' Ig asked him, stepping towards him.

At that, Cumstain leaped to his feet and backed a few steps off. 'Keep away from me.'

'Don't let him touch you,' Rory said.

Ig met Cumstain's gaze and said, in the most patient voice he could muster, 'I was just trying to help.'

Cumstain's upper lip was drawn back in a disgusted sneer, but his eyes had in them the dazed and distant look with which Ig was becoming familiar – the look that said the horns were taking hold and casting their influence.

'You didn't help,' Cumstain said. 'You fucked everything up.'

'They were burning you,' Ig said.

'So what? All the freshmen who make swim team get a mark. All I had to do was suck a little snake to show I enjoy the taste of blood, and then I was going to be solid with them. And you went and ruined it.'

'Get the hell out of here. Both of you.'

Rory and Cumstain ran. The other two were waiting at the treeline for them, and when Rory and Cumstain reached them, they all held up for a moment, in the fir-scented gloom under the trees.

'What is he?' Jesse asked.

'Scary,' said Rory. 'He's scary.'

'I just want to go,' said the fat boy, 'and forget about this.'

Ig had an idea then, and he stepped forward and called to them, 'No. Don't forget. Remember that there's something scary out here. Let everyone know. Tell them to stay away from the old foundry. This place is mine now.' He wondered if it was within the scope of his new powers to persuade them *not* to forget, as everyone else seemed to forget him. He could be very persuasive on other matters, so maybe he could have his way on this too.

The boys stared at him, rapt, for a moment longer, and then Fatboy broke and ran, and the others went after him. Ig watched until they were gone. Then he picked up the decapernated snake with the end of the fork – blood dripped steadily from the open hose of her neck – and carried her into the foundry, where he buried her under a cairn of bricks.

26

Mid-morning he walked into the woods to take a shit, hanging his can over the side of a stump, his shorts pushed down to his ankles. When he pulled them up, there was a foot-long garter curled in his boxers. He screamed and grabbed it and whipped it into the leaves.

He wiped with some old newspaper but still felt unclean and walked down the Evel Knievel trail to wade naked into the water. The river was deliciously cool against his bare skin, and he shut his eyes and pushed out from the bank, gliding into the current. The locusts thrummed, their timbales producing a harmonic that swelled and faded, swelled and faded, like breath. He was breathing easy, but when he opened his eyes, he saw water snakes zooming like torpedoes beneath him, and he screamed again and scrambled back to shore. He stepped carefully over what he thought was a long river-softened log, then jumped and shivered when it slid away through the wet grass, a rat snake the length of his own body.

He retreated into the foundry to escape them, but there was no escape. He watched, squatting in the furnace, as they gathered on the floor beyond the hatch, slipping through holes in the mortar between bricks, falling in through open windows. It was as if the room beyond the blast furnace was a tub and someone had turned the faucets on the cold and hot running snakes. They piddled in, spilling across the floor, a rippling liquid mass of them.

Ig regarded them unhappily, his head a nervous hum of thought that corresponded in pitch and urgency to the throb of the locusts. The forest was filled with locust song, the males calling the females to them with that single maddening transmission that went on and on without cessation.

The horns. The horns were transmitting a signal, just like the fuck-melody of the locusts. They were broadcasting a continuous call on WSNK, Radio Snake: *This next tune is for all you skin-shedding lovers out there.* Cue 'Tube Snake Boogie'. The horns called snakes and sins alike from the shadows, beckoning them out of hiding to show themselves.

He considered, not for the first time, sawing the horns right off his head. There was a long rusted hook-toothed saw in the wheelbarrow. But they were a part of his body, fused to his skull, joined to the rest of his skeleton. He pressed his thumb into the point of the left-hand horn until he felt a sharp prick and pulled his hand back and he saw a ruby-red drop of blood. His horns were the realest and most solid thing in his world now, and he tried to imagine dragging a saw back and forth across one. He flinched from the thought, envisioned spurting blood, tearing pain. It would be like dragging the saw across his ankle. The removal of the horns would require heavy-duty drugs and a surgeon.

Except any surgeon exposed to them would use the heavy-duty drugs on the nurse and then fuck her on the operating table after she passed out. Ig needed a way to cut off the signal without cutting off parts of his body, needed a way to take Radio Snake off the air, put it to sleep somehow.

Lacking that, his second-best plan was to go where the snakes weren't. He hadn't eaten in twelve hours, and Glenna worked at the salon Saturday mornings, styling hair and waxing eyebrows. She'd be gone, and he'd have the apartment and her fridge to himself. Besides, he had left cash there, and most of his clothes. Maybe he could leave her a note about Lee ('*Dear Glenna – stopped by for a sandwich, got some things, going to be gone a while. Avoid Lee Tourneau, he murdered my last girlfriend, Love, Ig*').

He climbed into the Gremlin and stepped out fifteen minutes later on the corner in front of Glenna's building. The heat walloped into him; it was like throwing open the door to an oven set to broil. Ig didn't mind it, though.

He wondered if he should've circled the block a couple of times, to make sure there weren't cops watching the place for him, ready to pick him up for pulling a knife on Lee Tourneau the day before. Then he thought he'd rather just walk in and take his chances. If Sturtz and Posada were waiting for him, Ig would give them a blast with the horns, have 'em sixty-nine each other. The thought made him grin.

But Ig had no company in the echoing stairwell except his shadow, twelve feet tall and horned, leading the way to the top floor. Glenna had left the door unlocked when she went out, which was unlike her. He wondered if her mind had been on other things when she left the building, if she was worrying about him, wondering where he was. Or maybe she had simply overslept and gone out in a hurry. More likely that was it. Ig was her alarm clock, the one who shook her awake and made the coffee. Glenna wasn't a morning person.

Ig eased the door inwards. He had walked out of the place just yesterday morning, and yet looking at it now, he felt as if he'd never lived here and was seeing Glenna's rooms for the first time. The furniture was cheap yard-sale stuff: a stained second-hand corduroy couch, a split beanbag with synthetic fluff hanging out. There was hardly anything of himself in this place, no photos or personal items, just some paperbacks on the shelf, a few CDs, and a varnished oar with names written on it. The oar was from his last summer at Camp Galilee – he had taught javelin and swimming – when he was voted Counsellor of the Year. All the other counsellors had signed it, as had the kids in his cabin. Ig couldn't remember how it had wound up here or what he'd meant to do with it.

He looked into the kitchen by way of the pass-through window. An empty pizza box sat on a crumb-littered counter. The sink was piled with chipped dishes. Flies hummed over them.

She had mentioned to him now and then that they needed new dishes, but Ig hadn't taken the hint. He tried to remember if he had ever bought Glenna anything nice. The only thing that came to mind was beer. When she was in high school, Lee Tourneau had at least been kind enough to steal her a leather jacket. The idea sickened him: that Lee could've been a better man than he was in any way.

He didn't want Lee in his head right now, making him feel unclean. Ig meant to cook himself a light breakfast, pack his things, clean up the kitchen, write a note, and depart – in that order. He didn't want to be here if someone came looking for him: his parents, his brother, the police, Lee Tourneau. It was safer back at the foundry, where the likelihood of encountering anyone else was low. And anyway, the dim and still atmosphere of the apartment, the humid, weighted air, disagreed with him. He had never realised it was such a dank little place. But then, the shades were pulled down over the windows, Ig didn't know why. They hadn't been pulled down in months.

He found a pot, filled it with water, put it on the stovetop, turned the heat to high. There were just two eggs left. He settled them into the water and left them to boil. Ig made his way down the short corridor to the bedroom, stepping around a skirt and a pair of panties that Glenna had taken off and left in the hall. The shades were down in the bedroom, too, although that was normal. He didn't bother with the lights, didn't need to see. He knew where everything was.

He turned to the dresser, then paused, frowning. The drawers were all hanging out, hers and his both. He didn't understand, he never left his drawers that way. He wondered if someone had been through his things – Terry maybe, trying to figure out what had happened to him. But no, Terry wouldn't play private detective like that. Ig felt little details connecting to make a larger picture: the front door unlocked, the shades pulled down so no one could see into the apartment, the dresser rifled. These things all went together in some way, but before he could figure out how, he heard the toilet splutter and flush in the bathroom.

He was startled, hadn't seen Glenna's car in the side parking lot, couldn't imagine why she might be home. He was opening his mouth to call to her, let her know he was here, when the door opened and Eric Hannity stepped out of the crapper.

He was holding up his pants with one hand and had a magazine in the other, a *Rolling Stone*. He lifted his gaze and stared at Ig. Ig stared back. Eric let the *Rolling Stone* slide out of his hand and fall to the floor. He lifted his pants and buckled his belt. For some reason he was wearing blue latex gloves.

'What are you doing here?' Ig asked.

Eric slid a wooden billyclub, cherry-stained, out of a loop on his belt. 'Well,' Eric said, 'Lee wants to talk to you. You had your say the other day, but he hasn't had his. And you know Lee Tourneau. He likes to get in the last word.'

'He sent you?'

'Just to watch the apartment. See if you came by.' Eric frowned to himself. 'It's the damndest thing about you showing up at the congressman's. I think those horns of yours fiddle-fucked with my mind. I forgot right until this minute you even had them. Lee says you and me talked yesterday, but I have no idea what we talked about.' He swung the club slowly back and

223

forth in his right hand. 'Not that it really matters. Most talk is bullshit. Lee is a talker. I'm more of a doer.'

'What were you going to do?' Ig asked.

'You.'

Ig's kidneys felt as if they were floating in very cold water. 'I'll scream.'

'Yeah,' said Eric. 'I'm kind of looking forward to it.'

Ig sprang for the door. The exit, though, was in the same wall as the door into the bathroom, and Eric lunged to his right to cut him off. Ig put on a burst of speed, shrinking away from Eric and trying to get out the door ahead of him, and at the same time a shrill, terrible thought flashed through his mind: *Not going to make it.* Eric had his cherry club back over one arm, as if it were a football and he was about to go long.

Ig's feet snarled in something and when he tried to step forward, he couldn't. His ankles caught, he plunged off balance. Eric came around with the club and Ig heard the low whistle of it passing behind his head, then a loud, brittle crunch as it caught the doorframe and tore away a chunk of wood the size of a baby's fist.

He got his forearms up just before he crashed to the floor, which probably saved him from breaking his nose for the second time in his life. He looked down between his elbows and saw that his feet had caught in a pair of Glenna's discarded panties, black silk, with little red devils printed on them. He was already kicking them away. He felt Eric stepping up behind him and knew if he tried to stand, he was going to catch that ironwood club in the back of the head. He didn't try to stand but pitched himself forward in a kind of mad scramble. The officer of the law put his size-thirteen Timberland in Ig's ass and shoved, and Ig went down on his chin. He slid on his face across the varnished pine floor. His shoulder batted the oar that was leaned against the wall and it fell over on top of him.

Ig rolled, grabbing blindly at the oar, trying to get it off him so he could stand up. Eric Hannity came at him, raising the club again. His eyes were blind and his face was blank, the way a face looked when someone was under the influence of the horns. The horns were good at making people do terrible things, and Ig understood they were an invitation now to Eric to do his worst.

He moved without thinking, holding the oar up in both hands, almost like an offering. His eyes focused on something written across the handle: *To Ig, from your best pal, Lee Tourneau – here's something for the next time you're up the creek.*

Eric came down with the club. It snapped the oar in two, at the narrowest point on the handle, and the paddle flipped into the air and swatted him across the face. He grunted and took an off-balance step back. Ig threw the knotty handle at his head. It struck him above the right eye and bounced off, bought enough time for Ig to push himself up off his elbows and onto his feet.

Ig wasn't ready for Eric to recover as quickly as he did, but he was at Ig again, as soon as he was up, coming around with the club. Ig jumped back. The head of the club brushed so close it caught the fabric of his T-shirt and tore it. It kept going around and hit the screen of the television. The glass spider-webbed, and there was a loud crack and a white snap of light somewhere inside the monitor.

Ig had backed right up into the coffee table and for an instant he was dangerously close to toppling over it. But he steadied himself while Hannity twisted the club free from the caved-in television screen. Ig turned, stepped onto the coffee table, across to the couch, and over the back, putting it between himself and Eric. In two more steps, Ig was in the kitchen.

He turned. Eric Hannity stared in at him by way of the pass-through window. Ig crouched, breathing hard, a stitch in his side. There were two ways out of the kitchen – he could go left or he could go right – but either way would dump him back into the living room with Eric, and he'd have to get by him to reach the stairwell.

'I didn't come here to kill you, Ig,' Eric Hannity said. 'I really just wanted to knock some sense into you. Make an impression on you, learn you to stay the fuck away from Lee Tourneau. But it's a goddamn thing. I can't stop thinking that I ought to smash your lunatic skull in like you did to Merrin Williams. I don't think someone with horns coming out of their head ought to be allowed to live. I think it'd be a fucking service to the state of New Hampshire to kill you.'

The horns. It was the horns working on him.

'I forbid you to hurt me,' Ig said, trying to bend Eric Hannity to his will, putting all the concentration and force behind his horns that he could muster. They throbbed, but painfully, without any of the usual thrill. They didn't work that way. They wouldn't play that song, wouldn't discourage sin, no matter how much Ig's life depended on it.

'You forbid shit,' Eric Hannity said.

Ig stared at him through the pass-through window, the blood rushing in him, making a dull roar in his ears like water coming to the boil. Water coming to the boil. Ig looked back over his shoulder at the pot on the stovetop. The eggs floated, while bubbles raced up and around them.

'I want to kill you and cut those fucking things off,' Eric said. 'Or maybe cut them off and *then* kill you. I bet you have a kitchen knife that's big enough. No one will know I did it. After what you did to Merrin Williams, there's probably a hundred people in this town who want to see you dead. I'd be a hero, even if no one but me knows it. I'd be someone my dad was proud of.'

'Yes,' Ig said, pushing his will behind the horns again. 'Come and get me. You know you want to do it. Don't wait, do it, do it *now*.'

It was music to Hannity's ears, and he lunged, not going

around the island but coming straight at the pass-through window, his upper lip drawing back to show his teeth, bared in what was either a grimace of fury or a terrible grin. He put a hand on the counter and went up and head first through the window, and Ig took the pot by the handle and flung it.

Hannity was fast, got his free hand up to protect his face as half a gallon of scalding water hit him, dousing his arm, spraying past to spatter his big bald head. He screamed and pitched to the kitchen floor, and Ig was already moving, rushing for the door. Hannity still had time to get up and throw the club at him. It hit a lamp on an end-table, and the lamp exploded. By then Ig was in the stairwell, flying down the steps, taking them five at a time, as if he had not grown horns but wings.

27

Somewhere south of town, he pulled over to the side of the road and got out to stand on the embankment, holding himself and waiting for the shakes to pass.

The tremors came in furious bursts, racking his limbs, but the longer he stood there, the longer between fits. After a while they had passed completely, leaving him weak and dizzy. He felt as light as a maple leaf – and as likely to be sent spinning by the next stiff breeze. The locusts droned, a sci-fi sound: alien death ray.

So he was right, had read the situation correctly. Lee was in some way beyond the reach of the horns. Lee had not forgotten seeing Ig yesterday – as others had forgotten – knew that Ig was a threat to him. He would be looking to get at Ig before Ig found a way to get at him. Ig needed a plan, which was bad news; so far he hadn't even come up with a workable plan for breakfast, he was lightheaded with hunger.

He got back into the car and sat with his hands on the steering wheel, trying to decide where to go now. It came to him, almost randomly, that today was his grandmother's eightieth birthday and that she was lucky to see it. His next thought was that it was already midday, and his entire family would be at the hospital to sing 'Happy Birthday' and eat cake at her bedside, which meant that Mama's fridge would be undefended. Home was the one place you could always count on for a meal when there was nowhere else to go – wasn't that some kind of saying?

Of course, visiting hours might be later in the day, he thought, already turning the car back onto the road. There was no guarantee the house would be empty. But would it matter if his family was home? He could walk right past them and they would forget seeing him the moment he left the room. Which raised a good question: would Eric Hannity forget what had just happened in Glenna's apartment? After Ig had boiled his head? Ig didn't know.

He didn't know if he really could walk right past his family either. He *knew* he couldn't walk right past Terry. He needed to deal with Lee Tourneau, yes, but he needed to see to Terry as well. It would be a mistake to leave him out of it, let him slide away back to his life in LA. The notion of Terry returning to LA to play his razzy little show tunes on *Hothouse* and wink at movie stars appalled Ig and filled him with an inspiring hate. Fucking Terry had a few things to answer for. Wouldn't it be something to find him home alone? That would be too much to hope for. That would be the luck of the devil.

Ig considered parking on the fire road a quarter of a mile away and hiking around to the back of the house, scaling the wall, sneaking in, but then said fuck it and steered the Gremlin right up the drive. It was too hot for stealth, and he was too hungry.

Terry's rent-a-Mercedes was the only car in the driveway.

Ig pulled up alongside it and sat with the engine off, listening. A cloud of glittering dust had chased him up the hill and roiled around the Gremlin. He considered the house and the hot, drowsing stillness of the early afternoon. Perhaps Terry had left his car and gone to the hospital with his parents. That was the most likely thing, only Ig didn't believe it, knew he was in there.

Ig made no effort to be quiet. In fact, when he got out of

the car, he slammed the door of the Gremlin and then hesitated, watching the house. He thought he would see movement on the second floor, Terry twitching aside a curtain to look out, see who was there. But he observed no sign of anyone alive inside.

He let himself in. The TV was off in the media room, the computer shut down in his mother's office. In the kitchen, stainless-steel appliances hushed efficiently. Ig pulled a stool up, opened the door and ate straight from the refrigerator. He drank half a carton of cold milk in eight hard swallows and then waited out the inevitable dairy headache, a sharp rush of pain behind the horns and a momentary darkening of his vision. When the headache subsided and he could see clearly again, he discovered a platter of devilled eggs under Saran Wrap. His mother had probably made them up for Vera's birthday, but she wasn't going to need them. Ig assumed that Vera was having something nutritious through a tube this afternoon. He ate them all, stuffing them into his mouth with his fingers, one after the other. He was sure they were 666 times better than the boiled eggs he'd been making for himself at Glenna's.

He was turning the plate in his hands like a steering wheel and running his tongue over it when he thought he heard a muttering male voice somewhere above. He froze, listening intently. After a bit he heard the voice again. He set the plate in the sink and took a kitchen knife from the magnetic strip on the wall, the biggest he could find. It came loose with a soft musical chime of steel against steel. He wasn't sure what he planned to do with it, only that he felt better holding it. After what had happened in his apartment, he thought it was a mistake to go anywhere unarmed. He climbed the stairs. His brother's old room was at the far end of the long second-floor gallery.

Ig held up in the partly open door with the knife. It had been made over into a guest room a few years earlier and was as coolly impersonal as a room at the Ramada. His brother slept on his back, a hand flung over his eyes. He made a muttering sound of disgust, and smacked his lips. Ig's gaze swept the night table, and he saw a box of Benadryl. Ig had got the asthma, while his brother was allergic to everything: bees, peanuts, pollen, cat hair, New Hampshire, anonymity. The muttering and the mumbling – that was the allergy medication, which always put Terry into a heavy, though curiously restless, sleep. He made thoughtful humming sounds, as if coming to grave but important conclusions.

Ig crept to the bedside and sat on the night table, holding the knife. Without any heat or rage in him at all he considered sinking it into Terry's chest. He could conceptualise the act quite clearly, how he would put a knee on him first to pin him to the bed, find a space between two ribs, and push the knife in with both hands while Terry struggled up towards consciousness.

He wasn't going to kill Terry. Couldn't. Ig doubted he could even stab Lee Tourneau to death while he slept.

'Keith Richards,' Terry said quite clearly, and Ig was so surprised he jumped lightly to his feet. 'Love the fuckin' show.'

Ig studied him, waited for him to lift his arm away from his eyes and sit up, blinking blearily, but he wasn't awake, just talking in his sleep. Talking about Hollywood, about his fucking job, rubbing elbows with famous rock stars, getting big ratings, nailing models. Vera was in the hospital, Ig had gone missing, and Terry was dreaming about the good times in the land of *Hothouse*. For a moment Ig was breathless with hate, his lungs struggling to fill with oxygen. Terry undoubtedly had a flight back to the West Coast tomorrow; he hated Bumpkinville, never stayed a minute longer than necessary, even before Merrin died. Ig saw no reason to let him go back with all his fingers. Terry was so out of it that Ig could take his right hand, the trumpet hand, put it on the nightstand and remove the fingers with one whack, all before he woke. If Ig had lost his great love, Terry could get by without his. Maybe he could learn to play the fucking kazoo.

'I hate you, you selfish motherfucker,' Ig whispered, and took his brother's wrist to draw it away from his eyes, and in that moment—

Terry twitches awake and glances blearily around and doesn't know where he is. An unfamiliar car, on a road he doesn't recognise, rain coming down so hard the wipers can't keep up, the night world beyond a blur of storm-lashed trees and boiling black sky. He scrubs his face with one hand, trying to clear his head, and looks over and up, for some reason expecting to see his little brother sitting beside him, but instead there's Lee Tourneau, steering them into darkness.

The rest of the night begins to come back to him, facts falling into place, in no particular order, like chips dropping through the pins in a game of Plinko. He has something in his left hand – a pinched-out joint, and not some little twist of grass either, but a thick blunt of Tennessee Valley weed, the size of his thumb. Tonight he has been to two bars and a bonfire on the sandbar under the Old Fair Road Bridge, making the rounds with Lee. He has smoked too much and drunk too much and knows he will repent of it in the morning. In the morning he has to drive Ig to the airport, because little brother has a flight to catch for Merrie Olde England, God save the queen. The morning is already only a few hours away. Terry is currently in no shape to drive anyone, and when he closes his eyes, it feels as if Lee's Cadillac is sliding to the left, like a pat of butter greasing its way across a pan tipped on its side. It is this motion-sick sensation that woke him from his doze.

He sits up, forcing himself to concentrate on their surroundings. It looks as if they are on the meandering country highway that circumscribes the town, making a three-quarter crescent along Gideon's outer limits, but that doesn't make any sense – there's nothing out here except the old foundry and The Pit, and they wouldn't have a reason to go either place. After they left the sandbar, Terry had assumed that Lee was taking him home, and he was glad of it. At the thought of his own bed, of crisp white sheets and his puffy down comforter, he had gone almost shivery with pleasure. The best thing about being home is waking up in his old room, in his old bed, with the smell of coffee brewing downstairs and sunlight showing around the shades, the whole bright day waiting for him to step into it. The rest of Gideon, though, Terry is just as glad to have left behind.

Tonight is a case in point, a perfect illustration of what he hasn't *been missing. Terry spent an hour at the bonfire without feeling in any way a part of it, might as well have been watching from behind glass – the pickup trucks parked on the embankment, the drunken friends wrestling in the shallows while their girls whooped it up, fucking Judas Coyne on the boombox, a guy whose idea of musical complexity is a song with four power chords instead of three. Life among the rednecks. When the thunder began to roll overhead and the first hot, fat drops of rain began to fall, Terry counted it a lucky break. Terry doesn't know how his father has lived here for twenty years. Terry can barely get through seventy-two hours of the place.*

His primary coping mechanism is currently cupped in his left hand, and even knowing he's already past his limit, a part of him itches to light up and have another toke. He would, too, if it were anyone but Lee Tourneau sitting next to him. Not that Lee would complain or give him so much as a dirty look, but Lee is an aide to a War on Drugs congressman, a Super-Christian Family Values man, and it would be his ass if he got pulled over in a car filled with ganja smoke.

Lee had come by the house around six-thirty to say good-bye to Ig. He stuck around to play Texas Hold 'Em with Lee and Ig and Terry and Derrick Perrish, and Ig won every hand, took them all for three hundred bucks. 'There,' Terry said, throwing a fistful of twenties at his younger brother. 'When you and Merrin are having your post-coital bottle of champagne, think fondly of us. We paid for it.' Ig had laughed and looked delighted with himself, and embarrassed, and got up. He had kissed his father and then he had kissed Terry, too, on the side of the head, an unexpected gesture that caused Terry to twitch in surprise. 'Keep your tongue out of my ear,' Terry said, and Ig laughed again and was gone.

'And what are you doing with the rest of your evening?' Lee had asked as Ig departed, and Terry said, 'I dunno – I was going to see if Family Guy *was on. What about you? Anything happening around town?' Two hours later they were at the sandbar and a friend from high school whose name Terry couldn't exactly remember was handing him a joint.*

They had gone out, ostensibly, to have some drinks and say hello to the old crowd, but there on the sandbar, standing back from the bonfire, Lee told Terry that the congressman loved the show and wanted to meet him sometime. Terry took it in his stride, tipped the neck of his beer bottle to Lee, and said definitely, they ought to make it happen one of these days. He had thought it was possible Lee would work his way around to something along those lines and does not hold it against him. Lee has a job to do, same as anyone else, same as Terry. And Lee's job involves doing a lot of good; Terry knows about his work with Habitat for Humanity, knows Lee gives time every summer to work with poor and disadvantaged urban kids at Camp Galilee, Ig right at his side. Being around Lee and Ig has, for years, made Terry feel a little guilty. He never wanted to save the world himself. The only thing Terry ever wanted was for someone to pay him for goofing off with his horn. Well, that and maybe a girl who likes to party – not an LA model, not someone hung up on her cell phone and her car. Just someone fun and real and a little dirty in the sack. Someone East Coast, with working-class jeans and a few CDs by Foreigner. He's got the sweet gig, so he's halfway to happiness anyway.

'Fuck we doing out here?' Terry asks now, staring into the rain. 'Thought we were calling it a night.'

Lee says, 'I thought you called it a night about five minutes ago.

I'm pretty sure I heard you snoring. I can't wait to tell people that the Terry Perrish drooled all over my front seat. That'll impress the honeys. It's like my own little piece of TV history.'

Terry opens his mouth for a comeback — he will clear more than two million dollars this year, partly on the strength of a sublime gift for verbally cutting other wiseasses down — and finds he has nothing to say, is a perfectly empty head. He shows Lee Tourneau his middle finger instead.

'You think Ig and Merrin are still at The Pit?' Terry asks. The place will be coming up on the right at any moment.

'We'll see,' Lee says. 'Be there in another minute.'

'Are you screwing with me? We don't want to go see them. I know they don't want to see us. It's their last night.'

Lee gives Terry a surprised, curious look out of the corner of his good eye. 'How do you know? Did she tell you?'

'Tell me what?'

'That she's breaking up with him. This is their last night.'

A statement that instantly jolts Terry out of his baked, thoughtless state, as startling as sitting down on a tack.

'The fuck you mean?'

'She thinks they got involved too young. She wants to see other guys.'

Terry marvels at the news, recoils from it, is baffled by it. He thoughtlessly lifts the joint cupped in his hand to his lips, then remembers it isn't lit.

'You really didn't know?' Lee asks.

'I just meant it's their last night before Ig goes to England.'

'Oh.'

Terry stares blankly into the rain, which is coming down so hard the wipers can't keep up, so it's like being in a car wash, the way the water pours down the glass. He cannot imagine Ig without Merrin, cannot imagine who that person would be. Dazed by the news, it takes an interminable time before the obvious question occurs to him.

'How do you know all this?'

'She talked to me about it,' Lee says. 'She's scared to hurt him. I've been in Boston a lot this summer, doing things for the congressman, and she's there, too, so we get together and talk sometimes. I've probably seen her more than Ig has over the last month.'

Terry looks out at the underwater world, sees a reddish haze of light approaching on the right. They're almost there.

'So why would you want to come by here now?'

'She said she'd call me if she needed a ride home,' Lee says. 'And she hasn't called.'

'So she doesn't need you, then.'

'But she might not call if she's upset. I just want to see if Ig's car is still there or not. Parking's up front. We don't even need to pull in.'

Terry doesn't follow Lee, can't figure out why he would want to drive by and look for Ig's car. He also can't imagine Merrin wanting to be around either of them if things have ended badly.

But Lee is already slowing, turning his head to look past Terry at the parking lot on the right.

'I don't . . .' Lee says, talking to himself now. 'It's not . . . I don't think she would've gone home with him . . . .' Sounding worried, almost.

Terry is the one who sees her, Merrin standing in the rain out by the side of the road, under a walnut with a great spreading crown. 'There. Lee, right there.'

She seems to spot them at the same moment and steps out from beneath the tree, one arm raised. With the water coming down the passenger-side window, Terry sees her as through carnival glass, an impressionistic painting of a girl with copper-wire hair, holding aloft what at first seems to be a white votive candle. As they grind to a stop and she moves to the side of the car, Terry sees she is merely holding up a finger to get their attention as she breaks from cover and runs barefoot through the rain, holding her black heels in one hand.

The Caddy is a two-door, and even before Lee tells him to get in *back, Terry is unbuckling his belt and turning to loft himself over the front seat. As he is about to pitch into the rear, Lee thuds an elbow into his ass, tipping him off-balance, and instead of landing in the seat, Terry dives into the footwell. For God knows what reason, there's a metal toolbox on the floor and Terry catches it on the temple, flinches at a sharp stab of pain. He pulls himself up onto the seat and pushes the ball of his hand hard against his banged-up head. It was a mistake to go leaping around, has set off the strongest wave of motion sickness yet, so it feels as if the whole car has been picked up off the ground by a giant who is shaking it slowly, like a cup with dice in it. Terry shuts his eyes, fighting to suppress that sudden nauseating sensation of reckless motion.*

By the time things have settled enough for him to risk looking around, Merrin is in the car and Lee Tourneau is turned sideways to face her. Terry looks at his palm and sees a bright drop of blood. He scraped himself good, although that initial sharp pain has already mostly subsided, leaving behind a dull ache. He wipes the blood on his leg and looks up.

It is easy to see that Merrin has only just stopped crying. She is pale and shaking, like someone either recovering from or beginning to succumb to illness, and her first attempt at a smile is a miserable, painful thing to look at.

'Thanks for picking me up,' she says. 'You just saved my life.'

'Where's Ig?' Terry asks.

Merrin glances back at him but has trouble making eye contact, and Terry is immediately sorry he asked.

'I d–don't know. He left.'

Lee says, 'You told him?'

Merrin's chin wrinkles, and she turns to face forward. She looks out the window at The Pit and doesn't reply.

'How'd he take it?' Lee asks.

Terry can see her face reflected in the glass, can see her biting her lips and struggling not to cry. Her answer is, 'Can we just go?'

Lee nods and puts on his blinker, then pulls a U-ie in the rain.

Terry wants to touch her shoulder, wants to reassure her in some way, let her know that whatever happened in The Pit, he doesn't hate her or hold it against her. But Terry doesn't touch her, won't touch her, never touches her. In a decade of knowing her, he has kept her at a friendly distance, even in his imagination, has never once considered allowing her into his sexual fantasies. There would be no harm in such a thing, yet he senses he would be placing something at risk all the same. What he would be placing at risk, he cannot say. To Terry the word 'soul' first refers to a kind of music.

Instead he says, 'Hey, girl, you want my jacket?' Because she is shivering helplessly and steadily in her wet clothes.

For the first time, Lee seems to notice the way she's trembling as well – which is funny, since he keeps shooting her glances, looking at her as much as he's looking at the road – and turns down the air-conditioner.

'S-s'all right,' she says, but Terry already has his coat off and is handing it forward. She spreads it across her legs. 'Thank you, Terry,' she says in a small voice, and then, 'You m-must think—'

'I don't think anything,' Terry says. 'So relax.'

'Ig—'

'I'm sure Ig is fine. Don't you worry yourself.'

She gives him a pained, grateful smile and then leans back towards him and says, 'Are you all right?' She reaches out to lightly touch his brow, where he went face first into Lee's toolbox. He flinches almost instinctively from her touch. She draws her fingers back, blood on the tips of them, looks at her hand, then back at him. 'You ought to have some g-gauze for that.'

'It's fine. No worries,' Terry says.

She nods and turns away, and immediately the smile is gone and her eyes come unfocused, staring at nothing anyone else can see. She is folding something in her hands, over and over, and unfolding it, and then starting up again. A tie, Ig's tie. This is somehow worse than seeing her in tears, and Terry has to look away. Being stoned no longer feels good in the slightest. He would like to lie motionless somewhere and close his eyes for a few minutes. Nap some and wake up fresh and himself again. The night has turned rancid on him, very quickly, and he wants someone to blame, someone to be irritated with. He settles on Ig.

It irritates him that Ig would peel off, leave her standing in the rain, an act so immature it's laughable. Laughable but not surprising. Merrin has been a lover, a comfort blanket, a guidance counsellor, a defensive barrier against the world, and a best friend to Ig. Sometimes it seems they have been married since Ig was fifteen. But for all that, it began as and always was a high-school relationship. Terry is sure Ig has never even kissed another girl, let alone fucked one, and he has wished for a while now that his brother had more experience. Not because Terry doesn't want him to be with Merrin but because . . . well, because. *Because love requires context. Because first relationships are by their very nature immature. So Merrin wanted them both to have a chance to grow up. So what?*

Tomorrow morning, on the drive to Logan Airport, Terry will have Ig alone and a chance to set him straight about a couple of things. He will tell Ig that his ideas about Merrin, about their relationship — that it was meant to be, that she was more perfect than other girls, that their love was more perfect than other loves, that together they dealt in small miracles — was a suffocating trap. If Ig hated Merrin now, it was only because he had discovered she was a real person, with failings and needs and a desire to live in the world, not in Ig's daydreams. That she loved him enough to let him go, and he had to be willing to do the same, that if you loved someone, you could set them free, and — fuck, that was a Sting song.

'Merrin, are you all right?' *Lee asks. She is still shivering almost convulsively.*

'No. Y—yes. I— Lee, please pull over. Pull over here.' *These last three words said with an urgent clarity.*

The road to the old foundry is coming up on the right, quickly, too quickly to turn in, really, but Lee turns in anyway. Terry plants one hand on the back of Merrin's seat and bites down on a cry. The

239

passenger-side tyres catch soft gravel and fling it into the trees, leave a deep four-foot-long gouge.

Brush scrapes at the bumper. The Cadillac thumps and bangs in the ruts, still going too fast, the highway disappearing behind them. Up ahead is a chain stretched across the road. Lee brakes hard, the steering wheel shimmying in his hands, back end slewing. The car stops with the headlights touching the chain, actually stretching it across the grille. Merrin opens her door, sticks her head out, and retches. Once. Again. Fucking Ig; right now Terry hates him.

He's not feeling too high on Lee either, flinging the car around like that. They've definitely come to a stop, and yet a part of Terry feels as if they're still moving, still sliding to the side. If he had his joint on hand, he'd hurl it out the window – the thought of putting the thing in his mouth repulses him, would be like swallowing a live cockroach – only he doesn't know what he did with it, doesn't seem to be holding it anymore. He touches his scraped and tender temple again and winces.

Rain taps slowly on the windshield. Except it isn't rain, not anymore. Just water drops blowing from the branches above. Not five minutes before, the rain was coming down so hard that the drops bounced when they hit the road, but in the usual way of summer thundershowers the storm has blown away as quickly as it blew in.

Lee gets out and goes around the side of the car and crouches beside her. He murmurs something to her, his voice calm, reasonable. However she answers him, he doesn't like it. He repeats his offer, and this time her reply is audible, her tone unfriendly. 'No, Lee. I just want to go home and get into some dry things and be by myself.'

Lee stands up, walks around to the trunk, pops it, fishes something out of it. A gym bag.

'Got gym clothes. Shirt. Pants. They're dry and warm. Plus, there's no sick on them.'

She thanks Lee and climbs out into the humid, buggy, wet, blowing night, hangs Terry's sports coat over her shoulders. Merrin reaches for the bag, but for a moment Lee doesn't release it.

'You had to do it, you know. It was crazy, thinking that you could – that either *of you could—'*

'I just want to change, okay?'

Pulling the gym bag away from him and starting down the road, Merrin crosses through the headlights, her skirt swishing around her legs and her blouse rendered briefly transparent by the intense glare, Terry catches himself staring, forces himself to look away, and so sees Lee staring as well. He wonders, for the first time, if maybe good old Lee Tourneau is carrying a little bit of a torch for Merrin Williams – or at least a hard-on. Merrin continues down the road, walking at first in the tunnel of brightness carved out by the headlights, then stepping off the gravel and into darkness. It is the last time Terry will ever see her alive.

Lee stands by the open passenger door, staring after her, like he doesn't know whether to get back in the car or not. Terry wants to tell him to sit down but can't summon up the will or the energy. Terry stares after her himself for a short time, and then he can't hack it. He doesn't like the way the night seems to be breathing, *swelling and contracting. The headlights are catching one corner of the open field below the foundry, and he doesn't like the way the wet grass lashes at the darkness, in constant uneasy motion. He can hear it through the open door. It hisses, like the snake exhibit at the zoo. Also: he still has a faint but stomach-turning sensation of sideways motion, of sliding helplessly away towards someplace he doesn't want to go. The ache in his right temple isn't helping either. He picks up his feet and lies down on the back seat.*

That's better. The mottled brown upholstery is moving, too, like billows of slow-moving cream in a lightly stirred cup of coffee, but that's okay, a good thing to see when you're stoned, a safe thing. Not like wet grass swaying ecstatically in the night.

He needs something to think about, something soothing, needs a daydream to ease his queasy mind. Production is lining up guests for next season, the usual mix of what's happening and what happened, black and white, Mos Def and Def Leppard, the Eels and the Crowes

241

and every other animal in the pop-culture zoo, but what Terry is really excited about is Keith Richards, who was in the Viper Room with Johnny Depp a few months ago and told Terry he thought the show was fuckin' darlin' and said he'd be de-fuckin'-lighted to be on, anytime, all roit, just fuckin' ask already, and wot took you so fuckin' long? That'd be a hell of a thing, get Richards on, give him the whole last half hour. The execs at Fox hate when Terry dumps the usual format and turns the show into a concert – he has been told it sends half a million viewers right over to Letterman – but as far as Terry is concerned, the execs can suck Keith Richards' stringy, overworked cock.

In a while he begins to drift. Perrish the Thought is performing with Keith Richards in front of a festival crowd, maybe eighty thousand people, who have, for some reason, gathered at the old foundry. They're playing 'Sympathy for the Devil', and Terry has agreed to do the lead vocal because Mick is in London. Terry glides towards the mike and tells the leaping, ecstatic crowd that he is a man of wealth and taste, which is a line from the song but which is also true. Then Keith Richards lifts his Telecaster and plays the old devil blues. His ragged-ass, broken-bottle guitar solo is an unlikely lullaby, but good enough to ease Terry Perrish down into fitful sleep.

He wakes once, briefly, when they're back on the road, the Caddy rushing along a smooth ribbon of night, Lee behind the wheel and the passenger seat empty. Terry has his sport coat back, spread carefully across his legs and lap, something Merrin must've done when she returned to the car, a typically thoughtful gesture. Although. The coat is soaking wet and dirty and there's something heavy holding it in his lap, lying on top of it. Terry gropes for it, picks up a wet stone the size and shape of an ostrich egg, wiry strands of grass and muck on it. That stone means something – Merrin stuck it there for a reason – but Terry is too dazed and muzzy-headed to get the joke. He puts the rock on the floor. It's got sticky stuff on it, like snail guts, and Terry wipes his fingers on his shirt, straightens his sport coat across his thighs, and settles back down.

His left temple is still throbbing where he banged it diving in back – feels sore and raw – and when he presses the back of his left hand to it, he sees he is bleeding again.

'Did Merrin get off okay?' Terry asks.

'What?' Lee says.

'Merrin? Did we take care of her?'

Lee drives for a while without reply. Then he says, 'Yes. Yes we did.'

Terry nods, satisfied, and says, 'She's a good kid. I hope her and Ig work it out.'

Lee just drives.

Terry feels himself sliding back into his dreams of being onstage with Keith Richards before an ecstatic crowd that is performing for him as much as he is performing for them. But then, tottering on the very edge of consciousness, he hears himself ask a question he didn't know was even on his mind.

'What's with the rock?'

Lee says, 'Evidence.'

Terry nods to himself – this seems a reasonable answer – and says, 'Good. Let's stay out of jail if we can.'

Lee laughs, a harsh, wet, coughlike sound – cat with a hairball in its throat – and it comes to Terry that he has never heard the guy laugh before and doesn't much like it. Then Terry is gone, settling himself back into unconsciousness. This time, though, there are no dreams waiting for him, and he frowns in his sleep, wearing the look of a man trying to work out a nagging clue in a crossword puzzle, something he should know the answer to.

Sometime later he opens his eyes and realises the car isn't moving. The Caddy has, in fact, been parked for a while. He has no idea how he can know this, only that he does.

The light is different. It isn't morning yet, but the night is in retreat, has already scooped up most of its stars and put them away.

Fat, pale, mountainous clouds, the shreds of last night's thunder-storm, drift vividly against a backdrop of darkness. Terry has a good view of the sky, staring up through one of the side windows. He can smell dawn, a fragrance of rain-saturated grass and warming earth. When he sits up, he sees that Lee has left the driver's door ajar.

He reaches on the floor for his sport coat. It must be down there somewhere; he assumes it slipped off his lap while he was asleep. There's the toolbox, but no coat. The driver's seat is folded forward, and Terry climbs out.

His spine cracks as he puts his arms out to his sides and stretches his back, and then he goes still — arms reaching out into the night like a man nailed to an invisible cross.

Lee sits smoking on the steps of his mother's house. His house now, Terry remembers, Lee's mother is six weeks in the ground. Terry can't see Lee's face, only the orange coal of his Winston. For no reason Terry can put his finger on, the sight of Lee waiting for him there on the porch steps unsettles him.

'Some night,' Terry says.

'It isn't over yet.' Lee inhales, and the coal brightens, and for a moment Terry can see part of Lee's face, the bad part, the part with the dead eye in it. In the morning gloom, that eye is white and blind, a glass sphere filled with smoke. 'How's your head?'

Terry reaches up to touch the scrape on his temple, then drops his hand. 'Fine. No big deal.'

'I had an accident, too.'

'What accident? You okay?'

'I am. But Merrin isn't.'

'What do you mean?' Abruptly, Terry is aware of the clammy-sick hangover sweat on his body, a kind of unpleasant dewy sensation. He looks down at himself and sees black finger smears on his shirt, mud or something, with only a vague memory of wiping his hand on himself. When he looks back at Lee, he is suddenly afraid to hear what he has to say.

'It really was an accident,' Lee said. 'I didn't know how serious it was until it was too late to help her.'

Terry stares, waiting on the punchline. 'You're moving too fast, buddy. What happened?'

'That's what we have to figure out. You and me. That's what I want to talk about. We need to have our story straight, before they find her.'

Terry does the reasonable thing and laughs. Lee has a famously dry, flat sense of humour, and if the sun was up and Terry wasn't so dreadfully sick, he might appreciate it. Terry's right hand, however, doesn't think Lee is funny. Terry's right hand has, all on its own, begun to pat Terry's pockets, feeling for his cell phone.

Lee says softly, 'Terry. I know this is terrible. But I'm not kidding. We're in a real mess here. Neither of us is to blame – this is no one's fault – but we're in about the most awful trouble two people can be in. It was an accident, but they'll say we killed her.'

Terry wants to laugh again. Instead he says, 'Stop it.'

'I can't. You need to hear this.'

'She is not dead.'

Lee sucks at his cigarette, and the coal brightens, and the eye of pale smoke stares at Terry. 'She was drunk, and she came on to me. I guess it was her way of getting even with Ig. She had her clothes off, and she was all over me, and when I pushed her away – I didn't mean to. She fell over a root or something and landed on a rock. I walked away from her, and when I came back – just awful. I don't know if you'll believe this, but I'd rather take out my other eye than have ever caused her pain.'

Terry's next breath is a lungful not of oxygen but of terror; he inhales a chestful of it, as if it were a gas, an airborne toxin. There is a churning feeling in both stomach and head. There is a feeling of the ground tilting underfoot. He has to call someone. He has to find his phone. He has to get help; this is a situation that calls for calm authorities with experience handling emergencies. He turns to the car, leans into the back seat looking for his sport coat. His cell phone *must be in his coat. But the coat isn't on the floor where he thought it would be. It isn't in the front seat either.*

Lee's hand on the nape of his neck causes Terry to jump upright, crying out, a soft sobbing shout, and to pull away from him.

'Terry,' Lee says, 'we need to figure out what we're going to say.'

'There's nothing to figure out. I need my phone.'

'You can use the one in the house if you want.'

Terry stiff-arms Lee, pushing him aside, and marches towards the porch. Lee pitches his cigarette and follows, in no particular hurry.

'You want to call the cops, I won't stop you. I'll go with you to meet them at the foundry,' Lee says, 'show them where to find her. But you better know what I'm going to tell them before you pick up the phone, Terry.'

Terry takes the steps in two bounding leaps, crosses the porch, jerks open the screen door and pushes the front door in. He takes a stumbling step into a dark front hall. If there's a phone here, he can't see it in all the shadows. The kitchen is through to the left.

'We were all so drunk,' Lee says. 'We were drunk, and you were high. She was the worst, though. That's what I'll tell them first. She was coming on to the both of us from the moment she got in the car. Ig called her a whore, and she was determined to prove him right.'

Terry is only half-listening. He moves swiftly through a small formal dining room, barking his knee on a straight-backed chair, stumbling, then going on into the kitchen. Lee comes after him, his voice unbearably calm.

'She told us to pull over so she could change out of her wet clothes, and then she put on a show, standing in the headlights. The whole time you didn't say anything, just watching her, listening to her talk about how Iggy had a few things coming to him for the way he treated her. She made out with me awhile, and then she went to work on you. She was so drunk she couldn't see how angry you were. In the middle of giving you her little lap dance, she started talking about all the money she could get, selling the story of Terry Perrish's

246

private gang-bang to the tabloids. That it would be worth doing to get even with Ig, just to see his face. That was when you hit her. You hit her before I knew what was happening.'

Terry is in the kitchen, at the counter, his hand on the beige phone, but he doesn't pick it up. For the first time, he turns his head and looks back at tall, wiry Lee with his crown of golden-white hair, and his terrible, mysterious white eye. Terry puts a hand in the centre of Lee's chest and shoves him hard enough to slam him back into the wall. The windows rattle. Lee doesn't look too upset.

'No one's going to believe that horseshit.'

'Who knows what they'll believe?' Lee Tourneau says. 'It's your fingerprints on the rock.'

Terry pulls Lee by the shirt, away from the wall, and smashes him into it again, pins him there with his right hand. A spoon falls from the counter, strikes the floor, rings like a chime. Lee regards him, unperturbed.

'You dropped that big fat joint you were smoking right next to the body. And she's the one gave you that scrape,' Lee says. 'Fighting you. After she was dead, you cleaned yourself off with her underwear. It's your blood all over her panties.'

'What the fuck are you talking about?' Terry asks. The word 'panties' also seems to ring in the air, just like the spoon.

'The scrape on your temple. I cleaned it with her underwear, while you were passed out. I need you to understand the situation, Terry. You're in this thing as much as me. Maybe more.'

Terry brings the left hand back, squeezing his fingers into a fist, then catches himself. There is a kind of eagerness in Lee's face, a bright-eyed anticipation, his breathing shallow and fast. Terry doesn't hit him.

'What are you waiting for?' Lee asks. 'Do it.'

Terry has never hit another man in anger in his life; he is thirty years old and has never thrown a punch. He has never even been in a school-yard brawl. Everyone in school liked him.

'If you hurt me in any way at all, I'll call the police myself. That'll

247

make things look even better for me. I can say I tried to defend her.'

Terry takes an unsteady step back from him and lowers his hand. 'I'm going. You ought to get yourself a lawyer. I know I'm going to be talking to mine inside of twenty minutes. Where's my coat?'

'With the stone. And her panties. In a safe place. Not here. I stopped somewhere on the way home. You told me to collect the evidence and get rid of it, but I didn't get rid of it—'

'Shut the fuck up—'

'—because I thought you might try to put it all on me. Go ahead, Terry. Call them. But I promise *if you lay this shit on me, I'll drag you down with me. Up to you. You just got* Hothouse. *You're going back to LA in two days to hang with movie stars and underwear models. But go ahead and do the right thing. Satisfy your conscience. Just remember, no one will believe you, not even your own brother, who will hate you forever for killing his best girl when you were drunk and stoned. He might not believe it at first, but give him time. You'll have twenty years in jail to pat yourself on the back for your upstanding morals. For the love of God, Terry. She's been dead for four hours already. If you wanted to look clean, you should've reported it while the body was still warm. Now it's bound to look like you at least thought about hiding it.'*

'I'll kill you,' Terry whispered.

'Sure,' Lee said. 'Okay. Then you've got two bodies to explain. Knock yourself out.'

Terry turns away, stares desperately at the phone on the counter, feeling like if he doesn't pick it up and call someone in the next few moments, every good thing in his life will be taken away from him. And yet he can't seem to lift his arm. He is like a castaway on a desert island, watching an airplane glitter in the sky forty thousand feet overhead, with no way to signal it and his last chance at rescue sailing away.

'Or,' Lee says, 'the other way it could've happened, if it wasn't you and it wasn't me, is she was killed by a random stranger. It happens all the time. It's like every Dateline *ever. No one saw us*

pick her up. No one saw us turn in to the foundry. As far as the world knows, you and I drove back to my place after the bonfire and played cards and passed out in front of the two a.m. SportsCenter. *My house is on the exact opposite side of town from The Pit. There's no reason we would've gone out there.'*

Terry's chest is tight, and his breath is short, and he thinks, randomly, that this must be how Ig feels when he's in the grip of one of his asthma attacks. Funny how he can't get his arm up to reach for the phone.

'There. I've said my piece. Basically, it comes down to this: you can live life as a cripple or a coward. What happens now is up to you. Trust me, though. Cowards have more fun.'

Terry doesn't move, doesn't reply, and can't look at Lee. His pulse trip-traps *in his wrist.*

'Tell you what,' Lee says, speaking in a tone of soothing reason. 'If you took a drug test right now, you'd fail. You don't want to go to the cops like this. You've had three hours' sleep, tops, and you aren't thinking clear. She's been dead all night, Terry. Why don't you give yourself the morning to think about this thing? They might not find her for days. Don't rush into anything you can't take back. Wait until you're sure you know what you want to do.'

This is a dreadful thing to hear – They might not find her for days *– a statement that brings to mind a vivid image of Merrin lying amid ferns and wet grass, with rainwater in her eyes and a beetle crawling through her hair. This is followed by the memory of Merrin in the passenger seat, shivering in her wet clothes, looking back at him with shy, unhappy eyes.* Thanks for picking me up. You just saved my life.

'I want to go home,' Terry says. He means it to sound belligerent, hard-assed, righteous, but instead it comes out in a cracked whisper.

'Sure,' Lee says. 'I'll drive you. But let me get you one of my shirts before we go. You've got her blood all over that one.' He gestures towards the filth Terry rubbed off on the front of his shirt, which

only now, in the pearly, opalescent light of dawn, can be identified as dried blood.

Ig saw it all in a touch, just as if he had sat in the car with them, the whole way to the old foundry – saw it all, and more besides. He saw the desperate and pleading conversation Terry had with Lee, thirty hours later, in Lee's kitchen. It was a day of impossible sunshine and unseasonably cool weather; kids shouted in the street, some teenagers splashed in a swimming pool next door. It was almost too jarring, trying to match the bright normalcy of the morning with the idea that Ig was locked up and Merrin was in a refrigerated cabinet in a morgue somewhere. Lee stood leaning against a kitchen counter, watching impassively, while Terry leaped from thought to thought and emotion to emotion, his voice sometimes strangled with rage, sometimes with misery. Lee waited for him to spend his energy, then said, *They're going to let your brother go. Be cool. The forensic evidence won't match, and they'll have to publicly clear him.* He was passing a golden pear from hand to hand.

What forensic evidence?

Shoe prints, Lee said. *Tyre prints. Who knows what else? Blood, I guess. She might've scratched me. My blood won't match with Ig, and there's no reason they'd ever test me. Or at least you better hope they don't test me. You wait. They'll let him go inside of eight hours, and he'll be clear by the end of the week. You just need to stay quiet a while longer, and you and him will both be out of this thing.*

They're saying she was raped, Terry said. *You didn't tell me you raped her.*

I didn't. It's only rape if she doesn't want you to do it, Lee said, and he lifted the pear and took a wet bite.

Worse than that was the glimpse Ig had of what Terry had attempted to do five months later, sitting in his garage, in the driver's seat of his Viper, the windows down and the garage door shut and the engine running. Terry was on the twitching edge of unconsciousness, exhaust boiling up around him, when the garage door rumbled open behind him. His housekeeper had never once in her life shown up on a Saturday morning, but there she was, gaping at Terry through the driver's-side window, clutching his dry cleaning to her chest. She was a fifty-year-old Mexican immigrant who understood English well enough, but it was unlikely she could read the part of the folded note sticking out of Terry's shirt pocket:

TO WHOM IT MAY CONCERN,

Last year my brother, Ignatius Perrish, was taken into custody under suspicion of assaulting and murdering Merrin Williams, his closest friend. HE IS INNOCENT OF ALL CHARGES. Merrin, who was my friend, too, was assaulted and murdered by Lee Tourneau. I know because I was present, and although I did not assist him in the crime, I am complicit in covering it up, and I cannot live with myself another—

But Ig didn't get any further than that, dropped Terry's hand, reacting as if he'd been zapped by static electricity. Terry's eyes opened, his pupils huge in the darkness.

'Mom?' Terry said in a doped, heavy voice. It was dark in the room, dark enough so Ig doubted he could make out anything more than the vague shape of him standing there. Ig held his hand behind his back, squeezing the hilt of the knife.

Ig opened his mouth to say something; he meant to tell Terry to go back to sleep, which was the most absurd thing he could say, except for any other thing. But as he spoke, he felt a throb of blood surge up into the horns, and the voice that came from his mouth was not his own, but his mother's. Nor was it an imitation, a conscious act of mimicry. It was her. '*Go back to sleep, Terry,*' she said.

Ig was so surprised at himself he stepped back and thumped a hip into the nightstand. A glass of water clashed softly against the lamp. Terry shut his eyes again but began to stir feebly, as if in another moment he might sit up.

'Mom,' he said, 'what time is it?'

Ig stared down at his brother, not wondering how he'd done it – how he had summoned Lydia's voice – but only if he could do it again. He already knew how he'd done it. The devil could, of course, speak in the voice of loved ones, telling them the things they most wanted to hear. The gift of tongues ... the devil's favourite trick.

'*Shh*,' Ig said, and the horns were filled with pressure, and his voice was the voice of Lydia Perrish. It was easy – he didn't even have to think about it. '*Shh, dear. You don't need to do anything. You don't need to get up. Rest. Take care of yourself.*'

Terry sighed and rolled away from Ig, turning a shoulder to him.

Ig had been prepared for anything except to feel sympathy for Terry. There was no cheapening what Merrin had been put through, but in a sense – in a sense Ig had lost his brother that night, too.

He crouched in the darkness, looking at Terry lying on his side under the sheets, and thought for a spell, considering this newest manifestation of his powers. Finally he opened his mouth, and Lydia said, '*You should go home tomorrow. Get back to your life, dear. You've got rehearsals. You've got things you need to do. Don't you worry about Grandma. Grandma is going to be fine.*'

'What about Ig?' Terry asked. He spoke in a low murmur, with his back turned. 'Shouldn't I stay until we know where Ig went? I'm worried.'

'*Maybe he needs to be alone right now,*' Ig said in his mother's voice. '*You know what time of year it is. I'm sure he's fine and would want you to take care of work. You need to think about yourself – for once. Straight back to LA tomorrow, Terry.*' Making it an order, pushing the weight of his willpower behind the horns so they tingled with delight.

'Straight back,' Terry said. 'Okay.'

Ig retreated, backing for the door, for daylight.

Terry spoke again, before Ig could go. 'Love you,' he said.

Ig held up in the door, his pulse tripping strangely in his throat, his breath short.

'*I love you, too, Terry*,' he said, and gently shut the door between them.

28

In the afternoon Ig drove up the highway to a small country grocery. He picked out some cheese and pepperoni, brown mustard, two loaves of bread, two bottles of red wine and a corkscrew.

The shopkeeper was an old man with a scholarly look, in granny glasses and a sweater that buttoned up the front. He slumped behind the counter with his chin on his fist, leafing through the *New York Review of Books*. He glanced at Ig without interest and began to ring up his purchases.

As he pressed the keys of the cash register, he confessed to Ig that his wife of forty years had Alzheimer's, and he had been thinking about luring her to the basement stairs and pushing her down them. He felt sure a broken neck would be ruled an accident. Wendy had loved him with her body, and written him letters every week while he was in the army, and given him two fine daughters, but he was tired of listening to her rave and washing her, and he wanted to go live with Sally, an old friend, in Boca Raton. When his wife died, he could collect an insurance payment of almost three-quarters of a million dollars, and then there would be golf and tennis and good meals with Sally for however many years he had left. He wanted to know what Ig thought about it. Ig said he thought he would burn in hell. The shopkeeper shrugged and said of course – that went without saying.

He spoke to Ig in Russian, and it was in this language that Ig gave his reply, although he didn't know Russian, had never studied it. Yet he was entirely unsurprised by his sudden, undeserved fluency. After speaking to Terry in their mother's voice, it seemed a small enough thing. Besides: the language of sin was universal, the original Esperanto.

Ig started away from the cash register, thinking how he'd fooled Terry, how something in him had been able to bring forth just exactly the voice Terry wanted to hear. He wondered at the limits of such a power, wondered how completely he could lead another mind astray. He stopped at the door and looked back, staring with interest at the shopkeeper, who sat behind the counter looking at his paper once again.

'Aren't you going to answer your phone?' Ig asked.

The shopkeeper lifted his head to stare at him, his eyebrows bunched together in puzzlement.

'It's ringing,' Ig said. The horns pounded with a feeling of pressure and weight, entirely pleasurable.

The shopkeeper frowned at the silent phone. He picked it up and put it to his ear – although even from across the room, Ig could hear the dial tone.

'*Robert, it's Sally,*' Ig said – but the voice that came from his lips was not his own. It was hoarse, deep, but unmistakably female, and with a Bronx twang; a voice entirely unfamiliar, and yet he was sure it was the one that belonged to Sally Whoever.

The shopkeeper screwed up his face in confusion and said to the empty line, 'Sally? We just talked a few hours ago. I thought you were trying to save on the long distance.'

The horns throbbed, in a state of sensual exhilaration.

'*I'll save money on long distance when I don't have to call you every day,*' Ig said in the voice of Sally-in-Boca Raton. '*When are you coming down here? This waiting is killing me.*'

The shopkeeper said, 'I can't. You know I can't. Do you

know what it would cost to put Wendy in a home? What would *we* live on?' Speaking to a dead line.

'*Who said we need to live like Rockefellers? I don't need oysters. Tuna salad will do. You want to wait until she dies, but what if I go first? Then where are we? I'm not a young woman, and you aren't a young man. Put her in a place where people will care for her, and then get on a plane and come down here so someone can care for you.*'

'I promised her I wouldn't put her in a home while she was alive.'

'*She isn't the person you made that promise to anymore, and I'm scared what you might do if you stay with her. Pick a sin we can both live with, is what I ask. Give me a call when you've got a ticket, and I'll come get you at the airport.*'

Ig broke the connection then, let go; the painful-sweet feeling of pressure drained from the horns. The shopkeeper drew the phone away from his ear and stared at it, lips parted slightly in confusion. The dial tone droned. Ig eased himself out the door. The shopkeeper didn't look up, had forgotten all about him.

Ig built a fire in the chimney, then opened the first bottle of wine and drank deeply, without waiting for it to breathe. The fumes filled his head, dizzying him, a sweet asphyxiation, loving hands around his throat. He felt he ought to be working on a plan, ought to have decided by now the proper way to deal with Lee Tourneau, but it was hard to think while staring into the fire. The ecstatic movement of the flames transfixed him. He marvelled at the whirl of sparks and the orange tumble of falling coals, marvelled at the bitter-harsh taste of the wine, which peeled away thought like paint stripper going to work on old paint. He tugged restlessly at his goatee, enjoying the feel of it, glad for it, felt that it made his thinning hair more acceptable. When Ig was a child, all his heroes had been bearded men: Jesus, Abraham Lincoln, Dan Haggerty.

'Beards,' he muttered. 'I am blessed in facial hair.'

He was on the second bottle of wine when he heard the fire whispering to him, suggesting plans and schemes, offering encouragement in a soft, hissing voice, putting forth theological arguments. Ig canted his head and listened to it, listened carefully, in a state of fascination. Sometimes he nodded in agreement. The voice of the fire said the most sensible things. Over the next hour, Ig learned a great deal.

After it was dark, he opened the hatch and found the teeming faithful gathered in the room beyond, waiting to hear The Word. Ig emerged from the chimney, and the crawling carpet of snakes – a thousand of them at least, lying on top of one another, braided together in mad tangles – cleared a path for him to the heap of bricks in the centre of the floor. He climbed to the top of the little hill and settled himself with his pitchfork and his second bottle of wine. From his perch upon the low mound, he ministered to them.

'It is a matter of faith that the soul must be guarded, lest it be ruined and consumed,' Ig told them. 'Christ himself forewarned his apostles to beware him who would destroy their souls in Hell. I advise you now that such a fate is a mathematical impossibility. The soul may not be destroyed. The soul goes on forever. Like the number pi, it is without cessation or conclusion. Like pi it is a constant. Pi is an irrational number, incapable of being made into a fraction, impossible to divide from itself. So, too, the soul is an irrational, indivisible equation that perfectly expresses one thing: you. The soul would be no good to the devil if it could be destroyed. And it is not lost when placed in Satan's care, as is so often said. He always knows exactly how to put his finger on it.'

A thick brown rope of snake dared to climb the pile of bricks. Ig felt it moving across his bare left foot but paid it no mind at first, attending instead to the spiritual needs of his flock.

'Satan has long been known as the Adversary, but God fears women even more than He fears the devil – and is right to. *She*, with her power to bring life into the world, was truly made in the image of the Creator, not man, and in all ways has proved Herself a more deserving object of man's worship than Christ, that unshaven fanatic who lusted for the end of the world. God saves – but not now, and not here. His salvation is on layaway. Like all grifters, He asks you to pay now and take it on faith that you will receive later. Whereas women offer a different sort of salvation, more immediate and fulfilling. They don't put off their love for a distant, ill-defined eternity but make a gift of it in the here and now, frequently to those who deserve it least. So it was in my case. So it is for many. The devil and woman have been allies against God from the beginning, ever since Satan came to the first man in the form of a snake and whispered to Adam that true happiness was not to be found in prayer but in Eve's cunt.'

The snakes writhed and hissed and fought for space at his feet. They bit one another, in a state close to rapture.

The thick brown snake at Ig's feet began to twist around one of his ankles. He bent and lifted her in one hand, peering down at her at last. She was the colour of dry, dead autumn leaves, aside from a single orange stripe that ran along her back, and at the end of her tail was a short, dusty rattle. Ig had never seen a rattle on a snake, outside of Clint Eastwood movies. She allowed herself to be hoisted in the air, made no effort to get away. The serpent peered back at him through golden eyes, crinkled like some kind of metallic foil and with long slotted pupils. Her black tongue flicked out, tasting the air. The cool material of her skin felt as loose on the muscle beneath as an eyelid closed over an eye. Her tail (but perhaps it was wrong to speak of tails; the whole thing was a tail, with a head stuck on one end) hung down against Ig's arm. After a moment Ig looped the viper over his shoulders, wearing her like a loose scarf, or an unknotted tie. Her rattle lay against his naked chest.

He stared out at his audience, had forgotten what he was saying. He tipped his head back and had a sip of wine. It burned going down, a sweet swallowed flame. Christ, at least, was right in his love of the devil drink, which, like the fruit of the garden, brought with it freedom and knowledge and certain ruination. Ig exhaled smoke and remembered his argument.

'Look at the girl I loved and who loved me and how she ended. She wore the cross of Jesus about her neck and was faithful to the church, which never did anything for her except take her money from the collection plate and call her a sinner to her face. She kept Jesus in her heart every day and prayed to him every night, and you see the good it did her. Jesus on His cross. So many have wept for Jesus on His cross. As if no one else has ever suffered as He suffered. As if millions have not shuffled to worse deaths, and died unremembered. Would I had lived in the time of Pilate. It would have pleased me to twist the spear in His side myself, so proud of His own pain. Merrin and I were to each other like man and wife. But she wanted more than me, wanted freedom, a life, a chance to discover herself. She wanted other lovers and wanted me to take other lovers as well. I hated her for this. So did God. For simply imagining she might open her legs to another man, He turned His face from her, and when she called to Him, as she was raped and murdered, He pretended He did not hear. He felt, no doubt, that she received her due. I see God now as an unimaginative writer of popular fictions, someone who builds stories around sadistic and graceless plots, narratives that exist only to express His terror of a woman's power to choose who and how to love, to redefine love as she sees fit, not as God thinks it ought to be. The author is unworthy of His own characters. The devil is first a literary critic, who delivers this untalented scribbler the public flaying He deserves.'

The serpent around his neck let her head fall to lovingly graze against Ig's thigh. He stroked her gently as he came to the point, the crux of his fire sermon. 'Only the devil loves humans for what they are and rejoices in their cunning schemes against themselves, their shameless curiosity, their lack of self-control, their impulse to break a rule as soon as they hear tell of it, their willingness to forsake their immortal soul for nookie. The devil knows that only those with the courage to risk their soul for love are entitled to have a soul, even if God does not.

'And where *does* this leave God? God loves man, we are told, but love must be proved by facts, not reasons. If you were in a boat and did not save a drowning man, you would burn in Hell for certain; yet God, in His wisdom, feels no need to use His power to save anyone from a single moment of suffering, and in spite of his inaction He is celebrated and revered. Show me the moral logic in it. You can't. There is none. Only the devil operates with any reason, promising to punish those who would make earth itself Hell for those who dare to love and feel.

'I do not claim that God is dead. I tell you He is alive and well but in no position to offer salvation, being damned Himself for His criminal indifference. He was lost the moment He demanded fealty and worship before He would offer His pro-tection. The unmistakable bargain of a gangster. Whereas the devil is anything but indifferent. The devil is always there to help those who are ready to sin, which is another word for "live". His phone lines are open. Operators are standing by.'

The viper around Iggy's shoulders gave her rattle a dry little shake of approval, like castanets. He lifted her in one hand and kissed her cold head, then set her down. He returned to the chimney, the snakes boiling away from his feet to allow him to pass. He left his pitchfork leaning against the wall, just outside the hatch, and climbed inside but did not rest. For a time he read his Neil Diamond Bible by the firelight. He paused, twisting his goatee nervously, considering the law in Deuteronomy that forbade clothes with mixed fibres. A problematic bit of Scripture. A matter that required thought.

'Only the devil wants man to have a wide range of lightweight and comfortable styles to choose from,' he murmured at last, trying out a new proverb. 'Although there may be no forgiveness for polyester. On this one matter, Satan and the Lord are in agreement.'

29

Ig woke, stirred by a clang and a steely shriek. He sat up in the soot-smelling darkness, rubbing his eyes, the fire long out. He squinted to see who had opened the hatch and caught an iron wrench in the mouth, hard enough to snap his head to the side. Ig rolled onto his elbows and knees, his mouth already full of blood. He felt solid lumps rolling against his tongue. He spat a slimy string of blood; teeth came with it, three of them.

A hand in a black leather glove reached into the chimney and got Ig by the hair and dragged him out of the furnace, bouncing his head off the iron hatch on the way out. It made a brassy ringing sound, like someone striking a gong. Ig was dumped onto the concrete floor. He tried to pick himself up, doing a rough push-up, and caught a steel-tipped black boot in the side. His arms gave out and he went straight down, struck the concrete with his chin. His teeth banged together like a clapperboard: *Scene 666, take one, action!*

His pitchfork. He had leaned it against the wall, just outside the furnace. He rolled and flung himself at it. His fingers swatted the handle and it fell over with a clang. When he grabbed for the shaft, Lee Tourneau brought the heel of his boot down on Ig's hand, and Ig heard the bones snap with a brittle crunch. It sounded like someone breaking a fistful of dry twigs. He turned his head to look up at Lee as Lee came down with the wrench again and he was clubbed right between the horns. A white flash bomb went off in Ig's head, brilliant burning phosphorus, and the world disappeared.

He opened his eyes and saw the floor of the foundry sliding by beneath him. Lee had him by the collar of the shirt and was dragging him, his knees sliding across concrete. His hands were in front of his body, held together at the wrists by something. Duct tape, it felt like. He tried to leap up and only managed to weakly kick his feet. The world was filled with the infernal drone of the locusts, and it took him a moment before he understood that the sound was only inside his head, because locusts were silent at night.

It was wrong, when considering the old foundry, to think about an outside and an inside. There was no roof; the inside *was* the outside. But Ig was hauled through a doorway and sensed that somehow they had come out into the night, although there was still dusty concrete under his knees. He couldn't lift his head but had an impression of openness, of having left all walls behind. He heard Lee's Caddy idling some- where nearby. They were behind the building, he thought, not far from the Evel Knievel trail. His tongue moved sluggishly around in his mouth, an eel swimming in blood. The tip touched an empty socket where a tooth had been.

If he was going to try to use the horns on Lee, he was going to have to do it *now*, before Lee did what he had come here to do. But when he opened his mouth to speak, there came a black grinding shock of agony, and it was all he could do not to scream. His jaw was broken – shattered, maybe. Blood bubbled and ran from his lips, and he made a muzzy, damaged sound of pain.

They were at the top of a flight of concrete stairs, Lee breathing hard. He paused there.

'Christ, Ig,' Lee said. 'You don't look like you're that heavy. I'm not cut out for this kind of thing.'

He dropped Ig down the steps. Ig hit the first on his shoulder and the second on his face, and it felt like his jaw was breaking all over again, and he couldn't help it, he *did* scream this time, a gravelly, strangled sound. He rolled the rest of the way to the bottom and sprawled across the dirt, nose in the earth.

After he came to rest, he held himself perfectly still – it seemed important to be still, the most important thing in the world – waiting for the black throb of pain in his smashed face to relent, at least a little. Distantly he heard boots scuff on the concrete stairs and crunch away across the earth. A car door opened. A car door slammed. The boot heels came crunching back. Ig heard a tinny clang and a hollow sloshing sound, neither of which he could identify.

'I knew I'd find you out here, Ig,' Lee said. 'Couldn't stay away, could you?'

Ig fought to lift his head and look up. Lee squatted beside him. He wore dark jeans and a white button-down shirt, sleeves rolled back to show his lean, strong forearms. His face was calm, almost good-humoured. With one hand he absently picked at the cross nestled in the curls of golden hair on his chest.

'I've known I'd find you out here ever since Glenna called me a couple of hours ago.' A smile flickered at the corners of his mouth for a moment. 'She came home to find her apartment trashed. TV kicked in. Shit tossed everywhere. She called me right up. She was crying, Ig. She feels terrible. She thinks somehow you found out about our – what's the right language for this? – our parking-lot tryst and that you hate her now. She's scared you might hurt yourself. I told her I was more scared about you hurting *her* and that I thought she ought to spend the night with me. Would you believe she turned me down? She said she wasn't afraid of you and needed to talk to you, before things went any further between me and her. Good ol' Glenna. She's sweet, you know. A little too desperate to please. A lot insecure. Pretty slutty. The second-closest thing to a disposable human being I've ever met. You'd be the first.'

Ig forgot his shattered jaw and tried to tell Lee to stay the fuck away from her. But when he opened his mouth, all that came out was another scream. Pain radiated from his smashed jawbone, and a darkness rushed up with it, gathering at the corners of his vision and then closing in around him. He breathed out – snorted blood from his nostrils – and fought it, pushed the darkness back by sheer effort of will.

'Eric doesn't remember what happened in Glenna's place this morning,' Lee said, in such a soft voice Ig almost missed it. 'Why is that, Ig? He can't remember anything except you throwing a pot of water in his face and nearly passing out. But something happened in that apartment. A fight? *Something*. I maybe would've had Eric along with me tonight – I'm sure he'd like to see you dead – but his face. You burned his face real good, Ig. If it was any worse, he would've had to take himself to a hospital and make up some lie about how he got hurt. He shouldn't have gone in Glenna's apartment anyway. Sometimes I think that guy has no respect for the law.' He laughed. 'Maybe it's for the best, though, that he's not part of this. This kind of thing is just easier when there are no witnesses.'

Lee's wrists rested on his knees and the wrench hung from his right hand, twelve pounds of rusting iron.

'I can almost understand Eric not remembering what happened over at Glenna's. An iron pot to the head will shake up a person's memory. But I don't know what to make of what happened when you showed up at the congressman's office yesterday. Three people watched you walk in: Chet, our receptionist, and Cameron, who runs the X-ray, and Eric. Five minutes after you left, none of them could remember you being there. Only me. Even Eric wouldn't believe you'd been there until I showed him the video. There's video of the two of you talking, but Eric couldn't tell me what you talked about. And there's something else, too. The video. The video doesn't look right. Like there's something wrong with the tape . . .' His voice trailed off, and he was silent for a musing moment. 'Distortion. But just around you. What did you do to the tape? What'd you do to *them*? And why didn't it seem to touch me? That's what I'd like to know.' When Ig didn't reply, Lee lifted the wrench and poked him in one shoulder. 'Are you listening, Ig?'

Ig had listened to every word, had been getting ready while Lee blabbed away, gathering what strength he had left to spring. He had pulled his knees under him and got his breath back and had just been waiting for the right moment, and here it was at last. He came up, batting the wrench aside and throwing himself at Lee, nailed him in the chest with his shoulder, knocked him back onto his ass. Ig got his hands up and put them around Lee's throat—

—and in the moment of skin-to-skin contact nearly screamed again. He was, for an instant, in Lee's head, and it was like being in the Knowles River all over again; he was drowning in a rushing black torrent, pulled down into a cold, roaring place of darkness and desperate motion. In that one moment of contact, Ig knew *everything* and wanted not to, wanted to make it go away, to *unknow*.

Lee still had the wrench and he came up with it, pounded it into Ig's gut, and Ig coughed explosively. He was shoved off, but as Ig was jolted aside, his fingers caught on the golden chain around Lee's neck. It came apart with hardly a sound. The cross sailed away into the night.

Lee squirmed out from under him, climbed back to his feet. Ig was on elbows and knees, struggling to breathe.

'Try and choke me, you piece of shit,' Lee said, and kicked him in the side. A rib snapped. Ig groaned and slumped onto his face.

Lee followed with a second kick and a third. The third thudded into the small of Ig's back and sent a withering shock of pain through kidneys and bowels. Something wet hit the back of his head. Spit. Then, for a while, Lee was still, and they both had a chance to get their breath back.

And at last Lee said, 'What are those goddamn things on your head?' He sounded genuinely surprised. 'Jesus, Ig. Are those *horns*?'

Ig shivered against the waves of hurt and sick in his back, his side, his hand, his face. He scratched at the dirt with his left hand, digging furrows in the black earth, clawing at consciousness, fighting for each second of clarity. What had Lee just said? Something about the horns.

'*That's* what was on the video,' Lee said, a little breathlessly. 'Horns. Holy fucking shit. I thought it was bad tape. But it wasn't something wrong with the tape. It was something wrong with *you*. You know, I think I saw them yesterday, looking at you through my bad eye. Everything is just shadows through that eye, but when I looked at you, I thought, *Hunh . . .*' His voice trailed off and he touched two fingers to his bare throat. 'How about that.'

When Ig closed his eyes he saw a bright, brassy Tom Crown mute, pushed deep into a trumpet to choke off the sound. He had found a mute for the horns at last. Merrin's cross had choked off their signal, had made a circle of protection around Lee Tourneau that they couldn't get through. Without it Lee was open to the horns at last. Naturally, too late to do Ig any good.

'My cross,' Lee said, still touching his neck. 'Merrin's cross. You broke it. You broke it trying to strangle me. That was uncalled for, Ig. You think I *want* to do this to you? I don't. I *don't*. The person I want to do this to is a little fourteen-year-old girl who lives next door to me. She likes to sunbathe in her backyard and I watch her sometimes from my bedroom window. She looks real cherry in her American-flag bikini. I think about her the way I used to think about Merrin. Not that I'd ever *do* anything to her. Too big a risk. We're neighbours, I'd be a natural suspect. You don't shit where you eat. Unless – unless

267

you think maybe I could get away with it. What do you think, Ig? Do you think I ought to do her?'

Through the black spoke of pain in his shattered rib and the swelling heat in his jaw and smashed hand, Ig noted that Lee's voice was different now – that he was speaking in a dreamy, talking-to-himself kind of tone. The horns were going to work on Lee as they had gone to work on everyone else.

Ig shook his head and made a pained sound of negation. Lee looked disappointed.

'No. It isn't a good idea, is it? Tell you what, though. I *did* almost come out here with Glenna just a couple of nights ago. I wanted to like you wouldn't believe. When we walked out of the Station House Tavern together, she was really drunk, and she was going to let me give her a ride home, and I was thinking I could drive her out here instead and fuck her in the fat tits and then beat her head in and leave her. That would've been on you, too. Ig Perrish strikes again, kills another girlfriend. But then Glenna had to go and blow me in the parking lot, right in front of three or four guys, and I couldn't do it. Too many people could've placed us together. Oh, well. Another time. Thing about girls like Glenna, girls with rap sheets and tattoos, girls who drink too much and smoke too much – they disappear all the time, and six months later even people who knew them can't remember their name. And tonight, Ig – tonight, at least, I've got you.'

He bent and took Ig by the horns and dragged him through the weeds. Ig could not find the strength to so much as kick his feet. Blood ran from his mouth and his right hand beat like a heart, and the night swelled around him like a black balloon filling with air.

Lee opened the front door of Ig's Gremlin and then got him under the arms and heaved him into it. Ig sprawled face down across the seats, his legs hanging out. The effort of tossing him into the car almost pulled Lee over – he was tired, too, Ig could feel it – and he half fell into the Gremlin himself. He put a hand on Ig's back to steady him, his knee on Ig's ass.

'Hey, Ig. Remember the day we met? Out here on the Evel Knievel trail? Just think, if you went and drowned way back then, I could've had Merrin when she was cherry, and maybe none of the bad things would've happened. Although I don't know. She was quite the stuck-up little bitch even then. There's something you need to know, Ig. I've felt guilty about it for years. Well. Not guilty. But you know. *Funny.* Here it is: I really. Truly. Did not. Save you. From drowning. I don't know how many times I've told you that or why you never believed me. You swam out on your own. I didn't even smack your back to get you breathing again. I only kicked you by accident, trying to get away from you. There was this big fucking snake right next to you. I hate snakes. I have, like, an aversion. Hey, maybe the snake pulled you out. It sure was big enough. Like a fucking fire hose.' He patted a gloved hand on the back of Ig's head. 'There. I'm glad I got that off my chest. I feel better already. It's true what they say. Confession *is* good for the soul.'

He rose, got Ig's ankles and pushed his legs up and into the car. A tired part of Ig was glad he was going to die here. Most of the best times of his life had happened in the Gremlin. He had loved Merrin here, had had all his happiest conversations with her here, and had held her hand on long drives in the dark, neither of them speaking, just enjoying a shared quiet. He felt that Merrin was close to him now, that if he looked up, he might see her in the passenger seat, reaching to put her hand gently on his head.

He heard scuffling from behind him and then that echoing, tinny, sloshing sound, and at last he could identify the noise. It was the sound made by liquid slopping about in a metal can. He had just struggled up onto his elbows when he felt a cold, wet splashing over his back, soaking his shirt. The eye-watering reek of gasoline filled the cockpit.

Ig rolled over, struggled to sit up. Lee finished dousing him, gave the can a last shake, and tossed it aside. Ig blinked at the stinging fumes, the air wavering around him with gasoline stink. Lee fished a small box out of his pocket. He had picked up Ig's Lucifer Matches on the way out of the foundry.

'I've always wanted to do this,' Lee said, struck the match, and flicked it through the open window.

The burning match hit Ig's forehead, flipped, and fell. Ig's hands were taped together at the wrists, but they were in front of his body and he caught the match as it dropped through the air, not thinking about it, just acting on reflex. For a moment – just one – his hands were a cup filled with fire, brimming with golden light.

Then he wore a red suit of flame, became a living torch. He screamed, but couldn't hear his own voice, because that was when the interior of the car ignited, with a low, deep *whump!* that seemed to suck all the oxygen out of the air. He caught a glimpse of Lee staggering back from the Gremlin, the flame light playing across his startled face. Even braced for it, he had not been ready for it: the Gremlin become a roaring tower of fire.

Ig grabbed the door and tried to push it open and climb out, and Lee stepped forward and kicked it shut. The plastic of the dashboard blackened. The windshield began to soot over. Through it Ig could see the night, and the drop of the Evel Knievel hill, and the river was down there somewhere. He reached blindly through the flames and found the gearshift, slammed it into neutral. With his other hand, he released the parking brake. As he lifted his palm from the gearshift, tacky strands of plastic came away, fusing with skin.

He looked again through the open driver's window and saw Lee sliding away from him. His face was pale and stunned in the glow of the moving inferno. Then Lee was behind him, and trees were beginning to rush past as the Gremlin tilted forward down the hill. Ig did not need the headlights to see ahead of him. The interior of the car produced a soft golden rush of light, was a burning chariot that cast a reddish glow ahead of it into the darkness. *Comin' for to carry me home*, Ig thought randomly.

The trees closed in from above and brush swiped at the sides of the car. Ig had not been on the trail since that time on the shopping cart, ten years before, and had never ridden it at night, or in a car, or while burning alive. But for all that, he knew the way, knew the trail by the plunging sensation in his bowels. The hill got steeper and steeper as he went, until it seemed almost as if the car had been dropped off the side of a cliff. The back tyres lifted off the ground and then came back down with a metallic, bashing sound. The passenger window exploded out from the heat. The evergreens whipped audibly by. Ig had the steering wheel in his hands. He didn't know when he had grabbed it. He could feel it softening in his grip, melting like one of Dalí's watches, sagging in on itself. The front driver's-side tyre struck something, and he felt the wheel try to twist free from his grip, turn the burning Gremlin sideways, but he pulled against it, held it on the trail. He couldn't breathe. All was fire.

The Gremlin hit the slight dirt incline at the bottom of the Evel Knievel trail and was catapulted into the stars, out over the water, a burning comet. It left a coil of smoke behind, like a rocket. The forward motion opened the flames in front of Ig's face, as if invisible hands had parted a red curtain. He saw the water rushing up at him, like a road paved in slick black marble. The Gremlin hit with a great wallop that smashed the windshield in at him, and water followed after.

30

Lee Tourneau stood on the riverbank and watched the current slowly turn the Gremlin around so it was pointed downriver. Only the back end stuck out of the water. The fire was out, although white smoke still poured from around the edges of the hatchback. He stood with the wrench, while the car listed and sank a little deeper, following the current. He stared until a sliding movement near his foot caught his attention. He looked down, then leaped back with a revolted little cry, kicking at a water snake in the grass. It slipped past him and plopped into the Knowles. Lee retreated, his upper lip curled in disgust, as a second and then a third slithered into the water, causing the moonlight on the river to shiver and break into silver pieces. He cast a final look out towards the sinking car and then turned and set off up the hill.

He was gone by the time Ig rose from the water and climbed the embankment into the weeds. His body smoked in the darkness. He walked six shaky paces across the dirt, and sank to his knees. As he pushed himself onto his back in the ferns, he heard a car door slam at the top of the hill and the sound of Lee Tourneau turning his Caddy around and driving away. Ig lay there, resting beneath the trees along the riverbank.

His skin was no longer a pale fish-belly white but had assumed a deep red burnish, like certain varnished hardwoods. His breathing had never been so easy, nor his lungs so full. The bellows of his ribs expanded effortlessly with each inhalation. He had heard one of those ribs snap, not twenty minutes before, but he felt no pain. He did not note until much later the faint discolorations of month-old bruises on his sides – all that remained to show he'd been attacked. He opened and closed his mouth, wiggling his jaw, but there was no pain, and when his tongue searched for the missing teeth, it found them, smooth and whole, back where they belonged. He flexed his hand. It felt fine. He could see the bones in the back of it, the rods even and undamaged. He had not been aware of it at the time but saw now that he'd never been in pain, all the while he burned. He had, instead, come out of the fire unharmed and made whole. The warm night air was redolent with the smell of gasoline and melted plastic and scorched iron, a fragrance that stirred something in Ig, in much the same way Merrin's odour of lemons and mint and girl-sweat had stirred him. Iggy Perrish closed his eyes and drew restful breath after restful breath, and when next he looked up, it was dawn.

His skin felt stretched tight across muscle and bone, felt clean. He had never felt cleaner. This was how baptism was supposed to feel, he thought idly. The banks were crowded with oaks, and their broad leaves fluttered and waved against a sky of precious and impossible blue, their edges shining with a golden green light.

Merrin had seen the tree house among leaves that were lit just so. She and Ig were pushing their bikes along a trail in the woods, coming back from town, where they had spent the morning as part of a volunteer team painting the church, and they were both wearing baggy T-shirts and cutoffs spattered in white paint. They had walked and biked this particular path often enough, but neither of them had ever seen the tree house before.

It was easy to miss it. It had been built fifteen feet off the ground, up in the broad, spreading crown of some tree Ig couldn't identify, hidden behind ten thousand slender leaves of darkest green. At first, when Merrin pointed, Ig didn't even think there was anything there. It wasn't there. Then it was. The sunlight reached through the leaves to shine against white clapboard. As they went closer, stepping under the tree, the house came into clearer view. It was a white box with wide squares cut out for windows, cheap nylon curtains hanging in them. It looked as if it had been framed out by someone who knew what he was doing, not a casual weekend carpenter, although there was nothing particularly showy about it. No ladder led to it, nor was one needed. Low branches provided a natural series of rungs leading to the closed trapdoor. Painted on the underside of the door in whitewash was a single, presumably comic sentence: BLESSED SHALL YOU BE WHEN YOU GO IN.

Ig had stopped to look at it – he snorted softly at what was written on the trap – but Merrin didn't lose a step. She set her bike down in the soft tufts of grass at the base and immediately began to climb, jumping with an athletic self-assurance from branch to branch. Ig stood below, watching her make the ascent, and as she worked her way up through the boughs, he was struck by her naked brown thighs, smooth and limber from a long spring of soccer. As she reached the trapdoor, she turned her head to look down at him. It was a struggle to move his gaze from her cutoffs to her face, but when he did, she was smirking at him. She did not speak but pushed the trapdoor back with a bang and wiggled up through the opening.

By the time he poked his head into the tree house, she was already pulling her clothes off. The floor had a little square of dusty carpet on it. A brass menorah, holding nine half-melted candles, stood on an end-table surrounded by small china figures. An easy chair with mouldering moss-coloured uphol-stery sat in one corner. The leaves moved outside the window, and their shadows moved over her skin, in constant rushing motion, while the tree house creaked softly in its cradle of branches, and what was the old nursery rhyme about cradles in trees? *Ig and Merrin up in a tree, K-I-S-S-I-N-G.* No, that wasn't the one. *Rock-a-bye baby, in the treetop.* Rock-a-bye. Ig closed the trapdoor behind him and moved the chair over it, so no one could enter and surprise them. He undressed, and for a while they went rock-a-bye together.

Afterwards she said, 'What's with the candles and those little glass guys?'

Ig got up on all fours to crawl towards them, and she sat up quickly and gave him a full-palmed smack on the ass. He laughed and jumped and scrambled away from her.

He knelt at the end-table. The menorah was set on a piece of dirty parchment with big block letters on it in Hebrew. The candles on the menorah had been melted down quite a bit, to leave a lacework of wax stalactites and stalagmites built up around the brass base. A china Mary – a really quite foxy Jewess in blue – was sunk down on one pious knee before an angel of the Lord, a tall, sinewy figure in robes arranged almost toga fashion. She was reaching up, presumably for his hand, although the figure had been manoeuvred so she was touching his golden thigh and looked like she was getting ready to reach for his crank. The Lord's messenger glared down at her with haughty disapproval. A second angel stood a little ways off from them, his face lifted to heaven, his back turned to the scene, mournfully blowing a golden trumpet.

Into this tableau some joker had stuck a grey-skinned alien with the black, multifaceted eyes of a fly. He was posed beside Mary, bent to whisper in her ear. This figure was not china but rubber, a posable figure from some movie; Ig thought maybe *Close Encounters.*

'Do you know what kind of writing this is?' Merrin asked. She had crawled over to kneel beside him.

'Hebrew,' Ig said. 'It's from a phylactery.'

'Good thing I'm on the pill,' she said. 'You forgot to put on your phylactery when we just did it.'

'That's not what a phylactery is.'

'I know it isn't,' she said.

He waited. Smiling to himself.

'So what's a phylactery?' she asked.

'You wear them on your head if you're Jewish.'

'Oh. I thought that was a yarmulke.'

'No. This is a different thing Jews wear on their head. Or maybe sometimes their arm. I can't remember.'

'So what's it say?'

'I don't know. It's Scripture.'

She pointed at the angel with his horn. 'Looks like your brother.'

'No it doesn't,' Ig said ... although, in fact, considering it again, it did rather resemble Terry playing his horn, with his broad, clear brow and princely features. Although Terry wouldn't be caught dead in those robes, except maybe at a toga party.

'What is all this stuff?' Merrin asked.

'It's a shrine,' Ig said.

'To what?' She nodded at the alien. 'You think it's the holy altar of ET?'

'I don't know. Maybe these figures were important to someone. Maybe they're a way to remember someone. I think someone made this to have a place to pray.'

'That's what I think, too.'

'Do you want to pray?' Ig asked automatically, and then swallowed heavily, feeling he had requested some obscene act, something she might judge offensive.

She looked at him under half-lowered eyelids and smiled in a sly sort of way, and it struck him for the first time ever that Merrin thought he had a streak of crazy in him. She cast her gaze around, at the window with its view of rippling yellow leaves, at the sunlight painting the weathered old walls, then looked back and nodded.

'Sure,' she said. 'Beats the heck out of praying at church.'

Ig put his hands together and lowered his head and opened his mouth to speak, but Merrin interrupted.

'Aren't you going to light the candles?' she asked. 'Don't you think we ought to create an atmosphere of reverence? We just treated this place like the set for a porno.'

There was a stained, warped box in the shallow drawer that had matches in it with funny black heads. Ig struck one, and it lit with a hiss and a sputter of white flame. He moved it from wick to wick, lighting each of the candles on the menorah. He was as quick at it as he could be, and yet still the match sizzled down to his fingers as he lit the ninth wick. Merrin shouted his name as he shook it out.

'Christ, Ig,' she said. 'You okay?'

'I'm fine,' he said, wiggling his fingertips. He really was. It didn't hurt even a little.

Merrin slid the tray back into the matchbox and made to put them away, then hesitated to look at them.

'Hah,' she said.

'What?'

'Nothing,' she said, and closed the drawer on them.

She bowed her head then and put her hands together and waited. Ig felt his breath go short at the sight of her, her taut, white, naked skin and smooth breasts and the dark red tumble of her hair. He had himself not felt so naked at any other time in his life, not even the first time he'd undressed before her. At the sight of her, patiently waiting for him to say his prayer, he felt a sweet, withering rush of emotion pass through him, almost more love than he could bear.

Naked together, they prayed. Ig asked God to help them be good to each other, to help them be kind to others. He was asking God to protect them from harm when he felt Merrin's hand moving on his thigh, slipping gently up between his legs. It required a great deal of concentration to complete the prayer, his eyes squeezed tightly shut. When he was done, he said 'Amen', and Merrin turned towards him and whispered 'Amen' herself as she placed her lips on his, and drew him towards her. They made love again, and when they had finished with each other, they dozed off in each other's arms, her lips against his neck.

When Merrin finally sat up – shifting his arm off her, rousing him in the process – some of the day's warmth had fled, and the tree house was filled with gloom. She hunched, covering her bare breasts with an arm, fumbling for her clothes.

'Shit,' she said, 'we need to go. My mom and dad were expecting us for dinner. They'll wonder where we are.'

'Get dressed. I'll blow out the candles.'

He bent sleepily in towards the menorah to blow out the candles – and then twitched unhappily, a weird, sick thrill passing through him.

He had missed one of the china figures. It was the devil. He was set on the base of the menorah and, like the tree house itself in its cloak of leaves, was easy to miss, half hidden behind the row of wax stalactites hanging from the candles above. Lucifer was convulsed with laughter, his gaunt red hands clenched into fists, his head thrown back to the sky. He seemed to be dancing on his little goaty hooves. His yellow eyes were rolled back in his head in an expression of delirious delight, a kind of rapture.

At the sight, Ig felt his arms and back prickle with cold gooseflesh. It should've been just another part of the kitschy scene arranged before him, and yet it wasn't, and he hated it, and he wished he hadn't seen it. That dancing little figurine was awful, a bad thing to see, a bad thing for someone to have left; not funny. He wished, suddenly, that he had not prayed here. He almost shivered, imagining it had dropped five degrees in the tree house. Only he wasn't imagining. The sun had gone behind a cloud and the room had darkened and chilled. A rough wind stirred in the branches.

'Too bad we have to go,' Merrin said, pulling on her shorts behind him. 'Isn't that air the sweetest thing?'

'Yes,' Ig said, although his voice was unexpectedly hoarse.

'So much for our little piece of heaven,' Merrin said, which was when something hit the trapdoor with a loud crash that caused them both to scream.

The trap banged hard into the chair set on top of it, with so much force that the whole tree house seemed to shake.

'What was that?' Merrin cried.

'Hey!' Ig shouted. 'Hey, is someone down there?'

The trap crashed into the chair again and the chair hopped a few inches on its legs, but remained on top of the hatch. Ig threw a wild look at Merrin, and then they were both grabbing at their clothes. Ig squirmed into his cutoffs while she refastened her bra. The trapdoor boomed against the underside of the chair again, harder than ever. The figurines on the end-table jumped, and the Mary fell over. The devil peered hungrily out from amid his cave of melted wax.

'Cut it the fuck out!' Ig yelled, heart throbbing in his chest.

Kids, he thought, *got to be fucking kids*. But he didn't believe it. If it was kids, why weren't they laughing? Why weren't they dropping out of the tree and sprinting away in a state of high hysterics?

Ig was dressed and ready, and he grabbed the chair to push it aside – then realised he was afraid to. He held up, staring at Merrin, who had frozen in the act of pulling on her sneakers.

'Go on,' she whispered. 'See who's out there.'

'I don't want to.'

He really didn't. His heart quailed at the thought of moving aside the chair and letting in whoever (*whatever*) was out there.

The worst of it was the sudden quiet. Whoever had been

pitching themselves into the trapdoor had quit, waiting for them to open it of their own volition.

Merrin finished tugging on her sneakers and nodded.

Ig called out, 'Listen, if there's someone down there . . . you had your fun. We're good and scared.'

'Don't tell him that,' Merrin whispered.

'We're coming out now.'

'Christ,' Merrin hissed, 'don't tell him that either.'

They traded a glance. Ig felt a rising dread, did not want to open the door, was seized with the irrational conviction that if he did, he would allow in something that would do them both irreparable harm. And at the same time, there was nothing to do but open the door. He nodded at her and shoved back the chair, and as he did he saw that something else was written on the *inside* of the trap, big capital letters in white paint, but he didn't pause to read what it said there, only flung back the hatch. He leaped down, not wanting to give himself time to think, grabbing the edge of the trap and lashing out with his legs, hoping to drive anyone who was on the branch off it, and fuck 'em if they broke their necks. He had assumed that Merrin would stay behind, that it was simply his role as the man to protect her, but she was going through the trapdoor with him and actually put her feet down on the branch below the tree house first.

Ig's heart was beating so fast that the whole world seemed to jump and twitch around him. He settled onto the branch beside her, his arms still reaching up, hands gripping the edges of the opening. He searched the ground below, breathing hard; she was breathing hard, too. There was no one. He listened intently for the sound of tramping feet, people rushing away, crashing in the brush, but heard only wind, and branches scraping against the outside of the treehouse.

He scrambled down out of the branches and made a series of widening circles around the tree, looking in the brush and along the path for signs of passers-by, but found nothing. When he returned to the trunk of the tree, Merrin was still up in it, sitting on one of the long boughs below the tree house.

'You didn't find anyone,' she said. It wasn't a question.

'Nope,' he said. 'Must've been the big bad wolf.'

It felt right to joke it off, but he was still uneasy, his nerves jangled.

If she was feeling jangled, she didn't show it. She had a last affectionate look up into the tree house and pulled the door shut. She hopped down out of the branches and scooped her bike up by the handlebars. They began to walk, leaving that bad moment of genuine fright further behind them with each step. The path was still in the last of the day's warm, generous light, and Ig became aware again of a pleasant, satisfied, freshly laid tingle. It was a good thing, to walk close to her, their hips almost touching and the sun on their shoulders.

'We'll have to come back out here tomorrow,' she said, and in almost the same moment Ig said, 'We could really do something with that place, you know?'

They laughed.

'We should get some beanbags for up there,' Ig said.

'A hammock. You put a hammock up in a place like that,' she said.

They were quiet, walking.

'Maybe grab us a pitchfork, too,' she said.

Ig stumbled, as if she had not just mentioned a pitchfork but pricked him with one, poking the tines into him from behind.

'Why a pitchfork?' Ig asked.

'To scare away the whatever. In case it comes back and tries to get in at us while we're naked.'

'Okay,' Ig said, already dry-mouthed at the thought of having her again up on the boards, in the cool-blowing breeze. 'It's a plan.'

But Ig was back in the forest, alone, two hours later, hurrying along the path through the town woods. He had remembered over dinner that neither of them had blown out the candles in the menorah, and he'd been in a state of high distress ever since, imagining the tree ablaze, the burning leaves drifting into the crowns of the surrounding oaks. He ran, in terror that at any moment he would catch a whiff of smoke.

He smelled only the early-summer fragrances of sun-baked grass and the distant cold, clean rush of the Knowles River, somewhere down the hill from him. He thought he knew exactly where to find the tree house and slowed as he neared the general vicinity. He searched the trees for the dim glow of candle flame and saw nothing but the velvety June darkness. He tried to find that tree, that enormous scaly-barked tree of a kind he didn't know, but in the night it was difficult to tell one leafy tree from another, and the trail didn't look the same as it had in the daylight. Finally he knew he had gone too far – way too far – and he started for home, breathing hard and proceeding slowly. He went back and forth on the trail, two, three times but couldn't find any sign of the tree house. He decided at last that the wind had blown the candles out, or they had guttered out on their own. It had always been a little paranoid to imagine them starting a forest fire. They were set in a heavy iron menorah, and unless it fell over, there wasn't much chance of them igniting anything. He could find the tree house another time.

Only he never did, not with Merrin and not on his own. A dozen afternoons he searched for it, walking the main trail and all the offshoots, in case they had somehow wandered onto a side path. He looked for the tree house with a methodical patience, but it wasn't to be found. They might as well have imagined the place, and in fact, in time, this was exactly what Merrin concluded: an absurd hypothesis but one that suited both of them. It had simply been there for an hour, one day, when they needed it, when they wanted a place to love one another, and then it was gone.

'We needed it?' Ig said.

'Well,' Merrin said, '*I* needed it. I was horny as hell.'

'We needed it, and it appeared. A tree house of the mind. The temple of Ig and Merrin,' Ig said. As fantastic and ludicrous as it seemed, the notion gave him a shiver of superstitious pleasure.

'That's my best guess,' she said. 'It's like in the Bible. You can't always get what you want, but if you really need something, you usually find it.'

'What part of the Bible is that from?' Ig asked her. 'The Gospel of Keith Richards?'

THE FIXER

31

His mother was dead in the next room, and Lee Tourneau was a little drunk.

It was only ten in the morning, but the house was already an oven. The fragrance of his mother's roses, planted on the path leading up to the house, drifted in through open windows, a light floral sweetness that mingled in a rather disagreeable way with a rank odour of human waste, so the whole place smelled just exactly like a perfumed turd. Lee felt that it was too hot to be drunk, but also that he could not bear the stink of her sober.

There was air-conditioning, but it was switched off. Lee had kept it off for weeks, because his mother had a harder time breathing with the humidity weighing on her. When Lee and his mother were alone in the house, he would kill the air-conditioner and put an extra comforter or two on top of the old cunt. Then he'd cut her morphine, to be sure she could really feel it: the weight and the heat. God knew Lee could feel it. By late afternoon he would be padding around the house naked, sticky with sweat, the only way he could stand it. He sat cross-legged by her bedside reading about media theory while she struggled weakly under her covers, too out of it to know why she was boiling in her parched yellow skin. When she shouted for something to drink – 'thirst' was about the only word his mother still seemed to know in her last days of senility and kidney failure – Lee would get up and fetch cold water. At the sound of ice clinking in the glass, her throat would start to work, in anticipation of slaking her thirst, and her eyes would begin to roll in their sockets, bright with excitement. Then he would stand over her bed, drinking it himself, where she could see him doing it – the eagerness draining out of her face, leaving her confused and forlorn. It was a joke that never got old. Every time he did it, she was seeing him do it for the first time.

Other times he brought her salt water and forced her to swallow it, half-drowning her. Just a mouthful would cause his mother to writhe and choke, trying to spit it out. It was a curious thing, how long she survived. He had not expected her to make it to the second week of June; against all odds she clung to her life right to the end of July.

He kept clothes in a pile on the bookshelf outside the guest-room door, ready so he could get dressed in a hurry in case Ig or Merrin made a surprise visit. He would not allow them to go in and see her, would tell them she had just fallen asleep, needed her rest. He didn't want them to know how hot it was in there.

Ig and Merrin brought him DVDs, books, pizza, beer. They came together or they came separately, wanted to be with him, wanted to see how he was holding up. In Ig's case Lee thought it was envy. Ig would've liked if one of his own parents were debilitated and dependent on his care. It would be an opportunity to show how self-sacrificing he could be, a chance to be stoically noble. In Merrin's case he thought she liked to have a reason to be in the hot house with him, to drink martinis and unbutton the top of her blouse and fan her bared breastbone. When it was Merrin in the driveway, Lee usually answered the door with his shirt off, found it thrilling to be in the house, half dressed, just the two of them. Well, the two of them and his mother, who didn't really count anymore.

Lee had instructions to call the doctor if his mother took a turn for the worse, but he thought in her case dying actually represented a turn for the better. With that in mind, the first person he called was Merrin. He was naked at the time, and it was a good feeling, standing there in the dim kitchen with nothing on, Merrin's solicitous voice in his ear. She said she just needed to get dressed and she'd be right over, and immediately Lee imagined her almost undressed herself, in her bedroom at her parents' house. Little silk drawers, maybe. Girlish panties with pink flowers on them. She asked if he needed anything. Lee said he just needed a friend.

After he hung up, he had another drink, rum and Coke. He imagined her picking out a skirt, turning this way and that to admire herself in the mirror on the back of her closet door. Then he had to stop thinking about it, was getting himself a little too turned on. He thought maybe he ought to get dressed himself. He debated with himself about putting on a shirt and finally decided it wouldn't do to be bare-chested this morning. Yesterday's stained white button-down and jeans were in the laundry cubby. He considered going upstairs to get something fresh, then asked himself WWID and decided to put on the old things. Wrinkled, unwashed clothes sort of completed the picture of painful loss. Lee had managed his own behaviour for almost a decade by asking WWID, and it had won him his life and kept him out of trouble, had kept him safe, safe from himself.

He thought she'd be along in another few minutes. Time to make some more calls. He called the doctor and said his mother was at rest. He called his father in Florida. He called the congressman's office and spoke with the congressman himself for a minute. The congressman asked if Lee wanted to pray with him, to have a silent prayer together, right there on the phone. Lee said he did. Lee said he wanted to thank God for giving him these last three months with his mother. They really had been precious. The two of them were quiet for a while, both of them on the phone but saying nothing. Finally the congressman cleared his throat, a little emotionally, and said Lee would be in his thoughts. Lee thanked him and said good-bye.

Last of all he called Ig. He thought maybe Ig would cry when he heard the news, but Ig pulled one of his not-infrequent surprises and was calm, quietly affectionate. Lee had spent the past five years in and out of college, had taken courses in psychology, sociology, theology, political science and media theory, but his real major was Ig Studies, and yet in spite of years of diligent coursework he was not always able to anticipate Ig's reactions.

'I don't know how she found the strength to hang on so long,' Lee said to Ig.

And Ig said, 'From you, Lee. She found it in you.'

There wasn't much Lee Tourneau found funny, but at this he barked with laughter, then turned it into a harsh, shuddering sob. Lee had discovered, years before, that he could cry whenever he needed to and that a crying person could steer a conversation in any direction he wanted to take it.

'Thank you,' he said, something else he'd learned from Ig over the years. Nothing made people feel better about themselves than being thanked, repetitively and needlessly. Then, in a hoarse, choked voice, he said, 'I have to go.' It was just the right line, perfect for that particular moment, but it was also true, since he could see Merrin pulling into the drive, behind the wheel of her daddy's station wagon. Ig said he'd be over soon.

Lee watched her through the kitchen window while she walked up the path, plucking at her blouse, dressed smartly in a blue linen skirt and a white blouse, unbuttoned to show her gold cross. Bare legs, navy slingbacks. She had thought about what to put on before she came here, had thought about how she wanted to be seen. He finished the rest of his rum and

Coke on his way to the door, opened it as she was raising her hand to knock. His eyes were still burning and watery from his conversation with Ig, and he wondered if he ought to blink some tears down his cheeks, then decided not to. It was better to look like he was fighting it than to actually do it.

'Hey, Lee,' she said. Merrin looked as if she were fighting tears herself. She cupped his face with one hand and then drew herself to him.

It was a brief hug, but for a moment his nose was in her hair and her small hands were against his chest. Her hair had a keen, almost-sharp smell of lemons and mint. Lee thought that was the most fascinating aroma he'd ever smelled, better even than the smell of wet pussy. He had laid plenty of girls, knew all their smells, all their flavours, but Merrin was different. Sometimes he thought if she just didn't smell that way, he could stop worrying about her.

'Who's here?' she asked, as she came into the house, her arm still around his waist.

'You're the first one . . .' Lee said. He almost finished it – *the first one I called* – then knew it would be the wrong thing, would be too . . . what? Unusual. Wrong for the moment. Instead he finished, '. . . to get here. I called Ig, and then I called you. I wasn't thinking. I should've called my father first.'

'Have you talked to him?'

'Just a few minutes ago.'

'Well. That's all right, Lee. Do you want to sit down? Do you want me to call people for you?'

He was leading her to the guest bedroom where his mother was. He didn't ask if she wanted to go, just started walking, and she went along with her arm around his waist and their hips touching. He wanted her to see his mother, wanted to see her face.

They stopped in the open doorway. Lee had propped the fan in the window and turned it on full blast as soon as he knew she was dead, but the room still contained a dry, fevery heat. His mother's withered arms were curled against her chest, her skinny hands hooked into claws, as if she were trying to push something away. She had been, had made a last fitful effort to try to shove off the comforters at around nine-thirty, but she was too weak. The extra comforters were now folded and put away. A single crisp blue sheet lay across her. In death she had become birdlike, looked like a dead chick dropped from a nest. Her head was tipped back, and her mouth was open, yawning wide to show her fillings.

'Oh, Lee,' Merrin said, and squeezed his fingers in hers. She had started to cry. Lee thought maybe it was time for him to cry, too.

'I tried putting a sheet over her face,' Lee said. 'But it didn't look right. She fought for so long, Merrin.'

'I know.'

'I don't like how she's staring. Will you close her eyes?'

'All right. You go sit down, Lee.'

'Will you have a drink with me?'

'Sure. I'll be right along.'

He went to the kitchen and mixed her a strong drink and then stood at the cabinet looking at his reflection and willing himself to start crying. It was harder than usual; he was, in truth, a little excited. As Merrin entered the kitchen behind him, tears were just beginning to spill down his face, and he bent forward and exhaled savagely, a noise much like a sob. Forcing those tears out was hard, painful work, like squeezing out a splinter. She came towards him. She was crying, too. He could tell by the soft struggling sound of her breath, although he couldn't see her face. She put a hand on his shoulder. She was the one who turned him to her, as his breath began to catch and then come out of him in hoarse, angry sobs.

Merrin put her hands behind his head and pulled him close and whispered to him, 'She loved you so much,' she said. 'You were there every day for her, Lee, and it meant everything to her.' And so on and so forth, a lot of stuff like that. Lee wasn't listening.

He was taller than her by almost a foot, and to be close she had to pull his head down. He pressed his face to her chest, to the cleft between her breasts, and shut his eyes, breathing in the almost-astringent mint smell of her. He took the hem of her blouse with one hand and tugged it down, pulling it tight against her body, but also deforming the opening, to show the lightly freckled tops of her breasts, the cups of her bra. His other hand was on her waist, and he moved it up and down over her hip, and she didn't tell him to stop. He wept against her breasts, and she whispered to him and rocked with him. He kissed the top of her left breast. He wondered if she noticed – his face was so wet that maybe she couldn't tell – and started to lift his face, to see her expression, to see if she liked it. But she pushed his face back down, holding him to her bosom.

'Go ahead,' she whispered, her voice soft, an excited whisper. 'Just go ahead. It's all right now. There's no one here but us. There's no one to see.' Holding his mouth to her breast.

He felt himself stiffening in his pants and became aware then of the way she was standing, his left leg planted between her thighs. He wondered if it had turned her on, the dead body. There was a strain of psychology that felt the presence of a corpse was an aphrodisiac. A corpse was a get-out-of-jail-free card, permission to do a crazy thing. After he had screwed her, she could assuage any guilt she felt, or thought she was supposed to feel – Lee didn't exactly believe in guilt, he believed in fixing things to satisfy social norms – by telling herself they were both carried away by their grief, by their desperate needs. He kissed her breast again and a third time, and she didn't try to get away.

'I love you, Merrin,' he whispered, the right thing to say, he knew it. It would make everything easier: for him and for her. As he said it, he had his hand on her hip and was swaying, forcing her to totter back on her heels so her rump was pushed up against the kitchen island. He had a fistful of skirt, pulling it up to mid-thigh, and his leg was well between her thighs, and he could feel the heat of her crotch against it.

'I love you, too,' she said, but her tone was off. 'We both do, Lee. Ig and I.' A strange thing to say, considering what they were doing, strange to bring Ig into it. She let go of the back of his head and dropped her hands to his waist, put them lightly on his hips. He wondered if she was feeling for his belt. He reached up to take her blouse, meaning to pull it open – if he busted a couple of buttons, then so be it – but his hand caught the little gold cross around her throat, and at the same time a completely unplanned convulsive sob passed through him. His hand jerked at the cross and there was a soft metallic chiming sound, and it came loose and slipped down the front of her blouse.

'Lee,' she said, pushing him back. 'My necklace.'

It fell softly against the floor. They stood looking down at it, and then Lee bent and got it and held it out to her. It shone in the sun and lit her face in gold.

'I can fix it,' Lee said.

'You did last time, didn't you?' she said, and smiled, her face flushed, her eyes weepy. She fidgeted with her blouse. A button had come undone, and he had left the top of her breast wet. She reached forward and put her hands over his, closed his fingers around the cross. 'Fix it and give it back to me when you're ready. You don't even have to use Ig as the middleman this time.'

Lee twitched in spite of himself, wondered for a moment if she could mean what he thought she meant by that. But of course she did, of course she knew exactly how he'd take it. A lot of what Merrin said had double meanings, one for public consumption and the other just for him. She'd been sending him messages for years.

She cast a discerning eye over him and said, 'How long have you been in those clothes?'

'I don't know. Two days.'

'All right. I want you to get out of those things and in the shower.'

He felt his heart tighten; his cock was hot against his thigh. He looked at the front door. There wasn't time for him to wash up before they had sex.

'People are coming,' he said.

'Well. No one is here yet. There's time. Go on. I'll bring you your drink.'

He walked ahead of her down the back hallway, as hard as he'd ever been in his life, grateful his underwear was holding it down against his leg. He thought she might follow him into the bathroom and reach around and unbutton his pants for him, but when he stepped in, she closed the door gently behind him.

Lee undressed and got into the shower and waited for her, the hot water hammering against him. Steam billowed. His pulse was quick and forceful, and his absurd erection wavered in the spray. When her hand reached around the curtain with his drink, another rum and Coke, he thought she would step in after it, clothes off, but as soon as he took the drink, she pulled her hand back.

'Ig's here,' she said. Her voice soft and full of regret.

'Made it in record time,' Ig said from somewhere behind her. 'How are you, man?'

'Hello, Ig,' Lee said, the sound of Ig's voice as unwelcome as if the hot water had cut out all at once. 'Doing okay. Given the circumstances. Thank you for coming.' The 'thank you' didn't come out quite right this time, but he decided Ig would hear the edge in his voice and write it off as emotional strain.

'I'll bring you something to wear,' Merrin said, and then they were gone; he heard the door shut with a click.

He stood in the hot water, half in a rage at the idea that Ig should be here already, wondering if he knew something – no – had an idea that – no, no. Ig had come at high speed because a friend needed him. That was Ig to the core.

Lee wasn't sure how long he'd been there before he realised that his right hand was hurting. He looked at it and found he was holding the cross, the gold chain wrapped around his hand, cutting into the skin. She had looked him in the eye, with her blouse half unbuttoned, and offered him her cross. She could not have offered herself to him any more plainly, his leg between her thighs while she surrendered it to him. There were things she did not dare say outright, but he understood the message she was sending him, understood her perfectly. He looped the chain of the cross around the showerhead, watched it swing, flashing in the late-morning light, flashing the all clear. Soon Ig would be in England and there would be no more reason for caution, nothing to stop them from doing what they both wanted.

32

After his mother died, Merrin called and e-mailed more frequently, under the pretence of checking to see how he was doing. Or perhaps that really was what she thought she was doing – Lee could not underrate the average person's ability to deceive themselves about what they wanted. Merrin had internalised a lot of Iggy's morality, and Lee thought she could only go so far, could only hint so much, and then he would have to take the lead. Also, even with Ig away in England, they wouldn't necessarily have a clear path at first. Merrin had settled on a set of rules about how people of high status acted. She would have to be persuaded that if she were going to fuck someone else, it was actually in Ig's best interests. Lee understood. Lee could help her with that.

Merrin left messages for him at home, at the congressman's office. She wanted to know how he was doing, *what* he was doing, if he was seeing anyone. She told him he needed a woman, he needed to get laid. She said she was thinking of him. It wasn't hard to see what she was working up to. He thought often she called after having a couple of drinks, could hear it in her voice, a kind of sexy slowness.

Then Ig went to New York City for his orientation with Amnesty International, and a few days later Merrin began pestering Lee to come see her. Her roommate was moving out, and Merrin was going to take her bedroom and would have twice as much space. There was a dresser she had left at home, in Gideon, that she wanted, and she e-mailed Lee, asked if he would bring it down the next time he got to Boston. She told him her Victoria's Secret things were in the bottom drawer, to save him the trouble of searching for them. She told him he could try on her fancy underwear, but only if he took pictures of himself and sent them to her. She texted him, said if he brought her the dresser, she would fix him up with a girl, a blonde, just like him, a snow queen. She wrote that the sex would be great, just like beating off in front of a mirror, only better, because his reflection would have tits. She reminded him that with her roommate gone there was an extra bedroom at her apartment in case he got lucky. Letting him know she would be alone.

By then Lee had learned to read her coded messages almost perfectly. When she talked about this other girl, she was talking about herself, what they had to look forward to. Still, he had not decided to bring the dresser, was not sure he wanted to meet her while Ig was in America, even if he was a few hundred miles away. They might not be able to keep their impulses in check. Things would be easier with Ig gone.

Lee had always assumed it would be Ig who discarded Merrin. It hadn't crossed his mind that *she* might want out, might be bored and ready finally to be done, and that Ig's going away for six months was her chance to make a clean break. Ig came from money, had a last name with some cachet, had a connected family, and it made sense for him to play the field. Lee had always assumed that Ig would dump her around the time they graduated from high school, and that would fix that; Lee could have his turn with her then. She was going to Harvard, and Ig was going to Dartmouth. Out of sight, out of mind, that was what Lee figured, but Ig figured different, was down in Boston fucking her every weekend, like a dog marking his territory.

All Lee could think was that on some level Ig held on to her out of a perverse desire to hold her *over* Lee. Ig was glad to have Lee as his sidekick – the reformation of Lee Tourneau had been Ig's high-school hobby – but he would want Lee to know there were limits to their friendship. He would not want Lee to forget who had won her. As if Lee did not remember every time he closed his right eye and the world became a dim shadowland, a place where ghosts crept through the darkness and the sun was a cold and distant moon.

A part of Lee respected how Ig had taken her away from him, back when they both had an equal shot at her. Ig had simply wanted that red pussy more than Lee, and under pressure he had become someone different, someone wily and smooth. With his asthma and bad hair and head full of Bible trivia, no one would ever think of Ig as ruthless or cunning. Lee had stayed close to Ig for most of ten years, following his lead. He thought of them as lessons in disguise, lessons in how to appear harmless, *safe*. Faced with any ethical quandary, Lee had learned it was best to ask, What Would Ig Do? The answer, usually, was apologise, abase himself, and then fling himself into some entirely unnecessary act of make-nice. Lee had learned from Ig to admit he was wrong even when he wasn't, to ask for forgiveness he didn't need, and to pretend he didn't want the things he had coming to him.

For a brief time, when he was fifteen, she had been his by right. For a few days he had worn Merrin's cross around his neck, and when he sometimes pressed that cross to his lips, he could imagine he was kissing it while she wore it about her throat – the cross and nothing else. But then he let her cross and his chance at her slip through his fingers, because even more than he wanted to see her pale and naked in the dark, he wanted to see something shatter, wanted to hear an explosion loud enough to deafen him, wanted to see a car erupt into flame. His mother's Caddy maybe, with her in it. The very thought made his pulse racy and strange in a way fantasies of Merrin couldn't match. So he gave her up, gave her back. Made his fool's deal with Ig – a deal with the devil, really. It had not just cost him the girl. It had cost him his eye. He felt there was meaning in this. Lee had done a miracle once, had touched the sky and caught the moon before it could fall, and ever since, God had pointed him towards other things that needed fixing: cats and crosses, political campaigns and senile old women. What he fixed was his forever, to do with as he liked, and only once had he given away what God put into his hands, and he had been blinded as a reminder not to do it again. And now the cross was his once more, proof, if he needed it, that he was being guided towards something, that he and Merrin were being brought together for a reason. He felt he was supposed to fix the cross and then fix her in some way, maybe simply by setting her free of Ig.

Lee might've kept his distance from Merrin all summer, but then Ig made it easy for him to go see her, sent him an e-mail from NYC:

Merrin wants her dresser but doesn't have a car and her dad's got work. I said ask you to bring it down and she said you aren't her bitch, but you and I both know you are, so bring it down next time you get to Boston for the congressman. Besides, she has snared an available blonde for you. Imagine the children this woman will bear you, little Vikings with eyes like the Arctic Ocean. Go to Merrin now. You cannot resist her summons. Let her buy you a nice dinner. You've got to be ready to leap in to do her dirty work now that I'm heading off. Are you hanging in there? – Ig

Lee didn't understand the last part of Ig's e-mail for hours – *Are you hanging in there?* – puzzled over it all morning, then remembered that his mother was dead, had been dead for two weeks. He was more interested in that line about leaping in to do Merrin's dirty work, a kind of message in and of itself. That night Lee suffered overheated, sexually complicated dreams; he dreamed that Merrin was naked in his bed, and he sat on top of her arms and held her down while he forced a funnel into her mouth, a red plastic funnel, and then poured gasoline into it, and she began to buck under him as in orgasm. He lit a match, holding the matchbook in his teeth to keep the strike strip steady, and dropped it down the funnel, and there was a whoosh, and a cyclone of red flames rose from the hole, and her surprised eyes ignited. When he woke, he found the sheets soaked. He had never before had a wet dream of such power, even as a young man.

Two days later it was Friday, and he drove to Merrin's to get the dresser. He had to move a heavy, rusting toolbox from the trunk to the back seat to make room for it, and even then he had to borrow straps from Merrin's father to keep the lid down and the dresser in place. Halfway to Boston, Lee pulled over at a rest area and sent her a text message: **Coming down to Boston tonight, got this heavy SOB in the trunk, you better be there to take it. Is my ice queen around, maybe I can meet her.**

There was a long wait before Merrin replied: **ah, sht Lee you are the best dam man for cuming to c me but shouldve told me you were on the wy no icequeen tonite shes workin guess youll have to make do with me.**

33

Merrin answered the door in sweatpants and a bulky hoodie, and her roommate was there, a butchy Asian girl with an annoying snicker. She was pacing around the living room, talking on a cell phone, her voice nasal and painfully cheerful.

'What do you have in this thing anyway?' Lee said. He leaned on the dresser, breathing hard and wiping sweat from his face. He had wheeled it in, strapped to a dolly that Merrin's dad had told him to take with him, banged it up seventeen steps to get it to the landing, nearly dumping it twice. 'Chainmail underwear?'

The roomie looked over Merrin's shoulder and said, 'Try a cast-iron chastity belt.' And wandered off, trailing goose-honk laughter.

'Thought your roomie moved,' Lee said when she'd got out of earshot.

'She's going away the same time Ig does,' Merrin told him. 'San Diego. After that I'll be all alone here for a while.'

Looking him in the eyes and smirking a little. Another message.

They wrestled the dresser in through the door, and then Merrin said just leave it and went into the kitchen to heat up some Indian food. She brought paper plates to a round, stained table under a window with a view of the street. Kids were skateboarding in the summer night, gliding out of the shadows and into the orange-tinted pools of light cast by the sodium-vapour streetlamps.

Merrin's notebooks and papers were spread all over one side of the table and she began collecting them in a pile to get them out of the way. Lee bent over her shoulder, pretending to look at her work while he drew in a long, sweet breath of her scented hair. He saw loose sheets of ruled notebook paper with dots and dashes arranged on them in a grid.

'What's with connect-the-dots?'

'Oh,' she said, collecting the papers and sticking them in a textbook and putting them up on the windowsill, 'my room-mate. We play that game, you know that game? Where you make all the dots, and then connect them into squares, and whoever has the most squares wins. Loser has to do laundry. She hasn't had to wash her own clothes in months.'

Lee said, 'You should let me have a look. I'm good at that game. I could help you with your next move.' He had only caught a brief glimpse of it, but it didn't even look like the grid had been drawn correctly. Maybe it was a different version of the game to the one he knew.

'I think that would be cheating. You're saying you want to make a cheater out of me?' she asked.

They held each other's stare for a moment. Lee said, 'I want what you want.'

'Well. I think I should try to win fair and square. No pun intended.'

They sat across from each other. Lee looked around, considering the place. It wasn't much of an apartment: a living room, a kitchenette, and two bedrooms on the second floor of a rambling Cambridge house that had been divided into five units. Dance music thumped overhead.

'Are you going to be able to cover the rent with no room-mate?'

'No. I'll have to find someone to shack up with eventually.'

'I bet Ig would help with the rent.'

She said, 'He'd pay the whole thing. I could be his kept mistress. I had an offer like that once, you know.'

'What offer?'

'One of my professors asked me out to lunch a few months ago. I thought we were going to talk about my residency. Instead he got us a two-hundred-dollar bottle of wine and told me he wanted to rent me a place in Back Bay. Sixty-year-old guy with a daughter two years older than me.'

'Married?'

'Of course.'

Lee sat back in his chair and whistled through his teeth. 'Ig must've shit himself.'

'I didn't tell him. And don't you say anything about it either. I shouldn't have mentioned it.'

'Why didn't you tell Ig?'

'Because I'm doing coursework with the guy. I wouldn't want Ig to report him for sexual harassment or something.'

'Ig wouldn't report him.'

'No. I guess not. But he would've wanted me to drop coursework with him. Which I didn't want to do. However he acts outside the classroom, the guy is one of the best oncologists in the country, and at the time I wanted to see what he could teach me. It seemed important.'

'It doesn't seem important any more?'

'Hell. I don't need to graduate first in anyone's class. I have mornings when I think I'll be lucky just to graduate at all,' she said.

'Ah, come on. You're doing great.' Lee paused and said, 'How'd the old bastard take it? When you told him to get screwed?'

'With good humour. The wine was nice. Early nineties from a little family vineyard in Italy. I have a feeling he's bought the exact same bottle for a few other girls. Anyway, I didn't tell him to get screwed. I told him I was in love with someone and also didn't think it would be appropriate while I was studying with him, but under other circumstances I would've been glad to entertain the idea.'

'That was kind of you.'

'It's true. If I weren't his student *and* if I'd never met Ig? I could imagine going out with him to a foreign film or something.'

'Get the hell out. Didn't you say he's old?'

'Old enough to qualify for AARP.'

Lee sank back into his chair, feeling something unfamiliar: disgust. And surprise. 'You're kidding.'

'Sure. He might teach me about wines. And books. And stuff I don't know about. What life looks like from the other end of the telescope. What it's like to be in an immoral relationship,' Merrin said.

'It'd be a mistake,' Lee said.

'I think maybe you have to make a few,' Merrin said. 'If you don't, you're probably thinking too much. That's the worst mistake you can make.'

'What about the old dude's wife and daughter?'

'Yeah. I don't know about that part. Course, it's the third wife, so it's not like she'd be terribly shocked.' Merrin narrowed her eyes and said, 'You think every guy gets bored sooner or later?'

'I think most guys fantasise about what they don't have. I know I've never been in a relationship in my life where I wasn't fantasising about other girls.'

'At what point? When in a relationship does a guy start thinking about other girls?'

Lee tipped his head back to stare at the ceiling, pretended to think. 'I dunno. About fifteen minutes into the first date? Depends if the waitress is hot.'

She smirked, then said, 'Sometimes I'll see Ig looking at a girl. Not often. If he knows I'm around, he keeps his eyes in his head. But, like, when we were down to Cape Cod this summer and I went to the car to get the suntan lotion and then remembered I'd stuck it in my windbreaker. He didn't think I'd be back so soon, and he was looking at this girl on her belly, with the back of her bikini top undone. Pretty girl, maybe nineteen, twenty. When we were in high school, I would've raked him up and down for looking, but now I don't say anything. I don't know what to say. He's never been with anyone except me.'

'Is that right?' Lee asked in an incredulous tone, although he already knew.

'Do you think when he's thirty-four he'll feel like I trapped him too young? You think he'll feel like he was cheated out of fun high-school sex and be fantasising about the girls he missed out on?'

'I'm sure he fantasises about other girls now,' said Merrin's roommate, passing through with a Hot Pocket in one hand, holding the phone to her ear with another. She continued on into her room and slammed her door. Not because she was angry, or even aware of what she was doing. Just because she was the kind of person who slammed doors without noticing.

Merrin sat back in her chair, arms crossed. 'True or false. What she said?'

'Not in a serious way. Like him checking out the girl on the beach. He might enjoy thinking about it, but it's just a thought, so what's it matter, right?'

Merrin leaned forward and said, 'Do you think Ig will do a little sleeping around in England? To get it out of his system? Or do you think he'd feel like he was stepping out in an unforgivable way on me and the kids?'

'What kids?'

'The kids. Harper and Charlie. We've been talking about them since I was nineteen.'

'Harper and Charlie?'

'Harper is the girl, after Harper Lee. My favourite one-book novelist. Charlie if it's a boy. 'Cause Ig likes when I say, "Solly, Cholly".' The way she said it made Lee not like her so much. She looked distracted and happy, and he could tell from the suddenly distant look in her eyes that she was imagining them herself.

'No,' Lee said.

'No what?'

'Ig won't sleep around on you. Not unless you slept around on him first and made sure he knew it. Then I guess, yeah. Maybe. Reverse this for a minute. Do you ever think maybe you'll be thirty-five and feel like *you* missed something?'

'No,' she said with a flat, disinterested certainty. 'I don't think I'll ever be thirty-five and feeling like I missed out on anything. That's an awful idea, you know.'

'What is?'

'Screw someone just to tell him about it.' She wasn't looking at him but staring out the window. 'The thought kind of makes me sick.'

The funny thing is, she looked a little sick right then. For the first time, Lee noticed how pale she was, dull pink circles under her eyes, her hair limp. Her hands were doing something with her paper napkin, folding it into smaller and smaller squares.

'Do you feel okay? You look a little off.'

The corners of her mouth twitched in a half-smile. 'I think I'm coming down with something. Don't worry about it. As long as we don't tongue each other, you won't catch it.'

He was fuming when he drove away an hour later. That was the way Merrin operated. She had lured him down to Boston, led him to imagine they would be alone together, then answered the door in her sweatpants, looking like warmed-over shit, her roomie wandering around, and they had spent the night talking about Ig. If she hadn't let him kiss her breast two weeks ago and given him her cross, he would've thought she had no interest in him at all. He was sick of being jerked around, and sick of her talk.

But as he crossed the Zakim Bridge, Lee's pulse began to slow and he began to breathe more normally, and it came to him that Merrin had never once mentioned the ice-queen blonde, not the whole time he was there. This was followed by another notion, that there was no ice queen, there was only Merrin, seeing how much she could get him worked up, keeping him thinking.

He was thinking, all right. He was thinking Ig would be gone soon enough, and so would her roommate, and sometime in the fall he would knock on her door, and when she opened it, she'd be alone.

34

Lee had hoped for a late night with Merrin, but it was just after ten when he crossed the border into New Hampshire and noticed he had a voicemail from the congressman. The congressman spoke in his slow, tired, migraine voice and said he hoped Lee would stop by tomorrow morning to talk over some news that had come in. The way he said it made Lee think he'd be just as glad to see him tonight, so instead of getting off I-95 to drive west to Gideon, he continued north and took the exit for Rye.

Eleven o'clock, Lee pulled into the congressman's driveway of crushed white seashells. The house, a vast white Georgian with a columned portico, sat on an acre of immaculately groomed green lawn. The congressman's twins were playing croquet with their boyfriends, all of them out in the front yard, in the floodlights. Champagne flutes stood on the path next to the girls' high heels; they were running around in bare feet. Lee got out of the Caddy and stood next to it, watching them play, two limber and brown-legged girls in summer dresses, one of them bent over her mallet and her date reaching around from behind, offering his help as an excuse to spoon against her. The laughter of the girls carried on air that smelled faintly of the sea, and Lee felt himself again in his element.

The congressman's girls loved Lee, and when they saw him

coming up the walk, they ran straight to him. Kaley put her arms around his neck, and Daley planted a kiss on the side of his face. Twenty-one and tanned and happy, but there had been hushed-up trouble with both: binge drinking, anorexia, a venereal disease. He hugged them back and kidded and promised to come out and play croquet with them if he could, but his skin crawled at their touch. They looked smooth and fine but were as rancid as chocolate-covered cockroaches; one of them was chewing a stick of spearmint, and he wondered if it was to cover up the odour of cigarettes, weed or dick. He would not have slept with both of them together at the same time in trade for a night with Merrin, who was, in some ways, still clean, still possessed of the body of a sixteen-year-old virgin. She had only ever slept with Ig, and knowing Ig as Lee did, that hardly counted. Ig probably kept a sheet between them the whole time.

The congressman's wife met Lee at the door, a small woman with feathered grey-and-black hair, thin lips frozen into a stiff smile from all the Botox. She touched Lee's wrist. They all liked to touch him, the congressman's wife and his children, and the congressman, too, as if Lee were some totem of good luck, a rabbit's foot – and he was, and he knew it.

'He's in his study,' she said. 'He'll be so glad to see you. You knew to come?'

'I knew. Headache?'

'Awful.'

'All right,' Lee said. 'No worries. The doctor is in.'

Lee knew where the study was and made his way there. He knocked on the pocket door but didn't wait to be told to enter before sliding it back. The lights were off, except for the television, and the congressman was on the couch in the dark with a wet washcloth folded into a band and laid across his eyes. *Hothouse* was on the TV. The volume was turned all the way down, but Lee could see Terry Perrish sitting behind his desk, interviewing some skinny Brit in a black leather jacket, a rock star, maybe.

The congressman heard the door, lifted one corner of the washcloth, saw Lee, and smiled with half his mouth. He dropped the washcloth back into place.

'There you are,' the congressman said. 'I almost didn't leave that message, because I knew you'd worry and come see me tonight, and I didn't want to bother you on your Friday evening. I take up too much of your life as it is. You should be out on the town with a girl.' He spoke in the soft, loving tones of a man on his deathbed speaking to a favourite son. It was not the first time Lee had heard him talking so, or the first time he'd tended to him while he suffered with one of his migraines. The congressman's headaches were closely associated with fund-raising and bad poll numbers. They'd been coming in bunches lately. Not a dozen people in the state knew it, but early next year the congressman would announce that he intended to run for governor against an incumbent who had won the last election in a landslide, but who had slid badly in the polls in the years since. Anytime her approval rating ticked up more than three points, the congressman needed to dry-swallow some Motrin and go lie down. He had never leaned on Lee's calm so much.

'That was the plan,' Lee said, 'but she bailed on me, and you're twice as cute, so no loss.'

The congressman wheezed with laughter. Lee sat on the coffee table, catty-corner to him.

'Who died?' Lee asked.

'The governor's husband,' the congressman said.

Lee hesitated, then said, 'Boy, I hope you're kidding.'

The congressman lifted the washcloth again. 'He has Lou Gehrig's. ALS. Was just diagnosed. There'll be a press conference tomorrow. They've been married twenty years next week. Isn't that the most awful thing?'

Lee had been ready for some bad internal-polling numbers, or maybe to learn that the *Portsmouth Herald* was going to run an unflattering story about the congressman (or the girls – there'd been more than a few of those). He needed a moment to process this one, though.

'God,' Lee said.

'What I said. It started with a thumb that wouldn't stop twitching. Now it's both hands. The course of the disease has apparently been quite rapid. You know not the day or the hour, do you?'

'No, sir.'

They sat together in silence. The TV played.

'My best friend in grammar school, his father had it,' the congressman said. 'The poor man would sit there in his easy chair in front of the TV, twitching like a fish on a hook, and sounding half the time like he was being choked to death by the Invisible Man. I am so sorry for them. I can't imagine what I'd do if one of the girls got sick. Do you want to pray for them with me, Lee?'

Not even a little, Lee thought, but he got on his knees at the coffee table and put his hands together and waited. The congressman got down on the floor next to him and bowed his head. Lee closed his eyes to concentrate, to work it through. It would boost her approval rating, for starters; personal tragedies were always good for a few thousand sympathy votes. Also, health care had always been her best issue, and this would play into that, give her a way to make the subject personal. Finally, it was difficult enough as it was to run against a woman, hard not to look like a chauvinist, a bully. But running against one who was heroically caring for an infirm spouse – who knew how *that* would play out over a campaign? Depended on the media, maybe, what angle they decided to work. Was there any angle that didn't wind up as a net plus for her? Maybe. Lee thought there was at least one possibility worth praying for – at least one way to fix it.

After a while the congressman sighed, an indication that prayer time was over. They continued to kneel together, quite companionably.

'Do you think I shouldn't run?' the congressman asked. 'Out of decency?'

'Her husband's illness is one kind of tragedy,' Lee said. 'Her policies are another. It's not just about her. It's about everyone in the state.'

The congressman shuddered and said, 'I'm ashamed to even be thinking about it. As if the only thing that matters are my goddamned political ambitions. Sin of pride, Lee. Sin of pride.'

'We don't know what's going to happen. Maybe she'll decide she needs to step down to care for him, won't run next time out, in which case better you than anyone else.'

The congressman shuddered again. 'We shouldn't talk this way. Not tonight. I really do feel indecent. This is a man's life and health. Whether I decide to run for governor or not is the least important thing in the world.' He rocked forward on his knees, staring blankly at the TV. Licked his lips. Then said, 'If she did step down, though, maybe it would be irresponsible *not* to run.'

'Oh, God, yes,' Lee said. 'Can you imagine if you didn't go for it and Bill Flores was elected governor? They'd be teaching sex ed in kindergarten, passing out rubbers to six-year-olds. Okay, kids, raise your hand if you think you know how to spell "sodomy".'

'Stop,' the congressman said, but he was laughing. 'You're awful.'

'You weren't even going to announce for five months,' Lee said. 'A lot can happen in a year. People aren't going to vote for her because her husband is sick. The sick spouse didn't help John Edwards in this state. Shoot, it probably hurt him. He looked like he was putting his career ahead of his wife's health.' Already thinking that it would look even worse, a woman giving speeches while her husband did a spastic dance in a wheelchair next to the podium. It would be a bad visual, and would people really want to vote for three more years of *that* on their TV? Or a woman who thought winning an election was more important than caring for her husband? 'People vote on the issues, not out of sympathy.' A lie; people voted with their nerve endings. That was how to fix it, to quietly, indirectly use her husband's illness to make her look that much more uncaring, that much less like a lady. There was always a way to fix it. 'It'll be old news by the time you get into things. People will be ready to change the subject.'

But Lee wasn't sure the congressman was listening anymore. He was squinting at the TV. Terry Perrish was slumped back in his chair, playing dead, his head cocked at an unnatural angle. His guest, the skinny English rock star in the black leather jacket, made the sign of the cross over his body.

'Aren't you friends with him? Terry Perrish?'

'More his brother. Ig. They're all wonderful people, though, the Perrish family. They were everything to me, growing up.'

'I've never met them. The Perrish family.'

'I think they lean Democrat.'

'People vote for friends before party,' the congressman said. 'Maybe we could all be friends.' He punched Lee in the shoulder, as if at a sudden idea. He seemed to have forgotten about his migraine. 'Hey, wouldn't it be something to announce the run for the governor's seat on Terry Perrish's show next year?'

'It would. It sure would,' Lee said.

'Think there's any way to fix it?'

'Why don't I take him out the next time he's around,' Lee said, 'and put in the good word for you. See what happens.'

'Sure,' the congressman said. 'You do that. Paint the town

red. Do it on my dime.' He sighed. 'You cheer me up. I'm a very blessed man, and I know it. And you are one of those blessings, Lee.' He looked at Lee with eyes that twinkled in a grandfatherly sort of way. He could do it on cue, make those Santa Claus eyes. 'You know, Lee, you aren't too young to run for congress yourself. My seat is going to be empty in a couple of years, one way or another. You have very magnetic qualities. You're good-looking and honest. You have a good personal story of redemption through Christ. You tell a mean joke.'

'I don't think so. I'm happy with the work I'm doing now – for you. I don't think running for office is my true calling,' Lee said, and without any embarrassment at all added, 'I don't believe that's what the Lord wants of me.'

'That's too bad,' said the congressman. 'The party could use you, and there's no telling how high you could climb. Heck, give yourself a chance – you could be our next Reagan.'

'Nah,' Lee said. 'I'd rather be the next Karl Rove.'

35

His mother didn't have a lot to say at the end. Lee wasn't sure how much she knew in the final weeks. Most days she spoke variations of only one word, her voice crazed and cracking: 'Thirst! Thirst-ee!' Her eyes straining from their sockets. Lee would sit by the bed, naked in the heat, reading a magazine. By midday it was ninety-five degrees in the bedroom, maybe fifteen degrees hotter under the piled comforters. His mother didn't always seem to know Lee was in the room with her. She stared at the ceiling, her weak arms struggling pitifully under the blankets, like a woman lost overboard, flailing to tread water. Other times her great eyes would roll in their sockets to point a pleading, terrified look in Lee's direction. Lee would sip his iced tea and pay no mind.

Some days, after changing a diaper, Lee would forget to put on a new one, and leave his mother naked from the waist down under the covers. When she peed herself, she would begin to call, 'Wet! Wet! Oh, God, Lee! Wet myself!' Lee was never in a hurry to change her sheets, a laborious, tiresome process. Her pee smelled bad, like carrots, like kidney failure. When Lee did change the sheets, he would ball up the wet linens and then press them down over his mother's face while she howled in a confused and strangled voice. Which was after all what his mother had done to him, rubbing his face in the sheets when he wet them. Her way of teaching him not to piss the bed, a problem in his youth.

'Do you need something to drink, Mom?' Lee would ask her in a mild tone of voice, squashing the piss-soaked sheets into her face. 'Are you awfully thirsty? Here you go, Ma. Drink up.'

His mother, however, had a single lucid moment towards the end of May, after weeks of incoherence – a dangerous moment of clarity. Lee had awoken before dawn in his bedroom on the second floor. He didn't know what had stirred him, only that something was wrong. He sat up on his elbows, listening intently to the stillness. It was before five, and there was a faint show of false dawn greying the sky outside. The window was open a crack, and he could smell new grass, freshly budded trees. The air wafting in had a warm, humid weight to it. If it was warm already, the day was going to be a scorcher, especially in the guest room, where he was finding out if it was possible to slow-cook an old woman. Finally he heard something, a soft thud downstairs, followed by a sound like someone scraping shoes on a plastic mat.

He rose and padded quietly downstairs to check on his mother. He thought he'd find her asleep, or maybe staring blankly at the ceiling. He didn't think he'd find her rolled on her left side, fumbling with one withered claw for the phone. She had knocked the receiver out of the cradle and it was hanging to the floor by the coiled beige wire. She had collected a bunch of the wire in one hand, trying to pull the receiver up to where she could reach it, and it was swinging back and forth, scraping the floor, occasionally batting lightly against the night table.

His mother stopped trying to collect the wire when she saw Lee standing there. Her harrowed, sunken face was calm, almost expectant. She had once had thick, honey-coloured hair, which for years she'd kept short but full, her curls feathering her shoulders. Farrah Fawcett hair. Now, though, she was balding, thin silver strands combed sideways across her liver-spotted dome.

'What are you doing, Mom?' Lee asked.

'Making a call.'

'Who were you going to call?' As he spoke, he registered the clarity in her voice and knew that she had, impossibly, surfaced from her dementia for the moment.

His mother gave him a long blank stare, then said, 'What are you?' Partially surfaced anyway.

'Lee. Don't you know me?'

'You aren't him. Lee is out walking on the fence. I told him not to. I said he'd pay the devil for it, but he can't help himself.'

Lee crossed the room and set the phone back in the cradle. Leaving an operating phone almost in arm's reach had been idiotically careless, and never mind her condition.

As he bent forward to unplug the phone from the wall, though, his mother reached out and grabbed his wrist. Lee almost screamed, he was so surprised at the ferocious strength in her gaunt and gnarled fingers.

'I'm going to die anyway,' she said. 'Why do you want me to suffer? Why don't you just stand back and let it happen?'

Lee said, 'Because I wouldn't learn anything if I just let it happen.'

He expected another question, but instead his mother said, in an almost-satisfied voice, '*Yes.* That's right. Learn about what?'

'If there are limits.'

'To what I can survive?' his mother asked, and then went on, 'No. No, that's not it. You mean limits to what you can do.' She sank back into her pillows – and Lee was surprised to see she was smiling in a knowing sort of way. 'You aren't Lee. Lee

318

is on the fence. If I catch him walking on that fence again, he'll feel the back of my hand. He's been told.'

She inhaled deeply, and her eyelids sank shut. He thought maybe she was settling down to go back to sleep – she often slipped into unconsciousness quite rapidly – but then she spoke again. There was a musing tone in her thin, old voice. 'Ordered an espresso maker from a catalogue one time. I think it might have been the Sharper Image. Pretty little thing, lot of copper trim. I waited a couple weeks and it finally showed up on the doorstep. I sliced open the box, and would you believe it? There was nothing in there but packaging. Eighty-nine dollars for bubble wrap and Styrofoam. Someone must've gone to sleep in the espresso-machine factory.' She exhaled a long, satisfied breath.

'And I care ... why?' Lee asked.

'Because it's the same with you,' she said, opening her great shining eyes and turning her head to stare at him. Her smile widened to show what teeth remained, small and yellow and uneven, and she started to laugh. 'You ought to ask for your money back. You got gypped. You're just packaging. Just a good-looking box with nothing in it.' Her laughter was harsh and broken and gasping.

'Stop laughing at me,' Lee said, which made his mother laugh more, and she didn't stop until Lee gave her a double dose of morphine. Then he went into the kitchen and drank a Bloody Mary with a lot of pepper, his hand shaking as he held the glass.

The urge was strong in Lee to pour his mother a scalding mug of salt water and make her drink the whole thing. Drown her with it.

Instead, though, he let her be; if anything, he looked after her with particular care for a week, running the fan all day, changing her sheets regularly, keeping fresh flowers in the room and the TV on. He was especially careful to administer the morphine on schedule, didn't want her going lucid again when the nurse was in the house. Telling tales out of school about her treatment when she was alone with her son. But his anxieties were misplaced; his mother was never clear in the head again.

36

He remembered the fence. He did not remember much about the two years they lived in Bucksport, Maine – did not, for example, even remember *why* they moved there, a place at the ass-end of nowhere, a small town where his parents knew no one. He did not recall why they had returned to Gideon. But he remembered the fence, and the feral tom that came from the corn, and the night he stopped the moon from falling out of the sky.

The tom came out of the corn at dusk. The second or third time it appeared in their backyard, crying softly, Lee's mother went outside to greet it. She had a tin of sardines, and she put it on the ground and waited as the cat crept close. The tom set upon the sardines as if he had not eaten in days – and maybe he hadn't – swallowing silver fish in a series of swift, jerky head motions. Then he twined smoothly between Kathy Tourneau's ankles, purring in a satisfied sort of way. It was a somehow rusty-sounding purr, as if the cat were out of practice being happy.

But when Lee's mother bent to scratch behind his ears, the tom slashed the back of her hand, laying the flesh open in long red lines. She shrieked and kicked him, and he ran, turning over the sardine tin in his haste to get away.

She wore a white bandage on her hand for a week and scarred badly. She carried her marks from the run-in with the tom all the rest of her life. The next time the cat came out of the corn, yowling for attention, she threw a frying pan at it, and it vanished back into the rows.

There were a dozen rows behind the Bucksport house, an acre of low, ratty corn. His parents hadn't planted it and did nothing to tend it. They weren't farmers, weren't even inclined to garden. Lee's mother picked some in August, tried to steam a few ears, but none of them could eat it. It was tasteless, chewy and hard. Lee's father laughed and said it was corn for pigs.

By October the stalks were dried out and brown and dead, a lot of them broken and tilting. Lee loved them, loved the aromatic scent of them on the cold fall air, loved to sneak through the narrow lanes between the rows, with the leaves rasping dryly around him. Years later he remembered loving them, even if he couldn't exactly recall how that love felt. For the adult Lee Tourneau, trying to remember his enthusiasm for the corn was a little like trying to get full on the memory of a good meal.

Where the tom spent the balance of his day was unknown. He didn't belong to the neighbours. He didn't belong to anyone. Lee's mother said he was feral. She said the word 'feral' in the same spitting, ugly tone she used to refer to 'The Winterhaus', the bar Lee's father stopped at every night for a drink (or two, or three) on his way home from work.

The tomcat's ribs were visible in his sides, and his black fur was missing in hunks, to show obscene patches of pink, scabby skin, and his furry balls were as big as shooter marbles, so big they jostled back and forth between his hind legs when he walked. One eye was green, the other white, giving him a look of partial blindness. Lee's mother instructed her only son to stay away from the creature, not to pet him under any circumstances, and not to trust him.

'He won't learn to like you,' she said. 'He's past the point where he can learn to feel for people. He's not interested in you, or anyone, and never will be. He only turns up hoping we'll put something out for him, and if we don't feed him, he'll stop coming around.'

But he didn't stop. Every night, when the sun went down but the clouds were still lit with its glow, the tomcat returned to cry in their backyard.

Lee went looking for him sometimes, as soon as he got home from school. He wondered how the tom spent his day, where he went and where he came from. Lee would climb onto the fence and walk the ties, peering into the corn for the cat.

He could only stay on the fence until his mother spotted him and yelled for him to get down. It was a split-tie, splintery wooden logs slotted into leaning posts, which enclosed the entire backyard, corn and all. The top rail was high off the ground, as high as Lee's head, and the logs shook as he walked across them. His mother said the wood had dry rot, that one of the ties would shatter underfoot, and then it would be a trip to the hospital (his father would wave a dismissive hand in the air and say, 'Whyn't you leave him alone and let him be a kid?'). But he couldn't stay off it; no kid could've. He didn't just climb on it or walk across it as if it were a balance beam, but sometimes he even ran across it, arms stuck out to either side, as if he were some gangly crane attempting to take off. It felt good, to run the fence, posts shaking underfoot and the blood pumping in him.

The tom went to work on Kathy Tourneau's sanity. He would announce his arrival from the corn with a plaintive, off-key wail, a single harsh note that he sang over and over again, until Lee's mother couldn't stand it anymore and burst from the back door to throw something at him.

'For God's sake, what do you want?' she screamed at the black tomcat one night. 'You aren't getting fed, so why don't you go away?'

Lee didn't say anything to his mother – but thought he knew

why the cat reappeared every evening. His mother's mistake was, she believed that the cat was crying for food. Lee, though, thought the tom was crying for the previous owners, for the people who lived in the house before them and who treated him the way he wanted to be treated. Lee imagined a freckly girl, about his age, in overalls and with long, straight red hair, who would set out a bowl of cat food for the black cat and then sit at a safe distance to watch him eat without troubling him. Singing to him, maybe. His mother's idea – that the cat had decided to torture them with incessant, shrill crying, just to see how much they could take – seemed an unlikely hypothesis to Lee.

He decided he would learn to be the tomcat's friend, and one night he sat out to wait for him. He told his mother he didn't want dinner, that he was full from the big bowl of cereal he ate when he got back from school, and could he just go outside for a while? She allowed he could, at least until his father got home, and then it was right up into his pyjamas and bed. He did not mention he planned to meet the cat or that he had sardines for him.

It got dark fast in mid-October. It was not even six when he went outside, but the only light left in the sky was a line of hot pink over the fields on the far side of the road. While he waited, he sang to himself, a song that was popular on the radio that year. '*Look at 'em go,*' he whisper-sang, '*look at 'em kiiick . . .*' A few stars were out. He tipped his head back and was surprised to see that one of these stars was moving, tracing a straight line across heaven. After a moment he realised that it had to be an airplane, or maybe a satellite. Or a UFO! What an idea. When he lowered his gaze, the tom was there.

The cat with the mismatched eyes poked his head from between the low stalks of corn to stare at Lee for a long, silent moment, not crying for once. Lee withdrew his hand from the pocket of his coat, moving slowly, so as not to scare it.

'Hey, bud-*dee*,' he said, dragging out the last syllable in a musical sort of way. 'Hey, bud-*dee*.'

The sardine tin made a sharp metal cracking sound as he popped it open and the tom flitted back into the corn, was gone.

'Oh, *no*, buddy,' Lee said, jumping to his feet. It was unfair. He had planned out the whole encounter, how he would lure the cat close with a soft, friendly song and then put the tin down for him, making no move to touch him tonight, just letting him eat. And now he was gone, without giving Lee a chance.

The wind lifted and the corn rustled uneasily, and Lee felt the cold through his coat. He was standing there, too disappointed to move, just staring blankly out at the corn, when the cat leaped into sight again, jumping onto the top rail of the fence. He turned his head to stare back at Lee with bright, fascinated eyes.

Lee was relieved the tom hadn't run off without a look back, was grateful to him for sticking around. Lee made no sudden moves. He crept, rather than walked, and did not speak to the cat again. He thought, when he got close, that the tom would drop back into the corn and vanish. Instead, though, when Lee had reached the fence, the cat took a few steps along the top rail, then paused to look back again, a kind of expectancy in his eyes. Waiting to see if Lee would follow, *inviting* him to follow. Lee took a post and climbed to the top rail. The fence shook, and he thought now, *now* the cat would jump and be gone. Instead the tomcat waited for the fence to stop moving and then began to stroll away, tail in the air to show his black asshole and big balls.

Lee tightroped after the tomcat, arms held out to either side for balance. He did not dare hurry, for fear of frightening him off, but moved at a steady walk. The cat strutted lazily on his way, leading him further and further from the house. The corn grew right up to the fence and dry, thick leaves swatted and brushed Lee's arm. He had a bad moment when one of the rails shook wildly underfoot and he had to crouch down and put a hand on a post to keep from falling. The cat waited for him to recover, crouching on the next tie. He still didn't move when Lee stood back up and crossed the wobbling log to him. Instead he arched his back, ruffling up his fur, and began to purr his strained, rusty purr. Lee was nearly beside himself with excitement, to be so close to him at last, almost close enough to touch.

'Hey,' he breathed, and the tom's purring intensified, and he lifted his back to Lee, and it was impossible to believe he didn't want to be touched.

Lee knew he had promised himself he wouldn't try to pet the tomcat, not tonight, not when they were just making first contact, but it would be rude to reject such an unmistakable request for affection. He reached up gently to stroke him.

'Hey, bud-*dee*,' he sang softly, and the cat squeezed his eyes shut in a look of pure animal pleasure, then opened them and lashed out with one claw.

Lee jerked upright, the claw swishing through the air not an inch from his left eyeball. The rail clattered violently underfoot and Lee's legs went rubbery, and he fell sideways into the corn.

The top rung was only about four feet from the ground in most places, but along that part of the fence the earth sloped away to the left, so the fall was closer to six feet. The pitchfork that lay in the corn had been there for over a decade, had been waiting for Lee since before he was born, lying flat on the earth with the curved and rusted tines sticking straight up. Lee hit it head first.

37

He sat up a while later. The corn whispered frantically, spreading false rumours about him. The cat was gone from the fence. It was full night, and when he looked up, he caught the stars moving. They were all satellites now, shooting in different directions, dropping this way and that. The moon twitched, fell a few inches, twitched again – as if the curtain of heaven were in danger of falling, and revealing the empty stage behind. Lee reached up and straightened the moon and put it back where it belonged. The moon was so cold in his hand that it made his fingers numb, like handling an icicle.

He had to get very tall to fix the moon, and while he was up there, he looked down on his little corner of West Bucksport. He saw things he could not possibly have seen in the corn, saw things the way God saw them. He saw his father's car coming down Pickpocket Lane and turning up the gravel road to their house. He was driving with a six-pack on the passenger seat and a cold one between his thighs. If Lee wanted to, he could've flicked his finger against the car and spun it off the road, tumbling it into the evergreens that screened their house from the highway. He imagined it, the car on its side, flames licking up from under the hood. People would say he was driving blind drunk.

He felt as detached from the world below as he would've been from a model railroad. West Bucksport was just as delightful and precious, with its little trees, and little toy houses, and little toy people. If he wanted to, he could've picked up his own house and moved it across the street. He could've put his heel on it and flattened it underfoot. He could wipe the whole mess off the table with one stroke of his arm.

He saw movement in the corn, an animate shadow sidling among other shadows, and recognised the cat, and knew he had not been raised to this great height just to fix the moon. He had offered food and kindness to the stray, and it had led him on with a show of affection and then lashed out at him and knocked him off the fence and might've killed him, not for any reason but because that was what it was built to do, and now it was walking away as if nothing had happened, and maybe to the cat nothing *had* happened, maybe it had already forgotten Lee, and *that would not do*. Lee reached down with his great arm – it was like being on the top floor of the John Hancock Tower and looking down the length of the glass tower at the ground – and pushed his finger into the cat, mashing it into the dirt. For a single frantic instant, less than a second, he felt a spasm of quivering life under his fingertip, felt the cat trying to leap away, but it was too late and he crushed it, felt it shatter like a dried seed pod. He ground his finger back and forth, the way he had seen his father grind out cigarettes in an ashtray. He killed it with a kind of quiet, subdued satisfaction, feeling a little distant from himself, the way he sometimes got when he was colouring.

After a while he lifted his hand and looked at it, at a streak of blood across his palm and a fluff of black fur stuck to it. He smelled his hand, which had on it a fragrance of musty basements mingled with summer grass. The smell interested him, told a story of hunting mice in subterranean places and hunting for a mate to screw in the high weeds.

Lee lowered his hand to his lap and stared blankly at the cat. He was sitting in the corn again, although he didn't remember sitting down, and he was the same size he'd always been, although he didn't remember getting any smaller. The tomcat was a twisted wreck. Its head was turned around backwards, as if someone had tried to unscrew it like a lightbulb. The tom stared up into the night with wide-eyed surprise. Its skull was battered and misshapen, and brains were coming out one ear. The unlucky black cat lay next to a flat piece of slate, wet with blood. Lee was remotely aware of a stinging in his right arm and looked at it and saw that his wrist and forearm were scratched up, scratches grouped together in three parallel lines, as if he had taken a fork to himself, gouging at his flesh with the tines. He couldn't figure out how the cat had managed to scratch him when he had been so much bigger, but he was tired now and his head hurt, and after a while he gave up trying to figure it out. It was exhausting, being like God, being big enough to fix the things that needed fixing. He pushed himself to his feet, his legs weak beneath him, and started back towards the house.

His mother and father were in the front room, fighting with each other again. Or, really, his father was sitting with a beer and *Sports Illustrated* and not replying while Kathy stood over him, yattering at him in a low, strangled voice. Lee had a little flash of the perfect understanding that had come over him when he was big enough to fix the moon, and he knew that his father went to The Winterhaus every night, not to drink, but to see a waitress, and that they were special friends. Not that either of his parents said anything about the waitress; his mother was furious about a mess in the garage, about him wearing his boots into the living room, about her work. Somehow, though, the waitress was what they were really arguing about. Lee knew, too, that in time – a few years, maybe – his father would leave, and he would not take Lee with him.

It didn't bother him, the way they were fighting. What bothered him was the radio, on in the background, making a clashing, dissonant sound: like pots thrown down a staircase, while someone hissed and sputtered, like a kettle coming to the boil. The sound of it grated on him, and he swerved towards the radio to turn it down and it was only as he was reaching for the volume that he recognised it was that song 'The Devil Inside'. He had no idea why he'd ever liked it. In the weeks to follow, Lee would discover he could not bear almost any music running in the background, that songs no longer made sense to him, were just a mess of aggravating sounds. When a radio was on, he'd leave the room, preferring the quiet that went with his own thoughts.

He felt light-headed climbing the stairs. The walls sometimes seemed to be pulsing, and he was afraid if he looked outside, he might see the moon twitching in the sky again, and this time he might not be able to fix it. He thought it might be best if he lay down before it fell. He said good night from the stairs. His mother didn't notice. His father didn't care.

When Lee woke the next morning, the pillowcase was soaked with dry bloodstains. He studied it without alarm or fear. The smell, an old copper-penny odour, was especially interesting.

A few minutes later he was in the shower and happened to look down between his feet. A thin thread of reddish-brown was racing in the current and whirling down the drain, as if there were rust in the water. Only it wasn't rust. He lifted a hand absently to his head, wondering if he had cut himself when he fell from the fence the night before. His fingers prodded a tender spot on the right side of his skull. He touched what felt like a small depression, and for a moment it was as if someone had dropped a hair dryer into the shower with him, a hard jolt of electricity that made the world flash, turn into a photographic negative for an instant. When the sickening shocked feeling passed, he looked at his hand and found blood on his fingers.

He did not tell his mother he had hurt his head – it didn't

seem important – or explain the blood on his pillow, although she was horrified when she saw the mess.

'Look at this,' she said. 'This is ruined! Completely ruined!' Standing in the middle of the kitchen with the blood-soaked pillowcase in one hand.

'Lay off,' said Lee's father, sitting at the kitchen table holding his head between his hands as he read the sports. He was pale and bristly and sick-looking but still had a smile ready for his boy. 'Kid gets a nosebleed, you act like he killed someone. He ain't murdered anyone.' His father winked at Lee. 'Not yet anyhow.'

38

Lee had a smile ready for Merrin when she opened the door, but she didn't appreciate it, hardly looked at him.

He said, 'I told Ig I had to be in Boston today for the congressman, and he told me if I don't take you out someplace for a nice dinner, he won't be my friend anymore.'

Two girls sat on the couch watching TV, the volume turned up on a rerun of *Growing Pains*. Piled between them and at their feet were stacks of cardboard boxes. Slants, like Merrin's roommate. The roomie sat on the arm of a chair, hollering cheerfully into her cell. Lee didn't think much of Asians in general, hive creatures fixated on phones and cameras, although he did like the Asian-schoolgirl look, black buckled shoes and high socks and pleated skirts. The door to the roomie's bedroom was open and there were more boxes piled on a bare mattress.

Merrin surveyed this scene with a kind of wondering hopelessness, then turned back to Lee. If he had known she was going to be as grey as dishwater, no make-up, hair unwashed, in her baggy old sweats, he would've skipped a visit. Total turn-off. He was already sorry he'd come. He realised he was still smiling and made himself stop, felt for the right thing to say.

'God, are you still sick?' he asked.

She nodded absently and then said, 'Want to go on the roof? Less noisy.'

He followed her up the stairs. They didn't appear to be going out to dinner, but she brought a pair of Heinekens from the fridge, which was better than nothing.

It was going on eight o'clock, but still not dark. The skateboarders were down in the road again, their boards clattering and banging on the asphalt. Lee walked across the roof deck to look over the edge at them. A couple had fauxhawks and wore ties and button-down shirts that were buttoned only at the collar. Lee had never been interested in skateboarding as anything more than a look, because you came off as alternative with a board under your arm, a little dangerous, but also athletic. He didn't like falling, though; just the idea of falling made one whole side of his head go cold and numb.

Merrin touched the small of his back, and for just a moment he thought she was going to push him over the side of the roof, and he was going to twist and grab her by her pale throat and pull her with him. She must've seen the shock on his face, because she smiled for the first time and offered him one of the Heinekens. He nodded thanks and took it and held it in one hand while he lit up with the other.

She sat on an air-conditioning unit with her own beer, not drinking it, just spinning the wet neck around and around in her fingers. Her feet were bare. Her little pink feet were cute anyway. Looking at them, it was easy to imagine her placing one foot between his legs, her toes gently kneading his crotch.

'I think I'm going to try what you said,' she told him.

'Voting Republican?' he asked. 'Progress at last.'

She smiled again, but it was a morose, wan sort of smile. She looked away and said, 'I'm going to tell Ig that when he goes to England, I want to take a relationship vacation. Like a trial break-up, so we can both see other people.'

Lee felt as if he had tripped over something, even though he was standing still. 'When were you planning to lay this on him?'

'When he gets back from New York. I don't want to tell him on the phone. You can't say anything, Lee. You can't even hint.'

'No. I won't.' He was excited and knew it was important not to show it. He said, 'You're going to tell him he should see other people? Other girls?'

She nodded.

'And . . . you, too?'

'I'll tell him that I want to try a relationship with someone else. I'm not going to tell him anything more than that. I'll tell him that whatever happens while he's away is off the books. I don't want to know who he's seeing, and I won't be reporting in to him about my relationships. I think that'll . . . that'll make things easier all around.' She looked up then, a rueful amusement in her eyes. The wind caught her hair and did pretty things with it. She looked less ill and wan out under the pale violet sky at the end of day. 'I feel guilty already, you know.'

'Well. You don't need to. Listen, if you really love each other, you'll know it for sure in six months, and you'll want to get back together.'

She shook her head and said, 'No, I . . . I do think this is looking a little more than temporary. There are some things I've learned about myself this summer, some things I know, that have changed how I feel about my relationship with Ig. I know I can't be married to him. After he's been over in England for a while, after he's had time to meet someone, I'll finish it for good.'

'Jesus,' Lee said softly, playing it again in his head: *There are some things I've learned about myself this summer.* Remembering what it was like in the kitchen with her, his leg between hers, and his hand on the smooth curve of her hip, and her soft, fast breath in his ear. 'Just a couple of weeks ago, you were telling me what you were going to name the kids.'

'Yeah. But when you know something, you know something.

I know I'm never going to have kids with him now.' She seemed calmer, had relaxed a little. She said, 'This is the part where you step up to defend your best friend and talk me out of it. You mad at me?'

'No.'

'Do you think less of me?'

'I'd think less of you if you pretended you still want to be with Ig when you know in your heart there's no future for the two of you.'

'That's it. That's exactly it. And I want Ig to have other relationships, and be with other girls, and be happy. If I know he's happy, it'll be easier for me to move on.'

'Jesus, though. You guys have been together forever.' His hand almost trembled as he shook a second cigarette from his pack. In a week Ig would be gone and she would be alone, and she would not be reporting in to him about who she was fucking.

She nodded at the pack of cigarettes. 'One for me?'

'Seriously? I thought you wanted me to quit.'

'*Ig* wanted you to quit. I was always kind of curious, but, you know. Figured Ig would disapprove. Guess I can try them now.' She rubbed her hands on her knees and said, 'So. Are you going to teach me how to smoke tonight, Lee?'

'Sure,' he said.

In the street a skateboard banged and crashed, and some of the teens shouted in a mixture of appreciation and dismay as a boarder went sprawling. She looked over the edge of the roof.

'I'd like to learn how to skateboard, too,' she said.

'Retarded sport,' Lee said. 'Good way to break something. Like your neck.'

'I'm not too worried about my neck,' she said, and turned and stood on her tiptoes and kissed the corner of his mouth. 'Thank you. For talking me through some things. I owe you, Lee.'

Her tank-top clung to her breasts, and in the cool night air her nipples had crinkled, dimpling the fabric. He thought of reaching up and putting his hands on her hips, wondered if they could get started with a little touch and feel tonight. Before he could reach for her, though, the roof door banged open. It was the roommate, chewing gum, looking at them askance.

'Williams,' said her roommate, 'your boyfriend is on the phone. I guess him and his Amnesty International friends waterboarded each other today, just to see what it feels like. He's all excited, wants to give you the rundown. Sounds like he's got a great job. Did I interrupt something?'

'No,' Merrin said, and turned back to Lee and whispered, 'She thinks you're one of the bad guys. Which, of course, you are. I should go talk to Ig. Raincheck on dinner?'

'When you do talk to him – are you going to say anything about – *us*, the stuff we've talked about—?'

'Oh, hey. No. I can keep a secret, Lee.'

'Okay,' he said, dry-mouthed, wanting her.

'I have one of those butts?' said the fat, butchy slant, coming towards them.

'Sure,' Lee said.

Merrin flapped one hand up in a little wave, crossed the roof, and was gone.

Lee shook a Malboro out for the roommate and lit it for her.

'Heading to San Diego, huh?'

'Yeah,' said the girl. 'I'm moving in with a friend from high school. It's going to be cool. She's got a Wii and everything.'

'Does your old high-school friend play the game with the dots and the lines, or are you going to have to start doing your own laundry?'

The slant squinted at him, then waved one chubby hand, swiping away the curtain of smoke between them. 'What are you talking about?' she asked.

336

'You know that game, where you put a whole bunch of dots in a row and then take turns making lines, trying to build squares? Don't you play that game with Merrin to see who does the laundry?'

'Do we?' said the girl.

39

~e~

He looked back and forth with his one good eye, searching the parking lot for her, everything lit up by the weird, infernal glow of the red neon sign that towered above all – THE PIT – so the rain itself fell red through the hazy night, and then there she was out, under a tree in the rain.

'There, Lee, right there,' Terry told him, but Lee was already pulling over.

She'd told him she might need a ride back from The Pit, if Ig was very angry, after 'The Big Talk'. Lee had promised he'd drive by to check on her, which she said he didn't need to do, but smiling and looking grateful, so he knew she really wanted him to. The thing about Merrin was that she didn't always mean what she said but often said things that were in direct opposition to her intentions.

When Lee saw her, in her soaked blouse and clinging skirt, her eyes reddened from crying, he felt his insides contract with nervous excitement, the thought in him that she was out there waiting for him, wanted to be with him. It had gone badly, Ig had said terrible things, had finally cast her aside, and there was no reason now to wait; he thought there was a good chance when he asked her to come home with him, she would agree, would say yes, in a gentle, accepting voice. As he slowed, she saw him and raised one hand, already stepping towards the side of the car. Lee regretted not bringing Terry home before coming here now, wanted her alone. He thought if it were just the two of them in the car, she might lean against him in her wet clothes for warmth and comfort, and he could put his arm around her shoulders, maybe work his hand into her blouse.

Lee wanted her up front and turned his head to tell Terry to get in back, but Terry was already up, about to pull himself over the front seat. Terry Perrish was trashed, had smoked half of Mexico in the last couple of hours, and moved with the grace of a tranquillised elephant. Lee reached past him to open the passenger-side door for her, and as he did, he put his elbow in Terry's ass to move him along. Terry fell into the back and Lee heard a soft, metallic bashing sound as he came down on the toolbox open on the floor.

She got in, pushing the wet strings of her hair out of her face. Her small, heart-shaped face – still the face of a girl – was wet and white and cold-looking, and Lee was seized with an urge to touch her, to gently stroke her cheek. Her blouse was soaked through, and her bra had little roses printed on it. Before he knew he was doing it, he was reaching out to touch her. But then his gaze shifted and he saw Terry's joint, a fat blunt as long as a ladyfinger, sitting on the seat, and he dropped his hand over it, palmed it before she could see it.

Instead *she* was the one who touched *him*, lightly putting her icy fingers on his wrist. He shivered.

'Thanks for picking me up, Lee,' she said. 'You just saved my life.'

'Where's Ig?' Terry asked in a thick, stupid voice, ruining the moment. Lee looked at him in the rearview. He was hunched forward, his eyes unfocused, one hand pressed to his temple.

Merrin pushed her wrist into her stomach, as if just the thought of Ig caused her physical pain.

'I d-don't know. He left.'

'You told him?' Lee asked.

Merrin turned her head to look out at The Pit, but Lee

could see her reflection in the glass, could see her chin dimpling with the effort it took not to cry. She was shivering helplessly, so her knees almost knocked.

'How'd he take it?' Lee asked, couldn't help himself.

She gave a quick shake of the head and said, 'Can we just go?'

Lee nodded and pulled out into the road, swinging the car back the way they'd come. He saw the rest of the evening as a set of clearly ordered steps: drop Terry at home, then drive her to his house without discussion, tell her she needed to get out of her wet things and into a shower, in the same calm, decisive voice she'd told him to get into the shower the morning his mother died. Only when he brought her a drink, he would gently draw the curtain aside to look at her in the spray and would already be undressed himself.

'Hey, girl,' Terry said. 'You want my jacket?'

Lee shot an irritated look into the rearview at Terry, had been so preoccupied with thoughts of Merrin in the shower that he'd half-forgotten Terry was there. He felt a low current of loathing for smooth, funny, famous, good-looking and basically dull-witted Terry, who had ridden a minimal talent, family connections, and a well-known last name to wealth and his pick of the finest pussy in the country. It made sense to try to twist Terry's faucet, see if there wasn't a way to make him pour some celebrity the congressman's way, or at least some money; but in truth Lee had never much liked him, a loudmouth and an attention hog who had gone out of his way to humiliate Lee in front of Glenna Nicholson the very first day they met. It sickened him, watching the oily fuck turn on the charm for his brother's girlfriend, not ten minutes after they broke up, as if he were entitled, as if he had any right. Lee reached for the air-conditioner, annoyed with himself for not turning it off sooner.

"S-s all right,' Merrin said, but Terry was already handing his coat forward. 'Thank you, Terry.' Her tone so ingratiating and needy that Lee wanted to backhand her. Merrin had her qualities, but fundamentally she was a woman like other women, aroused and submissive in the face of status and money. Take away the trust fund and the family name and Lee doubted she ever would've looked at sorry Ig Perrish twice. 'You m-must think—'

'I don't think anything. Relax.'

'Ig—'

'I'm sure Ig is fine. Don't worry yourself.'

She was still trembling, hard – a little bit of a turn-on, actually, the way her breasts were quivering – but she pivoted to reach a hand into the back seat. 'Are you all right?' When she drew her hand back, Lee saw blood on her fingertips. 'You ought to have some g-gauze for that.'

'It's fine. No worries,' Terry said, and Lee wanted to backhand *him*. Instead he pushed down on the pedal, in a hurry to dump Terry at his house, get him out of the picture as quickly as possible.

The Cadillac rose and fell, swooping along the wet road and swaying around the curves. Merrin hugged herself under Terry's coat, still shivering furiously, her bright, stricken eyes staring out from the tangled nest of her hair, a mess of wet red straw. All at once she reached up and put one hand against the dash, her arm stiff and straight, as if they were about to pitch off the road.

'What? Merrin? Are you all right?'

She shook her head. 'No. Y-yes. I— Lee, please pull over. Pull over here.' Her voice was thin with tension.

When he glanced at her again, he saw she was going to be sick. The night was shrivelling around him, slipping beyond control. She was going to puke in the Caddy, a thought that frankly appalled him. His favourite thing about his mother's illness and subsequent death was that it left him sole right of the Cadillac, and if Merrin threw up in it, he was going to be

341

pissed. You couldn't get the smell out no matter what you did.

He saw the turnoff to the old foundry coming up on the right, and he veered off the road into it, still going too fast. The front right tyre bit into the dirt at the shoulder of the road and flung the back end out to the side, not the thing you wanted to do with a sick girl in the passenger seat. Still decelerating, he pointed the Caddy up the rutted gravel fire lane, brush swatting at the sides of the car, rocks pinging against the undercarriage. A chain stretched across the road rose in the headlights, rushed towards them, and Lee kept the pressure on the brakes, slowing steadily, evenly. At last the Caddy whined to a soft stop, bumper right against the chain.

Merrin opened the door and made an angry retching sound, almost like a wet cough. Lee slammed it into park. He felt a little tremulous himself, with irritation, and made a conscious effort to regain his inner calm. If he was going to get her into the shower tonight, he was going to have to take it a step at a time, lead her by the hand. He could do it, could steer her where they were both headed anyway, but he had to get control of himself, of the wilting night. Nothing had happened yet that couldn't be fixed.

He stepped out, the rain plopping around him, dampening the back and shoulders of his shirt. Merrin had her feet on the ground and her head between her knees. The storm was already tapering off, just dripping quietly in the leaves overhanging the dirt road now.

'You all right?' he asked. She nodded. He went on, 'Let's take Terry home, and then I want you to come over to my place and tell me what happened. I'll fix you a drink, and you can unload. That'll make you feel better.'

'No. No thank you. I just want to be alone right now. I need to do some thinking.'

'You don't want to be alone tonight. In your state of mind, that'd be the worst thing. Hey, and look. You *have* to come to

342

my place. I fixed your cross. I want to put it on you.'

'No, Lee. I just want to go home and get into some dry things and be by myself.'

He felt another flash of annoyance – it was just like her to think she could put him off indefinitely, to expect him to pick her up from The Pit and dutifully drive her where she wanted to go with nothing in return – and then he pushed the feeling aside. He eyed her in her wet skirt and blouse, shivering steadily, then stood and went around to the trunk. He got his gym duffel, brought it back and offered it to her.

'Got gym clothes. Shirt. Pants. They're dry and they're warm, and there's no sick on them.'

She hesitated, then took the strap of the bag and rose from the car. 'Thank you, Lee.' Not meeting his eyes.

He didn't let go of the bag, held onto it, held on to *her* for a moment, kept her from striding away into the night to change. 'You had to do it, you know. It was crazy, thinking that you could – that *either* of you could—'

She said, 'I just want to change, okay?' She tugged the bag out of his hand.

Merrin turned and walked stiffly away, her tight skirt stuck to her thighs. She passed through the headlights, and her blouse went as clear as waxed paper. She stepped around the chain and continued on into the dark, up the road. But before she disappeared, she turned her head and gave Lee a frowning look, one eyebrow raised in a way that seemed to ask a question – or offer an invitation. *Follow me.* Then she was gone.

Lee lit a cigarette and smoked it, standing next to the car, wondering if it would be all right to go after her, not sure he wanted to head into the woods with Terry watching. But in a minute or two, he checked and saw that Terry had stretched out across the back seat with an arm over his eyes. He had rapped his head pretty good, had a red scrape close to the right temple, and he'd been pretty out of it even before that, as baked

343

as a Thanksgiving turkey. It was funny, being out here at the foundry, where he had first met Terry Perrish the day he blew up the big frozen bird with Eric Hannity. He remembered Terry's joint and felt in his pocket for it. Maybe a couple of tokes would settle Merrin's stomach and make her less shrill.

He watched Terry another minute, but when he didn't stir, Lee flipped his cigarette butt into the wet grass and started up the road after her. He followed the gravel ruts around a slight curve and up a hill, and there was the foundry, framed against a sky of boiling black clouds. With its towering smokestack, it looked like a factory built to produce nightmares in mass quantities. The wet grass glistened and shook in the wind. He thought perhaps she had walked up to the crumbling keep of black brick and shadows, was changing there, but then he heard her hiss at him from the dark, to the left.

'Lee,' she said, and he saw her, twenty feet off the path.

She stood below an old tree, the bark peeling away to show the dead, white, leprously spotted wood beneath. She had pulled on his grey sweatpants but was clutching Terry's sport jacket to her thin, bare chest. The sight was an erotic shock, like something from a lazy afternoon masturbation fantasy: Merrin with her pale shoulders and slim arms and haunted eyes, half-naked and shivering in the woods, waiting for him alone.

The gym bag was at her feet, and her wet clothes were folded and set to one side, her heels placed neatly on top of them. Something was tucked into one shoe − a man's tie, it looked like, folded many times over. How she did like to fold things. Lee sometimes felt she had been folding him into smaller and smaller slices for years.

'There's no shirt in your bag,' she said. 'Just sweats.'

Lee said, 'That's right. I forgot.' Walking towards her.

'Well, shit,' she said. 'Give me your shirt.'

'You want me to take off my clothes?' he said.

She tried to smile but let out a short impatient breath. 'Lee – I'm sorry, I'm just . . . I'm not in the mood.'

'No. Of course you aren't. You need a drink and someone to talk to. Hey, I've got weed if you really need something to relax.' He held up the joint and smiled, because he felt she needed a smile right then. 'Let's go to my house. If you're not in the mood tonight, another time.'

'What are you talking about?' she asked, frowning, eyebrows knitting together. 'I mean I'm not in the mood for comedy. What kind of mood are you talking about?'

He leaned forward and kissed her. Her lips were wet and cold.

She flinched, took a startled step back. The jacket slipped, and she caught it to hold it in place, keep it between them. 'What are you doing?'

'I just want you to feel better. If you're miserable, that's at least partly my fault.'

'Nothing's your fault,' she said. She was watching him with wide, wondering eyes, a terrible kind of understanding dawning in her face. So like a little girl's face. It was easy to look at her and imagine she was not twenty-four but still sixteen, still cherry. 'I didn't break up with Ig because of you. It has nothing to do with you.'

'Except that now we can be together. Wasn't that the reason for this whole exercise?'

She took another unsteady step back, her face becoming incredulous, her mouth widening as if to cry out. The thought that she might be about to yell alarmed him, and he felt an impulse to step forward and get a hand over her mouth. But she didn't yell. She laughed – strained, disbelieving laughter. Lee flinched; for a moment it was like his senile mother laughing at him: *You ought to ask for your money back.*

'Oh, fuck,' she said. 'Oh, Jesus fuck. Aw, Lee, this is a really bad time for some kind of shitty joke.'

345

'I agree,' Lee said.

She stared. The sick, confused smile faded from her face, and her upper lip lifted in a sneer. An ugly sneer of disgust.

'That's what you think? That I broke up with him … so I could fuck *you*? You're his *friend. My* friend. Don't you understand anything?'

He took a step towards her, reaching for her shoulder, and she shoved him. He wasn't expecting it, and his heels struck a root, and he went straight down onto his ass in the wet, hard earth.

Lee stared up at her and felt something rising in him, a kind of thunderous roar, a subway coming through the tunnel. He didn't hate her for the things she was saying, although that was bad enough, leading him on for months – years, really – then ridiculing him for wanting her. What he hated mostly was the look on her face. That look of disgust, the sharp little teeth showing under her raised upper lip.

'What were we talking about, then?' Lee asked patiently, ludicrously, from his spot on the damp earth. 'What have we spent the whole last month discussing? I thought you wanted to fuck other people. I thought there were things you knew about yourself, about how you feel, that you had to deal with. Things about me.'

'Oh, God,' she said. 'Oh, Jesus, Lee.'

'Telling me to meet you for dinners. Writing me dirty messages about some mythical blonde who doesn't even exist. Calling me up at all hours to find out what I'm doing, how I am.' He reached out with one hand and put it on that neat pile of her clothes. He was getting ready to stand up.

'I was worried about you, you dick,' she said. 'Your *mother* just died.'

'You think I'm stupid? You were climbing all over me the morning she passed away, dry humping my leg with her dead in the next room.'

'I *what?*' Her voice rose, shrill and piping. She was making too much noise, Terry might hear, Terry might wonder why they were arguing. Lee's hand closed around the tie tucked into her shoe, and he clenched it in his fist as he started to push himself to his feet. Merrin went on, 'Are you talking about when you were drunk and I gave you a hug and you started fondling me? I let it go because you were fucked up, Lee, and that's all that happened. That's *all.*' She was beginning to cry again. She put one hand over her eyes, her chin trembling. She still held the sport coat to her chest with the other hand. 'This is so fucked. How could you think I'd break up with Ig so I could screw you? I'd rather be dead, Lee. *Dead.* Don't you know that?'

'I do now, bitch,' he said, and jerked the jacket out of her hands, threw it on the ground, and put the loop of the tie around her throat.

40

After he hit her with the stone, Merrin stopped trying to throw him off, and he could do what he wanted, and he loosened his grip on the tie around her throat. She turned her face to the side, her eyes rolled back in their sockets, her eyelids fluttering strangely. A trickle of blood ran from under her hairline and down her dirty, smudged face.

He thought she was completely out of it, too dazed to do anything except take it while he fucked her, but then she spoke, in a strange, distant voice.

'It's okay,' she said.

'Yeah?' he asked her, pushing with more force, because it was the only way to stay hard. It wasn't as good as he thought it'd be. She was dry. 'Yeah, you like that?'

But he had misunderstood her again. She wasn't talking about how it felt.

'I escaped,' she said.

Lee ignored her, kept working between her legs.

Her head turned slightly, and she stared up into the great spreading crown of the tree above them.

'I climbed the tree and got away,' she said. 'I finally found my way back, Ig. I'm okay. I'm where it's safe.'

Lee glanced up into the branches and waving leaves, but there was nothing up there. He couldn't imagine what she was staring at or talking about, and he didn't feel like asking. When he looked back into her face, something had fled from her eyes, and she didn't say another word, which was good, because he was sick and tired of all her fucking talk.

THE GOSPEL
ACCORDING TO
MICK AND KEITH

41

It was early when Ig collected his pitchfork from the foundry and returned, still naked, to the river. He waded into the water up to his knees and did not move while the sun climbed higher in the cloudless sky, the light warm on his shoulders.

He didn't know how much time had passed before he observed a brown trout, perhaps a yard from his left leg. It hovered over the sandy bottom, waving its tail back and forth and gazing stupidly at Ig's feet. Ig cocked the pitchfork, Poseidon with his trident, twirled the shaft in his hand, and threw. It struck the fish on the first try, as if he had spent years spear fishing, as if he had thrown the fork a thousand times. It wasn't so different from the javelin, that he'd taught at Camp Galilee.

Ig cooked the trout with his breath, on the riverbank, driving a smothering blast of heat up from his lungs, strong enough to distort the air and blacken the flopping fish, strong enough to bake its eyes the colour of cooked egg yolk. He was not yet able to breathe fire, like a dragon, but he assumed that would come.

It was easy enough to bring forth the heat. All he had to do was concentrate on a pleasurable hate. Mostly he focused on what he'd seen in Lee's head, Lee slow-roasting his mother in the oven of her deathbed, Lee pulling the tie around Merrin's throat to stop her from shouting. Lee's memories crowded Ig's head now, and it was like a mouthful of battery acid, a toxic, burning bitterness that had to be spat out.

After he ate, he returned to the river to wash the trout grease off him, while water snakes slid around his ankles. He dunked himself and came up, cold water drizzling down his face. He wiped the back of one gaunt red hand across his eyes to clear them, blinked, and stared into the river at his own reflection. Maybe it was a trick of the moving water, but his horns seemed larger, thicker at the base, the points beginning to hook inward, as if they were going to meet over his skull. His skin had been cooked a deep, full shade of red. His body was as unmarked and supple as sealskin, his skull as smooth as a doorknob. Only his silky goatee had, inexplicably, not been burned away.

He turned his head this way and that, considering his profile. He thought he was the very image of the romantic, raffish young Asmodeus.

His reflection turned its head and eyed him slyly.

Why are you fishing here? said the devil in the water. *For are you not a fisher of men?*

'Catch and release?' Ig asked.

His reflection contorted with laughter, a dirty, convulsive shout of crowlike amusement, as startling as a string of fire-crackers going off. Ig jerked his head up and saw that it was indeed only the sound of a crow, lifting off from Coffin Rock and skimming away over the river. Ig toyed with his chinlock, his little schemer's beard, listening to the woods, to the echoing silence, and at last became aware of another sound, voices drifting upriver. After a while there sounded the brief, distant squawk of a police siren, a long way off.

Ig climbed back up the hill to dress. Everything he had brought with him to the foundry had burned in the Gremlin. But he recalled the mildewed old clothes strung in the branches of the oak that overhung the top of the Evel Knievel trail: a stained black overcoat with a torn liner, a single black sock, and a blue lace skirt that looked like something from an early-eighties Madonna video. Ig tugged the filthy garments from the branches. He pulled the skirt up over his hips, remembering the rule of Deuteronomy 22:5, that a man shall not put on a woman's garment, for all that do so are an abomination unto the Lord thy God. Ig took his responsibilities as a budding young lord of Hell seriously. In for a penny, in for a pound of flesh (his own, most likely). He put the sock on under the skirt, though, because it was a short skirt, and he was self-conscious. Last he added the stiff black overcoat, with its oilskin lining.

Ig set out, his blue lace skirt flouncing about his thighs, fanning his bare red ass, while he dragged the pitchfork in the dirt. He had not reached the tree line, though, when he saw a flash of golden light to his right, down in the grass. He turned, searching for the source, and it blinked and blinked again, a hot spark in the weeds, sending him an urgent and uncomplicated message: *Over here, chump, look over here.* He bent and scooped Merrin's cross from the grass. It was warm from an entire morning of heating in the light, a thousand fine scratches in its surface. He held it to his mouth and nose, imagining he might smell her on it, but there was no smell at all. The clasp was broken again. He breathed on it gently, heating it to soften the metal, and used his pointed fingernails to straighten the delicate gold hoop. He studied it for a moment and then lifted it and hung it around his own neck. He half expected it to sizzle and burn, to sear into the red flesh of his chest, leaving a black, cross-shaped blister, but it rested lightly against him. Of course nothing that had been hers could really ever do him harm. Ig drew a sweet breath of morning air and went on his way.

They had found the car. It had followed the current right through Parkham Marsh and out the other end, winding up on the sandbar below the Old Fair Road Bridge, where the local kids had their yearly bonfire to mark the end of summer. The Gremlin looked as if it had tried to drive right up out of the river, the front tyres embedded in the soft sand, the rear end underwater. A few cop cars and a tow truck had driven partly out onto the sandbar towards it. Other cars – police cruisers, but also local yokels who had pulled over to stare – were scattered on the gravel landing below the bridge. Still more cars were parked up on the bridge itself, people lined along the rail to look down. Police scanners crackled and babbled.

The Gremlin didn't look like itself, with the paint cooked right off it and the iron body beneath baked black. A cop in waders opened the passenger-side door, and water flooded forth. A sunfish spilled out in the torrent, its scales iridescent in the late-morning sunshine, and landed in the wet sand with a splat. The cop in rubber boots kicked it into the shallows and it recovered itself and shot away.

A few uniformed cops stood in a knot on the sandbar, drinking coffee and laughing, not even looking at the car. Snippets of their conversation came to Ig, carried on the clear morning air.

'—fuck is it? A Civic, you think?'

'—dunno. Something old and shitty.'

'—someone decided to get the bonfire goin' a couple days early—'

They gave off an air of summery good humour and ease and masculine indifference. As the tow truck slammed into gear and began to roll forward, hauling the Gremlin out, water gushed from the rear windows, which had shattered. Ig saw that the licence plate had been removed from the back end. Probably gone from the front, too. Lee had thought to remove them before he hauled Ig out of his chimney and put him into it. The police didn't know what they had, not yet.

Ig made his way down through the trees and settled at last on some rocks above a steep drop, to watch the sandbar through the pines from a distance of maybe twenty yards. He didn't look down until he heard the sound of soft laughter directly below. He took a casual glance over the edge and saw Sturtz and Posada, in full uniform, standing side by side, holding each other's prick while they urinated into the brush. When they locked mouths, Ig had to grab a low nearby tree to keep from toppling off the rocks and falling onto them. He scrambled back to where he wouldn't be seen.

Someone shouted, 'Sturtz! Posada! Where the fuck are you guys? We need someone on the bridge!' There was a whisper and the rustle of the two men adjusting their clothing and Posada laughing, and then they started back. Ig took another peek over the side to watch them go. He had meant to turn them against each other, not turn them *on* to each other, and yet was not altogether surprised by this outcome. It was, perhaps, the devil's oldest precept, that sin could always be trusted to reveal what was most human in a person, as often for good as for ill.

Ig moved to a position higher on the slope, where he had a better view of both the sandbar and the bridge, and that was when he saw Dale Williams. Merrin's father stood at the railing among the other onlookers, a pasty man with a buzz cut in a striped short-sleeved shirt.

The sight of the nuked car seemed to hold Dale fascinated. He leaned against the rusted railing, his fat fingers entwined, staring at it with a stricken, empty expression on his face. Maybe the cops didn't know what they'd found, but Dale did. Dale knew cars, had sold them for twenty years, and he knew this car. He hadn't just sold it to Ig, he'd helped Ig fix it up and had seen it in his driveway almost every night for six years. Ig could not imagine what Dale saw now, looking over the bridge at the fire-blackened ruin of the Gremlin on the sandbar and believing that his daughter had taken her last drive in it.

There were cars parked along the bridge and on the sides of the road at either end of the span. Dale stood on the eastern tip of the bridge. Ig began to cross the hill, angling through the trees towards the road.

Dale was moving too. For a long time, he had simply been

standing there staring at the burned-out shell of the Gremlin, the water pouring off it. What finally broke him out of his trance was the sight of a cop – it was Sturtz – coming up the hill to provide some crowd control. Dale began to squeeze by the other onlookers, making his slow water-buffalo way off the bridge.

As Ig reached the verge of the road, he spotted Dale's ride, a blue BMW; Ig knew it was his by the dealer plates. It was parked in the gravel breakdown lane, in the shadow of a stand of pines. Ig stepped briskly from the woods and climbed into the back, shut the door behind him, and sat there with his pitchfork across his knees.

The rear windows were tinted, but it hardly mattered. Dale was in a hurry and didn't glance into the back seat. Ig understood he might not want to be seen hanging around. If you made a list of the people in Gideon who would most want to see Ig Perrish burned alive, Dale would definitely be in the top five. The car salesman opened the door and dropped behind the wheel.

He took his glasses off with one hand, covered his eyes with the other. For a while he just sat there, his breathing ragged and soft. Ig waited, not wanting to interrupt.

There were pictures taped to the dash. One was of Jesus, an oil painting, Jesus with his golden beard and his swept-back golden hair, staring, in an inspired sort of way, into the sky while shafts of golden light broke through the clouds behind him. '*Blessed are they that mourn*,' read the caption, '*for they shall be comforted.*' Taped next to it was a picture of Merrin at ten, sitting behind her father on the back of his motorcycle. She wore aviator goggles and a white helmet with red stars and blue racing lines on it, and her arms were around him. A handsome woman with cherry-red hair stood behind the bike, one hand on Merrin's helmet, smiling for the camera. At first Ig thought it was Merrin's mother, then realised she was too young and that it had to be Merrin's sister, the one who'd died when they lived in Baltimore. Two daughters, both gone. Blessed are they that mourn, for they shall be kicked in the nuts as soon as they try to get back up. That wasn't in the Bible, but maybe it should've been.

When Dale had regained control of himself he reached for the keys and started the car, pulled out onto the road with a last sidelong glance in the driver's-side mirror. He swiped at his cheeks with his wrists, stuck his glasses back on his face. He drove for a while. Then he kissed his thumb and touched it to the little girl in the photo of the motorcycle.

'That was his car, Mary,' he said, his name for Merrin. 'All burned up. I think he's gone. I think the bad man is gone.'

Ig put one hand on the driver's seat and the other on the passenger seat and hoisted himself between them, sliding up front to sit next to Dale.

'Sorry to disappoint you,' Ig said. 'Only the good die young, I'm afraid.'

As Ig climbed forward into view, Dale made a gobbling noise of fright and jerked at the wheel. They swerved hard to the right, into the gravel breakdown lane. Ig fell hard against the dash and almost crashed to the floor. He could hear rocks clanging and bashing against the undercarriage. Then the car was in park and Dale was out of it and running up the road, running and screaming.

Ig pushed himself up. He couldn't make sense of it. No one else screamed and ran when they saw the horns. Sometimes they wanted to kill him, but no one screamed and ran.

Dale reeled up the centre of the road, looking back over his shoulder at the station wagon and uttering vaguely birdlike cries. A woman in a Sentra blasted her horn at him as she blew by – *Get the hell out of the road.* Dale staggered to the edge of the highway, a thin strip of dirt crumbling off into a weedy ditch. The earth gave way under Dale's right foot and he went tumbling down.

Ig got behind the wheel and rolled slowly after him.

He pulled alongside as Dale rose unsteadily to his feet. Dale began to run once again, in the ditch now. Ig pressed the button to lower the passenger window and leaned across the seat to call out to him.

'Mr Williams,' Ig said, 'get in the car.'

Dale didn't slow down but ran on, gasping for breath, clutching at his heart. Sweat gleamed on his jowls. There was a split in the back of his pants.

'Get away!' Dale cried, his words blurring together. *Geddway*. 'Gedawayalp!' He said it twice more before Ig realised that 'alp' was panic-ese for 'help'.

Ig looked blankly at the picture of Christ taped to the dash, as if hoping Big J might have some advice for him, which was when he remembered the cross. He looked down at it, hanging between his clavicles, resting lightly on his bare chest. Lee had not been able to see the horns while he wore the cross; it stood to reason that if Ig was wearing the cross, *no one* could see them or feel their effects, an astonishing proposition, a cure for his condition. To Dale Willliams, Ig was himself: the sex murderer who had bashed his daughter's head in with a rock and who had just climbed out of the back seat in a skirt, armed with a pitchfork. The golden cross looped about Ig's throat was his own humanity, burning brightly in the morning light.

But his humanity was of no use to him, not in this situation, nor any other. It had been of no use to him since the night Merrin was taken. Was, in fact, a weakness. Now that he was used to it, he far preferred being damned. The cross was a symbol of that most human condition: suffering. And Ig was sick of suffering. If someone had to get nailed to a tree, he wanted to be the one holding the hammer. He pulled over, unclasped the cross and put it in the glove compartment. Then he sat up straight behind the wheel again.

He sped up to get ahead of Dale, then stopped the car. He

reached behind him and awkwardly lifted the pitchfork from the back and got out. Dale was just stumbling past, down in the ditch, up to his ankles in muddy water. Ig took two steps after him and threw the pitchfork. It hit the marshy water in front of him and Dale shrieked. He tried to go back too quickly and sat down with a great splash. He paddled about, scrambling to find his feet. The pole of the pitchfork stood straight up from the shallow water, shivering from the force of its impact.

Ig slid down the embankment with all the grace of a snake greasing its way through wet leaves and grabbed the pitchfork before Dale could stand. He jerked it free from the mud and pointed the business end at him. There was a crawfish stuck to one of the tines, writhing in its death throes.

'Enough running. Get in the car. We have a lot to talk about.'

Dale sat breathing strenuously in the muck. He looked up the shaft of the pitchfork and squinted into Ig's face. He shaded his eyes with one hand. 'You got rid of your hair.' Paused, then added, almost as an afterthought, 'And grew horns. Jesus. What *are* you?'

'What's it look like?' Ig asked. 'Devil in a blue dress.'

42

'I knew it was your car right away,' Dale said, behind the wheel and driving again. He was calm now, at peace with his own private demon. 'Soon as I looked at it, I knew someone had set fire to it and pushed it into the river. And I thought you were probably in it at the time, and I felt ... felt so ...'

'Happy?'

'Sorry. I felt sorry.'

'Really?'

'That I wasn't the one who did it.'

'Ah,' Ig said, looking away.

Ig held the pitchfork between his knees, the tines sticking into the fabric of the roof, but after they'd been driving for a bit, Dale seemed to forget about it. The horns were doing what they did, playing their secret music, and as long as Ig wasn't wearing the cross, Dale was helpless not to dance along.

'I was too scared to kill you. I had a gun. I bought it just to shoot you. But the closest I ever came to killing anyone with it was myself. I put it in my mouth one night to see how it tasted.' He was silent briefly, remembering, then added, 'It tasted bad.'

'I'm glad you didn't shoot yourself, Mr Williams.'

'I was scared to do that, too. Not because I'm afraid I'll go to hell for committing suicide. It's because I'm afraid I *won't* go to hell ... that there isn't a hell to go to. No heaven either. Just nothing. Mostly I think there must be nothing after we die.

Sometimes that seems like it would be a relief. Other times it's the most awful thing I can imagine. I don't believe a merciful God would've taken both my little girls from me. One from the cancer and the other killed out in the woods that way. I don't think a God worth praying to would've put either of them through what they went through. Heidi still prays. She prays like you wouldn't believe. She's been praying for you to die, Ig, for a year now. When I saw your car in the river I thought ... I thought ... well. God finally came through on something. But no. No, Mary is gone forever, and you're still here. You're still here. You're ... you're ... the fucking *devil*.' Panting for breath. Struggling to go on.

'You make that sound like a bad thing,' Ig said. 'Turn left. Let's go to your house.'

The trees growing alongside the road delineated an avenue of bright and cloudless blue sky. It was a nice day for a drive.

'You said we have things to discuss,' Dale said. 'But what could we possibly have to talk about, Ig? What did you want to tell me?'

'I wanted to tell you that I don't know if I loved Merrin as much as you did, but I loved her as much as I knew how. And I didn't kill her. The story I told the police, about passing out drunk behind Dunkin' Donuts, was true. Lee Tourneau picked Merrin up from in front of The Pit. He drove her to the foundry. He killed her there.' After a beat, Ig added, 'I don't expect you to believe me.' Except: he did. Maybe not right away, but soon enough. Ig was very persuasive these days. People would believe almost any awful thing their private devil told them. In this case it was true, but Ig suspected that if he wanted to, he could probably convince Dale that Merrin had been killed by clowns who had picked her up from The Pit in their teeny-tiny clown car. It wasn't fair. But then, fighting fair was what the old Ig did.

However, Dale surprised him, said, 'Why should I believe you? Give me a reason.'

Ig reached over and put his hand on Dale's bare forearm for a moment, then took it away.

'I know that after your father died, you visited his mistress in Lowell and paid her two thousand dollars to go away. And you warned her if she ever called your mother drunk again, you'd go looking for her, and when you found her, you'd knock her teeth in. I know you had a one-night stand with a secretary at the dealership, at the Christmas party, the year before Merrin died. I know you once belted Merrin in the mouth for calling her mother a bitch. That's probably the thing in your life you feel worst about. I know you haven't loved your wife for going on ten years. I know about the bottle in the bottom left-hand desk drawer at work, and the skin magazines at home in the garage, and the brother you don't talk to because you can't stand that his children are alive and yours are dead and—'

'Stop. Stop it.'

'I know about Lee the same way I know about you,' Ig said. 'When I touch people, I know things. Stuff I shouldn't know. And people tell me things. Talk about the things they want to do. They can't help themselves.'

'The bad things,' Dale said, rubbing two fingers against his right temple, stroking it gently. 'Only they don't seem so bad when I look at you. They seem like they might be ... *fun*. Like I've been thinking how when Heidi gets on her knees to pray tonight, I ought to sit on the bed in front of her and tell her to blow me while she's down there. Or the next time she tells me God doesn't give anyone burdens they can't bear, I could slug her one. Hit her again and again until that bright look of faith goes out of her eyes.'

'No. You aren't going to do that.'

'Or it might be good to skip work this afternoon. Lie down for an hour or two in the dark.'

'That's better.'

'Have a nap and then put the gun in my mouth and be done with this hurt.'

'No. You aren't going to do that either.'

Dale sighed tremulously and turned in to his driveway. The Williamses owned a ranch on a street of identically dismal ranches, one-storey boxes with a square of yard in back and a smaller square in front. Theirs was the pale, pasty green of some hospital rooms, and it looked worse than Ig remembered it. The vinyl siding was mottled with brown splotches of mildew where it met the concrete foundation, and the windows were dusty, and the lawn was a week overdue for a mow. The street baked in the summery heat, and nothing moved on it, and the sound of a dog barking down the road was the sound of heatstroke, of migraines, of the indolent, overheated summer staggering to its end. Ig had hoped, perversely, to see Merrin's mother, to find out what secrets she hid, but Heidi wasn't home. No one on the whole street seemed to be home.

'What about if I blow off work and see if I can get shitfaced by noon? See if I can't get myself fired. I haven't sold a car in six weeks – they're just looking for a reason. They only keep me on out of pity as it is.'

'There,' Ig said. 'Now that's what I call a plan.'

Dale led him inside. Ig didn't bring the pitchfork, didn't think he needed it now.

'Iggy, would you pour me a drink out of the liquour cabinet? I know you know where it is. You and Mary used to sneak drinks out of it. I want to sit in the dark and rest my head. My head is all woffly inside.'

The master bedroom was at the end of a short hall done in chocolate shag carpeting. There had been pictures of Merrin along the whole corridor, but they were gone now. There were pictures of Jesus there instead. Ig was angry for the first time all day.

'Why did you take her down and put Him up?'

'Those were Heidi's idea. She took Mary's photos away.' Dale kicked off his black loafers as he wandered down the hall. 'Three months ago she packed up all of Mary's books, her clothes, her letters from you, and shoved them in the attic. Merrin's bedroom is her home office now. She works in there stuffing envelopes for Christian causes. She spends more time with Father Mould than she does with me, goes to the church every morning and all day Sunday. She's got a picture of Jesus on her desk. She doesn't have a picture of me or either of her dead daughters, but she has a picture of Jesus. I want to chase her out of the house, shouting her daughters' names at her. You know what? You should go up in the attic and get down the box. I'd like to dig out all Mary's and Regan's photos. I could throw them at Heidi until she starts to cry. I could tell her if she wants to get rid of our daughters' pictures, she's going to have to eat them. One at a time.'

'Sounds like a lot of work for a hot afternoon.'

'It would be fun. Be a hell of a good time.'

'But not as refreshing as a gin and tonic.'

'No,' Dale said, standing now at the threshold of his bedroom. 'You get it for me, Ig. Make it stiff.'

Ig returned to the den, a room that had once been a gallery on the subject of Merrin Williams' childhood, filled with photographs of her: Merrin in war paints and skins, Merrin riding her bike and grinning to show a mouthful of chrome wire, Merrin in a one-piece swimsuit sitting on Ig's shoulders, Ig up to his waist in the Knowles River. They were all gone now, and it looked as if the room had been furnished by a real-estate agent in the most banal fashion possible, for a Sunday-morning open house. As if no one lived here anymore.

No one lived here anymore. No one had lived here in months. It was just a place Dale and Heidi Williams stored their things, as detached from their interior lives as a hotel room.

The liquour was where it had always been, though, in the cabinets above the TV set. Ig mixed Dale a gin and tonic, using tonic water from the fridge in the kitchen, throwing in a sprig of mint, cutting a section of orange, too, and pushing it down into the ice. On the way back to the bedroom, though, a rope hanging from the ceiling brushed against Ig's right horn, threatened to snag there. Ig looked up and—

—*there it was, in the branches of the tree above him, the bottom of the tree house, words painted on the trap, the whitewash faintly visible in the night:* BLESSED SHALL YOU BE WHEN YOU GO IN. *Ig swayed, then—*

—shook off an unexpected wave of dizziness. He used his free hand to massage his brow, waiting for his head to clear, for the sick feeling to abate. For a moment it was there, what had happened in the woods when he went drunk to the foundry to rave and wreck shit, but it was gone now. Ig put his glass down on the carpet and pulled the string, lowering a trapdoor to the attic with a loud shriek of springs.

If it was hot in the streets, it was suffocating in the low, unfinished attic. Some plywood had been laid across the beams to make a rudimentary floor. There was not enough headroom to stand under the steep pitch of the roof, and Ig didn't need to. Three big cardboard boxes with the word MERRIN written on their sides in red Sharpie had been pushed just to the left of the open trap.

He carried them down one at a time, set them on the coffee table in the living room and went through them. He drank Dale Williams' gin and tonic while he explored what Merrin had left behind when she died.

Ig smelled her Harvard hoodie and the ass of her favourite jeans. He went through her books, her piles of used paperbacks. Ig rarely read novels, had always liked non-fiction about fasting, irrigation, travel, camping, and building structures out of recycled materials. But Merrin preferred fiction, high-end book-club stuff. She liked things that had been written by people who had lived short, ugly and tragic lives, or who at least were English. She wanted a novel to be an emotional and philosophical journey and also to teach her some new vocabulary words.

She read Gabriel García Márquez and Michael Chabon and John Fowles and Ian McEwan. One book fell open in Ig's hands to an underlined passage: 'How guilt refined the methods of self-torture, threading the beads of detail into an eternal loop, a rosary to be fingered for a lifetime.' And then another, a different book: 'It goes against the American storytelling grain to have someone in a situation he can't get out of, but I think this is very usual in life.' Ig stopped flipping through her paperbacks. They were making him uneasy.

Some of his books were mixed in with hers, books he had not seen in years. A guide to statistics. *The Camper's Cookbook*. *Reptiles of New England*. He drank the rest of his gin and thumbed through *Reptiles*. About a hundred pages in, he found a picture of the brown snake with the rattle and the orange stripe down the back. She was *Crotalus horridus*, a pit viper, and although her range was largely south of the New Hampshire border – she was common to Pennsylvania – she could be found as far north as the White Mountains. They rarely attacked humans, were shy by nature. More people had been killed in the last year by lightning than had died in the whole last century from run-ins with *horridus*; yet for all that, its venom was accounted the most dangerous of any American snake, neurotoxic, known to paralyse lungs and heart. He put the book back.

Merrin's medical texts and ring-binder notebooks were piled in the bottom of the box. Ig opened one, then another, grazing. She kept notes in pencil, and her careful, not-particularly-girlish cursive was smeared and fading. Definitions of chemical compounds. A hand-drawn cross section of a breast. A list of apartments in London – flats – that she had found online for Ig. At the very bottom of the box was a large manila envelope. Ig almost didn't bother with it, then hesitated, squinting at some pencil marks in the upper left-hand corner of the envelope. Some dots. Some dashes.

He opened the envelope and slid out a mammogram, a blue-and-white teardrop of tissue. The date was sometime in June last year. There were papers, too, ruled notebook papers. Ig saw his name on them. They were pencilled all over in dots and dashes. She had done the up-and-down lines in pen to let him know they didn't matter. He slid the papers and the mammogram back into the envelope.

He made a second gin and tonic and walked it down the hall. When he let himself into the bedroom, Dale was passed out on the covers, in black socks pulled almost to his knees and white jockey shorts with pee stains on the front. The rest of him was a stark white expanse of male flesh, his belly and chest matted in dark fur. Ig crept to the side of the bed to set down the drink. Dale stirred at the clink of the ice cubes.

'Oh. Ig,' Dale said. 'Hello. Would you believe I forgot you were here for a minute?'

Ig didn't reply. He stood by the bed with the manila envelope. He said, 'She had cancer?'

Dale turned his face away. 'I don't want to talk about Mary,' Dale said. 'I love her, but I can't stand to think about her and ... and any of it. My brother, you know, we haven't spoken in years. But he owns a bike and jet ski dealership in Sarasota. Sometimes I think I could go down there and sell his bikes for him and look at girls on the beach. He still sends me Christmas cards asking me to visit. I think sometimes I'd like to get away from Heidi, and this town, and this awful house, and how bad I feel about my shitty, fucked-up life, and start all over again.

369

If there's no God and no reason for all this pain, then maybe I should start again before it's too late.'

'Dale,' Ig said softly. 'Did she tell you she had cancer?'

He shook his head, without lifting it from the pillow. 'It's one of these genetic things, you know. Runs in families. And we didn't learn about it from her. We didn't know about it at all until after she was dead. The medical examiner told us.'

'There was nothing in the paper about her having cancer,' Ig said.

'Heidi wanted them to put it in the paper. She thought it would create sympathy and make people hate you more. But I said Mary didn't want anyone to know and we should respect that. She didn't tell us. Did she tell you?'

'No,' Ig said. What she told him instead was that they should see other people. Ig had not read the two-page note in the envelope but thought he already understood. He said, 'Your older daughter. Regan. I've never talked to you about her. I didn't think it was my business. But I know it was hard losing her.'

'She was in so much pain,' Dale said. His next breath shuddered strangely. 'It made her say awful things. I know she didn't mean a lot of it. She was such a good person. Such a beautiful girl. I try to remember that, but mostly ... mostly I remember how she was at the end. She was barely eighty pounds, and seventy pounds of that was hate. She said unforgivable things to Mary, you know. I think she was mad because Mary was so pretty, and – Regan lost her hair, and there was, you know, a mastectomy and a surgery to remove a block on her intestines, and she felt ... she felt like Frankenstein, like something from a horror movie. She told us if we loved her, we'd put a pillow over her face and get it done. She told me I was probably glad it was her dying and not Merrin, because I always liked Merrin better. I try to put it all out of my mind, but I wake up some nights thinking about it. Or thinking about how Mary died.

You want to remember how they lived, but the bad stuff kind of crowds out the rest. There's probably some sound psychological reason for that. Mary took courses in psychology, she would've known why the bad stuff leaves a deeper mark than the good stuff. Hey, Ig. You believe my little girl got into Harvard?'

'Yes,' Ig said. 'I believe it. She was smarter than you and me put together.'

Dale snorted, face still turned away. 'Don't you know it. I went to a two-year college, all my old man would pay for. God, I wanted to be a better father than he was. He told me what classes I could take and where I could live and what I'd do for work after I graduated to pay him back. I used to say to Heidi I'm surprised he didn't stand in my bedroom on our wedding night and instruct me in the approved method of screwing her.' He smiled, remembering. 'That was back when Heidi and I could joke about those kinds of things. Heidi had a funny, dirty streak before she got a head full of Christ. Before the world stuck its taps in her and drained out all the blood. Sometimes I want so bad to leave her, but she doesn't have anyone else. She's all alone ... except for Jesus, I guess.'

'Oh. I don't know about that,' Ig said, and let out a slow, seething breath, thinking about how Heidi Williams had pulled down all Merrin's pictures, had tried to shove her daughter's memory up away into dust and darkness. 'You should drop in on her some morning when she's working for Father Mould at the church. As a surprise. I think you'll find she has a much more active ... *intercourse* with life than you give her credit for.'

Dale flicked a questioning look at him, but Ig remained poker-faced and said no more. Finally Dale offered a thin smile and said, 'You should've shaved your head years ago, Ig. Looks good. I used to want to do that, go bald, but Heidi always said if I ever did it, I could consider our marriage over. She wouldn't even let me shave it to show my support for Regan, after Regan had chemo. Some families do that. To show they're all in it together. Not our family, though.' He frowned and said, 'How did we get off on this? What were we talking about?'

'When you went to college.'

'Yeah. Well. My father wouldn't let me take the theology course I wanted, but he couldn't stop me from auditing it. I remember the teacher, a black woman, Professor Tandy, she said that Satan turns up in a lot of other religions as the good guy. He's usually the guy who tricks the fertility goddess into bed, and after a bit of fiddling around they bring the world into being. Or the crops. Something. He comes into the story to bamboozle the unworthy or tempt them into ruination, or at least out of their liquour. Even Christians can't really decide what to do with him. I mean, think about it. Him and God are supposed to be at war with each other. But if God hates sin and Satan punishes the sinners, aren't they working the same side of the street? Aren't the judge and the executioner on the same team? The Romantics. I think the Romantics liked Satan. I don't really remember why. Maybe because he had a good beard and was into girls and sex and knew how to throw a party. Didn't the Romantics like Satan?'

'*You're whisperin' in my ear,*' Ig whispered. '*Tell me alla things I wanna hear.*'

Dale laughed again. 'No. Not *those* Romantics.'

Ig said, 'They're the only ones I know.'

He eased the door gently shut on his way out.

372

43

~℮

Ig sat at the bottom of the chimney, in a circle of hot afternoon light, holding the glossy mammogram of Merrin's breast over his head. Lit from behind by the August sky, the tissues within looked like a black sun, going nova, looked like the End of Days, and the sky was as sackcloth. The devil turned to his Bible: not to the Old Testament, nor to the New, but to the back page, where years before he had copied the key to the Morse Code alphabet from his brother's encyclopaedia. Even before he translated the papers within the envelope, he knew they were a testament of a different sort: a final one. Merrin's final testament.

He started with the dots and dashes on the front of the package, a simple enough sequence. It spelled FUCK OFF, IG.

He laughed – a dirty, convulsive shout of crowlike amusement.

He slipped out the two pages of notebook paper, covered in dots and dashes, both sides, the labour of months, of an entire summer. Working with his Bible, Ig set to translating them, occasionally fingering the cross around his neck, Merrin's cross. He had put it back on as soon as he left Dale's. It made him feel she was with him, was close enough to lay her cool fingers on the nape of his neck.

It was slow work, converting those lines of dots and dashes

to letters and words. He didn't care. The devil had nothing but time.

Dear Ig,

You will never read this while I'm alive. I'm not sure I want you to read it even if I'm dead.

Whoo, this is slow writing. I guess I don't mind. It passes the time when I'm stuck in a lobby somewhere waiting on the result of this or that test. Also forces me to say just what needs to be said and no more.

The sort of cancer I have is the same that struck my sister down, a sort known to run in families. I won't bore you with the genetics. It is not advanced yet, and I'm sure if you knew, you would want me to fight. I know I should, but I'm not going to. I have made up my mind not to go like my sister. Not to wait until I'm filled with ugliness, not to hurt the people I love and who have loved me, and that is you, Ig, and my parents.

The Bible says suicides go to hell, but hell is what my sister went through when she was dying. You don't know this, but my sister was engaged when she was diagnosed. Her fiancé left her months before she died. She drove him away, one day at a time. She wanted to know how long he'd wait after she was buried to fuck someone else. She wanted to know if he'd use her tragedy to win sympathy from girls. She was horrible. I would've left her.

I'd just as soon skip all that, thanks. But I don't know how to do it yet, how to die. I wish God would find a way to do it to me all at once, when I'm not expecting it. Put me in an elevator and then have the cable snap. Twenty seconds of flight and it's over. Maybe as a bonus I could fall on someone bad. Like a child-molesting elevator repairman or something. That would be all right.

I'm afraid if I tell you I'm sick, you will give up your future and ask to marry me, and I will be weak and say yes, and then you'll be shackled to me, watching while they cut pieces off and I shrink and go bald and put you through hell, and then I die anyway and ruin what was best in you in the process. You want so much to believe that the world is good, Ig, that people are good. And I know when I'm really sick I won't be able to be good. I will be like my sister. I have that in me, I know how to hurt people, and I might not be able to help myself. I want you to remember what was good in me, not what was most awful. The people you love should be allowed to keep their worst to themselves.

You don't know how hard it is not to talk about these things with you. That's the reason I'm writing this, I guess. Because I need to talk to you, and this is the only way. A bit of a one-sided conversation, though, huh?

You're so excited to go to England, to be up to your neck in the world. Remember that story you told me about Evel Knievel Hill and the shopping cart? That's you every day. Ready to fly bare-naked down the steep pitch of your own life and be flung into the human stream. Save people drowning in unfairness.

I can hurt you just enough to push you away. I'm not looking forward to it, but it will be kinder than letting this thing play itself out.

I want you to find some girl with a trashy Cockney accent and take her back to your flat and screw her out of her knickers. Someone cute and immoral and literary. Not as pretty as me, I'm not that generous, but it's okay if she's not terrible-looking. Then I'm hoping she will callously dump you and you will move on to someone else. Someone better. Someone earnest and caring and with no family history of cancer, heart disease, Alzheimer's, or any other bad stuff. I also hope by then I am long dead so I don't have to know anything about her.

You know how I want to die? On the Evel Knievel trail, roaring down it on a cart of my own. I could close my eyes and imagine your arms around me. Then go right into a tree. She never knew what hit her. That's how. I would like very much to believe in a Gospel of Mick and Keith, where I can't get what I want – which is you, Ig, and our children, and our ridiculous daydreams – but at least get what I need, which is a quick, sudden ending and the knowledge that you got away clean.

And you will have some stout and kindly mother-wife to give you children, and you will be a wonderful, happy, energetic father. You will see all of the world, every corner of it, and you will see pain, and you will *ease* some of it. You will have grandchildren, and great-grandchildren. You will teach. You will go for long walks in the woods. On one of these walks, when you are very old, you will find yourself at a tree with a house in its branches. I will be waiting for you there. I will be waiting by candlelight in our tree house of the mind.

This is a lot of lines and dots. Two months of work, right here. When I started writing, the cancer was a pea in one breast and less than a pea in my left armpit. Now, wrapping up, it's … well. From small things, Mama, big things one day come.

I'm not sure I really needed to write so much. Probably could've saved myself a lot of effort and just copied out the first message I ever sent you, flashing you with my cross. US. That says most of it. Here's the rest: I love you, Iggy Perrish.

Your girl, Merrin Williams

44

After he had read Merrin's final message, and set it aside, and read it again, and set it aside once more, Ig climbed out of his chimney, wanted to be away from the smell of cinder and ash for a while. He stood in the room beyond, breathing deeply of the late-afternoon air, before it came to him that the snakes had not gathered. He was alone in the foundry, or almost. A single snake, the pit viper, lay coiled in the wheelbarrow, sleeping in fat loops of herself. He was tempted to go close and stroke her head, even took a single step towards her, then stopped. *Better not*, he thought, and looked down at the cross around his neck, then shifted his gaze to stare at his shadow climbing the wall in the last of the day's red light. He saw the shadow of a man, long and skinny. He still felt the horns at his temples, felt the weight of them, the points slicing into the cooling air, but his shadow showed just himself. If he walked to the snake now, with Merrin's cross around his throat, he thought there was a good chance she would bury her fangs in him.

He considered the black length of his body, climbing the brick wall, and understood that he could go home if he wanted. With the cross about his throat, his humanity was his again, if he wanted it. He could put the last two days behind him, a nightmare time of sickness and panic, and be who he had always been. The thought brought with it an almost painful sense of relief, was an almost sensual pleasure: to be Ig Perrish and not the devil, to be a man and not a walking furnace.

He was still thinking it over when the serpent in the wheelbarrow lifted her head, white lights washing over her. Someone was coming up the road. Ig's first thought was Lee, coming back to look for his lost cross and any other incriminating evidence he might've left behind.

But as the car rolled up in front of the foundry, he recognised it as Glenna's battered emerald Saturn. He could see it through the doorway that opened on a six-foot drop. She climbed out, trailing veils of smoke behind her. She pitched her cigarette into the grass and ground it out with her toe. She had quit twice in the time Ig had been with her – once for as long as a week.

Ig watched her from the windows while she made her way around the building. She had on too much make-up. She always had on too much make-up. Black cherry lipstick and a big hair perm and eyeshadow and shiny pink paste-ons. She didn't want to go inside, Ig could tell from the look on her face. Beneath her painted mask, she looked afraid and miserable, and pretty in a plain, forlorn sort of way. She wore tight low-riding black jeans that showed the crack of her ass, and a studded belt and a white halter which bared her soft belly and exposed the tattoo on her hip, the Playboy Bunny rabbit head. It hurt Ig, looking at her and seeing how it was all put together in a kind of desperate plea: *Want me, somebody want me.*

'Ig?' she called. 'Iggy! Are you in there? Are you around?' She cupped a hand to her mouth to amplify her voice.

He didn't reply, and she dropped the hand.

Ig went from window to window, watching her stride through the weeds, around to the back of the foundry. The sun was on the other side of the building, the red tip of a cigarette sizzling through the pale curtain of the sky. As she crossed to the Evel Knievel trail, Ig slipped down through an open doorway and circled behind her. He crept through the grass and the day's dying-ember light: one crimson shadow among many. Her back was to him, and she did not see him coming towards her.

Glenna slowed at the top of the trail, seeing the scorch mark on the earth, the blasted place where the soil had been cooked white. The red metal gas can was still there, lying in the undergrowth on its side. Ig crept on, continuing across the field behind her, and into the trees and brush, on the right-hand side of the trail. In the field around the foundry, it was still late afternoon, but under the trees it was already dusk. He played restlessly with the cross, rubbing it between thumb and fore-finger, his mind on how to approach Glenna and what he should say to her. What she deserved of him.

She looked at the burn in the dirt and then at the red metal gas can and, finally, down the trail, towards the water. Ig could see her putting the parts together, figuring it out. She was breathing faster now. Her right hand dived into her purse.

'Oh, Ig,' she said. 'Oh goddamn it, Ig.'

The hand came out with her phone.

'Don't,' Ig said.

She tottered in her heels. Her phone, as pink and smooth as a bar of soap, slipped from her hand, hit the ground, bounced into the grass.

'What the hell are you doing, Ig?' Glenna said, shifting from grief to anger in the time it took to get her balance back. She peered past a screen of blueberry bushes and into the shadows under the trees. 'You scared the shit out of me.' She started towards him.

'Stay where you are,' he told her.

'Why don't you want me to—?' she began, then stopped. 'Are you wearing a skirt?'

Some faint, rose-coloured light reached through the branches and fell upon the skirt and his bare stomach. From the chest up, though, he remained in shadow.

379

The flushed and angry look on her face gave way to a disbelieving smile that did not express amusement so much as fright. 'Oh, Ig,' she breathed. 'Oh, baby.' She took another step forward, and he held up a hand.

'I don't want you to come back here.'

She came no closer.

'What brings you to the foundry?'

'You trashed our place,' she said. 'Why'd you do that?'

He didn't answer, didn't know what to say.

She dropped her gaze and bit her lip. 'I guess someone told you about me and Lee the other night.' She forced herself to look back up. 'Ig, I'm sorry. You can hate me if you want. I got that coming, I guess. I just want to be sure you're okay.' Breathing softly, and in a small voice, she said, 'Please let me help you.'

Ig shivered. It was almost more than he could bear, to hear another human voice offering to help him, to hear a voice raised in affection and concern. He had been a demon for just two days, but the time when he knew what it was like to be loved seemed to exist in a hazily recalled past, to have been left behind long ago. It amazed him to be talking with Glenna in a perfectly ordinary way, was an ordinary miracle, as simple and fine as a cold glass of lemonade on a hot day. Glenna felt no impulse to blurt her worst and most shameful impulses; her guilty secrets were just that, secrets. He touched the cross about his neck again, Merrin's cross, enclosing a small, precious circle of humanity.

'How did you know to find me here?'

'I was watching the local news at work, and I saw about the burned-out wreck they found on the sandbar. The TV cameras were too far back, so I couldn't tell if it was the Gremlin, and the newslady said the police hadn't confirmed a make or model. But I just had a feeling, a kind of bad feeling. So I called Wyatt Farmer, do you remember Wyatt? He glued a beard on my cousin Gary once when we were kids, see if they couldn't buy some beer.'

'I remember. Why did you call him?'

'I saw it was Wyatt's tow truck that pulled the wreck off the sandbar. That's what he does now. He has his own business in auto repair. I figured he could tell me what kind of car it was. He said it was so toasted they hadn't figured it out yet, 'cause there was nothing to work from except the frame and the doors, but he thought it was a Hornet or a Gremlin, and he was thinking Gremlin because they're more common these days. And I thought, oh, no, someone burned your car. Then I thought what if you were in it when it caught on fire. I thought what if you went and burned yourself up. I knew if you did it, you would've done it out here. To be close to her.' She gave him another shy, frightened look. 'I get why you trashed our place—'

'Your place. It was never ours.'

'I tried to make it ours.'

'I know. I think you tried your best. I didn't.'

'Why'd you burn your car? Why are you out here, wearing ... that?' Her hands were balled into fists pressed into her bosom. She fought for a smile. 'Aw, baby. You look like you've been through hell on earth.'

'You could say that.'

'Come on. Come get in my car, Ig. We'll go back to the apartment and get you out of that skirt and get you cleaned up, and you'll be yourself again.'

'And we'll go back to the way things were before?'

'Yes. Just like the way things were before,' she said.

That was the problem right there. With the cross around his neck, he could be his old self again, he could have it all back if he wanted it, but it wasn't worth having. If you were going to live in hell on earth, there was something to be said for being one of the devils. Ig reached behind his neck and unclasped

Merrin's cross and hung it from a branch overhead, then shoved aside the bushes and stepped into the light, let her see him for what he was now.

For one moment she quailed. Glenna took a staggering, unsteady step back, a heel sinking into soft earth and turning under her so she nearly twisted her ankle before she recovered. Her mouth opened to scream, a real horror-movie scream, a deep and tortured wail. But the scream didn't come. Almost immediately her plump, pretty face smoothed itself back out.

'You hated the way things were,' spoke the devil.

'I hated it,' she agreed, and a kind of grief stole over her face again.

'All of it.'

'No,' she said. 'There were a couple of things I liked. I liked when we'd make love. You'd close your eyes and I'd know you were thinking of her, but I wouldn't care because I could make you feel good and that was all right. And I liked when we made breakfast together on Saturday mornings, a big breakfast, bacon and eggs and juice, and then we'd watch stupid TV, and you seemed like you'd be happy to sit by me all day. But I hated knowing I'd never matter. I hated we didn't have a future, and I hated hearing you talk about the funny things she said and the clever things she did. I couldn't compete. I was never going to be able to compete.'

'Do you really want me to come back to the apartment?'

'*I* don't even want to go back. I hate that apartment. I hate living there. I want to go away. I want to start again somewhere else.'

'Where else would you go? Where could you go to be happy?'

'To Lee's house,' she said, and her face shone, and she smiled in a sweet, surprised way, like a girl catching her first sight of Disney World. 'Go in my raincoat with nothing on underneath and give him a real thrill. Lee wants me to come by and see him sometime. He sent me a text message this afternoon saying if you didn't turn up, we should—'

'*No,*' Ig said, his voice harsh and black smoke gushing from his nostrils.

She cringed, stepped away.

He inhaled, sucking the smoke back in. Took her arm and turned her in the direction of the car and started walking. The maiden and the devil walked in the furnace light at the end of the day, and the devil admonished her, 'You don't want to have anything to do with him. What'd he ever do for you besides steal you a jacket and treat you like a hooker? You need to tell Lee to fuck off. You need better than him. You have to give less and take more, Glenna.'

'I like to do nice things for people,' she said in a brave little voice, as if embarrassed.

'You're people, too. Do something nice for yourself.' And as he spoke, he put his will behind the horns and felt a shock of white pleasure pass through the nerves in them. 'Besides, look at how you've been treated. I wrecked your apartment, you haven't seen me for days, and then you come out here and find me fagging around in a skirt. Screwing Lee Tourneau won't pull you even. You need to think bigger than that. You got a little revenge coming to you. Go on home and get the bank card, empty the account, and . . . give yourself a vacation. Haven't you ever wanted to take off for a little *you* time?'

'Wouldn't that be something?' she said, but her smile faltered after a moment, and she said, 'I'd get in trouble. I was in jail once, thirty days. I don't ever want to go back.'

'No one's going to bother you. Not after you drove by the foundry and spotted me out here in my little lace skirt, playing the nancy boy. My parents aren't going to sic a lawyer on you. That's not the kind of thing they want getting out to the general public. Take my credit card, too. I bet my folks won't even put a stop on it for a few months. The best way to get even with anyone is to put them in the rearview mirror on your way to something better. You deserve something better, Glenna,' Ig said.

They were beside her car. Ig opened the door and held it for her. She looked down at his skirt, then up into his face. She was smiling. She was also crying, big black mascara tears.

'Was that your thing, Ig? Skirts? Is that why we didn't have us too much fun? If I knew, I would've tried to ... I dunno, tried to make that work.'

'No,' Ig said. 'I'm only wearing this because I didn't have red tights and a cape.'

'Red tights and a cape?' Her voice was dazed and a little slow.

'Isn't that what the devil is supposed to wear? Like a super-hero costume. In a lot of ways, I guess Satan was the first superhero.'

'Don't you mean supervillain?'

'Nah. Hero, for sure. Think about it. In his first adventure, he took the form of a snake to free two prisoners being held naked in a Third World jungle prison by an all-powerful meg-alomaniac. At the same time, he broadened their diet and introduced them to their own sexuality. Sounds kind of like a cross between Animal Man and Dr Phil to me.'

She laughed – weird, disjointed, confused laughter – and then hiccoughed, and the smile faded.

'So where do you think you'll go?' Ig asked.

'I dunno,' she said. 'I always wanted to see New York City. New York City at night. Taxis going by with strange foreign music coming out the windows. People selling those peanuts, the sweet peanuts, on the corners. Don't they still sell those peanuts in New York?'

'I don't know if they do anymore. They used to. I haven't been there since just before Merrin died. Go find out, why don't you. It's going to be great. Time of your life.'

'If taking off is so great,' she said, 'if getting even with you is so wonderful, why do I feel so shitty?'

'Because you aren't there yet. You're still here. And by the time you drive away, all you're going to remember is you saw me dressed up for the dance in my best blue skirt. Everything else – you're going to forget.' Putting the weight and force of the horns behind this instruction, pushing the thought deep into her head, a more intimate penetration than anything they had ever done in bed.

She nodded, staring at him with bloodshot, fascinated eyes. 'Forget. Okay.' She started to get into the car, then hesitated, looking at him over the door. 'First time I ever talked to you was out here. You remember? Bunch of us were cooking a turd. What a thing, huh?'

'Funny,' Ig said. 'That's kind of what I'm planning on this evening. Go on now, Glenna. Rearview mirror.'

She nodded and began to lower herself into the car, then straightened and bent over the door and kissed him on the forehead. He saw some bad things about her he hadn't known; she had sinned often, always against herself. He was startled and stepped back, the cool touch of her lips still on his brow and the cigarette and peppermint smell of her breath in his nostrils.

'Hey,' he said.

She smiled. 'Don't get hurt out here, Ig. Seems like you can't spend an afternoon at the foundry without nearly getting yourself killed.'

'Yeah,' he said. 'Now that you mention it, it is getting to be something of a habit.'

Ig walked back to the Evel Knievel trail to watch the smouldering coal of the sun sink into the Knowles River and gutter out. Standing there in the tall grass, he heard a curious musical chirrup, insectlike, but no insect he knew. He heard it quite distinctly – the locusts had gone quiet in the dusk. They were dying anyway, the droning machinery of their lust winding down with the end of the summer. The sound came again, to the left, in the weeds.

He crouched to investigate and saw Glenna's phone in its pink semi-transparent shell, lying in the straw-coloured grass where she had dropped it. He tugged it from the weeds and flipped it open. There was a text from Lee Tourneau on the Home screen:

WHAT R U WEARING?

Ig twisted his goatee, nervously considering. He still didn't know if he could do it over a phone, if the influence of the horns could be shot from a radio transmitter and bounced off a satellite. On the other hand, it was a well-known fact that cell phones were tools of the devil.

He selected Lee's message and pressed CALL.

Lee answered on the second ring. 'Just tell me you've got on something hot. You don't even have to be wearing it. I'm great at pretend.'

Ig opened his mouth but spoke in Glenna's soft, breathless, buttery voice. '*I'm wearing a bunch of mud and dirt, is what I'm wearing. I'm in trouble, Lee. I need someone to help me. I got my goddamn car stuck.*'

Lee hesitated, and when he spoke again, his voice was low and measured. 'Where did you get yourself stuck, lady?'

'*Out at the goddamn fuckin' foundry,*' Ig said in Glenna's voice.

'The foundry? Why are you out there?'

'*I came looking for Iggy.*'

'Why would you want to do that? Glenna, that wasn't thinking. You know how unstable he is.'

'*I know it, but I can't help it, I'm worried about him. His family is worried, too. There isn't anyone knows where he's at, and he*

386

missed his grandma's birthday, and he won't answer his phone. He could be dead for all anyone knows. I can't stand it, and I hate thinking he's messed up and it's my fault. It's part your fault, too, you shithead.'

He laughed. 'Well. Probably. But I still don't know why you'd be out at the foundry.'

'He likes to go out here this time of year, 'cause of this is where she died. So I thought I'd poke around, and I drove in, and got the car stuck, and of course Iggy isn't anywhere around. You were nice enough to give me a ride home the other night. Treat a lady twice?'

He paused for a moment. Then he said, 'Have you called anyone else?'

'You were the first person I thought of,' Ig said in Glenna's voice. 'Come on. Don't make me beg. My clothes are all muddy, and I need to get out of them and wash off.'

'Sure,' he said. 'All right. As long as I can watch you. Wash off, I mean.'

'That depends how fast you get here. I'm sittin' inside the foundry waitin' on you. You'll make fun of me when you see where I got my car stuck. When you get out here, you're going to absolutely die.'

'I can't wait,' he said.

'Hurry up. It's kind of creepy out here by myself.'

'I bet. No one out there but the ghosts. You hold on. I'm coming for you.'

Ig hung up without saying good-bye. Then he crouched for a while over the scorch mark on the top of the Evel Knievel trail. The sun had gone down while he wasn't paying attention. The sky was a deep, plummy shade of purple, the first stars lighting it in pinpricks. He rose at last to walk back to the foundry and get ready for Lee. He stopped and collected Merrin's cross from where he'd hung it in the branches of the oak. He grabbed the red metal gas can, too. It was still about a quarter full.

45

He figured Lee would need at least half an hour to get there, more if he was coming all the way from Portsmouth. It didn't feel like a lot of time. Ig was just as glad. The longer he had to think about what he needed to do, the less likely he was to do it.

Ig had come around to the front of the foundry and was about to hoist himself up through the open door into the great room when he heard a car thudding in the rutted road behind him. Adrenaline came up in an icy rush, filling him with its chill. Things were moving fast, but they couldn't be going that fast, not unless Lee had already been in his car when Ig called, and driving out this way for some reason. Only it wasn't Lee's big red Caddy, it was a black Mercedes, and for some reason Terry Perrish was behind the wheel.

Ig sank into the grass, set the half-full gas can down against the wall. He was so unprepared for the sight of his brother – here, *now* – that it was hard to accept what he was seeing. His brother couldn't be here because by now Terry's plane was on the ground in California, and Terry was out in the semi-tropical heat and Pacific sunlight of LA. Ig had told him to go, to give in to what he wanted to do most anyway – which was cut and run – and that should've been enough.

The car turned and slowed as it approached the building, creeping along through the high, wiry grass. The sight of Terry infuriated and alarmed Ig. His brother didn't belong here, and there was hardly any time to get rid of him.

Ig scampered along the concrete foundation, staying low. He reached the corner of the foundry as the Mercedes crunched by, quickened his pace, and grabbed the passenger-side door. He popped it open and leaped in.

Terry looked at him and screamed and fell back against the driver's door, hand fumbling for the latch. Then he recognised Ig and stopped himself.

'Ig,' he panted. 'What are you—?' His gaze dropping to the filthy skirt, then rising to his face. 'What the fuck did you do to yourself?'

Ig didn't understand at first, couldn't make sense of Terry's shock. Then he felt the cross, still clasped in his right hand, the chain wound around his fingers. He was holding the cross, and it was muting the horns. Terry was seeing Ig for himself, for the first time since he'd come home. The Mercedes jostled along through the high summer weeds.

'Want to stop the car, Terry?' Ig said. 'Before we go down the Evel Knievel trail and into the river?'

Terry's foot found the brake, and he brought the car to a halt.

The two brothers sat together in the front seat. Terry's breath came fast and quick through his open mouth. For a long moment, he gaped at Ig, his face vacant and baffled. Then he laughed. It was shaky, horrified laughter, but with it came a nervous twitch of the lips that was almost a smile.

'Ig. What are you doing out here ... like this?'

'That's my question. What are you doing out here? You had a flight today.'

'How do you—?'

'You need to get away from here, Terry. We don't have a lot of time.' As he spoke, he looked into the rearview mirror, checking the road. Lee Tourneau would be coming any minute.

'Time before what? What's going to happen?' Terry hesitated, then said, 'What's with the skirt?'

'You, of all people, ought to know a Motown reference when you see it, Terry.'

'Motown? You aren't making sense.'

'Sure I am. I'm telling you that you need to get the fuck out of here. What could make more sense than that? You are the wrong person in the wrong place at the exact wrong time, Terry.'

'What are you talking about? You're scaring me. What's going to happen? Why do you keep looking in the rearview mirror?'

'I'm expecting someone.'

'Who?'

'Lee Tourneau.'

Terry blanched. 'Oh,' he said. 'Oh. Why?'

'You know why.'

'Oh,' Terry said again. 'You know. How ... how much?'

'All of it. That you were in the car. That you passed out. That he fixed it so you couldn't tell.'

Terry's hands were on the steering wheel, his thumbs moving up and down, his knuckles white. His face, in the gloom of the car, was as pale as the rising August moon. 'All of it. How do you know he's on his way?'

'I know.'

'You're going to kill him,' Terry said. It wasn't a question.

'Obviously.'

Terry considered Ig's skirt, his grimy bare feet, his reddened skin, which might just have been a particularly bad sunburn. He said, 'Let's go home, Ig. Let's go home and talk about this. Mom and Dad are worried about you. Almost in a panic, you want to know the truth. Let's go home so they can see you're all right, and then we'll all talk. We'll figure things out.'

'My figuring is done,' Ig said. 'You should've left. I told you to leave.'

Terry shook his head. 'What do you mean, you told me to leave? I haven't seen you the whole time I've been home. We haven't talked at all.'

Ig looked in the rearview and saw headlights. He twisted around in the seat and stared through the back window. A car was passing out on the highway, on the other side of that thin strip of forest between the foundry and the road. The headlights blinked between the trunks of the trees in a rapid staccato, a shutter being opened and closed, blink-blink-blink, sending a message: *Hurry, hurry*. The car went past without turning in, but it was a matter of minutes until a car came that would *not* pass but instead would swing up the gravel road and head their way. Ig's gaze dropped, and he saw a suitcase on the back seat and Terry's trumpet case beside it.

'You packed,' Ig said. 'You must've planned to go. Why didn't you?'

'I did,' Terry said.

Ig sat up and looked a question at him.

Terry shook his head. 'It doesn't matter. Forget it.'

'No. Tell me.'

'Later.'

'Tell me now. What do you mean? If you left town, how come you're back?'

Terry gave him a bright and blank-eyed look. After a moment he began to speak, careful and slow. 'It doesn't make sense, okay?'

'No. It doesn't make sense to me either. That's why I want you to tell me.'

Terry's tongue darted out and touched his dry lips. When he spoke, his voice was calm but a little rushed. He said, 'I decided I was going back to LA. Getting out of the madhouse. Dad was pissed at me. Vera's in the hospital, and no one knows where you've been. But I just got it in my head that I wasn't doing any good in Gideon and that I needed to go, get back to LA, get busy with rehearsals. Dad told me he couldn't imagine anything more selfish than me taking off with things like they are. I knew he was right, but somehow it didn't seem to matter. It just felt good driving away.

'Except the further I got from Gideon, the less good I felt. I'd be listening to the radio, and I'd hear a song I like, and I'd start thinking about how to arrange it with the band. Then I'd remember I don't have a band anymore. There's no one to rehearse with.'

'What do you mean there's no one to rehearse with?'

'I don't have a job,' Terry said. 'I quit. Walked away from *Hothouse.*'

'What are you talking about?' Ig asked. He hadn't seen anything about this on his trip into Terry's head.

'Last week,' Terry said. 'I couldn't stand it. After what happened to Merrin, it wasn't fun anymore. It was the opposite of fun. It was hell. Hell is being forced to smile and laugh and play party songs when you want to scream. Every time I played the horn, I was screaming. The Fox people asked me to take the weekend and think it over. They didn't come right out and threaten to sue me for breach of contract if I don't show up for work next week, but I know that's in the air. I also know I don't give a shit. There's nothing they got that I need.'

'So when you remembered you didn't have a show anymore – was that when you turned around and came home?'

'Not right away. It was scary. Like ... like being two people at the same time. One minute I'd be thinking I needed to get off the interstate and head back to Gideon. Then I'd go back to imaginary rehearsals again. Finally, when I was almost to Logan Airport – you know that hill with the giant cross on it? The one just past the Suffolk Downs racetrack?'

Ig's arms prickled with cold and gooseflesh. 'About twenty

feet tall. I know it. I used to think it was called the Don Orsillo, but that's not right.'

'Don Orione. That's the name of the nursing home that takes care of the cross. I pulled over there. There's a road that leads up through the projects to the thing. I didn't go all the way up. I just pulled over to think, parked in the shade.'

'In the shade of the cross?'

His brother nodded in a vague sort of way. 'I still had the radio on. The college station, you know. The reception gets crackly that far south, but I hadn't got around to changing it. And the kid came on for the local news, and he said the Old Fair Road Bridge in Gideon was open again after being closed for a few hours in the middle of the day while police salvaged a firebombed car from off the sandbar. Hearing about that car gave me a kind of sick feeling. Just because. Because we hadn't heard from you in a couple of days and the sandbar is downriver from the foundry. And this is around the same time of year that Merrin died. It all felt connected. And suddenly I didn't know anymore why I was in such a hurry to get out of Gideon. I didn't know why it was so important for me to go. I turned around. I came back. And as I was pulling in to town, I thought maybe I should check the foundry. In case you came out here to be close to Merrin and . . . and something happened to you. I felt like I had no business doing anything until I knew you were okay. And . . . and here I am. And you're not okay.' He looked Ig over again, and when he spoke, his voice was halting and afraid. 'How were you going to . . . kill Lee?'

'Quickly. Which is better than he deserves.'

'And you know what I did . . . and you're letting me off? Why not kill me, too?'

'You aren't the only person to fuck a thing up because he was scared.'

'What's that mean?'

Ig thought for a moment before he replied, 'I hated the way

393

Merrin used to look at you, when you'd play the trumpet at your performances. I was always afraid she'd fall in love with you, instead of me, and I couldn't stand it. Do you remember the flow charts you used to draw, making fun of Sister Bennett? I wrote the note telling on you. The one that got you suspended and thrown out of the end-of-year recital.'

Terry goggled at him for a moment, as if Ig had spoken to him in an incomprehensible tongue. Then he laughed. It was a strained, thin sound, but real. 'Oh shit. My ass is still sore from the beating Father Mould gave me.' But he couldn't hold on to the smile, and when it was gone, he said, 'That isn't the same as what I did to you. Not in kind and not in degree.'

'No,' Ig agreed. 'I just mention it to illustrate the principle. People make lousy decisions when they're afraid.'

Terry tried to smile but looked closer to crying. He said, 'We need to go.'

'No,' Ig said. 'Just you. Now.' As he spoke, he was already lowering the passenger window. He balled the cross up and threw it out into the grass, got rid of it. In the same moment, he put his weight and will behind the horns, calling to all the snakes of the forest, calling for them to join him in the foundry.

Terry made a sound, down in his throat, a long hiss of surprise. '*Haaaahorns.* You ... you have horns. On your head. What ... my God, Ig ... what are you?'

Ig turned back. Terry's eyes were lamps, shining with an elevated kind of terror, a terror that approached awe.

'I don't know,' Ig said. 'Demon or man, I'm not sure. The crazy thing is, I think it's still up in the air. I know this, though: Merrin wanted me to be a person. People forgive. Demons – not so much. If I'm letting you go, it's as much for her as for you, or me. She loved you, too.'

'I need to go,' Terry said in a thin, frightened voice.

'That's right. You don't want to be here when Lee Tourneau arrives. You could be hurt if things go wrong, and even if you aren't, think of the damage you could do to your reputation. This has nothing to do with you. It never did. In fact, you will forget this conversation. You never came here, and you never saw me tonight. That's all gone now.'

'Gone,' Terry said, flinching and then blinking rapidly, as if someone had dashed a handful of cold water in his face. 'Jesus, I need to get out of here. If I'm ever going to work again, I need to get the fuck out of this joint.'

'That's right. This conversation is gone, and so are you. Take off. Drive home, and tell Mom and Dad you missed your flight. Be with the people who love you, and have a look at the newspaper tomorrow. They say they never report good news, but I think you'll feel a whole lot better about your life after you see the front page.' Ig wanted to kiss his brother's cheek but was afraid – was worried he would discover some hidden deed that would make him rethink his desire to send him away. 'Good-bye, Terry.'

He got out of the car and stood back from it as it started to move. The Mercedes rolled slowly forward, crushing the tall grass before it. It went into a big, lazy turn, circling behind a great heap of rubbish, bricks, old boards, and cans. Ig turned away then, didn't wait to see the Mercedes come around the other side of the midden heap. He had preparations to attend to. He moved quickly along the outer wall of the foundry, casting glances towards the line of trees that screened the building from the road. Any moment now he expected to see headlights through the firs, slowing as Lee Tourneau turned in.

He climbed into the room beyond the furnace. It looked as if someone had come in with a couple of buckets of snakes, tossed them, and run. Snakes slid from the corners and dropped from piles of bricks. The timber rattler uncoiled from the wheelbarrow and fell with an audible thump to the floor. There were only a hundred or so. Well. That was enough.

He crouched and lifted the timber rattler into the air, hand under her midsection; he was not afraid of being bitten now. She narrowed her eyes in a sleepy expression of affection and her black tongue flicked at him, and for a moment she whispered cool, breathless endearments in his ear. He kissed her gently on the head and then walked her to the furnace. As he carried her, he realised he could not read her for any guilt or sin, that she had no memory of ever having done a wrong. She was innocent. All snakes were, of course. To slip through the grass, to bite and shock into paralysis, either with poison or with the swift crunch of the jaws, to swallow and feel the good, furry, slick lump of a field mouse go down the throat, to drop into a dark hole and curl up on a bed of leaves – these were pure goods, the way the world was supposed to be.

He leaned into the chimney and set her in the stinking blanket on the mattress. Then he bent over her and lit each of the candles, creating an intimate and romantic ambience. She settled down into a contented coil.

'You know what to do if they get by me,' Ig said. 'The next person to open this door, I need you to bite and bite and bite. Do you understand?'

Her tongue slipped out of her mouth and lapped sweetly at the air. He folded the corners of the blanket over her, to hide her, and then set upon it the smooth pink soap shape of Glenna's phone. If by some chance Lee killed him, instead of the other way around, he would go in there to blow out the candles, and when he saw the phone, would want to take it with him. It had been used to call him, after all, and it wouldn't do to leave evidence lying around.

Ig eased himself out of the hatch and pushed the door almost all the way shut. Candlelight flickered around its edges, as if the old furnaces had been lit once more, as if the foundry were returning to life. He grasped his pitchfork, which was leaning against the wall just to the right of the hatch.

'Ig,' Terry whispered from behind him.

Ig spun around, his heart lunging in him, and saw his brother standing outside, rising on his tiptoes to look through the doorway.

'What are you still doing here?' Ig asked, flustered by the sight of him.

'Are those snakes?' Terry asked.

Terry stepped back from the door as Ig dropped through it. Ig still had the box of matches in one hand, and he flipped them to the side, onto the can of gas. Then he turned and jabbed the pitchfork in the direction of Terry's chest. He craned his head to look past him, into the dark field. He didn't see the Mercedes.

'Where's your car?'

'Behind that pile of shit,' Terry said, gesturing back towards a particularly large mound of trash. He reached up with one hand and gently pushed aside the tines of the pitchfork.

'I said to go.'

Terry's face gleamed with sweat in the August night. 'No,' he said.

It took Ig a moment to process Terry's unlikely reply.

'*Yes.*' Pushing with the horns, pushing so hard that the feeling of pressure and heat in them was, for once, almost painful – a disagreeable soreness. 'You don't want to be here, and I don't want you here.'

Terry actually staggered, as if Ig had shoved him. But then he got his feet set and remained where he was, an expression of grim strain on his features.

'And I said no. You can't make me. Whatever you're doing to my head, it has its limits. You can only make the offer. I have to accept. And I don't accept. I'm not driving away from this place and leaving you here to face Lee alone. That's what I did to Merrin, and I've been living in hell ever since. You want me to go, get in my car and come with me. We'll figure this out.

We'll figure how to deal with Lee in a way where no one gets killed.'

Ig made a choked sound of rage in his throat and came at him with the pitchfork. Terry danced back, away from the tines. It infuriated Ig that he couldn't make his brother do what he wanted. Each time Ig came towards him, prodding with the fork, Terry faded out of reach, a weak, uncertain grin on his face. Ig had the helpless sensation of being ten years old and forced into some backyard game of grab-ass.

Headlights wavered on the other side of the line of trees that screened the foundry from the road, slowing steadily as someone prepared to turn in. Ig and Terry both stopped, looking up at the road.

'It's Lee,' Ig said, and focused his furious gaze back on Terry. 'Get in your car and out of sight. You can't help me. You can only fuck things up. Keep your head down and stay out of the way where you won't get your ass killed.' Urging him back with another thrust of the pitchfork and at the same time putting one last blast of will behind the horns, trying to *bend* Terry.

Terry didn't fight this time but turned and ran, through the tall grass, back towards the midden heap. Ig watched until he had reached the corner of the building. Then he pulled himself through the high doorway and into the foundry. Behind him the headlights of Lee Tourneau's Cadillac were sliding through the air, slicing the darkness like a letter opener cutting into a black envelope.

46

No sooner had he pulled himself into the room than the headlights swept through the windows and doors. White squares of brightness streamed over the graffiti-covered walls, picking out ancient messages: TERRY PERRISH BLOWS, PEACE '79, GOD IS DEAD. Ig stepped away from the light to one side of the doorway. He removed his coat and threw it into the middle of the floor. Then he crouched in the corner and used his horns to call to the snakes.

They came from the corners, fell from holes in the wall, oozed out from under the heap of bricks. They glided towards the coat, sliding over one another in their haste. The overcoat began to squirm and boil as they gathered beneath it. Then it began to sit up. The coat rose and straightened, and the shoulders began to fill out, and the sleeves moved, swelling, as if an invisible man were pushing his arms into them. Last rose a head, with hair that writhed and spilled over the collar. It looked as if a long-haired man, or perhaps a woman, were sitting in the middle of the floor, meditating, head down. Someone who was shivering steadily.

Lee honked his horn.

'Glenna?' he called out. 'What are you doing, babe?'

'*I'm in here,*' Ig called in Glenna's voice. He squatted just to the right of the door. '*Aw, Lee, I twisted my goddamn ankle.*'

A car door opened and slammed. Footsteps approached through the grass.

'Glenna?' Lee said. 'What's up?'

'*I'm just sittin' here, honey,*' said Ig, Glenna-voiced. '*I'm just sittin' right here.*'

Lee set a hand on the concrete and hoisted himself up through the door. He had put on a hundred pounds and shaved his head since the last time Ig had seen him, a transformation almost as astonishing as growing horns, and for a moment Ig couldn't make sense of it, couldn't assimilate what he was seeing. It wasn't Lee at all. It was Eric Hannity, in his blue latex gloves, holding his nightstick, and his head all blistered and burned. In the headlights the bony curve of his scalp was as red as Ig's own. The blisters on his left cheek were thick and broad and looked full of pus.

'Hey, lady,' Eric said softly. His eyes darted this way and that, looking around the vast, dark room. He didn't see Ig with the pitchfork, not where he was crouching to the right, in the deepest of shadows. Eric's eyes hadn't adjusted yet. With the headlights pouring in through the door around him, they never would. Lee was out there somewhere. Somehow Lee knew that it wasn't safe and had come with Eric, and how did he know that? He didn't have the cross to protect him anymore. It didn't make sense.

Eric took small, scuffling steps towards the figure in the overcoat, the club swinging in slow, lazy arcs from his right hand.

'Say something, bitch,' Eric said.

The coat shivered and flapped an arm weakly and shook its head. Ig didn't move, was holding his breath. He couldn't think what to do. It was supposed to be Lee who came through the door, not someone else. But then, that was the story of his brief life in the demon trade, Ig thought. He had done his Satanic best to come up with a nice and simple murder, and now it was all blowing away, like so much cold ash in the wind. Maybe it was always like that, though. Maybe all the schemes of the devil were nothing compared to what men could think up.

Eric crept forward until he was standing right behind the thing in the coat. He lifted the club with both hands and brought it down, onto its back. The coat collapsed, and snakes gushed out, a great sack splitting open and spilling everywhere. Eric made a sound, a strangled, disgusted cry and almost tripped over his own Timberlands, stepping away.

'What?' Lee shouted from somewhere outside. 'What's happening?'

Eric brought his boot down on the head of a garter snake, wiggling between his heels. It shattered with a fragile crunch, like a lightbulb breaking. He made a pained sound of revulsion, kicked away a water snake, backing up, backing towards Ig. He was wading in them, a geyser of serpents. He was turning to get out when he stepped on one and his ankle rolled under him. He did a surprisingly graceful pirouette, spinning all the way around, before unbalancing and coming down hard on one knee, facing Ig. He stared with his small, piggy eyes in his big, burnt face. Ig held the pitchfork between them.

'I'll be goddamned,' Eric said.

'You and me both,' Ig said.

'Go to hell, you fuck,' Eric said, and his left hand started to come up, and for the first time Ig saw the snub-nosed revolver.

Ig lunged, not giving himself time to think, rising and slamming the pitchfork into Eric's left shoulder. It was like driving it into the trunk of a tree. A shivering impact ran up the shaft and into Ig's hands. One of the tines shattered Eric's clavicle; another punctured his deltoid; the middle tine got his upper chest. The gun went off, fired into the sky, a loud crack like a cherry bomb exploding, the sound of an American summer. Ig kept going, carrying Eric off-balance, driving him onto his ass. Eric's left arm flew out and the gun sailed away into the dark and fired again when it hit the floor and a rat snake was torn in two.

Hannity grunted. It looked as if he were straining to lift some terrible weight. His jaw was clenched and his face, already red, was approaching a shade of crimson, spotted with fat white blisters. He dropped his nightstick, reached across his body with his right hand and took the pitchfork by the iron head, as if he meant to pry it out of his torso.

'Leave it,' Ig said. 'I don't want to kill you. You'll hurt yourself worse trying to pull it out.'

'I'm not,' Hannity panted. 'Trying. To pull. It out.'

And he swung his body to the right, dragging the handle of the pitchfork and Ig with it, out of the darkness and into the brightly lit doorway. Ig didn't know it was going to happen until it had happened, until he had been tugged staggering from the shadows. He recoiled, yanking at the pitchfork, and for an instant the barbed points caught on tendon and flesh, and then they sprang free and Eric screamed.

Ig had no doubt what was about to happen and tried to get out of the doorway, which framed him like a red target on black paper, but he was too slow. The boom of the shotgun was a single deafening clap, and the first casualty was Ig's hearing. The gun spat red fire, and Ig's stunned eardrums flatlined. The world was instantly swaddled in an unnatural, not-quite-perfect silence. It felt as if Ig's right shoulder had been clipped by a passing school bus. He staggered forward and slammed into Eric, who made a harsh, wet, coughing noise, a kind of doglike bark.

Lee grabbed the doorframe with one hand and pulled himself up and in, a shotgun in his other hand. He came to his feet, in no rush. Ig saw him work the slide, saw very clearly as the spent cartridge jumped from the open chamber and leaped in a parabolic arc away through the darkness. Ig tried to leap in an arc of his own, to break to the left, make himself a moving target, but something had him by the arm – Eric. Eric had his elbow and was hauling on him, either to use him as a crutch or to hold him in place as a human shield.

Lee fired again, and a shovel struck Ig in the legs. They folded beneath him. For one instant he was able to keep his feet: he put the shaft of the pitchfork on the floor and leaned his weight against it to stay up. But Eric still had him by the arm and had caught spray himself, not in the legs but the chest. Eric went straight back and jerked Ig over with him.

Ig caught a whirling glimpse of black sky and luminescent cloud where once, almost a century before, there had been ceiling. Then he hit the concrete on his back with a resounding thud that rattled his bones.

He lay next to Eric, his head almost resting on Eric's hip. He couldn't feel his right shoulder anymore, or anything below his knees. Blood rushed from his head, the darkness of the sky deepening dangerously, and he made a thrashing, desperate effort to hang on to consciousness. If he passed out now, Lee would kill him. This was followed by another thought, that his relative consciousness didn't make any difference, because he was going to be killed here regardless. He noted, almost as a distant afterthought, that he had held on to his pitchfork.

'You hit *me*, you fuckhead!' Eric cried. His voice was muffled. Ig felt as if he were hearing the world through a motorcycle helmet.

'It could be worse. You could be dead,' Lee told Eric, and then he was standing over Ig, pointing the barrel into Ig's face.

Ig stabbed out with the pitchfork and caught the barrel of the gun between the tines. He wrenched it up and to the right, so when it went off, it exploded in Eric Hannity's face. Ig turned his head in time to see Eric Hannity's head burst like a cantaloupe dropped from a great height. Blood lashed Ig in the face, so hot it seemed to scald, and Ig thought, helplessly, of the turkey coming apart with a sudden annihilating crack.

Snakes sighed and slid through the blood, fleeing, heading to the corners of the room.

'Ah, shit,' Lee said. 'It just got worse. Sorry, Eric. I was trying to kill Ig, I swear.' And then he laughed, hysterical, unfunny laughter.

Lee took a step back, sliding the barrel free from between the tines of the pitchfork. He lowered the gun, and Ig jabbed at it with the fork again, and the shotgun slammed for a fourth time. The shot went high, caught the shaft of the pitchfork itself, and shattered it. The trident head of the fork spun away into the darkness and clanged off the concrete, leaving Ig holding a splintered and useless wooden spoke.

'You want to please hold still?' Lee asked, working the slide on the shotgun again.

He took a step back and, from a safe distance of four feet away, pointed the gun once more into Ig's face and pulled the trigger. The hammer fell with a dry clack. Lee scowled, lifted the .12-gauge, and looked at it with disappointment.

'What, these things only carry four bullets?' Lee said. 'It's not mine. It's Eric's. I would've used a gun on you the other night, but, you know, forensics. In this case, though, there's nothing to worry about. You killed Eric, and he killed you, and I'm out of it, and everything makes sense. I'm just sorry Eric ran out of shells and had to club you to death with his gun.'

He turned the 12-gauge around, took the barrel in both hands, and lifted it back over his shoulder. Ig had an instant to note that it looked as if Lee had been spending some time on the golf course – he had an easy, clean stroke, bringing the shotgun around – and then he smashed it into Ig's head. It struck one of the horns with a splintering crack, and Ig was flung away from Eric, rolled across smooth floor.

He came to rest face up, panting, a hot stitch in one lung, and waited for the sky to stop spinning. The heavens swayed, stars flying around like flakes in a snow-globe that someone has given a good shake. The horns hummed, a great tuning fork. They had absorbed the blow, though, kept his skull together.

Lee stalked towards him and lifted the shotgun and brought it down on Ig's right knee. Ig screamed and sat straight up, grabbing his leg with one hand. It felt as if the kneecap had split into three large pieces, as if there were broken shards of plate shifting around under the skin. He had hardly thought that, though, when Lee came around again. He caught Ig a glancing blow across the top of the head and knocked him onto his back once more. The spoke of wood Ig had been holding, the sharp spear that had been the shaft of the pitchfork, flew from his hand. The sky continued its nauseating snow-globe whirl.

Lee swung the butt of the shotgun, with as much force as he could muster, between Ig's legs, struck him in the balls. Ig could not scream, could not find the air to scream. He twisted, jerking onto his side and doubling over. A hard white knot of pain rose from his crotch and into his bowels and intestines, expanding, like poisonous air filling a balloon, into a withering sensation of nausea. Ig's whole body tightened as he fought the urge to vomit, his body clenching like a fist.

Lee tossed the shotgun and Ig heard it clatter on the floor next to Eric. Then he began to pace around, looking for something. Ig couldn't speak, could hardly get air down into his lungs.

'Now, what did Eric do with that pistol of his?' Lee said in a musing voice. 'You know, you had me fooled, Ig. It's amazing the things you can do to people's heads. How you can make them forget things. Blank out their memory. Make them hear voices. I really thought it was Glenna. I was on the way here when she called me from the salon to tell me I could go fuck myself. More or less just like that. You believe it? I said, "Okay, I'll go fuck myself, but how did you get your car unstuck?" And she said, "What in God's name are you talking about?" You can't imagine how that felt. Like I was losing my mind. Like the whole world was knocked out of whack. I felt something like that once upon a time, Ig. When I was little, I fell off a fence and hurt my head, and when I got up, the moon was trembling like it was about to fall out of the sky. I tried to tell you about it once, you know. I fixed it. Fixed the moon. I set heaven back in order. And I'll fix you, too.'

Ig heard the door to the blast furnace open with a squeal of iron hinges and felt a brief, almost painful surge of hope. The timber rattler would get Lee. He would reach into the chimney, and the viper would bite him. But then he heard Lee moving away, heels scuffing on concrete. He had only opened the door, perhaps for more light to see by, still searching for the gun.

'I called Eric, told him I thought you were out here, playing some kind of game, and that we had to step on you and I wasn't sure how hard. I said because you used to be a friend, I thought we should deal with you off the books. 'Course, you know Eric. I didn't have to work too hard to talk him into it. I didn't need to tell him to bring his guns either. He did that all on his own. You know I've never shot a gun in my life? Never so much as loaded one. My mother used to say they're the devil's right hand and wouldn't keep them in the house. Ah. Well. Better than nothing.' Ig heard a metallic scrape, Lee picking something off the floor. The waves of nausea were coming slower now, and Ig could breathe, in tiny little swallows. He thought that with another minute to rest he might have the strength to sit up. To make one final effort. He also thought that in another minute there would be five .45-calibre slugs in his head.

'You are just full of tricks, Iggy,' Lee said, walking back. 'Truth is, just a couple of minutes ago? When you were shouting to us in your Glenna voice from in here? A part of me half-believed it all over again, really thought it was her, even though rationally I knew she was at the salon. The voices are great, Ig, but not as great as coming out of a burning wreck without a mark on you.' He paused. He was standing over Ig, not with the pistol but with the head of the pitchfork. He said, 'How did it happen? How did you become like this? With the horns?'

'Merrin,' Ig said.

'What about her?'

Ig's voice was weak, shaking, hardly louder than an exhaled breath. 'Without Merrin in my life . . . I was this.'

Lee lowered himself to one knee and stared at Ig with what seemed real sympathy. 'I loved her too, you know,' Lee said. 'Love made devils of us both, I guess.'

Ig opened his mouth to speak, and Lee put his hand on Ig's neck, and every evil thing Lee had ever done poured down Ig's throat like some icy, corrosive chemical.

'No, I think it would be a mistake to let you say any more,' Lee said, and he raised the pitchfork overhead, the prongs aimed at Ig's chest. 'And at this point I don't really think there's anything left for us to talk about.'

The blast of the trumpet was a shrill, deafening squall, the sound of a car accident about to happen. Lee jerked his head to look back at the doorway, where Terry balanced on one knee, his horn lifted to his lips.

In the instant he looked away, Ig shoved himself up, pushing aside Lee's hand. He took hold of the lapels of Lee's sport coat and drove his head into his torso: slammed the horns into Lee's stomach. The impact reverberated down Ig's spine. Lee grunted, the soft, simple sound of all the breath being forced out of him.

A feeling of wet suction grabbed at the horns and held them, so it was hard to pull free. Ig twisted his head from side to side, tearing the holes wider. Lee wrapped his arms around Ig's head, trying to force him back, and Ig gored him again, thrusting deep into an elastic resistance. He smelled blood, mingled with another odour, a foul old garbage stink – a perforated bowel, perhaps.

Lee put his hands on Ig's shoulders and shoved, trying to extricate himself from the horns. They made a wet, sucking sound as they came loose, the sound a boot makes as it is pulled out of deep mud.

Lee folded and rolled onto his side, his arms wrapped around his stomach. Ig couldn't sit up any longer either and toppled, slumping to the concrete. He was still turned to face Lee, who was almost foetal, hugging himself, his eyes shut and his mouth a great open hole. Lee wasn't screaming anymore, couldn't get the breath to scream, and with his eyes shut he couldn't see the black rat snake sliding past him. The rat snake was looking for a place to hide, a way out of bedlam. It turned its head as it glided past, giving Ig a frantic look with eyes of gold foil.

There, Ig told it with his mind, gesturing with his chin towards Lee. *Hide. Save yourself.*

The rat snake slowed and looked at Lee, then back to Ig. Ig felt there was unmistakable gratitude in the rat snake's gaze. It swerved, gliding elegantly through the dust on the smooth concrete, and slithered head first into Lee's yawning mouth.

Lee's eyes sprang open, the good eye and the blind eye alike, and they were bright with a kind of ecstatic horror. He tried to snap his jaws shut, but when he bit the three-inch-thick cable of the snake, he only startled it. Its tail shivered furiously back and forth, and it began to hurry, pumping itself down Lee's throat. Lee groaned, choking on it, and let go of his mauled stomach to grab at it, but his palms were soaked with blood, and it squirmed slickly from within his fingers.

Terry was coming across the floor at a stumbling run. 'Ig? Ig, are you—' But when he saw Lee thrashing on the floor, he stopped where he was and stared.

Lee rolled onto his back, screaming now, although it was hard to make any sound with his throat full of snake. His heels beat against the floor. His face was deepening to a colour that was almost black in the night. And branches of veins stood out in Lee's temples. The bad eye, the eye of ruin, was still turned towards Ig, and it stared at him with something very close to wonder. That eye was a bottomless dark hole containing a circular staircase of pale smoke, leading down to a place where a soul might go and never return. His hands fell to his sides. A good eight inches of rat snake hung from his open mouth, a long black fuse drooping from a human bomb. The snake itself was motionless, seemed to understand that it had been lied to, had made a grave error trying to hide itself in the wet, tight tunnel of Lee Tourneau's throat. It could go forward no further, nor could it slide itself out. Ig was sorry for it. That was a bad way to die: stuck inside Lee Tourneau.

The pain was returning, pouring into the centre of him from crotch and devastated shoulder and smashed knees, like four polluted tributaries emptying into a deep reservoir of sick feeling. Ig shut his eyes to concentrate on managing his pain. Then, for a while, it was quite still in the old foundry, where the man and the demon lay side by side – although which was which would perhaps have been a matter for theological debate.

47

Shadows lapped unsteadily at the walls, rising and falling, the darkness coming in waves. The world was ebbing and flowing around him in waves, and Ig struggled to hold onto it. A part of him wanted to go under, to escape the pain, turn the volume down on his ruined body. He was already drifting away from himself, the hurt balanced by a dreamy, growing sensation of buoyancy. The stars swam slowly along overhead, drifting from left to right, so it was as if he were floating on his back in the Knowles River, letting the current carry him steadily downstream.

Terry bent over him, his face anguished and confused. 'All right, Ig. You're all right. I'm going to call someone. I have to run back to my car and get my phone.'

Ig smiled in a way he hoped was reassuring and tried to tell Terry all he needed to do was set him on fire. The gas can was outside, against the wall. Slosh some unleaded on him and throw a match, he'd be fine. But he couldn't find the air to push out the words, and his throat was too raw and tight for talking. Lee Tourneau had done a number on him, all right.

Terry squeezed his hand, and Ig knew, randomly, that his older brother had copied answers on a seventh-grade geography test from the boy sitting in front of him. Terry said, 'I'll be back. Do you hear me? Right back. One minute.'

Ig nodded, grateful to Terry for taking care of things. Terry's hand slipped from Ig's, and he rose out of sight.

Ig tipped his head back and looked at the reddish candlelight washing over the old bricks. The steady, shifting movement of the light soothed him, added to his feeling of suspension, of floating. His next thought was that if there was candlelight, the hatch to the furnace must be open. That's right, Lee had opened it to throw more light on the concrete floor.

And then Ig knew what was about to happen, and the shock of it brought him up out of his dreamy, floating stupor. Terry was about to see the phone, Glenna's phone, carefully set on the blanket in the furnace. Terry could not put his hand in there. Terry, of all people – Terry, who had nearly died at fourteen from a bee sting – needed to stay the fuck away from the furnace. Ig tried to call for him, to shout, to warn him, but could not produce anything except a cracked and tuneless whistle.

'One minute, Ig,' Terry said from across the room. He seemed, in truth, to be talking to himself. 'You hang in there and— Wait! Hey, Ig, we're in luck. Got a phone right here.'

Ig turned his head and tried again, tried to stop him, and did in fact manage a single word: 'Terry.' But then that tight, painful feeling of compression settled back into his throat, and he could say no more, and anyway, Terry did not look back at the sound of his name.

His brother bent into the hatch, grabbing for the phone on the lumpy blanket. When he picked it up, one fold flopped back and Terry hesitated, looking down at the loops of snake beneath, the scales like brushed copper in the candlelight. There was a dry rattle of castanets.

The viper uncoiled and struck Terry in the wrist, with a sound Ig could hear twenty-five feet away, a meaty thump. The phone flew. Terry screamed and went up and straight back and banged the iron frame of the hatch with his skull. The impact dropped him. He got his hands up, stopped himself before he could go face first into the mattress, the lower half of his body hanging out through the hatch.

The snake still had him by the wrist. Terry grabbed it and jerked. The timber rattler slashed his wrist open as her fangs were tugged loose, and she coiled and hit him again, in the face, sinking her teeth into his left cheek. Terry grabbed her about halfway up the body and pulled, and she let go and bunched up and hit him a third time, a fourth. Each time she pounded into him, it made a sound like someone drilling the speed bag in a gym.

Ig's brother sank back out of the hatch, dropping to his knees. He had the snake low, close to the end of her tail. He pulled her off him and lifted her in the air and smashed her against the floor, like someone banging a broom against a rug to knock the dust out of it. A black spray of blood and snake brain dashed across the concrete. Terry flipped her away from himself, and she rolled and landed on her back. Her tail whipped madly about, slapping at the concrete. The thrashing slowed a little at a time, until her tail was only waving gently back and forth, and then it stopped completely.

Terry knelt at the door of the furnace with his head bowed, like a man in prayer, a devout penitent in the church of the holy and everlasting chimney. His shoulders rose and fell, rose and fell with respiration.

'Terry,' Ig managed to call out, but Terry did not lift his head and look back at him. If Terry heard him – Ig wasn't sure he had – he couldn't reply. Terry had to save each precious breath for the effort of getting the next lungful of oxygen. If it was anaphylactic shock, then he would need an EpiPen in the next few minutes, or he'd suffocate on the swollen tissues of his own throat.

Glenna's phone was somewhere in the furnace, not thirty feet away, but Ig didn't know where Terry had dropped it and didn't want to drag himself around looking for it while Terry choked. He felt faint and wasn't sure he could even clear the hatch to the furnace, two and a half feet off the floor. Whereas the tank of gas was just outside.

He knew that starting would be hardest. Just the thought of trying to roll onto his side lit up vast and intricate networks of pain in shoulder and crotch, a hundred fine burning fibres. The more time he gave himself to think, the worse it was going to be. He turned on his side, and it felt as if there were a hooked blade buried in his shoulder being turned back and forth – a continuous impalement. He shouted – he hadn't known he *could* shout until he did it – and closed his eyes.

When his head cleared, he reached out with his good arm and grabbed at the concrete and pulled, dragging himself about a foot. And cried out again. He tried to push himself forward with his legs, but he couldn't feel his feet, couldn't feel anything below that sharp, persistent ache in his knees. His skirt was wet with his blood. The skirt was probably ruined.

'And it was my favourite,' he whispered, nose squashed against the floor. 'I was going to wear it to the dance.' And laughed – a dry, hoarse cackle that he thought sounded particularly crazy.

He pulled himself another foot with the good arm and the knives sank deep into his right shoulder once more, the pain radiating into his chest. The doorway didn't look any closer. He almost laughed again at the amusing futility of it all. He risked a glance at his brother. Terry still knelt before the hatch, but his head drooped so that his forehead was almost touching his knees. From where Ig was, he could no longer see through the hatch into the chimney. Instead he was looking at the half-open iron door and the way the candlelight wavered around it and—

—there was a door up there, with a light wavering around it.

He was so drunk. He had not been this drunk since the night Merrin had been killed, and he wanted to get drunker still. He had pissed on the Virgin Mother. He had pissed on the cross. He had pissed quite copiously upon his own feet and laughed about it. He was tucking himself into his pants with one hand and tipping his head back to drink straight from the bottle when he saw it above him, cradled in the diseased branches of the old dead tree. It was the underside of a tree house, not fifteen feet off the ground, and he could see the wide rectangle of the trapdoor, delineated by a faint, wavering candlelight that showed around the edges. The words written upon that door were barely visible in the gloom: BLESSED SHALL YOU BE WHEN YOU GO IN.

'Hunh,' Ig said, absentmindedly pushing the cork back in the bottle, then letting the bottle drop from his hand. 'There you are. I see you up there.'

The Tree House of the Mind had played a good trick on him – on him and Merrin both – hiding from them out here all these years. It had never been there before, not any of the other times he had come to visit the place where Merrin had been killed. Or perhaps it had always been there and he hadn't been in the right frame of mind to see it.

Pulling his zip up with one hand, he swayed and then began to move—

—another foot across the smooth concrete floor. He didn't want to lift his head to see how far he had gone, was afraid he would be no closer to the door now than he'd been a few minutes ago. He reached out with his left arm and—

—*grabbed the lowest branch and began to climb. His foot slipped, and he had to clutch at a bough to keep from falling. He waited out a bad moment of dizziness with his eyes shut, feeling that the tree was about to come uprooted and fall over with him in it. Then he recovered himself and went on, climbing with the drunkard's thoughtless, liquid grace. Soon enough he found himself on the branch directly below the trapdoor, and he went straight up to throw it open. But there was a weight resting on top of it, and the trap only banged noisily in its frame.*

Someone cried out, softly, from within – a voice he recognised.
'What was that?' Merrin cried.

'Hey,' said someone else, a voice he knew even better: his own.
Coming from within the tree house, it was muffled and remote. 'Hey,
is someone down there?'

For a moment Ig couldn't move. They were there, on the other
side of the trapdoor, Merrin and himself, both of them still young
and undamaged and perfectly in love. They were there, and it was
not too late to save them from the worst of what was coming for
them, and he rose hard and fast and hit the trapdoor again with his
shoulders—

—and opened his eyes and looked blearily around. He had
winked out for a while, maybe as long as ten minutes. His pulse
was slow and heavy. His right shoulder had been hot before.
Now it was cold and wet. The cold worried him. Dead bodies
got cold. He lifted his head to orient himself and found he was
only a yard from the doorway and from the six-foot drop beyond
that he'd been trying not to think about. The can was down
there, just to the right. All he had to do was get through the
door and—

—he could tell them what was going to happen, could warn
them. He could tell his younger self to love Merrin better and trust
her, to stay close to her, that their time was short, and he hit the trap
again and again, but each time the door only rose an inch or so before
smashing back down.

'Cut it the fuck out!' shouted the young Ig, inside the tree house.

Ig paused, readying himself for another go at the trapdoor – and
then held himself back, recalling when he had been the one on the
other side of the door.

He'd been afraid to open the trap, had only worked up his nerve
to pull back the hatch when the thing that was waiting outside
stopped trying to force its way in. And there had been nothing there.
He wasn't there; or they weren't.

'Listen,' said the person he'd been, on the other side of that door,

'if there's someone down there ... you had your fun. We're good and scared. We're coming out now.'

The chair legs thumped and squeaked as they were pushed back, and Ig hit the trapdoor from beneath in the same moment the young Ig threw it open. Ig thought he saw the shadows of the two lovers leaping out and past him for a moment, but it was only a trick of the candlelight within, making the darkness seem briefly alive.

They had forgotten to blow out the candles, and when Ig stuck his head through the open door, he found them still lit, so—

—he stuck his head through the door, and his body tumbled after it. He hit the dirt on his shoulders, and a black electric shock went through his right arm, an explosion, and he felt he might be fragmented from the force of it, blown into pieces. They would find parts of him in the trees. He rolled onto his back, his eyes open and staring.

The world shivered from the force of the impact. Ig's ears were filled with an atonal hum. When he looked into the night sky, it was like the end of a silent movie: a black circle began to shrink, closing in on itself, erasing the world, leaving him—

—alone in the dark of the tree house.

The candles had melted to misshapen one-inch plugs. Wax ran in thick and glistening columns, almost completely obscuring that crouching devil who squatted on the base of the menorah. The flame light flickered around the room. The mould-spotted easy chair stood to the left of the open trap. The shadows of the china figures wavered against the walls, the two angels of the Lord and the alien. Mary was tipped over on her side, just as he remembered leaving her.

Ig cast his gaze about him. It was as if only a few hours had passed since he'd last been in this place, and not years.

'What's the point?' he asked. At first he thought he was speaking to himself. 'Why bring me here if I can't help them?' Growing angry as he said it. He felt a heat in his chest, a fuming tightness. The room smelled of burning candles.

There had to be a reason, something he was supposed to do, to find. Something they had left behind maybe. He looked at the end-table with the china figures on it and noticed that the little drawer was open a quarter of an inch. He strode to it and pulled it back, thinking there might be something in it, something he could use, something he could learn from. But there was nothing in there except a rectangular box of matches. A black devil leaped on the cover, head thrown back in laughter. The words LUCIFER MATCHES were written across the cover in ornate nineteenth-century script. Ig grabbed them and stared at them, then closed his fist on them, wanting to crush them. He didn't, though. He stood there holding them, staring down at the little figures – and then his eyes refocused on the parchment beneath them.

The last time he'd been in this tree house, when Merrin was alive and the world was good, the words on the parchment had been in Hebrew and he hadn't had any idea what they said. He'd believed it was Scripture, a scroll from a phylactery. But in the wavering light of the candle flame, the ornate black letters swayed, like living shadows somehow magically pinned to paper, spelling a message in plain, simple English:

THE TREE HOUSE OF THE MIND

Tree of Good & Evil
1 Old Foundry Road
Gideon, NH 03880

RULES AND PROVISOS:

Take What You Want While You're Here
Get What You Need When You Leave
Say Amen on Your Way Out the Door
Smoking Is NOT prohibited

L. MORNINGSTAR, PROPRIETOR

Ig swayed, staring down at it, not sure he understood it any better now, even knowing what it said. What he wanted was Merrin, and he was never going to have her again, and, lacking that, he wanted to burn this fucking place to the ground and smoking was not prohibited and before he knew what he was doing, he swept his hand across the table, throwing the lit menorah across the room, crashing over the little figures. The alien tumbled and bounced, rolled off the table. The angel who resembled Terry, and who held a horn to his lips, dropped off the table and into the half-open drawer. The second angel, the one who had stood over Mary, looking aloof and superior, hit the table with an almost musical crack. His aloof, superior head rolled off.

Ig turned in a furious circle—

—turned his body in a painful circle and saw the gas can where he had left it, against the stone wall, below and to the right of the doorway. He shoved himself through a clump of high grass, and his hand swatted the can, producing a bonging sound and a watery slosh. He found the handle, tugged on it. It surprised him how heavy the thing was. As if it were full of liquid concrete. Ig felt along the top of the gasoline tank for the box of Lucifer Matches and set them aside.

He lay still for a while, gathering his strength for the last necessary act. The muscles in his left arm were trembling steadily, and he wasn't sure he could do what he needed to. Finally he decided he was ready to try, and he made an effort to lift the can and upend it over himself.

Gasoline splattered down on him in a reeking, glittering rain. He felt it in his mutilated shoulder, a sudden stinging burst. He screamed, and a mushroom cloud of grey smoke gushed from his lips. His eyes watered. The pain was smothering, caused him to let go of the can and double over. He shivered furiously in his ridiculous blue skirt, a series of tremors that threatened to become a full-blown convulsion. He flailed with his right hand, didn't know what he was reaching for until he found the box of Lucifer Matches in the dirt.

The August-night sounds of crickets and cars humming past on the highway were very faint. Ig tapped open the box. Matches flew from his shaking hand. He picked out one of the few that remained and dragged it across the strike strip on the side of the box. A white lick of fire rose from its head.

The candles had dropped to the floor and rolled every which way. Most of them were still lit. The grey rubber alien figure had come to rest against one, and a white lick of fire was blackening and lique-fying the side of its face. One black eye had already melted away to reveal a hollowness within. Three other candles had wound up against the wall, beneath the window, with its sheer white curtains rippling gently in the August breeze.

Ig grabbed fistfuls of curtains, tore them from the window and hung them over the burning candles. Fire climbed the cheap nylon, rushing up towards his hands. He threw them onto the chair, just looking for something else that would go up without too much trouble.

Something popped and crunched underfoot. He looked down and saw he had put his heel on the figure of the china devil. He had crushed the body, although the head remained intact, wobbling on the planks. The devil grinned maniacally, teeth showing in his goatee.

Ig bent and picked the head up from the floor. He stood in the burning tree house, considering Satan's urbane, handsome features, the little needles of his horns. Streamers of fire unrolled up the wall, and black smoke gathered beneath the banked ceiling. Flames boiled over the easy chair and end-table alike. The little devil seemed to regard him with pleasure, with approval. He appreciated a man who knew how to burn a thing down. But Ig's work here was done now, and it was time to move on. The world was full of other fires waiting to be lit.

He rolled the little head between his fingers for a moment, then returned to the end-table. He picked up Mary and kissed her small face, said, 'Good-bye, Merrin.' He set her right.

He lifted the angel who had stood before her. His face had been imperious and indifferent, a holier-than-thou, how-dare-you-touch-me face, but the head had snapped off and rolled somewhere. Ig put the devil's head in its place, thought Mary was better off with someone who looked like he knew how to have a good time.

Smoke caught and burned in Ig's lungs, stung his eyes. He felt his skin going tight from the heat, three walls of fire. He made his way to the trapdoor, but before stepping through it, he lifted it partway to see what was written on the inside; he remembered very clearly that there was something painted there in whitewash. It said, BLESSED SHALL YOU BE WHEN YOU GO OUT. Ig wanted to laugh but didn't. Instead he smoothed his hand over the fine grain of the trap and said 'Amen', then eased himself through the hole.

With his feet on the wide branch directly below the trap, he paused for a last look around. The room was the eye at the centre of a churning cyclone of flame. Knotholes popped in the heat. The chair roared and hissed. He felt, all in all, happy with himself. Without Merrin the place was just kindling. So was all the world, as far as Ig was concerned.

He shut the trapdoor behind him and started to pick a slow and careful route down. He needed to go home. He needed some rest.

No. What he really needed was to get his hands on the throat of the person who had taken Merrin away from him. What had it said on the parchment in the Tree House of the Mind? That you would get what you needed on your way out? A guy could hope.

He stopped just once, halfway to the ground, to lean against the trunk and rub the palms of his hands into his temples. A dull, dangerous ache was building there, a sensation of pressure, of some-thing with sharp points pushing to get out of his head. Christ. If this was how he felt now, he was going to have one hell of a hangover in the morning.

Ig exhaled – did not notice the pale smoke wafting from his own nostrils – and continued down and out of the tree, while above him heaven burned.

420

He stared at the burning match in his hand for exactly two seconds – *Mississippi one, Mississippi two* – and then it sizzled down to his fingers, touched gasoline, and he ignited with a whump and a hiss, exploded like a cherry bomb.

48

Ig stood, a burning man, devil in a gown of fire. For half a minute, the gasoline flames roiled off him, streamed away from his flesh in the wind. Then, as quickly as it had come roaring to life, the blaze began to flutter weakly and sputter out. In a few moments, it was gone entirely, and a black, oily smoke rose from his body in a thick, choking column. Or what would've been choking to any man but was, to the demon in the centre of it, as sweet as an alpine breeze.

He cast off his robe of smoke, stepped forth from it entirely naked. The old skin had burned away, and the new skin beneath was a deeper, richer shade of carmine. His right shoulder was still stiff, although the wound had healed to a tormented mass of whitish scar tissue. His head was clear; he felt well, felt as if he had just run a mile and was ready for a swim. The grass around him was black and smouldering. A burning red line was marching across the dry weeds and bunches of grass, moving towards the forest. Ig looked beyond it to the dead cherry tree, pale against its background of evergreens.

He had left the Tree House of the Mind in flames, had burned down heaven, but the cherry still stood undamaged. A wind rose in a hot gust, and the leaves thrashed, and even from here Ig could see there was no tree house up there. It was funny, though – the way the fire seemed to be *aimed* at it, burning a path through the high grass to its trunk. It was the wind, funnelling it straight across the field, pouring fire at the old town woods.

Ig climbed through the foundry doorway. He stepped over his brother's trumpet.

Terry knelt before the open door of the furnace, head bowed. Ig saw his perfect stillness, the calm look of concentration on his face, and thought his brother looked good even in death, his shirt drawn smoothly across his broad back, cuffs folded carefully past his wrists. Ig lowered himself to his knees beside Terry. Two brothers in the pews. He took his brother's hand in his and saw that when Terry was eleven, he had stuck gum in Ig's hair on the school bus.

'Shit,' Ig said. 'It had to be cut out with scissors.'

'What?' Terry asked.

'The gum you put in my hair,' Ig said. 'On Bus Nineteen.'

Terry inhaled a small sip of air, a whistling breath.

'Breathing,' Ig said. 'How are you breathing?'

'I've got,' Terry whispered, 'very strong. Lungs. I do. Play the horn. Now. And then.' After a moment he said, 'It's a miracle. We both. Got out. Of this. Alive.'

'Don't be so sure about that,' Ig said.

Glenna's phone was in the furnace, had hit the wall and cracked. The battery cover had come off. Ig thought it wouldn't work, but it beeped to life as soon as he flipped it open. Luck of the devil. He dialled emergency services and told an impersonal operator that he had been bitten by a snake, that he was at the foundry off Route 17, that people were dead and things were burning. Then he broke the connection and climbed out of the chimney to crouch beside Terry again.

'You called,' Terry said. 'For help.'

'No,' Ig said. '*You* called for help. Listen closely, Terry. Let me tell you what you're going to remember – and what you're going to forget. You have a lot to forget. Things that happened tonight and things that happened *before* tonight.' And as he spoke, the horns throbbed, a hard jolt of animal pleasure. 'There's only room for one hero in this story – and everyone knows the devil doesn't get to be the good guy.'

Ig told him a story, in a soft and pleasing voice, a good story, and Terry nodded as he listened, as if to the beat of a song he particularly liked.

In a few minutes, it was done. Ig sat with him for a while longer, neither of them speaking. Ig was not sure Terry still knew he was there; he had been told to forget. He seemed to be asleep on his knees. Ig sat until he heard the distant wail of a trumpet, playing a single, razzy note of alarm, a musical sound of panicked urgency: the fire trucks. He took his brother's head in his hands and kissed his temple. What he saw was less important than what he felt.

'You're a good man, Ignatius Perrish,' whispered Terry, without opening his eyes.

'Blasphemy,' Ig said.

49

He climbed down from the open doorway and then, as an afterthought, reached up and took his brother's trumpet. Then he turned and looked across the open field, along the avenue of fire, which reached in a straight line towards the cherry tree. The blaze leaped and flickered around the trunk for a moment – and then the tree itself erupted into flames, as if it were soaked in kerosene. The crown of the tree roared, a parachute of red and yellow flame, and in its branches was the Tree House of the Mind. Curtains of flame billowed in the windows. The cherry alone burned in the wood, the other trees were untouched by fire.

Ig strode along the path the fire had cut through the field, a young lord on the red carpet that led to his manor. By some trick of optics, the headlights of Lee's Caddy fell upon him and cast a vast, looming, four-storey-high shadow against the boiling smoke. The first of the fire trucks was thumping its slow way down the rutted dirt road, and the driver, a thirty-year veteran named Rick Terrapin, saw it, a horned black devil as tall as the foundry's chimney, and he cried out and jerked at the wheel, took the fire truck right off the road and clipped a birch tree. Rick Terrapin would retire three weeks later. Between the devil in the smoke and the horrors he saw inside the foundry, he didn't much feel like putting out fires anymore. After that he was just as happy to let shit burn.

Ig went with his stolen trumpet into the yellow blaze and came at last to the tree. He did not lose a step but started straight up the burning ladder of its branches. He thought he heard voices above, irreverent, cheerful voices, and laughter – a celebration! There was music, too, kettledrums and the saucy bump-and-grind of trumpets. The trapdoor was open. Ig climbed through, into his new home, his tower of fire, which held his throne of flame. He was right; there was a celebration under way – a wedding party, *his* wedding party – and his bride awaited him there, with her hair aflame, naked but for a loose wrap of fire. And he took her into his arms, and her mouth found his, and together they burned.

50

~e

Terry came back home in the third week of October, and the first warm afternoon with nothing to do he drove out to the foundry for a look around.

The great brick building stood in a blackened field, amid the trash heaps that had gone up like bonfires and were now hills of ash, smoked glass and burnt wire. The building itself was streaked with soot, and the whole place had a faint odour of char about it.

But around back, at the top of the Evel Knievel trail, it was nice, the light good, coming sideways through the trees in their Hallowe'en costumes of red and gold. The trees were on fire, blazed like enormous torches. The river below made a soft rushing sound that played in gentle counterpoint to the easy soughing of the wind. Terry thought he could sit there all day.

He had been doing a lot of walking the last few weeks, a lot of sitting and watching and waiting. He had put his LA house on the market in late September and moved back to New York City, went to Central Park almost every day. The show was over, and without it he didn't see any reason to hang around in a place where there weren't seasons and where you couldn't walk to anything.

Fox was still hoping he'd come back, had issued a statement that in the aftermath of his brother's murder Terry had opted to take a professional sabbatical; this conveniently overlooked the fact that Terry had in fact formally resigned, weeks before the incident at the foundry. The TV people could say what they wanted to say. He wasn't coming back. He thought maybe in another month or two he might go out, do some gigging in clubs. He wasn't in any hurry to work again, though. He was still getting unpacked, trying not to think too much. Whatever happened next would happen on its own schedule. He'd find his way to something eventually. He hadn't even bought himself a new horn.

No one knew what had happened that night at the foundry, and since Terry refused to provide a public comment and everyone else at the scene was dead, there were a lot of crazy ideas going around about the evening Eric and Lee died. TMZ had published the craziest account. They said Terry had gone out to the foundry looking for his brother and found Eric Hannity and Lee Tourneau there, the two of them arguing. Terry had overheard enough to understand they had murdered his brother, burned him alive in his car, and were out there looking for evidence they might have left behind. According to TMZ, Lee and Eric caught Terry trying to slip away and dragged him into the foundry. They had meant to kill him, but first they wanted to know if he had called anyone, if anyone knew where he was. They locked him in a chimney with a poisonous snake, trying to scare him into talking. But while he was in there, they began to argue again. Terry heard screams and gunshots. By the time he got out of the chimney, things were on fire and both men were dead, Eric Hannity by shotgun, Lee Tourneau by pitchfork. It was like the plot of a sixteenth-century revenge tragedy; all that was missing was an appearance by the devil. Terry wondered where TMZ got their information, if they had paid someone off in the police department – Detective Carter, perhaps; their outlandish report read almost exactly like Terry's own signed testimony.

Detective Carter had come to see Terry on his second day

in the hospital. Terry didn't remember much about the first day. He recalled being wheeled into the emergency room, remembered someone pulling an oxygen mask over his face, and a rush of cool air that smelled faintly medicinal. He remembered that later he had hallucinated, had opened his eyes to find his dead brother sitting on the edge of his hospital cot. Ig had Terry's trumpet and was playing a little bebop riff. Merrin was there, too, pirouetting barefoot in a short dress of crimson silk, spinning to the music so her red hair flew. As the sound of the trumpet resolved to the steady bleep of the EKG machine, both of them faded away. Still later, in the early hours of the morning, Terry had lifted his head from the pillow and looked around to find his mother and father sitting in chairs against the wall, both of them asleep, his father's head resting on his mother's shoulder. They were holding hands.

But by the afternoon of the second day, Terry merely felt as if he were recovering from a very bad flu. His joints throbbed and he could not get enough to drink, and he was aware of an all-body weakness . . . but otherwise he was himself. When the doctor, an attractive Asian woman in cat's-eye glasses, came in the room to check his chart, he asked her how close he had come to dying. She said it had been one-in-three that he would pull through. Terry asked her how she came up with odds like that, and she said it was easy. There were three kinds of timber rattlers. He had run into the kind that had the weakest venom. With either of the other two, he would've had no chance at all. One-in-three.

Detective Carter had walked in as the doctor was walking out. Carter took Terry's statement down impassively, asking few questions but allowing Terry to shape the narrative, almost as if he were not a police officer but a secretary taking dictation. He read it back to Terry, making occasional corrections. Then, without looking up from his lined yellow notepad, he said, 'I don't believe a word of this horseshit.' Without anger or

429

humour or much inflection at all. 'You know that, don't you? Not one goddamn word.' Finally lifting dull, knowing eyes.

'Really?' Terry had said, laying in his hospital bed, one floor below his grandmother with her busted face. 'What do you think happened, then?'

'I've come up with lots of other explanations,' said the detective, his small, pale eyes sullen and cool. 'And they all make even less sense than this pile of crap you're handing me. I'll be damned if I have any idea what happened. I'll just be damned.'

'Aren't we all,' Terry said.

Carter gave him a hard and unfriendly glare.

'I wish I could tell you something different. But that's what really happened,' Terry said. And most of the time, at least when the sun was up, Terry really believed it *was* what had happened. After dark, though, when he was trying to sleep . . . after dark sometimes he had other ideas. Bad ideas.

The sound of tyres on gravel roused him, and he lifted his head, looked back towards the foundry. In another moment an emerald Saturn came bumping around the corner, trolling across the blasted landscape. When the driver saw him, the car whined to a stop and sat there for a moment idling. Then it came on, finally pulling in not ten feet away.

'Hey, Terry,' said Glenna Nicholson as she eased out from behind the wheel. She seemed not in the least surprised to see him – as if they had planned to meet here.

She looked good, a curvy girl in stonewashed grey jeans, a sleeveless black shirt and a black studded belt. He could see the Playboy Bunny on her exposed hip, which was a trashy touch, but who hadn't made mistakes, done things to themselves they wished they could take back?

'Hey, Glenna,' he said. 'What brings you out here?'

'Sometimes I come here for lunch,' she said, and held up a

sub in one hand, wrapped in white waxed paper. 'It's quiet. Good place to think. About Ig and . . . stuff.'

He nodded. 'What've you got?'

'Eggplant parm. Got a Dr Pepper, too. You want half? I always get a large, and I don't know why. I can't eat a large. Or I shouldn't. I guess sometimes I do.' She wrinkled her nose. 'I'm really trying to take off ten pounds.'

'Why?' Terry asked, looking her over again.

She laughed. 'Stop it.'

He shrugged. 'I'll eat half your sandwich, if it helps with the diet. But you don't have anything to worry about. You're all right.'

They sat on a fallen log along the side of the Evel Knievel trail. The water was spangled gold in the late-afternoon light. Terry didn't know he was hungry until she gave him half her sandwich and he started to eat. Soon it was gone, and he was licking his fingers, and they were sharing out the last of the Dr Pepper. They didn't talk. Terry was fine with that. He didn't want to make small talk, and she seemed to know it. The silence didn't make her nervous. It was funny, in LA no one ever shut up; everyone there seemed terrified by a moment of silence.

'Thanks,' he said finally.

'Don't mention it,' she said.

He pushed a hand back through his hair. At some point in the last few weeks, he had discovered a thinness at the crown, and he had responded by letting it grow out until it was almost shaggy. He said, 'I should've come by the salon, had you give me a cut. My shit is getting out of control.'

'I don't work there anymore,' she said. 'Gave my last cut yesterday.'

'Get out.'

'Mm-hm.'

'Well. Here's to going on to other things, then.'

'Here's to going on to other things.'

431

They each had a sip of Dr Pepper.

'Was it a good cut to end on?' Terry asked. 'Did you give someone a completely awesome trim to finish up?'

'I shaved a guy bald. An older guy, actually. You don't usually get older guys asking for a buzz job. That tends to be more of a younger-dude thing. You know him – Merrin Williams' dad. Dale?'

'Yeah. I kind of know him,' Terry said, and grimaced, fought back an almost tidal surge of sadness that didn't entirely make sense.

Of course Ig had been killed over Merrin; Lee and Eric had burned him to death because of what they thought he had done to her. Ig's last year had been so bad, so unhappy, Terry almost couldn't bear to think about it. He was sure Ig hadn't done it, could never have killed Merrin. He supposed that now no one would ever know who had really killed her. He shuddered, remembering the night Merrin had died. He had been with fucking Lee Tourneau then – the revolting little sociopath – had even enjoyed his company. A couple of drinks, some cheap ganja out on the sandbar – and then Terry had dozed off in Lee's car and not woken again until dawn. It sometimes seemed like that had been the last night he was really happy, playing cards with Ig and then aimlessly driving around and around Gideon through an August evening that smelled of the river and firecrackers. Terry wondered if there was any smell in all the world so sweet.

'Why'd he do it?' Terry asked.

'Mr Williams said he's moving down to Sarasota, and when he gets there, he wants to feel the sun on his bare head. Also, because his wife hates men with shaved heads. Or maybe she's his ex-wife now. I think he's going to Sarasota without her.' She smoothed a leaf out on her knee, then picked it up by the stem, lifted it into the breeze and let go, watched it sail away. 'I'm moving too. 'S why I quit.'

'Where to?'

'New York,' she said.

'City?'

'Uh-huh.'

'Hell. Look me up when you get there, why don't you? I'll show you some good clubs,' Terry said. He was already writing the number to his cell on an old receipt in his pocket.

'What do you mean? Aren't you in LA?'

'Naw. No reason to hang around without *Hothouse*, and I'd take New York over LA anytime. You know? It's just a lot more ... real.' He handed her his number.

She sat on the ground, holding the scrap of paper and smiling up at him, her elbows back on the log and the light dappling her face. She looked good.

'Well,' she said, 'I think we'll be living in different neighbourhoods.'

'That's why God invented cabs,' he said.

'He invented them?'

'No. Men invented them, so they could get home safely after a night of drunken carousing.'

'When you think about it,' she said, 'most of the good ideas came along to make sin a whole lot easier.'

'True that,' he said.

They got up to walk off their sandwiches, went for a meandering stroll around the foundry. As they came to the front, Terry paused again, looking at that wide swathe of burned earth. It was funny the way the wind had channelled the fire straight to the town woods and then set just a single tree aflame. *That* tree. It still stood, a rack of great blackened antlers, terrible horns clawing at the sky. The sight of it gave him pause, held him briefly transfixed. He shivered; the air suddenly felt cooler, more like late October in New England.

'Lookit,' Glenna said, bending and picking something out of the burnt undergrowth.

It was a gold cross, threaded on a delicate chain. She held it up, and it swung back and forth, flashing a golden light into her smooth, pretty face.

'Nice,' she said.

'You want it?'

'I'd probably catch fire if I put this thing on,' she said. 'Go for it.'

'Nah,' Terry said. 'This is for a girl.' He carried it over to a sapling growing up against the foundry, hung it on one of the branches. 'Maybe whoever left it will come back for it.'

They went on their way, not talking much, just enjoying the light and the day, around the foundry and back to her car. He wasn't sure when they took each other's hand, but by the time they reached the Saturn, they had. Her fingers slid from his with unmistakable reluctance.

A breeze lifted, raced across the yard, carrying that smell of ash and the fall chill. She hugged herself, trembled pleasurably. Distantly there came the sound of a horn, a saucy, jaunty thing, and Terry cocked his head, listening, but it must've been music from a car passing on the highway, because in a moment it was gone.

'I miss him, you know,' Glenna said. 'Like I can't say.'

'Me, too,' he said. 'It's funny, though. Sometimes ... sometimes he's so close it's like I might turn around and see him. Grinning at me.'

'Yeah. I feel that, too,' she said, and smiled: a tough, generous, real smile. 'Hey. I should go. See you in New York, maybe.'

'Not maybe. Definitely.'

'Okay. Definitely.' She got into her car and shut the door and waved to him before she began to back away.

Terry stood there after she was gone, the breeze tugging at his overcoat, and looked again at the empty foundry, the blasted field. He knew he should've been feeling something for Ig, should've been racked with grief ... but instead he was wondering how long after he got to New York it would be before Glenna called, and where he ought to take her. He knew some places.

The wind gusted again, not just chilly but genuinely cold, and Terry cocked his head once more, thought for a moment he heard another distant snatch of trumpet, a dirty salute. It was a beautifully wrought little riff, and in the moment of hearing it he felt, for the first time in weeks, the impulse to play again. Then the sound of the horn was gone, carried away on the breeze. It was time for him to go, too.

'Poor devil,' Terry said, before he got into his rent-a-car and drove away.

ACKNOWLEDGMENTS, NOTES, CONFESSIONS

Experts disagree about the lyrics of The Romantics' seminal 1980s hit, 'What I Like About You'. Ig sings it *'you're whispering in my ear'*, but many other listeners claim that Jim Marinos is hollering *'warm whispering in my ear'*, or even, *'phone whispering in my ear'*. Given the widespread popular confusion, I felt I could allow Iggy to have it his way, but I apologise to rock purists who feel I got it wrong.

While ransacking Merrin's old books, Ig comes across two underlined sentences. Credit where credit is due: the first is from *Atonement* by Ian McEwan (Vintage), the second from *Wampeters, Foma and Granfalloons* by Kurt Vonnegut (Jonathan Cape).

The copy-editors on this book noted, correctly, that locusts die off in July, but the author chose to pretend otherwise, for those famous artistic reasons we're always hearing so much about.

My thanks to Dr Andy Singh, for providing me with a rough sketch of BRCA1, the form of cancer that claimed Merrin's sister, and might've claimed her, if my plot didn't demand otherwise. Any errors regarding medical fact are, however, the author's own. Thanks as well to Kerri Singh, and the rest of the Singh clan, for indulging my hand-wringing over this particular novel, during the course of a variety of evenings.

Much gratitude as well to Danielle and Dr Alan Ades. When I needed a place to work where no one would bother me, they found me one. Thanks as well to the folks at Lee Mac's for feeding me for four months. I'm grateful to my friends Jason Ciaramella and Shane Leonard, who both read this book in manuscript form and provided me with a good deal of helpful feedback.

Thanks to Ray Slyman, who filled me in on the Don Orione cross; to my sister, the minister Naomi King, who pointed me to several useful passages in the Bible. A book, *God's Problem: How the Bible Fails to Answer Our Most Important Question – Why We Suffer* by Bart Ehrman (HarperOne) also proved a helpful resource. I read *God's Problem* while I was neck-deep in the fifth draft. I suspect that if I had read it earlier on, this would've been a very different novel. Not better or worse, just different.

A dedicated team of passionate book people worked on *Horns* behind the scenes at William Morrow/HarperCollins: Mary Schuck, Ben Bruton, Tavia Kowalchuk, Lynn Grady, Liate Stehlik, Lorie Young, Nyamekye Waliyaya, and copy-editor Maureen Sugden. My thanks to the whole crew for doing so much to make me look good.

There was a point at which I came to feel that this book itself was the devil; I'm grateful to my editors, Jen Brehl, Jo Fletcher and Pete Crowther, and to my agent, Mickey Choate, both for their patience while I struggled with the thing and for all the help they offered to guide me through the nettles of my own story. Finally, love to my folks, Leanora, and my boys; without them, I wouldn't have had a hope in hell of finishing *Horns*.

J.H., August 2009